LIGHTNING
SEEDS

The Stars Hereafter Chronicles, Book I: *Lightning Seeds*

ISBN-13: 978-1-9990749-1-3

Cover design, illustration, book design and image editing by Robert Grey.

Map, sword-and-snake, and lock-and-key engravings by Channarong Pherngjan.
The first door original image by Sebelas Studio.
Perkona Ola and Baille Ghrommet original images by Icon Ade.
Badlands original image by Turan Israyilli.
Mudredd Vale original image by Md Faruk Mia.
Longbow Domain original image by Vecstock.
Masks original image by Michael Külbel.
Devastation of Perkona Ola original image by Freepik.
Samarit and Rowan (original background image only) by Art_Dreams.

LIGHTNING SEEDS

THE STARS HEREAFTER CHRONICLES | BOOK ONE

RUPERT SMITHSON

HUMMINGBIRD HILL

CONTENTS

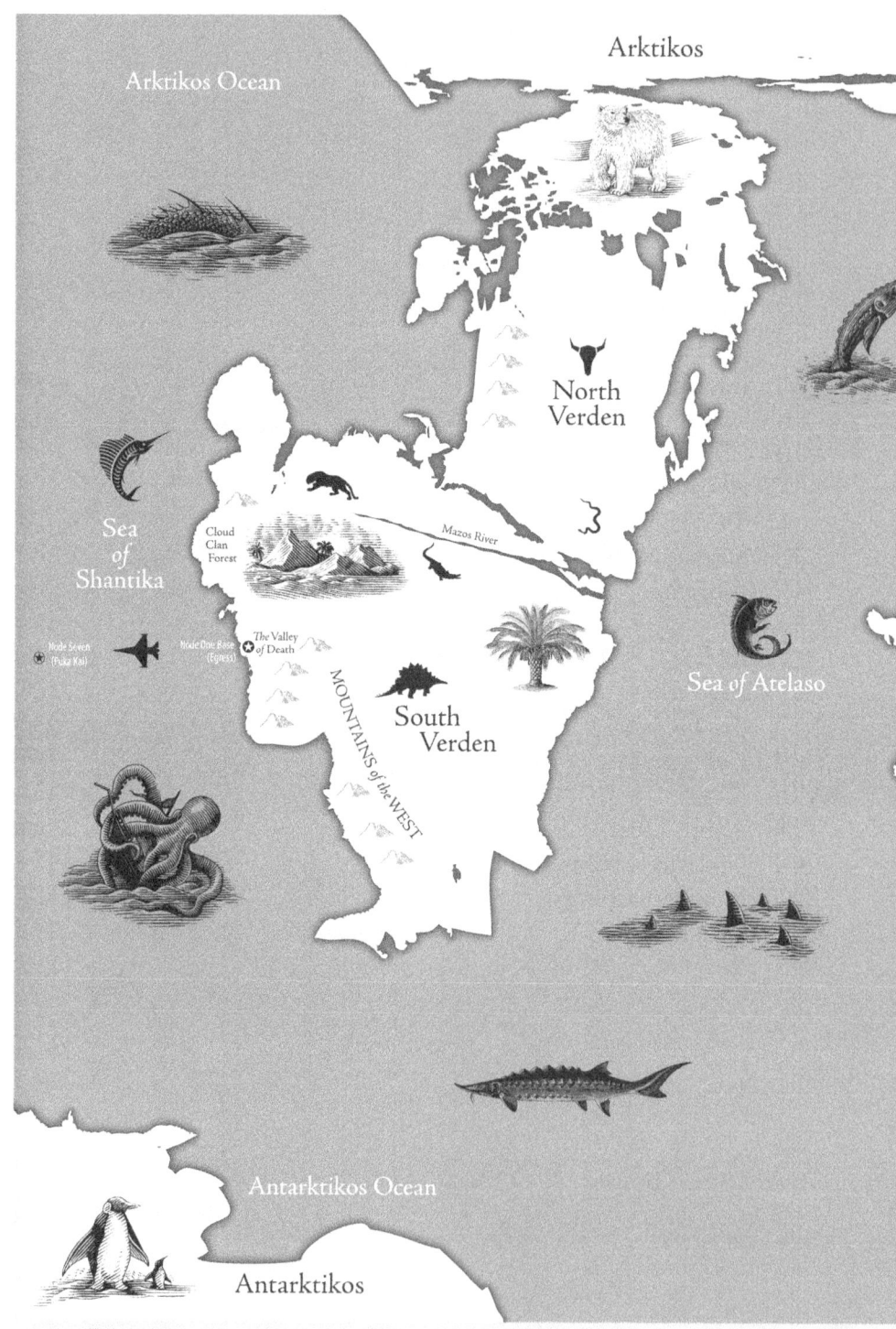

Arktikos

Arktikos Ocean

North
Verden

Sea
of
Shantika

Cloud
Clan
Forest

Mazos River

Node Seven
(Puka Kai)

Node One Base
(Egress)

The Valley
of Death

Sea of Atelaso

MOUNTAINS of the WEST

South
Verden

Antarktikos Ocean

Antarktikos

Continent of Evrys

Continent of Aja

Continent of Afara

Sea of Sindhu

Iningizimu

Nordmark

Finnmark

Ryglaland

Tatutland

Nordsee

Seaxland

Pole Land

Frankenland

Rostova

Vugh Deep

Longbow
Domain

KEO RANGE

FELL RANGE

WHITE MTS.

Mt.
Torra

Suro

Middle
Sea

Garden
of
Desire

Bearan
Island

Gate of the
Shining Ones

Mudredd
Vale

Bay of
Sahmanheyd

Inland
Sea

Aha
Domain

Serq
Sea

Tel Ba'al

Ushu

Zau

Akhmim

Black Land (Khemia)

Devil's
Doorway

Abdju

IRON DESERT

Waka
the Song Eyes)

Bharat

"The world as we know it has grown out of seeds scattered from a mighty tree shattered by lightning."

◆

Samarit Longbow

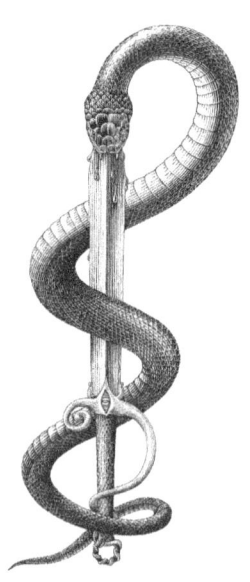

I

The Rule

THE MORNING OF that day fifty-two thousand years ago began like most, with the wake-up whistle that never failed to scour Syx's skull like a length of barbed wire strung between his ears. He stood up in as close to an instant as possible and opened his eyes to stare at the straw on the flagstones beneath his dirty bare feet, and in peripheral vision the other ragged orphans.

The head boy not much older than Syx announced the dawn each day with a crack of his short rigid hunting crop on the wall, and shouted: "*Who are you!*"

Each dawn the boys of all ages stumbled to an upright position and answered in unison: "I have no name, Master Hepta."

"*What are you!*"

"I am a Syx, Master Hepta."

"*What do you know!*"

"What you tell me, Master Hepta, and the Rule."

"*And what is the Rule!*"

"Bigger is better, Master Hepta."

"*Wake and work, Syx!*"

The particular Syx whose story this is knew how to count to ten on his fingers. But even if he possessed five times as many, the orphans' number exceeded that sum. The lads lined the inside perimeter of a stable whose stalls had been torn out. Centuries old, the hovel leaned against the bailey, the castle's outer walls. The boys bowed their heads and closed their eyes, ready for the Hepta to begin the "wake" part of the morning ritual. Very rarely did a new boy, or "noob" as we say to this day, not follow the elder inmates' example and keep his head down.

The boys' genus, *Felis*, and species, *sapiens*, or "felid" in the vernacular, differed only a little from *Homo sapiens* that grew to dominate later epochs in their timeline. For example, felids' sensitive ears stood out shaped like a cat's, although not many had eyes with vertical slit pupils. Like most, our Syx's pupils were round like those of felids' ancient lion ancestor. The males at puberty grew catlike whiskers on their upper lips, some on their brows; some like our Syx had faint striped patterns in the skin of their faces, unlike him some with matching downy vellus hair. Had there been humans as we understand the primate genus *Homo* today, specifically the species *sapiens*, a comparison of the two would highlight felids' greater independence. However, as social animals, like humans of our era, most felids feared exclusion from the tribe, especially in youth and old age.

Social anxiety made a noob's gaze automatically focus on his feet, unless his character had already grown unusually independent, a trait of undomesticated felids that had to be suppressed with brute force. The newcomer's crown in the first hour suffered a quick raze. Raw from the subsequent tattooed serial number, the noob invariably screamed like a wounded wildcat when the Hepta lashed that part of the boys' anatomies to begin the day's assignment to each individual. By the next morning the noob, now a rookie Syx with a tattoo, knew better because it had been explained no third morning would dawn for him if so much as a whimper escaped his lips next time. Otherwise, his corpse by default contributed to the food supply otherwise limited to a kind of hard tack made from whatever available flour, salt pork once a week, and nettles when in season. Our Syx when a rookie believed the other Syxes hungered for his failure to keep silent under the lash, a toxic fear that lingered. Uneducated, he did not know to call it paranoid alienation.

When each morning the Hepta stepped to the first Syx in line to "wake" him with a crack of his crop, its leather-covered cane shaft, and head loaded with steel or lead to give it more heft, he always shouted: *"Work!"* and for each boy added the particular job he must complete to perfection before being allowed to feed that day.

This dawn, two boys down the line, our Syx's turn came. The hem of Hepta's black robe and his grimy feet appeared before Syx's downcast eyes, the cue to squeeze his eyelids shut and hold his breath – but the fire on his shaven crown never came. The first time a delay like this had happened, Syx had choked on air befouled by the Heptas' fifteen-foot-tall master they called Lord Boss. Syx knew

better than to open his eyes, but after that incident held his breath for as long as it took for the usually brief inspection to pass by. If he had dared to look up, Syx knew what he would see: a reptilian humanoid three times his stature, with rows of outsized spiky teeth in its scaly blunt-nosed orange-eyed head. This morning Syx kept his eyes shut, but could not help but give ear to the pervasive unquiet gurgle of lizard breath pass in and out of the wet round nostrils of its lizard snout, slow and deep as the draught of the blacksmith's bellows.

With a grunt, the giant lizard man turned and lumbered out of earshot into the courtyard, possibly

Syx, one *of* many Syxes.

even the mysterious world beyond the drawbridge over the moat, in the past century drained, more of a soggy ditch now, as well as mosquito hatchery in warm weather.

For some reason the Hepta ignored the current noob's sigh of relief, a young lad only three feet tall who had arrived in the middle of the night. Sorely tempted to glance at the boy, Syx did not, not with the Hepta standing right in front of him with the crop in his hand. Instead of the expected command to wake, the master even lowered the whip, and skipped to: *"Work! Blood duty!"*

◆

Syx gagged. The catacombs beneath a remote part of the castle enclosure stank of putrid flesh worse than did Lord Boss. Even the sight of fresh gore made Syx want to retch, let alone gore three days old.

Nevertheless, he preferred blood duty for its solitude, out of sight of the Heptas and somewhat free of the group mind. For Syx, an empath, a person with the paranormal ability to perceive the mental and emotional states of others, lack of boundaries his parents would have encouraged to mature, had they lived, allowed the Heptas to abuse him freely in any way they chose short of actual murder. They had so far failed to break any of his bones, however. Blessed with a strong anatomy but weak personal boundaries, swamped by feelings or images that had nothing to do with him, he took responsibility for them as a way of controlling the consequent internal chaos. He even learnt to appreciate nausea when it displaced the knot in his middle that felt like his stomach eating itself.

Syx's hands grew red with blood as he worked. He tried to remember his mother and father, but as usual failed. Only vague impressions of a warm golden summer long ago brightened his thoughts, an obsession for as long as he could remember. Today he had scrubbed the bloody floor clean three times after he had stripped off the remaining clothing and stowed the body in a barrel – not the missing head, however – that as always had been removed to the shrine room first thing. And gratitude, as always, arose for being spared the sight of any dead one's face. But at times it seemed today's victim's ghost lingered as a shiver up the spine. Yet Syx refused to suspect the flesh would be salted and called pork. The Heptas never spoke of it either after the initial warning. A correlation stood out that no one admitted, however, between a death and the appearance of meat in their bowls.

Syx quickly scanned the work he had done. A felid's photoreceptors like a cat's included more of the rod type than cones, which meant Syx could see in the dark, although unlike cats felids retained perception of nearly the full range of colours in dim light. The subterranean cemetery had no lighting other than the occasional dim crystal sconce between the many dusty skulls of various humanoid hybrid species that lined the tunnels. He hurried to finish the job. The hypervigilant Hepta would soon shine a bright lantern on Syx's work.

None of the boys retained self-confidence in the way they might have done before they had been enslaved, but Syx had grown proficient in blood-duty work after the many years of experience he might have counted had he learnt to count beyond his ten fingers. He wiped his red hands on his tunic, and stood at attention for an indefinite period as he awaited inspection.

In time the Hepta showed up. On this occasion Syx passed muster. For the first time, however, blindfolded and ordered back up to the main floor of a smoky workshop via a hidden passageway, the intense heat of what must be the blacksmith's forge nearby threatened to singe his hair, face and bare arms, and even made his bloody tunic smoke. But the heat abated quickly.

"*Stop!*" the Hepta ordered. "*Stand still!*" And he tore the blindfold away.

The pale late afternoon light that stabbed its sharp slanted beams through the shutters stung Syx's eyes briefly until his lenses adjusted. He blinked, but did not look directly at the master; instead he closed his eyes, and bowed before him, who stood only an inch taller at six-foot-six.

"Stench," the Hepta said, "follow." Hepta led Stench (a name interchangeable with "Syx") along a dark passageway behind the forge at the end of which he shoved him through a doorway into the light of day. The slam of the heavy plank door behind him and the sharp clack of the iron bolt as it slid into place passed through one ear and out the other and jangled every nerve on the way. He found himself upright in momentary disbelief between the mossy walls of a narrow enclosure so high it must be a pen for creatures very thin and tall who in ancient times needed metal shoes the blacksmith made in the workshop behind him, then sold to local farriers. *But how would a beast that big get in here?*

He abandoned the curiosity as a sin. However, in the next instant his attention riveted on the even taller architectural feature called a "keep," a watchtower in ancient times that looked out over the countryside from where it stood on a mound of ground called a "motte," in this instance one that stood above a little river valley, although Syx knew nothing of the outside world. He only knew the workshops and the nettle patches within the walls. The keep, like a commanding finger, pointed to the blue vault of heaven.

Syx looked up, straight up. Had a vulture passed over the enclosure and looked down, it would have seen a dazzled young felid boy who looked up

4

awestruck at the blue firmament. He wanted to disappear into it, extinguish existence itself, a desire irrationally conflated with going "home." He rubbed his eyes to clear them, and told himself he must qualify for Hepta status first. If he performed well, the next step, tracker, a mythic role to a felid boy, would grant him freedom to roam outdoors to hunt down fugitives and dissidents, of course within limits imposed by a permanent collar tracked by something called the Eye in the Sky. The illicit urge to escape and go back home, the ultimate sin, inflamed his heart in the here and now. Guilt always followed. As penance he tore his gaze from the infinite blue above, and turned quickly to face the iron-studded streaked grey planks of the old enclosure door. The familiar called him back inside, however dank and dim until nettle season, but nostalgic already. Yet he dared not even think to knock. He had no right to ask for anything. Patient gazing at the door would be all that he could do, therefore he would gaze with all his might.

But this door – could not be the same door of a moment ago. Stunned, he only now noticed in fact two doors, as if a second one had magically appeared where only an instant ago the lichen-covered wall, part of the bailey itself, had been blank. A gap separated a pair of adjacent planks in the door where the wood had shrunk and worn away in the wind and rain. Attention of its own volition reached towards the narrow opening – *there's an "out there" out there* – all this flashed through Syx's body from his bare soles to his shaven crown. But he stood rooted, eyes closed tight to shut the mortal sin out.

The door back *to the* familiar.

II

The Foment

"HEY, YOU! I'M talking to you!"

Syx opened his eyes. That a rookie had just whispered from the other side of the bailey stirred his blood even more than did the blue sky or the glimpse of the world outside. The words that wanted to form in his mouth felt like something tough and sticky, like something he should spit out and forget.

"I'm your friend," the rookie said.

Syx stared, but nevertheless replied in near-whisper: "You... *go away!*"

"Don't tell me to go away, you great big pretty girly-man. Just stay right where you are and keep me company. What's your name?"

Syx never spoke to anyone other than to acknowledge the Heptas' demands, but to obey orders had become second nature, therefore he stood still and tried to peer through the narrow gap between the planks. On the other hand, the Rule affirmed his biggerness by far. *Girly* – the vague image of a girl child overlaid the scene. He squinted at it. Breathing grew more rapid. His mother – she had been a girl once. Was it her ghost? *But what is a ghost?* –

"Hey, you," the rookie said, "I asked you, what's your name? You look like you're in dreamland but your eyes are open."

The rookie surely must know his name, the same as his own. Maybe he really was a noob. Syx scratched his tattooed crown.

"You're not a number," the noob said. "Are you in a madhouse, Syx?"

"What's that?" Syx's scratchy voice sounded like a stranger's –

"I'm just teasing," the noob said. "I know all about what happens here. You should walk away. Just leave."

"Then you know there's no way out. Besides, I'll be a Hepta soon. After that I'll be a tracker. I'll go home..." To admit his secret plan to defy the world order made Syx spin about to look behind him. Unsure that he had not felt eyes staring at the back of his head, he lifted his brows as his gaze drifted upwards to the square black window that looked out from the top of the dark tower, the keep.

"I'm sorry to tell you your home is gone," the noob said, "no matter where you're from. That's why you're an orphan. No one here ever goes home. If you survive, you'll leave this place, but carted off somewhere and given milk of poppy if you behave. When you're worn out from hauling lizard shit all day long for years, you'll be force-fed a heroic dose and spend your last minutes as

6

a blinded competitor in fights with baby Reps for the titillation of the lizards and their ladies."

"That's ridiculous, I'll be a tracker..."

But the cocky noob's footfalls receded into the distance.

Syx wanted to jump out of his skin. But he exhaled – only then did he notice he had held his breath again. One ear remained cocked in the direction of the gap between the planks. But now only the wind soughed beyond the bailey, and whistled a little through the gap in the door. He blinked his staring eyes a few times, and sighed. His shoulders sagged. Maybe he had just had a waking dream.

The blue sky – like that other time – inside the tower, the dark keep that rose above this very enclosure – the pure blue had filled its square frame and implied a magical and vast enigma. The memory had been burnt into his brain, because a raven had flown up from below and rested its silhouette on the sill. The creature had tilted its black head and blinked back at him, called out a deep throaty rasp – *caw!* – and spread its broad wings and escaped from view. The shutters slammed shut, and a Hepta sprang out of the shadows behind him – pain followed, of course.

But it must be time to go back inside by now. He abandoned his vigil and stepped to the door that had admitted him, obviously more in use than the one that captured his attention while daydreaming. *Look... there, the grass in front of it is shorter, no weeds at the sill.* The feet of well-behaved felids like him had worn a shallow depression in the dirt just there. Syx relaxed into the knowledge of his good standing; after all, he had been allowed outdoors for the first time not in nettle season – surely a reward. Otherwise, to what purpose? He opened his eyes to stare at his feet. *Home.* His gaze again returned to the mysterious second door, and did again and again. No one came to order him back into the familiar darkness. At long last the bolt slid and the rusty hinges creaked. Syx turned to face the Hepta's feet, fortunately, because he had nearly succumbed to the urge to lie down on the ground to gaze into the blue sky.

✦

Soon the daydream sank into bottomless amnesia. The sleepwalk of daily drudgery lulled his mind into a familiar certainty. Apart from the hour in the enclosure, he knew exactly what to expect from dawn till dusk. The headmaster's sermons on the Rule in the shrine room droned on in the same voice as the one in his head: *Wrongthink is a sin: curiosity, disobedience, imagination, hope, doubt; compliance is a virtue: conformity, sufferance, forbearance, obedience...*

Yet certainty had thinned and grown tattered. Nocturnal dreams rippled the dark surface of Syx's mind: a shadowy figure or indistinct shape often approached, which made him sit bolt upright; he may even shout if this kept up. The Hepta stationed outside surely suspected a dangerous element fomented on the cold stone floor of the stable, to be silenced with a rag; it had happened before to others. The faint red fur on the backs of his hands (the Heptas called them paws) and the tops of his feet would fail to grow, a symptom of illness. Any sick boy disappeared quickly. As secretive as a rat, the memory of the daydream in the enclosure darted beneath his dimly lit mental furniture. He choked, and coughed into his sleeve. He looked about in the dark, but all remained still. *Girly-man…* He started. His eyes opened wide. *The Bailey Boy…* maybe one of the Heptas or even the headmaster had sprung a test on him well in advance of qualification for Hepta status – but Syx knew curiosity to be wrongthink, a sin, thus dismissed it.

◆

After some months, what he called fur expanded in the form of down across the backs of his hands and the tops of his feet. He often touched his chin and its soft tuft. It itched at times, but felt long enough to tug on. The whiskers on his upper lip felt stiffer to the touch too. His tunic now stretched tight across the chest. Care had to be taken not to part the seams as he laboured at his duties with more diligence than ever. The broadening shoulders beneath itched at times and needed frequent scratching. But he must not indulge in the sin of hope –

◆

The air cooled as autumn decayed. A Hepta thrust Syx into the enclosure for the second time. His heart thumped at the thought of another test. With gritted teeth he closed his eyes to temptation. When qualified as a tracker, somehow rid of the requisite collar that reported to the Eye in the Sky, he would disappear and go home, back to his dimly remembered birthplace. He drew a breath and squeezed his eyes shut tighter. He must not look at the sky, nor the dark tower. Instead he contemplated his future free life as a tracker – if he survived the orphanage. Nothing could be worse than orphan status. Things could only get better. Blood duty had desensitized him to a degree, surely an advantage. Gore and stench no longer made him want to faint, but the gag response remained, unfortunately. He reviewed eavesdropped information from the Heptas: trackers may be required to kill in self-defence, but mainly they captured fugitive slaves, of which only a rare few had trained in combat. Generally they were victims of wrongthink, a mental illness that made them run away from the breeding-mother egg pits – and the carrion fields where diggers pulled the entrails from dead bodies – and the skinners, who presumably had something to do with leather crafting – and the big workshops where whips, shovels, buckets, barrels, carts, pots and other things were made. The thought of the tool industry evoked the memory of mysterious "dragon ships" the Heptas whispered of – they claimed the reptilians travelled to Lunah and back through the sky, and had been born in the Sacred Sun – but the god Lord Kirzaka had come from another galaxy, whatever that was – another mystery he might solve once free.

Syx relished the thought of boyish life in the orphanage, secure though it may be, finished, done, behind him and over with. The sin of imagination gave rise to the sin of hope, which in turn gave rise to courage to face the alternative worst-case scenario – his own head on the hook dripping red death onto the altar in the shrine room, the ultimate punishment he had witnessed time and again – above the altar dedicated to Maçina the Artificer, Creator of the Sacred Sun. To attempt to portray this ultimate god even in imagination was said to be strictly forbidden on pain of mutilation, but not so his incarnation Kirzaka the Deathless, Talon of Maçina, a giant demigod twice the stature of his humanoid reptilian minions, with massive clawed legs and a long tail and small claw-like forelimbs. As proof, the altar painting showed how with such violent grace Kirzaka vanquished his foes, the non-reptoid hybrid species: canids, anders, felids, ferals – their heads, arms and legs flew skywards in sprays of blood; a lightning cloud towered behind the demigod, through which the Sacred Sun broke through in radiant splendour – Kirzaka's little yellow eyes matched the sun's luminance like two widely separated bright headlights. And behind the demigod's head, his nest Lunah in full-moon phase glowed white –

Roused from the sinful daydream, Syx opened his unruly eyes. The enclosure had changed little. Long years had streaked the old stone bailey walls with dark weathered stains, moss and lichen. The grass, dormant at this season, had faded to brown, like the dead broken weeds at the mystery door, which remained ancient and unused. Fortunately, the sky had grown overcast. The blue, blue sky faded to a memory only, much less of a temptation. And a few lazy drops of cold rain touched his face.

III
Vanishing Point

For the third time the enclosure door creaked and closed behind him with a slam that made Syx flinch, even though he braced himself in expectation of it. The lock slid shut with an undiminished clack. The air outdoors bit even colder than inside. He found it nearly impossible not to rush to the ancient unused mystery door to listen for the noob's voice, despite having told himself it was all the headmaster's doing. Syx made a supreme effort to appear calm. He wandered here and there in the small space, crouched to inspect the dead grass at close range, stretched his arms and back, rubbed his shaven tattooed crown encircled by a thick fringe of red hair. Only then did he casually amble towards the old abandoned door. The outside world beyond the only outdoors he knew, the courtyard and the nettle patches, still beckoned through the crack. It appeared to move if he cocked his head. In the distance he glimpsed not fields but bare hills under broken clouds – shafts of sacred sunbeams illumined a line of evergreen trees like emerald fire along the hills' sawtoothed crests. He stood on his toes, and marvelled at the gleam of a river below lined with bare trees. Its waters sparkled the reflection of columns of light that slanted from the heavens above, Maçina's revelation, its beauty denied to all inferiors like Syx. The sight set his heart aflame – but with a start he landed on his heels and spontaneously leapt backwards – a slice of a face and a single dark eye blocked the view –

A complementary urge intervened: to spin about half-circle to check if a Hepta watched from the dark window in the dark tower. But sudden movements may attract suspicion. He steeled himself, aided by the need to understand what he had just witnessed, and by doing so fell victim to the sin of curiosity. Eyes focused, he looked into that single dark brown eye in the hairless face – at least as far as he could tell its tanned skin was bare – and the pale pink lips blossomed full, shapely and unadorned yet by either down or whiskers – *Bailey Boy.*

"Who *are* you?" Syx whispered.

"I'm your friend." The pink lips parted, and added, "Remember, Syx?"

Eyes wide open, Syx stilled himself. The part of the face visible through the crack in no way resembled the headmaster, the oldest boy as tall as Syx. This little noob must be two heads shorter at least. And he had no other fur than a long dark wavy mane that grew in profusion out of his unshaven crown, loosely parted in the middle. His teeth looked white and even, with small bicuspids.

Syx ran his tongue along the edges of his own teeth, which felt like the noob's looked. Maybe it felt the same to the little lad when he tongued his own.

"You've really grown since last time," Bailey Boy said. "You're so furry! But so pretty. You look like a big burly fox kit."

"Well, *you're* no bigger. I don't know what you mean by a burly... or a kit, whatever that is. I'm a felid."

"You're very pretty all the same, big green eyes, and so strapping. And you have a lot to learn, don't you?"

Syx frowned, and narrowed his gaze, but answered: "I've learnt all there is to learn, the Rule. That's all anyone needs. Anyhow... no one has green eyes."

The noob's long-fingered hand covered a snigger.

Syx glared. "What's wrong with you," he said, a statement, not a question. "Bigger means better, that's the Rule. Don't you know that? You speak to a bigger only when spoken to. In fact we shouldn't be talking at all."

"Ooh, I'm so scared!" The noob lifted the back of his slender hand to his forehead, arched his fine dark brows, and rolled his dark eyes skywards.

Syx's face grew hot. "You're lucky you're safe on the other side of this wall..." But he did not know what to say next. What could he do? Shriek like a Hepta? That would be suicide, if he could even figure out how to shriek; it might require a scalping like the Heptas got when promoted from Syxes so a patch of skin from their backsides could be grafted to their crowns. Their tattoos never needed shaving after that. The dark tower loomed – and the watcher sure to be up there surely watched. Syx slowly turned, and leaned against the wall. A subtle movement at his feet caught his eye – a mantis bit the head off a smaller one. He crouched to watch, plucked a stalk of dry grass, and tickled the headless victim, but threw the grass away so the watcher in the tower would not accuse him of playing, the worst form of the sin of imagination.

"I'm not behind this wall, Syx, *you* are. I'm free. But I'll tell you a secret."

Syx sighed, and tilted his face in the direction of the gap to listen.

"I know you can hear me," the noob said. "You're no prisoner. You just think you are. But you will be forever if you don't do as I say."

Syx leaned towards the door again, and whispered out of the side of his mouth, "I'm a felid, not a fox, not a kit, not a prizner, whatever that is. Stop calling me names that don't mean anything. Call me Syx."

"Fine, Syxie. That's not your name anyway. Do you even remember your real name?"

Syx rubbed his tattooed crown. "I don't need one."

11

"No, you idiot, not your number. I mean the name your mother and father gave you when you were born."

"*Hey…* I know what an idiot is. They don't last long here. I'm a felid. I keep telling you."

"So remember your real name then, like a proper felid."

"And you're a cheeky *Stench*. You would never survive this side of the wall…" But Syx had lost the thread of the conversation. Bailey Boy was no Stench, as his crown had not been shaved and tattooed yet. Something irritated the inside of Syx's head, just behind his eyes, and scratched like a rat inside a wall.

"Listen, Syx, you must get out of here. Leave. You can walk away, escape. You can do it, and I'll help you."

Syx's face froze. Something wafted like a chill breeze through his entire body. His soles tingled.

"You can open this door," the noob said.

"Only a Hepta can open the door."

"No, Syx. I meant only *you* can open this door. I can't. There's no handle on the outside. But there's one on the inside. All you have to do is slide the bolt out of the brackets, then pull on the hand-hold."

Syx looked the door over. A slight hollow had been carved into the wood. *The hand-hold?…* and a horizontal piece of wood across the door's width in rusty iron things sort of like clamps attached to the wall. *The bolt?*

"Come on! Try it," the noob said. "The others were too afraid. It made them stupid. But something tells me you've got the balls."

"Balls? I don't know what you mean. My head will be cut off, everyone will watch it dripping over the altar. So no, I'm not going to do that." Syx relaxed a little after pointing out this obvious fact. The poor noob just did not know what went on in the orphanage. "Go away now or be punished."

"You don't want that. What you *want* is to know what's out here. What you *want* is freedom. Why put up with being crammed in a dark mouldy prison when you could be out here in the sun?"

"Are you crazy? Stay out of the sun if you want to live. And I only want to go home. I can't if my head's on the hook." *Obviously.*

"You *can* go home if you want, and right now too. Come on, just slide the bolt so I can push the door open a crack, just enough so you can see the view. That way I'll be to blame, and you'll at least get to see what you're missing before you decide one way or the other… stay a slave or go home."

For the second time Syx wanted to jump out of his skin. "It won't be my fault?"

"Yes, that's right, I'll take all the blame… you were only minding your own business."

"Well then," said Syx, quite suddenly even more unbelievably giddy, "I'm just going to take a quick look… then I'm going to push the door shut tight."

"Good. That's very good. Let's do it!"

The horizontal piece of wood, the bolt, broke in Syx's hands in a puff of ancient woody dust. His mouth agape, he stood paralyzed. Bailey Boy did not need to push on the door. It fell open by itself, and now barely hung by part of its lower hinge to reveal a much bigger view of the river valley below than a mere glimpse. Syx stared and stared –

"*Quick! Squeeze through,*" said Bailey Boy. "*Push!*" His slender hand grabbed at Syx's tunic. "*Girly-man.*" The noob's dark eyes flashed. "*I can see your la-dy parts,*" he taunted sing-song, "*I can see your pus-sy!*"

Syx stood stunned, but not by what the noob said, which he did not understand at all. He only knew he could *never* go back now. It would be a death sentence. There was no going back. There was only going *home*.

◆

"*Wait,*" Syx said as they hurried alongside a tall hawthorn hedge. "I can't run… my feet hurt."

"No worries, fox face." Bailey Boy seemed quite pleased with himself. Hands clasped to his hips, he shifted his weight to one leg, and stood looking Rowan over. "They won't be chasing us for long. If you're missed they'll say you've been shortlisted for some Rep's dinner party. Another of your cubby mates will get his head stuck on the hook as a warning."

The world spun. Syx squatted, and hung his head between his knees.

Bailey Boy cocked his head and winked. "I'm just teasing. It's more likely they'll just hide any evidence, otherwise the headmaster will get it in the neck for missing inventory."

Syx massaged his achy foot – in fact both ached in equal measure.

Bailey Boy watched him. "You know," he said, "undomesticated felids are an independent lot. Maybe you have a rival who wanted you out of the way, but in my opinion the Heptas secretly hope at least one of their kind one day will be true to themselves and brave enough to make a break for it. They knew I'd been snooping and decided to see what you would do. Curiosity is a sin, but only if you're not a Hepta. Congratulations, you're it. That's why they chucked you into the enclosure, and why the door had never been sealed up. But we really have to get you in shape. There's a long way to go if you're not used to hiking. Your feet will yowl like blinded felids tortured by Rep hatchlings."

Syx glanced at the noob. "I've heard the Heptas whisper about that. It's what they feared most. They said beheading was a better way to die."

"Hardly. But it would be quicker."

Syx peered at the noob's feet. As if there were only one broad toe on each, scuffed black coverings extended halfway to his knees. The willowy legs – *black skin?* For the first time he took in the noob's whole figure. Not only was he cheeky and disrespectful of his biggers, he lacked enough fur for even the youngest noob, although his head sprouted an exuberantly wavy, dark and bushy mane that spiralled with ringlets – but with no down at all in sight, not even on the rosy cheeks. Syx's gaze lowered to the slim waist, and drifted up to linger on the well-rounded bumps clearly visible on each side of his upper torso under the dark grey fitted tunic. *What a strange little creature…*

"Right, foxy man, time to ramble on. And please stop staring at my chest like that. It's impolite."

Syx blinked. Free of the need to whisper, his voice a stranger to his ears nevertheless resonated in parts of his body from his head to his belly. "Who *are* you?" he asked. "You're not like any felid I've ever seen. What's *your* name?" The sin of curiosity reared its beautiful head. He may as well wallow in it as long as possible. According to Bailey Boy, Syx's home had disappeared anyhow. Without warning his face grew long – he even forgot he had asked a question as yet unanswered.

"Oh, cheer up," said the noob. "Fine, I'll call you Syx instead of nicknames if you like. Is that better? This is day one of the best days of your life, if you can handle it. But I won't tell you my name until you remember yours. Deal?" The lad spit in his own palm, grinned and extended his slender little hand.

Syx stood up. "I don't know what you mean." He stared glassy-eyed at the outstretched palm, and shrugged. "I'm tired. I should go back before it's too late."

The noob withdrew his hand and clenched it into a fist between the bumps on his chest, wiped it on his thigh, and made it into a fist again. He said nothing, just frowned for a moment. "I understand," he said at last. "You want to go back to the familiar cage and take your punishment. That will make everything feel right again. Correct? Or maybe I'm mistaken and you expect to survive the penalty. How many times have you seen severed heads on the hook dripping over the altar? Have any of those lonely heads been placed back on their bodies? I mean in working order."

Syx opened his mouth to reply –

"None? Oh, really?" Bailey Boy set his hands on his hips. "Well then, I'm surprised at your choice. But fine, we'll go back."

Syx drew a deep breath, and moaned out loud for the first time in his life that he could recall. "You're right, they will take my head. I'll *never* go home now. *You've ruined everything!*"

Bailey Boy gasped. He raised his fingers to his mouth, and said, "You're the first one I've talked into escaping. It was so easy, but the others were too thick or too scared to get it. Besides, you have green eyes. I just want you to be free." The noob took Syx's hand. "Look, I don't want to hurt you. *Please* don't go back. We must keep going until we're home. It's a long way to go, but you're safe with me. Right?"

Home? Syx did not jerk his paw away at being touched. The noob's hand, too little to cause much pain, felt warm. He raised his gaze from the ground to look into the soft dark eyes in the noob's hairless face. Something in those kind eyes reminded him of Fuzzy, his only friend ever. When the two had been rookies, the fun-loving lad lost his head for lack of circumspection. Bailey Boy's eyes sparkled with the same beauty Fuzzy's had – and the narrow view through the gap between the planks in the mystery door he had glimpsed just a short time ago – the shafts of golden light on the emerald hills, the silvery river that shone below, so beautiful, so mysterious – the world, Maçina's vast world.

✦

"Am I too fast for you, Syx?" Bailey Boy asked. "We can stop for a bit."

Syx fell back onto his bottom, lifted his feet off the ground, and sighed.

The noob went on, "You know, tracking is instinctive to felids, and they love the chase, but it's doubtful the Heptas at your orphanage ever had to deal with a truant before, judging by how old that door was. And it's risky to allow Heptas to range beyond the walls. They might go feral if they're too long away. But that doesn't mean they're not following our trail. We can't rest too long. We must keep heading home as quickly as possible. I'm not allowed a weapon yet. I don't even know the Heptas' basic commands. No one's studied them. Maybe one day I'll make that a project for bonus credits."

Syx replied, "My feet hurt." His body remained planted on the damp grass beneath the shelter of a boulder. "I have no foot-coverings like yours, and my pads are raw." He wanted to lick them, but did not think his tongue could reach.

"They're called boots," the noob said. "They protect my feet. We'll get you some when we get home. Come on, get up. Let's go."

15

"What's 'basic commands'?" asked Syx.

"There's plenty of time for explanations… later… but for now, understand that the Heptas, all the Syxes, you too, in fact all the captives topside everywhere have been hypnotized to believe they're something they're not. Only slight variations in the basic program determine their roles in the system. But most importantly, they're taught self-hypnosis to make the false identity more efficient."

"I don't know what you mean," replied Syx. "What has that to do with basic commands?" His seated position made their eye level more equal. And he wanted to rest his feet a bit longer.

"I don't think you even know you hypnotize yourself. You've internalized the Rule. If I knew what the basic commands were, maybe I could cancel them. With a bit of interrogation, you could tell me, but it's probably not a good idea just yet. You might turn into a zombie. Each of the classes of *sapiens* the Primordial Architects made from splicing genes or whatever respond to specific commands."

Syx's brows drew together, and he peered at Bailey Boy.

"You know," the lad continued, "from the aboriginal hominid that was native to Eorthe? Felids, canids, anders and reptoids, or reptilians. Anders didn't come from the hominid so much, they came more from *Homo neanderthalensis*. We're all anthropoids. But they didn't teach you anything in there, did they?"

"They teach the Rule," Syx answered. "That's enough to work anything out. Bigger is better. I'm not totally ignorant, you know. I do understand who made us felids. The bosses did. I never heard of canids or… neanderwhatsits. Kirzaka the Deathless landed on Eorthe in his flying wagon ages ago, took some of the savage lions and made us. Later Lord Kirzaka taught the bosses how because he was busy with ruling the world. They needed workers to make the world great because wild animals are too stupid to get anything done. Now we can stand on two legs like them. Our forelimbs and paws are free to use tools. And we don't need tails. We can talk too, but aren't smart enough to read. They did us a favour and made our teeth dull like yours so we can't bite anyone to death, but even a real lion bite couldn't hurt them at all."

Bailey Boy *of the* outside world.

Bailey Boy smirked. "You've just made my case. They taught you nothing. That's all a load of lizard crap. Why do you call them 'paws'? They're just hands like mine, only big with a little fuzz like your arms. And you're looking at a canid right now." He pulled back his mane to reveal pointed ears. "See?" Small tufts of dark fur poked out of the canals. "I don't shave mine. Maybe I will when I move to Perkona Ola for good. Hairy ears are looked down upon there. Showing them hairy is as illegal as going topless in public or exposing your lady parts in the street, which is totally stupid, in my humble opinion. I mean about hairy ears, not… anyhow, I'm at school. This is sort of a field trip, a solo assignment you're helping me with."

"I've never seen ears like that!" Syx reached up to feel his own velvety cat ears. "What's Perkola?"

"*Per-ko-na O-la*. It's a big city in a cavern nation called Vugh Deep."

"View what?"

"You know, a deep cavern… underground? You look kind of like you think I'm lying. I'm not. Most of the world that isn't Rep lives underground, where it's safe and free. Perkona Ola is a huge city, but more than that, much more, called a 'prefecture.' It has vast fields of every kind of crop, factories, towers, airports, a portal station, a university, you name it. And a fantastic library and museum, the Hall of Memory. We'll go there! I'll show you everything. It all runs on crystal power from the Uaimh System, where they've grown as big as tree trunks since forever. When you're in Perkona Ola it's just like being topside on a super nice day. The ceiling is made that way. It's timed with the sun, moon and stars as they appear above the Surface so they're mirrored in it and move just right, synchronized. They even make clouds that rain.

"And that's only one cavern. There are hundreds around the world. Only one country on Eorthe I know of is above ground. That's Black Land, because it's mostly a huge river delta. Well, its real name is Khémia. It's one of the oldest nations on the planet, so old no one knows how it started. Khémians say they came from some legendary island that sank a long time ago when the world was young, ages before the Liminal Age started three hundred and fifty or so years ago, when the Reps began the terror campaigns that forced everyone else underground. They're mostly anders there. And they have real lions. If my ears are hidden, I look exactly like a Khémian ander. They look exactly like canids but don't have quite the same ears. Theirs are more round on top and don't have the tufts. Well, maybe some of the old men do, and no one cares if they show them since the women even go topless. It's really hot there, like summer on overdrive. Maybe they're throwbacks." Bailey Boy chuckled. "Come to think of it, some of them do have kind of heavy brows, like ape-men." He bounced up, stuck out his lower jaw, and ambled in circles hunched over, and dragged his knuckles on the ground, and vocalized something like, "*Ooh-ooh-ooh!*"

Syx did not blink once as he watched this mysterious behaviour –

The noob stood up, and puckered his lips into a rosebud shape. While he gazed at Syx, he moved the little pink pucker to the side of his face for a moment. "If I knew the right words," he said, "I could order the masters to stop the hunt, lie down and go to sleep, possibly even return to the orphanage without remembering anything. Right now that's still beyond my powers."

"You have powers?" Syx rubbed his pads. "The bosses have all powers." The pain would lessen in time; he had long experience with pain and its limits. And the more Bailey Boy talked the more he could rest.

"We really must be on the move now. Otherwise the truant officers will sniff us out." The noob's eyes acquired a strange heightened look, a sparkle, almost a smile: "Then they won't be able to stop themselves from tearing our limbs out of their sockets. Our heads will be stuck on poles as a warning to anyone who passes this way… they'll gorge themselves on the leftover bits! It's what they do!" Bailey Boy tickled Syx's ribs. "*Eek!*" he shrieked. "Come on, Syx, let's get out of here!"

Syx stood up, rigid as a post.

"Hey… I'm *joking*." Bailey Boy turned to go –

Syx noted a small circular mark on his wrist. "What's that?" he asked.

"What's what?" The noob looked down. "Oh that. Come on, for goodness' sake! I will explain later. You're like a little baby asking for a treat when the house is burning down." And he yanked on Syx's arm.

"All right, all right!" Syx growled, and jerked his arm away. "No need to tear my fur out." Neither the lash of a loaded crop nor the touch of another being, equal horrors, were welcome.

Bailey Boy raised his palms in peace, and turned to walk the path, which soon grew less steep and made a gentle descent around a crag to reveal the scene before them: the way's vaguely visible level ribbon wound through the foothills of a range of snowy peaks beyond. The clouds above moved towards the fugitives, and thickened into woolly shapes that weaved into a dark blanket.

"It will rain soon," said the noob, "a new experience for you, no doubt."

"I've seen a drop or two," muttered Syx, "in the enclosure."

Bailey Boy threw his head back and chortled.

Syx's ears stood upright and tingled at the noob's wordless spontaneity. Yet it stirred something deep inside. It nearly evoked the memory of the last time he had seen Fuzzy alive. One of his hands moved automatically to massage the resonance that reverberated in his chest. As the hour ripened and the clouds dropped lower, his feet gradually numbed to the pain, although he could not help but halt their progress from time to time.

"Well, rest then for a bit while I look around for a balm," said Bailey Boy. "I'll be quick, so don't nod off. Keep your eyes peeled and your ears pricked." The noob winked, and disappeared over a ledge.

Balm? Syx wondered in silence. Alone now, he took in his surroundings. The light had dimmed, yet he sat and visually explored the indistinct far horizon. Row upon row of gentle hills undulated below, their valleys laden with pale mist. His eyes struggled to search out where the orphanage must be, but it had vanished beyond the misty edge of the world. In fact his mind wrestled with the facts of nature that impinged on it, even the fresh cool air. Grey light above darkened the land below in a range of colours from tan to loden to burnt umber. He did not close his eyes, as he had been commanded to keep them peeled. Instead he studied the lichen on the rocks nearby. This too flooded the senses. Such a plethora of patterns, fresh and graceful tiny shapes!

His ears pointed in the direction the travellers had come, and swivelled at the subtle scrabble of gravel as it rolled downhill. There before him stood upright a chubby furred being, who stared through the gleam of little black beads for eyes. Syx sat as still as the rocks, yet his heart raced. As his mind adjusted, he understood the creature to be much smaller than him, even smaller than Bailey Boy. The two creatures faced each other. Like two boulders, neither moved. Its tiny stature encouraged Syx to ask: "Who are you?"

The little rounded ears of the thing twitched, but it said nothing. It made a sudden jerk, then another and disappeared before his eyes. Or seemed to – two high-pitched tones whistled – and the second receded into the distance.

Bailey Boy sprang over the ledge with a green plant in hand. He squatted and tore the leaves from the stem, and stuffed them into his mouth. When they had been sufficiently softened, he palmed the mash, and rubbed the stuff into Syx's foot pads. The noob even tore the bottom off his undershirt and used the ragged strip of white cloth to hold the goo in place.

"Ow!..."

"You *are* a girly-man, aren't you?" Bailey Boy spat several times. "You know, this stuff tastes like the most absolute crap."

To the surprise of them both, Syx growled a proper growl this time – a low, quiet snarl – but nevertheless, they both held their breath. He knew this when he heard the noob exhale.

"Whoa, it's beginning already!" exclaimed Bailey Boy, and grinned.

"Do you mean my feet won't hurt anymore? And I can walk?"

"Soon. But no, I mean you're waking up."

"I don't know what you mean… I am awake. And I'm a felid. I keep telling you. Nor am I a fox or a kit. I'm a felid, a…"

The boy glanced at him, stood up, and rubbed his hands together. Clumps of green flakes fell to the ground. "Listen, I apologize. Maybe it's fun for me, but not for you. I can see it's making you grouchy, along with the sore feet. Where I come from it's a game to tease each other when we're children. Sometimes it gets out of hand, so I'll try to stop before it gets nasty. It's kind of a habit."

"Habit?" Syx asked. "What's that?"

"You know… a habit is a behaviour that becomes automatic. Maybe it's good at first, but you outgrow it. In fact that's what the hypnotic techniques used by the Reps take advantage of. It has to be reinforced because it's possible for any being to revert to their original baseline freedom-loving nature."

"I don't know what you mean."

Bailey Boy shook his head, and said, "Never mind, stop stalling! Let's just keep moving. Stand up now, Syx… you should be able to walk better."

As commanded, Syx stood, and for the first time in many hours did not wobble. "Oh…" he murmured, and looked at the noob.

Bailey Boy returned his gaze, grinned, and replied, "You're welcome."

Syx's heart resonated again. His cheeks contracted. It occurred to him that he must be "smiling." His solar plexus warmed, and his heart glowed.

As the noob had predicted, rain fell, at first in quick washes of heavy mist, then in torrents. The trail soon turned into a rill. Thunder boomed around them, and echoed everywhere, preceded by bright flashes of blue light. Syx's ears flattened behind the matted fringe that dripped streams of water into his brows and cascaded from the tuft of fur on his chin. He stopped to crouch. The booming crash was not unfamiliar, but in the past he had only known it muffled by stone walls and leaky but heavy slate or lead roofs installed when the orphanage had been an aristocrat's motte-and-bailey castle long ago. Here thunder sounded like massive boulders that crashed into each other above his head. He stilled his steps and shivered.

"Keep moving, Syx! There's a cave around here somewhere. There has to be, I just know it." Another prediction came true: a dark opening appeared around the next bend. Inside, they found shelter. Outside, the storm beat without mercy in an irregular pattern. Bailey Boy stood and shivered with his arms folded around his middle, and moved close.

Syx stiffened and backed away a few steps. Thunder and lightning was bad enough, but close proximity to another being had always meant pain.

"Oh, for goodness' sake, I don't bite!" The noob stamped his feet. His dark eyes flashed in the darkness. "You smell rank when you're wet, but I'm freezing and don't care. Just stand still. Stop squirming, you wiggly worm!"

Syx did as commanded. He had not noticed his odour. Was it bad? He had been called Stench by the Heptas more times than he could count, although that was only to ten. Rank meant stinky. Although wet, Bailey Boy did not stink. In fact he smelled vaguely like the little wildflowers Syx had sat on and crushed, before the small furry creature had shown up. He sensed the noob's body heat where they touched. They stood huddled together in silence until the storm abated. The outer darkness decreased, but not to its former brightness. The day had ended.

The boy turned away, and stripped off his tunic and undershirt.

Syx's felid night vision made out narrow shoulders, a slender but strong, hairless back that narrowed where it disappeared into the skin-tight black leggings – not black skin after all. While the haunches where they met the slim waist looked firm and well-rounded, the arms and legs were slender and shapely. Bailey Boy's dark mane, lengthened by being wet, hung in waves that streamed down the shallow channel of muscle between his shoulder blades. The noob handed the wet clothing to Syx behind him to hold, while he bent over and wrung out his mane too, which exposed not only the pointed ears, but the large bumps on his chest that could be seen even from behind. Bailey Boy shook his head, which tickled Syx's nose with droplets, and the noob shook out the undershirt and tunic, and put them back on before he turned around.

"Brr, that's better," he said, "a little. Let's find a flat place to sit or lie down back to back to keep warm. I'll take the chance you don't have fleas or lice. Be warned that we both may need delousing if you do, but I'll be sure to explain that it was an emergency I could have avoided if I hadn't lost my gear. We should get some rest. Our scent will have been washed away somewhat by the rain, but other signs may linger, so we'll have to move on at daybreak. The storm is moving in a direction to our advantage. It would be good to be as dry as possible though, so that you're less stinky."

Darkness thickened too much to see more than greyish mottled shapes, but somehow Syx knew the boy must be smiling, which elicited an unfamiliar but not unpleasant sensation. So what if he stank? He had not been much cooled by the rain, and glad to warm his guide if necessary. And the smooth rock proved not much harder than his spot on the straw on the floor in the stable. Gradually resistance to Bailey Boy's touch receded upon this decision.

✦

"Your stomach is growling," said Bailey Boy. "It woke me up. Actually, I could eat a frozen goat myself."

"What's that?" asked Syx, and stretched his back in a long arch.

"You really do have a lot to learn, don't you? Well, it's an animal native to our region in the mountains high above our caverns. It loves to play on the cliff faces. I'm just pulling your leg when I say I could eat one. That's just an expression. It only means I'm really hungry too."

Syx's legs remained unpulled, both of them. Nevertheless, he looked up, and asked, "What's an 'expression'?"

"Well," replied the noob, "it's a word or phrase that's… I don't know, just a saying that kind of refers to something else… I guess."

"Then you're right. I could eat ten pieces of nutted corn tack, with loads of butter melted over them because they've just popped out of the ovens. And are still without mould," he said, deadpan, "as hot as my pretty ass."

Bailey Boy chortled again. "You're funny, foxy… I mean Syx."

The noob's strange wordless vocalizations resonated in Syx's heart, and set it aglow. He said, "That's just an *expression* I remember… from somewhere."

They moved to the cave mouth, and carefully examined the view beyond it. The noob turned to Syx, and said, "You know, I think you're waking up a bit faster than I thought. I feel wonderful. Thank you."

"But I am awake." Syx peered at the noob. "What is 'thank you'?"

Bailey Boy peered back. "I mean I feel honoured and grateful that you… that you have given me a gift that I treasure. The gift of hope."

"What's a 'gift'?"

The noob's eyebrows peaked. "Never mind, you big… thingy. Let's get going."

Syx opened his mouth to ask what "thingy" meant, but the noob had turned and already hurried up the trail.

IV

The Hidden Land

THE RISING SUN lit the translucent woolly mists from within, even where they caught in the furrows between the rounded green hills. The sky above domed vast, blue and cloudless. The Sacred Sun's corona remained shrouded, filtered by vapour. Syx did not know that Eorthe's local star hid just beneath the horizon. He found it difficult to not simply stop in his tracks and dissolve his mind into the blue. The last of the damp in his tunic, however, distracted enough to make him remember to keep Bailey Boy in view. The little noob seemed happy to bound ahead, perhaps in a hurry to eat a goat, whatever that was. If it resembled nutted corn tack in any way, that was quite understandable. He lifted his chin, and sniffed the air. His keen sense of smell had expanded its range. The wildflowers that interspersed the strewn boulders, although varied greatly in fragrance, grew more distinguishable from the boy's scent, unique and sweet as it may be. Knowing this allowed him to relax his pace. He would not lose the trail after all. The pads on his feet could be favoured a little, although they had been nearly healed by the herbal poultice.

"Hey, you, whatever your name is. *Syx!* Get your pretty ass up here." The noob looked as if he stood on the edge of the sky.

When Syx reached that high spot, he gazed out at a wilderness that extended to and across the wide horizon with absolutely no sign of habitation anywhere. In the alpine distance spired mountains and more mountains, countless jagged peaks topped with white under swept high clouds.

"Isn't it grand?" Bailey Boy smiled his beautiful smile. "We're home."

No castles in sight, no towers, not even one hut – "Where is it?"

"I told you, it's below ground! Not even the Reps' drones can find it, let alone the dragon ships way up in the stratosphere."

Syx peered at Bailey Boy.

"No worries," the lad said, "all shall be revealed, my friend. You know, I could kiss your beautiful whiskers!" Bailey Boy danced in circles, and leapt and hopped.

Syx looked on the display of exuberance, and a strange oscillation in his vocal cords produced rhythmic harmonics. An internal alarm went off. His eyes opened wide, certain that roots grew from his feet into the ground and lashed him to the spot he stood on.

Bailey Boy's fine dark eyebrows raised, but he turned to Syx, and said, "Hey, now *there's* a sign, no doubt about it."

"I… *I don't know what you mean!*" Syx moaned out loud for the second time. He had done something very wrong. He had made a very big mistake. Now he would be punished –

"Oh, stop saying that, for goodness' sake!" The noob formed a rosebud with his mouth again, and regarded the felid. "Syx, apologies. Never mind. I'll let my teacher explain. There's no one better at that." He reached out his slender hand to take Syx's into his warm firm grasp.

The noob's touch no longer made Syx flinch and withdraw. In fact it provided an anchor. The wide world had opened to his overwhelmed senses in little more than a day. Its tremendous mystery revealed vast ignorance. Only Bailey Boy made it somewhat intelligible. Curiosity drowned in remorse, however. He decided to try to stifle the other sin too, the urge to whine, as Bailey Boy had commanded, even though the noob ranked low in biggerness.

Together they descended into the wilderness below.

◆

"You said you were home," said Syx. "But we've been on the move for most of the day. I'm feeling dizzy. Can we rest?"

Bailey Boy replied, "I forgot you're a big furry thing and need your feed. I'm not sure about nutty corn tack, but there will be plenty of everything to keep Your Thinginess purring soon."

Syx almost choked on the question of what "purring" meant. Instead he sat down beneath a gnarled tree along the long ledge in the cliff face that towered above their path. Maybe the noob would find a goat – he might even share some. Syx stroked his chin tuft, and looked out over the fantastically rugged terrain revealed by the generous Sacred Sun, which allowed him to live if he stayed in the shadows.

"You sure were scared back there," said the noob, "when the sun cooked off the fog. You even scared me."

Syx did not remember any of that, but as commanded, said nothing.

"You know," the noob continued, "I've been watching your orphanage and a few other places within a day's march or two for a long time now. Orphanages are only for felids, you know. That's because they don't taste good, to the Reps, I mean… not that anyone else eats them."

Syx refrained from mentioning his doubt of salted "pork." It occurred to him he had no idea what that word meant anyhow.

"I was teasing about you being served up as a Rep's dinner," Bailey Boy admitted. "They're too hard to keep completely hypnotized for long. Some can't be hypnotized at all, but that's true of anyone. Those unfortunates get early retirement. But the good ones, felids I mean, are invaluable as trackers and exterminators once they grow up. *And* they have nine lives."

Syx counted on his fingers –

"There's an infinite number of numbers, you know, not just ten!..." The noob hitched his shoulders, and grimaced. "Sorry, I didn't mean... anyhow, don't listen to anyone who tells you you're stupid." He tickled Syx's ribs, looked up into his face, and winked. "Except me."

Syx gazed into Bailey Boy's eyes, and relaxed.

The noob twinkled, and said, "Felids' lifespans are so long they don't need replacement for a long time. It's called 'return on investment,' with a good ratio... never mind. The Reps could easily breed smaller reptiles for the job, but think *Reptilia* class is too good for that, except for the Snake People to guard the tunnels the lizard men are too big for, only *they're* so stupid they'll eat each other. That's what we're taught. I'd like to see for myself if that's true.

"Anyhow, Reps prefer their cultivated livestock, like bugs, rodents, various birds for the eggs, stuff like that. They like cattle too, and sheep, any fairly big wild animal when they hunt for sport, except wildcats. They drink blood, and they'll eat ander meat and love canid, especially if they've died of fright, and if the flesh is left to rot until it's ripe. They love brains. Sometimes they bury them, then dig them up again in two weeks. It's their idea of gourmet cuisine, only usually they're too impatient for that. But if they *are* patient, and if they kill their prey at the height of terror just right, they harvest a unique brain chemical so addictive that it's illegal, I mean in their realm. Felid brains are not valued for that. Not because they're stupid, but because they don't scare so well, so the drug is less potent.

"The facilities for other species are more like farms than orphanages. The young are wanted for their innocence. That's because the Reps have lost theirs, their innocence I mean. Or never had any to begin with, so this is how they get in touch with what they think they're missing and need more than anything in the whole wide world. It's so magical to them that they've figured out how to concentrate the chemical's unspoilt vibrations to almost pure psi energy.

"But I'm finally coming back with something to show for my efforts. And that's you. Big beautiful you." The cheerful noob sat down beside Syx on the flat rock. "This is a big achievement for me, one step closer to qualifying for military college."

Bailey Boy's warm body radiated like a little oven. Syx asked, "What do you eat when you're watching those places? Where do you sleep? In caves?"

"Sometimes in caves. Or in trees. Weird for a canine, right? But not for canids, like our hominid ancestor. Canids are mostly hominid, just like felids."

Syx felt his brow wrinkle all on its own.

"Never mind, Syx. I bring food along if it's far to go. I left my rucksack behind this time because I was too totally thrilled when the door fell open. I think it must have rolled into the moat, and sank in the stagnant water. The loss will cost a few percentage points, unfortunately. I'd brought enough rations for us both too. *And* my warm waterproof cape, plus an extra one. I lost my multi-tool knife too. I'll be fined for that… and I should have thought about your feet… anyway, we also learn how to go without, like now. It's part of our training. We just breathe in a special way, sometimes we have to sit in the sun for a while."

"You do? Felids die if we dare do that. The Sacred Sun hates to death ill-made beings like felids."

"That's crazy. No wonder you were so scared. Maçina didn't make the sun, you know. The god is just an idea, a concept… mistaken for something real. Don't ask, you'll find out what a concept is one day. Anyhow, are you dead? You've been exposed to the sun at least a few times since it came up."

Syx remained silent for a moment. "I don't think I'm dead. But what do you eat when you're away from home?"

"Listen, I'm hungry too, especially when you keep asking. There's nothing much to eat up here but rodents and the odd bird's egg if you can find them, but I'm trained to forage for wild fruit or herbs and nuts, seeds, roots, things like that. And berries. I never steal. That's wrong. That's what the Reps do."

"*Berry…?*"

The noob leaned away, and looked up at Syx's profile. "It's all right. A berry is a small sort of fruit with no stone, just seeds. Have you never eaten one? They're nice and sweet, sometimes sour. Don't eat the green ones. They're vile, unless it's a gooseberry or a green grape. Did you only eat nutty corn tack at the orphanage?"

"I don't know. Feed is the same every day. It has nuts. And corn."

"What? No veg? No fruit? No wine, ha ha? Not in a place like that, I guess, but I wasn't allowed wine either until I was legal."

"What's a 'legal'?"

"Just legal… of legal age. You know, a grown-up."

Syx stiffened. "You're a *grown-up?* But you're only a furless little boy!"

Bailey Boy stood up, and peered at him. "I'm a boy? That's hilarious. Don't you know anything? *I'm a girl! Look!*" The noob twirled about to display himself full-circle, and chortled. But he calmed down, looked the seated felid in the eyes, leaned in, and placed a slim hand on each of his big shoulders. "I can't seem to help teasing you. I hope you know it's all in good fun." Bailey Boy pulled on Syx's chin tuft, and said, "I forget what it must have been like to have spent your whole life in captivity, isolated." He stood upright, set his hands on his hips, and scowled. "It's terrible what they do. Just terrible!"

Syx merely gaped at the strange little creature.

"You look like you don't get it, Sir Thingy. Look, you don't know what I am, right? There are many species... kinds of creatures, in this great big world, not just reptilians and felids."

Syx remembered the praying mantis. And the strange little furry being he had met while he waited for the balm for his foot pads – the whistling one. And the raven, the big black bird on the window sill.

"Felids, canids, anders and reptoids aren't indigenous... look, you and I are related, both altered by the Primordial Architects. Madam Ellaern can explain it properly. For now just know that I'm technically what's called a canid. I'm a *girl* canid. You're a *boy* felid. I'm a *her* and a *she*, you're a *him* and *he*. Get it? You call yourself felids because you think you're... whatever it is you think you are... cat people, sort of. I would never say I'm a dog person... anyhow, it's better to say you're just a person, the same as me and the same as anders. You'll see plenty of them too in Perkona Ola. We're just persons, people. You and I are not so different really, only never forget that I'm a girl and you're a boy."

Girl, canid, ander – only *girl* rang a bell somewhere in the back of his mind –

"Never mind, Syx. Maybe it will make more sense after your need for feed has been freed." Bailey Boy – no, *girl* – Bailey Girl braced her palms on his shoulders again, and looked intently into his eyes. Her windblown hair framed a friendly pretty face.

He stared at her until he felt dizzy. He moaned aloud for the third time, and buried his face in his hands.

"Oh, what have I done now?" she murmured. "Look, I'm sorry I called you names. You're definitely not a fox nor even of the same genus. I just happen to think fox kits are sweet, and your face reminds me of one. Right?" She leaned in, clasped her arms around his neck, and peered into his eyes. "Listen," she said, "You don't look like a fox really, you look more like a great big kitten." She embraced him, and sighed.

Her two firm chest bumps pressed against him, and her fragrance grew even more sweet. He closed his eyes. His arms of their own volition wrapped around her body. A warm soft light appeared between their hearts. They had always been together like this: solid, safe, peace itself. His throat oscillated – but the oscillation stopped as she pulled away.

"Enough rest, Syx," she said, and touched his mouth with a forefinger. Her eyes went a tiny bit cross-eyed as she focused on it, but she said, "Let's move," raised her gaze to his eyes, and twinkled again. "Come on, we're nearly home." She stood up and tugged on his hand. "I promise."

◆

Bailey Girl had jogged ahead, but stopped and turned about to face him. "Listen, Syx, this may be another shock. We're here. We're home."

Home. Syx glanced down at her, and scanned the horizon – but no castles anywhere, no towers, no buildings, no huts – nothing but mountains.

"I know it's strange," she said, "but you have to try to remain calm. You're hungry. I am too." She winked, and took his hand. "Close your eyes, Syx. And don't worry."

He relaxed, and did as commanded. The cool air warmed a little, and wafted into a light breeze. His ears pricked into points, and swivelled.

Bailey Girl said, "Syx, when I say so, open your eyes."

Obedient, he stood and waited.

A raven cried, like that time the black silhouette in the square window in the dark tower did – the sky had shone so intensely blue behind it – the shutters slammed shut – and now that first *caw!* joined an increasing number jumbled in layered discord – *caw! caw! caw!* more and ever louder: *caw! CAW! CAW!* –

"Syx, dear, open your eyes!"

Beside Bailey Girl stood a felid a little taller, not quite as slender, with a tawny mane in a tidy bun, no striped patterns, only a few small faint freckles at the temples – and large golden eyes framed in dark lashes – and little oval windows stuck on her eyes! –

Syx's eyes could not open wider: a *girl* felid – *CAW!* – and he moaned aloud a fourth time. His eyes had been commanded to open, so he dropped on all fours and stared at the floor. *CAW! CAW! CAW!*

But Bailey Girl's hands touched him, and the harsh corvid cries faded.

Madam Ellaern *of* Vugh Deep.

28

"Madam Ellaern," she said, "this is Syx."

The tawny felid-girl teacher never took her golden eyes off him. "Welcome, Syx," she said. "You are most welcome," she repeated in speech more accented than Bailey Girl's. Her golden eyes drew him in and in and in, and she said: "I have looked forward to this meeting for a very long time. Syx, you forget your sorrows." And she clapped her hands together.

From out of nowhere appeared persons like Bailey Girl, of variant statures. Some had browner skin, some as light as his own. All wore similar clothes, like Bailey Girl's, only clean and crisp. Anders, he guessed, by the shape of their ears. They bowed to Madam Ellearn.

Syx at that instant noticed the edifice of white stone behind them. He gazed upwards. Towers with conical tops directed his eyes to a high concavity of buffed blue softly lit from within, but not the real sky, because no compulsion arose to dissolve into it. Brighter points of light glittered across the concavity. Glossy lines overlaid its matte surface. Pale line drawings of mythological creatures marked the ecliptic, although he did not know to call it that, nor had he any notion of *mythos*. But his stomach growled.

◆

"Please be seated, sir," said an ander, who smiled and gestured to one of two chairs, which he had pulled out from beneath a long wooden table polished to a natural glow, unlike the rough furniture of the orphanage.

On the other chair sat Bailey Girl. She nodded to Syx.

He looked back at her, and wrinkled his brow.

She frowned and nodded quickly towards the chair.

He did as commanded, and a big steaming bowl appeared before him. The aroma made him giddy. His throat lightly oscillated.

"Well," said Bailey Girl, "dive in as we used to say when we were little."

Happy to obey, Syx soon learned how to use the "spoon" when instructed in the technique. The ander took the empty bowl away. More deliciousness appeared, orders of magnitude better than nutty corn tack, even with nettles, even with rare butter. At length the need for feed had indeed been freed. Only then he noticed Bailey Girl's eyes.

She reached across the table, clasped his hands, and twinkled.

29

V

The Hall of Memory

His sleepy eyes opened upon an indecipherable view until he remembered Bailey Girl. Above, a pattern of soft green velvety shapes gently caressed the eye. Whatever created the velvet highlights made him turn to see where the light came from. No straw on the floor, and no other sleeping places beyond the velvety canopy of the soft bed, where he partially raised himself on one elbow – just a fireplace between two tall windows with long green velvety draperies at their sides, each panel of which hung from a horizontal metal rod with curled ends. In front of each window sat a wooden chair shaped like a scoop. One entire wall consisted of many empty wooden shelves and something like a table with drawers beneath it. A fire had been lit – or what looked much like a fire, but no smoke. Warm air, not his experience of waking on most mornings – and windows! He leapt out of bed and rushed to see outside. There below on the very flat grassless ground countless small beings moved across a large square, unwalled and surrounded by many buildings big and small. In the pale blue sky above drifted several objects. He moaned aloud a fifth time – but stopped too late – a rap of knuckles on wood, and the click of a door latch –

"Are you all right, sir?" a voice asked.

A sigh betrayed his hiding place behind the curtain. "No," he explained, "I'm Syx." He noticed that he held his breath, and exhaled. "Where is…?" He must not call her Bailey Girl.

"Sir, she is in her room. Soon the dining hall will open, where you can meet. Or else I can ask the young lady now if you wish." There stood the speaker, a boy, a hairy one – his voice low in pitch, and a figure more heavily built than other boys so far – and a dark mane, which hid the tops of his ears, with no fuzz in the canals. *Shaved? A neanderwhatsit?* He also had dark fur on his face, perhaps what his own must be like, but all over his lower face and longer, down to the middle of his wide chest. Since the boy wore clothes from neck to toe, Syx wondered whether fur grew on other parts of his body. "I'm not who you said," he repeated. "I'm Syx. I'm a felid."

"Very good, sir." The boy did not look at him, but into empty space, and explained: "I'm not to address you by name, I'm sorry to say. Orders from above, you see. You may not know my name either, for now. Rest assured I understand that you're a felid. I mean no disrespect addressing you as I do, sir."

The sin of curiosity displaced any anxiety. Syx stepped out into the room.

The furry boy raised his head enough to glance at him out of one eye, and straightened his posture, but did not look again at Syx. "With your permission, sir," he said, "Chancellor Ellaern requests that she be informed of your availability when you are ready."

Syx rubbed his tattooed crown. "I don't know what you mean," he replied. The stubble on his head grazed his palm like nettle spines.

"I beg your pardon, sir. I only mean that, if you are rested, the chancellor requests your company briefly. To prepare, may I suggest a bath and fresh attire?"

Syx did not know how to answer. "What am I to do? What are the chansler's orders?"

"If I may be so bold, sir, I shall groom you if you like, and suggest appropriate attire to replace your tunic, which we will clean and store for you if you wish.

Perkona Ola prefecture, Vugh Deep.

We shall then go directly to Chancellor Ellaern's office. Madam will answer the questions I cannot." The boy bowed again.

"You shouldn't bow like that. I'm a Syx, not a Hepta. What is 'groom'?"

"Ah, grooming is washing, trimming and brushing your hair to make it shine, and to don clean clothing for a neat and tidy appearance. But first, a bath. It's very good for you, sir, and makes a fine impression on the ladies." The furry boy leaned forward slightly, peered at Syx, and winked. "If you know what I mean." He straightened, and resumed the formal stance.

"I don't know what you mean. But I must not make the… the chansler angry. What is 'bath'?"

◆

Unexpected delight arose at the answer to that question, once he got over the embarrassment of persuasion to remove his tunic. But the sheer torture of a stiff brush dragged through the fringe of wet red mane made him squirm in ticklish convulsions. The fur on his shaggy head had become badly tangled. The boy warned him of an ordeal, but something called "frizz" should be avoided. Clippy-snippy sounds made Syx shut his eyes tight as he sat while the furry boy hovered over his head. When silence returned, the barber opened a drawer to withdraw a tool of some kind, so that Syx could view the progress of the job, he said, and approve the results. At first Syx did not see anything, just jittery images, jumpy shapes through the hoop or paddle the boy held in his hand. As it steadied, at once Syx recognized a felid – with *green eyes*. Impossible. How could he be looking at himself looking at himself – *looking at himself?* He stifled a sixth moan, a "habit" that never did any good. This small insight empowered a decision: he must not run away from what he did not understand. He must simply accept what is and see what happens, actually a big relief.

"You look exceedingly presentable, sir! A truly handsome young man."

Man?

"May I suggest a small tasteful brooch to complement the brocade?"

Unnoticed until the furry boy dragged it into view, in a glassy device similar to the paddle but full-length and rectangular – a "mirror" – and in it a complete felid with rich clothing that covered more than his old tunic had. But green eyes looked directly into his. A seventh moan had to be squeezed into a thin squeak that trailed off into silence – he summoned courage to look again at the felid face – but unlike any noob or rookie – nor did it resemble a Hepta, who typically wore a perpetual scowl and aged before his time. This face looked neither young nor old. Syx did not quite accept that it might be his own, but did perceive that it meant him no harm. And he moved without worry that seams might rip – interesting, the felid in the mirror thing moved at the same time, and copied whatever he did – in leg tubes too, like Bailey Girl's only not so tight. Over a very comfortable and clean soft white tunic that allowed free movement of shoulders and arms, slipped a warm black vest subtly patterned with leafy designs. He had already forgotten to ask about the "brooch" but the furry boy pinned it to the vest and told him to take care not to lose it.

Syx tilted his head forward and peered into the glassy mirror's reflective surface. The brooch thing had been shaped like the unforgettable silhouette of the raven he had glimpsed long ago – it had marks in the bright metal's edge, meaningless to the illiterate –

"Excellent, sir, dashing indeed. If you're fine to go unshod until later, when a visit to the bootmaker is on the agenda, the chancellor awaits."

◆

The click of the latch as it closed behind him sent a shiver up his spine. But Syx determined not to let his mind be overtaken by the girl-felid teacher a second time. *Chansler.* Yet her dark-rimmed intense golden gaze commanded total attention without her having spoken a word – no hint of a twinkle like Bailey Girl's – but her authority demanded a semblance of calm. The tawny blonde-tipped mane – the fine raiment that swaddled her, the waist narrow like Bailey Girl's, and the two rounded bumps on her chest that raised her shimmery gown – light from yet another tall window at her side reflected in the tiny flat fragments of shiny metal patterned in the fabric – sparkles when she moved even slightly entranced the eye, but – to look made him dizzy –

"Syx, please pay attention," Madam Ellaern said. "Staring at a woman's chest is impolite. And I have something important to say to you."

Womans? Her accent fascinated in a manner unlike Bailey Girl's –

Madam Ellaern gazed softly at him, but with great concentration.

His attention focused. A thought appeared: *I'll do anything you ask...* She did not shriek like a Hepta – insistent, but smooth and soft, like fresh butter –

"Syx!"

"I am a Syx," he said, and blinked.

"You do clean up nicely, I must say. Now, I know how strange everything must feel to you," she said, "but please remember that you are safe. I will be

33

brief. Now look into my eyes again. Relax, completely… good. You feel very calm, composed and attentive. Very good. You will forget the past. Forget now."

Syx blinked, ignorant of what she meant.

The chancellor studied him with intense focus. "Your squire will take you to the dining hall now. The young woman who brought you to us will meet you there. She will show you around later. Feel free to ask her anything you wish to know."

Syx stared at the teacher-chansler-felid-girl – *young woman?*

The door opened, and the same furry boy who had given him groom bowed. Syx looked to Madam Ellaern for instruction.

She nodded once at him, and looked towards the door, then back at him.

The furry boy straightened, and said, "Please, sir, follow me."

⬩

Bailey Girl smiled and waved when Syx spotted her among the many other persons in the dining hall, who all talked at once. The din threatened to send him reeling, but the furry squire boy led him to an empty chair at her side, which the squire pulled away and stood behind.

"Syx, for goodness' sake," Bailey Girl said, "sit down, please."

Bailey Woman, the voice in Syx's head corrected. Asked what he would like for breakfast, he replied that he would like her to choose. Another captivating meal appeared, worlds away from nutty corn tack yet so different from the first one. Syx at last looked up, and reminded himself: *Bailey Woman, a person.*

She twinkled at him, and hitched her shoulders. "Syx, I can't believe how good you look." Her pupils dilated subtly, but she looked away. Her palm swept one side of her hair back, and her cheeks reddened a little too before she looked up, and said, "But now we'll take a tour, if you like. We'll see as much as we can see in the next few hours. You may ask me anything. It's my duty and my joy to explain." Her dark eyes sparkled.

He mirrored her twinkle, stood up, and let her lead the way. Attention riveted on the way she walked, and the corners of his mouth turned up, thus the din receded into insignificance. The dining hall turned out to be part of a much larger building, itself part of a complex, so brightly lit by shutterless windows, and so clean. Eventually they emerged into the street. His mind boggled at the number of buildings big and small, mostly big. Persons walked everywhere. A few small furry persons walked along on all four limbs, and led two-legged persons by tethers. Most amazing of all: carts, with four wheels instead of two, sort of wagons but covered – and persons within looked out from windows, and rolled along somehow self-propelled.

"Those little furry persons," he said, "who are they?"

Bailey Woman chuckled. "They're *pets* called 'dogs.' Dogs are canines, like canids descended from the wolf, but not mixed with our hominid ancestor. They've been bred into all manner of styles, shapes and sizes. Pets are adorable animals that we care for and love. Some are felines, but not mixed with our ape-man ancestor like felids are. They're *Felis catus*, related to lions, tigers, lynxes, cougars, leopards, all kinds of wildcats, but they're too independent and dangerous to be led in the streets. Oh, and some pets are even related to reptoids, reptilians! Even birds are. Pets are raised as companions and give us much pleasure." Bailey Woman paused, and added, "Long ago they came from the wild, and some of those creatures were attracted to our activities, such as hunting and farming. We found them helpful, and they became our friends."

Syx stopped, overwhelmed by the "concept" of "pets." Just then he noticed that the furry boy-squire walked right behind them, so he turned around.

The squire bowed. The crowd of persons flowed around.

Syx sighed, and turned to his canid guide. "I must ask… what is 'squire'?"

Bailey Woman twinkled. "A squire is a special companion to one of high rank. You know… someone who's important, whom the squire escorts, and whose needs the squire takes care of, like a personal assistant."

Syx knew what rank meant: it turned a "smell" into a "stench." His brow wrinkled, but curiosity grasped at something he might understand more easily: "Is the squire then a pet?"

Bailey Woman chortled. "No! No, not a pet! Pets are *animals*. This squire of yours is a person like us. A *man* ander, by the way." She put her fingers to her mouth, and peered up at Syx. "Maybe," she said, "we should go to the White Tower. We can see much of the city from up there. Then we'll go to the Hall of Memory I told you about, where I'll show you pictures that will explain things a lot better than I can in words."

They wove their way through the traffic, persons on foot and self-propelled wagons, and entered the base of an extremely tall keep, the White Tower, aptly named, built of gleaming stone, and so finely crafted the perfectly chiselled blocks showed barely visible spaces between them. Inside many more persons milled about in no particular order, just as he had noticed when he first looked out from his high bedroom windows. They hardly glanced at the three tourists, who made their way to a door within. Bailey Woman led him through the door into an empty closet – a queasy place until a little bell chimed, and they stepped into a wide room where persons looked out through large windows to a vast horizon beyond immense natural stone pillars that seemed to hold up the sky. The pillars had windows too, many. Scattered between the pillars stood an orderly array of countless massive buildings of various shapes and sizes, divided by criss-crossing straight paths in a grid pattern. Above and below the vantage point drifted floating objects of the kind Syx had observed through his bedroom windows, unnoticed by the people who streamed like ants below. Lost for words, he remembered Madam Ellaern had said he could ask about anything. "What are those things floating in the sky? Why does no one notice?"

Bailey Woman replied, "They're… vehicles called discs. Instead of riding in grounders, ones that are meant for streets and roads, we can ride in discs through the air. It's quicker if we have to go far, and we can land in high places like birds, without having to climb cliffs. Does that make sense? Oh, and no one pays much attention. We're quite used to such marvels… but we take them for granted. In time you'll understand how they work. We'll even take a ride in one if you like!"

Syx's eyes opened wide. "Can we go back now?"

"Of course, right after we visit the Hall of Memory. This is probably a lot to take in right now, right?" She placed her slender hand on Syx's forearm. "It's all right, Syx, you'll master everything in no time. I know you will, and I'll help you. Madam Ellaern says you're my responsibility because I helped you escape from the orphanage, but I want to more than anything, really. We'll make it fun!"

"No…"

"Syx, don't be like that. You'll learn about everything. Your skills will take you to amazing places. You'll do great things with your life."

"I don't know what you mean. When can I go home?"

"You're like a man-sized kitten. That's not your fault. Yes, you'll find a home one day. That's why we busted you out of that prison, my one small contribution to freedom so far. And you were so brave. But you have to prepare. You can't just go home without understanding how to get there. You need to understand the world we're in. Come." She twinkled, and took his hand. "Let's begin."

✦

A wide building of many storeys, the Hall of Memory housed numerous large rooms, some with cases that held strange objects, all of them old, many broken. Syx wondered why they had not been thrown out in a world that enjoyed so much better. He recognized canes, whips, buckets, mops and floor brushes, but little else. They passed through rooms in which gilt-framed images, painted like

Kirzaka's portrait, populated with persons that displayed the kingdom's past, and pictures with nothing but trees and lakes and waterfalls and sunsets, sometimes a table with fruit. Often the painted persons wore nothing, stark naked or mostly so. The bare chest bumps on the girls stood out. Syx stopped to stare.

"Syx, please come away from there. Let's save looking at art for another time." Bailey Woman took his hand, and said, "Come." She kept him moving, their destination a large room where roamed many noisy little persons, cubs too, accompanied by grown-ups who herded them among rows of cubicles behind low walls.

At one vacant cubicle, Bailey Woman stopped, and said, "If you sit here and watch, Syx, you'll learn about animals that aren't pets, but live free in the wild, in nature." She pointed to a small wooden chair with an inclined board attached to it. "It's fun. Look into the screen. When I push the button, watch what happens. Remember, you're perfectly safe. I'll be away from you only a short while. I'll come back soon. Stay put until the movie, the picture story, is finished."

He sat.

She squeezed his shoulder, and left.

Syx, perched atop the low seat as well as he could, did as commanded. Before him the inclined board brightened and turned into a window. Within it a landscape moved as if the window itself turned this way and that. It made him dizzy at first. Often the scene changed before he knew what happened. Strange creatures appeared, and a pleasant voice gave them names and explained how the undomesticated beings roamed freely in the wild outdoors, ate things and ran and hid from others who wanted to eat them, terrible to witness, but the contrast between living beings and dead gore fascinated. The discomfort of sitting in an awkward position forgotten, he hunched low and leaned forward, and imagined he could almost smell what he saw.

Many strange creatures in a series of picture-stories later, his attention riveted on a large animal the voice identified as a lion, the wild being Kirzaka the Deathless, Talon of Maçina, had combined with some extinct creature to make the two-legged felids. The lion stood on all fours like a pet. Syx noted whiskers, a bit like his own, but its dark triangular nose resembled a pet's, and its mane encircled its whole face. And its paws looked the same as its feet, not like Syx's at all. He should not call his hands paws anymore. Also unlike him, a long tail grew from just above the lion's bum, like some of the other creatures, but with a tuft of dark fur at the tip. Its face looked much more like a pet than the face he remembered seeing in the mirror. Unlike a pet, the lion led no one by a tether. It seemed not to care about its stark-nakedness, and meandered through tall grass, its eyes intense. Its ears swivelled. Its head lifted higher, and it sniffed the air. It leapt ahead and ran on all four limbs. The scene changed to a group of anders like the squire, only beautifully dark-skinned and less furry. They carried long pointed sticks and something folded up like a blanket. The lion stopped, trapped. The anders made much noise, and yelled too. Some banged on upside down bucket-like things. Syx's ears rang – panic flared – but he remembered the command to stay put until the picture-story finished. The lion in the story-window crouched and opened its mouth wide, roared and displayed fearsome sharp fangs like a reptilian's. The roar caused Syx's teeth to chatter. But he stayed put, as commanded.

The anders surely wanted to capture the odd-looking lion because it had escaped, to return it for punishment as a lesson to others who might succumb to the same evil temptation –

Syx wrung his hands and rocked in place – but he did not look away.

The dark-skinned anders yelled and threw the ropy blanket, which had holes so large it was barely there.

The lion, covered with the net, stood up on its hind legs at last, but pawed and clawed in vain. Too late. The more it struggled, the more it got entangled.

Syx's heart grew heavy.

The noisy anders grew quiet, and fell to the ground on their knees, arms stretched out before them.

Through the tall grass that only reached its knees Lord Boss loomed into view, its scales iridescent where visible beneath black metallic armour that glinted in the Sacred Sun. The familiar heavy breath passed through wet round nostrils – in, out, in, out – and the grunt of approval –

But Syx did not look away. He even looked into the small orange eyes, even their black slit pupils. Syx's skin crawled as a splinter of sharp fear tried but failed to pierce his heart. The window grew dark. Syx closed his eyes to recall *the lion the bosses made felids from* –

Her gentle touch on his shoulder let him know Bailey Woman had returned. "The movie is over, Syx," she murmured in his ear. "You can stand up now. We'll come back another day. I told you it would be fun, right?"

VI
Inward Gaze

Syx watched Bailey Woman stroll towards his seat in the mezzanine he had claimed as a lookout over the campus.

She took his hand and tugged. "Come, cubby," she said. "Madam Ellaern sent me to fetch you. It's time you remembered your name. Then you'll learn mine. That will certainly make things easier for me. And you won't have to put up with my nicknames for you. Names have power, you know."

They did not meet in Madam Ellaern's office this time, but in a part of the campus far removed from the busy common areas. In a small quiet room with no windows, a low ceiling and soft lighting, the chancellor gestured towards a smooth white chair shaped like an egg, but with a section cut out of it to reveal a blue cushioned interior. And it hovered above the floor, with no visible means of support –

"Please sit inside the egg chair and make yourself comfortable," she instructed. "You will soon hear tones while inside this device that will relax you so completely you will think you are asleep and dreaming. You are perfectly safe, but I believe you know that now, and have known for several days, is that not so?"

Syx nodded assent, and replied, "I am a Syx." He chewed his lip, and held his breath. *What's wrong with me?* he asked himself. *She seems so nice.*

The chancellor fixed him in her gaze, and said, "No, Syx, I do not order it like a Hepta, I *facilitate*. It means I encourage. I make it easier for you to remember the time before you were taken from your home. By this means you will know you are completely safe. There is no danger, although what you will experience will seem quite real. You may see people you knew when you were very small. Ignore them. Only your mother and father you recall. Today you remember your given name. All right?"

"Yes. I want to know. I want to know everything." Syx entered the chair, which formed around him perfectly and straightened his spine. Soon he floated freely as the room went as black as the stable that had hosted his orphan nightmares. Instructed that he would seem to be all alone, but assured the teacher-chansler-felid Madam Ellaern and his canid friend Bailey Woman stood by, he had no trouble relaxing as if asleep while awake. Or perhaps the other way around. The external temperature increased slightly until his body lost its limits in the total silence that ensued. A light appeared in the distance. He had always known the light, only had forgotten it. Or not, not really. Maybe only the light existed, and he had dreamt a small room with an egg-shaped chair. But now time unfolded. Without effort he moved towards the light. Or perhaps it moved towards him. The light acquired definition. Colours and shapes formed within it. A scene congealed, and its parts moved into place. So familiar, it glowed with warmth. Rich with potential, it must be the stage on which his earliest life played. He saw through the little cub's eyes, in fact all the senses and the thoughts in his young mind now unavoidable.

Her familiar smile blessed him. Sunshine made a halo of golden mane around her head. *Mama!* His tiny body – joy itself. She lifted him to her face to be nuzzled by love. A little click made her hold him to her warm soft breast. She turned towards the wooden gate of the path to their hut. In strode his father, an even more lively jolly figure. *Papa!* Easily the cub flew between the two, then up into the air above his mother's head and back into his father's strong arms, safe. Papa set him on his little feet; his knees wobbled, but he looked up and adored the two giants, who kissed each other and twinkled as they looked into each other's eyes. If the little one had known the word "gratitude" he would have shouted it through the treetops to the sky. Instead the tyke just shouted in wordless glee. But not for long –

Solid wood smashed into splinters, louder than when Papa chopped wood for the cooking fire. The scintillating iridescent patterned scales that covered the intruders' muscular frames tall as trees amazed the little one nevertheless – his first brief sighting of a squad of armoured reptilians, their spines spiked with shiny metal protrusions below the blue-feathered combs that spumed through their hard metal helmets.

His mother covered his head with her itchy shawl and told him to always look away – and *never oh never* look again into the black slits of their widely separated eyes like small orange beads stuck on a lizard doll's face – they dragged his poor father off into the unknown, never to be seen again. Mama? *Gone.* Forever gone, lost. And he lost even the name they had given him.

Gravity tugged at his being. Until then he had forgotten it. It enfolded his heart, and he sank into the darkness. The atmosphere cooled, and the lighting of the small room with the egg-shaped chair returned. In fact he now understood he sat *in* the chair, and had not observed it from outside. He blinked, and tried to focus, but found himself again outside the chair somehow.

"Welcome back," said Madam Ellaern. "You are no longer to be called Syx. It is not a proper name, only the lowest rank, based on a number, six, the numeral of incompletion. You will now never become a Hepta, a seven, the numeral of so-called completion. You have been saved from that terrible fate. Tell me, what is your true name?"

He, formerly Syx, blinked at Madam Ellaern. "I'm called Rowan."

"Do you remember also the name of the place you were taken from?"

"The place is called Berry," he replied. "I'm Rowan Berry, born in that place." An eighth moan threatened – but dissipated.

"Turn around, Rowan Berry. Meet Samarit Longbow."

Rowan did as commanded. Bailey Woman – who had rescued him from slavery, his friend – "Samarit," he said, and savoured the sound. *Names have power.*

"Nice to meet you, Rowan." She smiled like his mother had in the vision, and extended her hand.

He looked down at it, and into her dark eyes. He took her small hand into both of his. "Nice to meet you, Samarit." *If I knew the proper words,* he thought, *I would shout them.*

•

"Samarit, why are you also called Longbow?" Her fresh pretty face said so much more than her words, but he loved to watch her do just about anything.

From their perch in the mezzanine, Samarit looked up from the campus square in evening light, much less travelled than during the day. "It's not a place like Berry," she said, "it's a clan… well, it's a job, maybe a role if you like. I'm a Wishbone Warren Longbow, one of the tribes of Longbows, a clan that in this part of the world has been soldiering for the kingdom and guarding the borders for centuries. Many of us belong to the warrior guild. A longbow is a weapon of ancient times, one that shoots feathered arrows, but it's kept by tradition as our emblem. And name." She bared the top of her wrist. "See? My tattoo shows a warrior drawing a bow and arrow. The arrow feathers were most prized when taken from dead reptoids. I'll show you traditional longbows next time we visit the Hall of Memory."

Rowan frowned as he slowly took in her words. "You mean you plucked them from bosses? Wait… did you *kill* them? Are you saying they can *die*? I don't know what you mean!"

"You don't? They try to convince the world they're immortal, right? It's pure lizard crap. You mustn't believe it."

Rowan held his breath.

Samarit sat up straight, turned to look at him, and lowered her brows. "Hey, they deserve it. We'd be a tasty snack otherwise, only a belch to remember us by. Now we have weapons that make arrows look like toothpicks…" She squinted at him, and asked, "Listen, did I say something wrong?"

"I don't know." Rowan sat hunched, rested his elbows on his knees, and stared unseeing at his feet.

"Now, hang on, cubby… Rowan. You're still hypnotized. I'll ask Madam Ellaern to fix that. It may take some work. The Reps are evil incarnate and every single one is a supremely nasty piece of work. You've got to drop this warm fuzzy thing you've got going for them. Remember, they killed your parents, and they kept you in the dark for dirty jobs like blood duty."

＊

Madam Ellaern remained seated behind her desk. "Please, sit down, Rowan," she said. "There is something we need to discuss."

He sat – and looked into her eyes – her golden eyes –

"Very good. Keep your eyes open and locked onto mine. You are relaxed, sleepy but not asleep. Dreamy, but you do not dream. I show you the real world. Berry, the hamlet where you were born, is gone. But you find a new home, where you are safe and happy."

"I'm happy now, madam, when I hear this. It's been my only wish… to go home." An oscillation formed in his throat.

She leaned back, and continued, "Rowan, you are three-and-sixty years of age, on the threshold of adulthood for our species. I am half felid. I come from a place far away, of a family of cottage-industry weavers for generations. That lifestyle came to end when a militant collective took over and forced everyone to work in factories to mass-produce what we had until then sold in our local marketplace. The whole region became enslaved to the clock. No one owned anything anymore, and our ancestral roots were torn… forgive me, we are here to talk about you, not me. I only add that I am one hundred and twelve years old. Much has changed in the world since we were younger. You could not have noticed while in captivity, isolated and uneducated. For you there was only the repetition of uneventful days on end, apart from the killings, only some of which were public executions if it suited the reptilians' purposes. Until now you were unprepared for life freed from captivity, still under their spell, hopeful of life as an exterminator or if very lucky a tracker. I here and now remedy that in short order, with methods I have developed over many long years, thanks to technology we have built based on the discoveries of archaeology here far below the Surface world, as well as borrowed from elsewhere."

"I don't know what you mean."

Her black-rimmed golden eyes narrowed. "Yes," she said, "but what I am saying is that I remedy that. Focus. You know for certain the reptilians are evil, our enemies who only want to destroy us. They deserve to die."

"Samarit said that too. But what is 'tek...' and the other thing?"

"Technology is the application of knowledge for practical purposes, machines and devices for the most part," she answered. "Archaeology is the study of the past through investigation of what has been left behind by people who came before us long ago. Very often no writings remain for historians, people who study past events, and for philologists, who study languages and how they develop, so we must infer, make smart guesses, about how they lived and what they knew, based on the objects and structures ancient peoples made that have survived."

"But... what is 'Surface world'?"

"Apologies, Rowan. As a former teacher I should know better than to not have your knowledge level tested before we attempt to explain too much, and in the wrong order. For now, think of the cave that you and Samarit took shelter from the storm in on your journey here. Where we are now is like that, only very much deeper underground, in a place that's very safe, however. No enemy means of detection can find us. Not yet."

Rowan stared at her. "But the cave was dark and cold." He recalled Samarit as she peeled off her soaked clothing and wrung it out – he had called her Bailey Boy, as if only boys existed. "Here everything's bright and warm," he said. "It doesn't seem like the cave at all. But how can the sky be so light then? Sometimes there's a bright spot... but where is the Sacred Sun?"

"Unlike that little natural cave, our city is part of a vast cavern that has been carefully carved out over a very long time. Its entrance is invisible. You would not have seen the door that only special people like Samarit can open. It is warm here because we are closer to the fiery forces of nature that flood beneath our world, where the rock is molten, so hot it is melted. The forces create great heat, but we know how to use it to our advantage. Water seeps from the Surface and also wells inside, and we capture it, and allow the fire below to heat it for various purposes. As to why the sky is bright, we have discovered long ago that the sun above the Surface world is itself a manifestation of a force that is everywhere, accessible by means of crystals. Through long study we have devised ways of making it useful, in the case of our inner sky to make it spread evenly across the carefully honed concave inner surface of our cavern. It is like a very strong upside down bowl. Understand? So the city below is lit as we prefer, without adding extra heat. The moonlight is just a limited version. All this is necessary because our ancestors originated on the Surface, so our bodies still have internal rhythms we cannot alter without making us ill."

"I want to learn." Rowan tried to hold all that she had said at once in one bundle in his thoughts, like too many sticks of firewood, some or all of which might fall on his toes. "The first thing," he said, "now that I know my name, and Samarit's name, is what exactly is 'boy' and 'girl'? I think I only know boy, except the bosses. They didn't seem to be boy *or* girl. But my mama and papa, they were the same as each other, but different too. Felids, like me…" Words welled up on their own all too quickly, but he did not know how to stop them, and spoke ever faster as he tried to match them to thoughts and keep up with the feelings they provoked: "Like *you* too, but *not* like the lion I saw in the picture-story at the Hall of Memory. Mama told me of her own mama. She was a 'woman' like Mama. Papa was a 'man' but not like the squire. But the Heptas made us Syxes believe the bosses *can't* die. They come from the Sacred Sun. They *can't* die. They know *everything*. Compared to them we're like the wiggly bugs in nutty corn tack are to us. They made us. We're *nothing*…" Rowan squirmed in his chair. "I'm not sure what I'm asking now…" His face tensed, his throat dried and scratched, which made him croak. "Asking is bad… a bad sin."

"Look at me, Rowan. Look into my eyes. Listen. Asking questions is *not* a sin. Curiosity is one of the capacities that helps you grow into a proper person. Do not worry, Rowan, we will teach you everything. It will not take long. Look at me." Madam Ellaern's golden eyes grew bright. "Your intelligence is awake." Her golden orbs held sadness deep inside, although she pretended otherwise for some reason.

But Rowan too brightened at her tacit promise. It calmed his mind. Something within resonated, so much so that his throat oscillated the loudest it ever had. "Pardon me. What *is* that sound I make?"

"It is called 'purring,' Rowan. We felids make that sound when we're truly happy. It is good, very good."

VII

Learning Curve

Rowan confirmed that Samarit had been right: *many* more numbers than just ten existed. He soon discovered that and much more as he took his place among the young anders and a few felid cubs in his local primary school. He towered above his classmates in stature only, and eagerness to learn precluded any embarrassment. The children soon accepted him as a fact like the furniture in the classroom, although at first they tugged at his hands to invite him to play during recesses. He wanted to please, but found their games confusing. The cubs especially fascinated him, yet they made him feel sad too. Soon they gave up and let him be.

When not at his studies, he sat by the tall windows in his room that overlooked White Tower Square, especially interested in the slow transition of soft even light above when it darkened to reveal the "moon" at "night." He had been taught the tiny creatures that lived on minerals in the rock served as the "stars." In confirmation as well of what Samarit had mentioned when they first met, the daily phases between light and dark had been carefully coordinated with the real sun, moon and stars above the Surface world, "topside." Often he sat in one of the hide chairs in the high place, the mezzanine, and watched the campus below the ever-changing skyscape. He sat there now one early afternoon, one of many in the past months, and listened to Samarit, and watched her face.

"Rowan, sorry I haven't had time lately to hang out. There's so much to do! I knew that when I signed up, but I have to come up for air once in a while."

"I don't know what you mean. We're sitting, not hanging." Interested to hear the response, he also simply loved to watch her.

"Well, it's just an expression that refers to taking a break, relaxing, maybe like laundry on a clothes line. It's a metaphor. Get it?"

"Well, it's not like we're wet, like in the little cave on our way here. Do wet clothes worry less while they hang?" Before she could respond, he asked, "So anyway, how's the training going?"

"You know I can't say anything about that," she replied. "I love it, but a girl just wants to have non-structured fun once in a while… you know?"

"I don't know what you mean," he replied. Before she could complain as she often did when he said that, he added, "I think you must be talking about play. Right? Anyhow, I thought you were a woman."

"You got it, felidelicious one, I am that. You know, it's not hard to imagine you playing with your classmates. Do you?"

He sighed. "Well, I've tried. I haven't got the 'hang' of it yet. All the jumping, bouncing and running… and I don't get game rules at all."

"I have a feeling you'll figure it out in no time. Play is a way of relaxing. We contact our inner being that way, which is always playing, 'appearances to the contrary notwithstanding' as Madam Ellaern often says. It's your true self that loves to play… Rowan, when you look at me like that I always know what you're going to ask."

"Oh?" He pretended to yawn. "And what's that?"

"What you always ask after a while."

"Hmm, let me see… what is a 'woman'… right?"

"Come to think of it, it's a good question." She looked away. "Thanks to you I had trouble answering it for a while. It seemed a no-brainer at first: a woman is an adult female person, full stop. If you keep going you'll find more shades of woman than you can shake a stick at, but I'm sticking with that one. Do you know we have a legend about a wise man of old who asked dumb questions? At first they seemed obvious, the answers I mean, like mine. But he kept digging deeper, never satisfied. After a while the public were annoyed by the old man and his stupid questions. They got really irritated. Finally they got angry and hanged him upside down until that was that. Peace at last."

"That's a sad story." He raised one eyebrow. "And your point is?"

Samarit twinkled and giggled and poked his ribs. "You *do* know what fun is."

"I don't know what you mean," he said, and grinned at her.

"Oh, *stop!*" she said, and punched his shoulder.

"*Ow!*"

"My little fist couldn't have hurt you. What a great actor!"

"Madam Ellaern says we're all actors, all day long," he said. "I stood at the back of the auditorium in the dark and audited her lecture." Rowan peered at Samarit, and curled his whiskers into curved points.

"How *do* you do that?" she asked.

"I'm gifted."

"That's a gift? Maybe it's a medical symptom." She twinkled up at him and giggled. "You should get it seen to while there's still time."

"If you say so. You know, I had a dream about you," he said. "We were flying, only without one of those disc thingies." He stood up, and pointed. "Like that one. *See?* It just came out from behind White Tower. What on Eorthe… well, under it… are they?"

"I told you before, they're vehicles. *Vee-hik-kuls.* Get it?" She jumped up, placed her hands on her hips, and with a glint in her eye said, "We can go for a ride somewhere, you know. Do you want to? *Let's!*" She jumped twice, and tugged his hand. "Come on, you. It's fun!"

"Right, fun… *that.*" Rowan feigned a yawn, but finally surrendered to her tug and stood up, stretched and yawned.

◆

"No way," said Rowan, "I can't do *that!*"

"Coward. Where's your sense of adventure? I've been doing this since I was fifteen. It's easy."

The silver disc they had rented from an airport agency at the end of a long journey by "grounder" (a self-propelled vehicle meant for paved streets), hovered silently high above a large field. The vehicle wobbled whenever he shifted his weight even slightly. He crouched and gripped the rail beside his empty seat at the inner circumference. Beyond the now translucent interior, grids of roads and patches of tiny trees spread far below – and between his feet, what may be a flock of white birds in flight over green fields – "I don't feel good," he muttered. "Let's go back." A ninth moan threatened. *"Please?"*

"Scaredy-cat!" Samarit had taken the central pilot's chair, which perfectly formed to her body. She faced an inclined desktop with round glowing dials in a grid at the top. Her hands appeared to have sunk into it. "Ha ha!" She held her arms up. "Look, no hands." The surface of the desk filled in smooth again, but the disc dropped by several feet in an instant and stopped.

Rowan's stomach churned.

"Anyone can learn this in five minutes," she said, "even an overgrown kitten like you." She stood up. "Here, try it!" The disc wobbled from side to side as she lightly stepped out of the seat and balanced with her arms spread with the grace of a dancer. She apparently had no need to hang on to the rail.

He peered at her, and shook his head. "I don't know what to do!"

"Rowan, listen. I assure you that you *do* know what to do. You just don't *know* that you know."

"Samarit, that makes no sense. Until now I've believed every word that passes your luscious lips, but this is too much."

Samarit's dark eyes opened wider – and she stared at him.

"I'm only just learning to read and write a bit," he explained, "not fly magical machines. What if I kill us both when we crash to the ground?"

47

The tip of her tongue made a brief appearance, and slid along her upper lip.

He watched it slide, and added: "I saw 'luscious' in an ad for lipstick in a shop window... my teacher told us to practise reading big words."

Samarit blinked. "Trust me, Rowan, maybe it looks wildly impossible, but it's not." She frowned. "Where's your lionheart?"

"My what?"

"Your *ly-on-hart*. You know, from the children's reader? When the fraidy-cat lion cub raised by a flock of sheep learns that he's king of the jungle? Maybe you haven't had that one yet. It was one of my faves when I was little. You should be able to relate to it even better, being a felid and all."

"You're still little, but my lionheart's been captured by poachers. *You* fly it!"

"No way." Saramit stamped her feet. "You can do it. Here, kitty baby." She danced over to Rowan's side of the disc, and tugged on his hand. Slowly the craft recovered its balance on its own. Rowan released his grip on the railing, and crawled towards the control desk on three limbs, while Samarit towed the other. The pilot's chair automatically expanded and conformed perfectly to his body. He exhaled in relief.

"Close your eyes, Rowan. Breathe slowly until you feel perfectly calm." She stood behind him, and stroked his red mane. "Ready? If you see anything but what I tell you, ignore it. You are an eagle, and you hover high above the world. You can see everything in absolute detail below, even bugs crawling on the ground. But you could not care less. You want nothing but to soar wherever you like, whenever you like. And you do. Now."

Rowan gasped. Her chest bumps pressed against him as she bent to touch something on the desk. But astonishment pervaded perception: with eyes firmly closed, he saw the ground far below, even blades of grass in the field, and within it a pond. The reflection of the disc's silvery circle rippled in its surface. In the distance the accretion of large buildings and towers stood among the massive natural stone columns that reached to the concave top of the cavern, where small white clouds had collected. Bodiless, gravity had vanished – until he thought of the vertical cliff face where the huge waterfall plunged; he had noticed it in wonder on the ride to the airport in the taxi. Velocity increased as he spun about and sped towards it. The cliff approached alarmingly *fast...!*

Samarit had to shout over the din of the cascade to be heard: "*Whoa there, flying felid! That was great! See? You can do it!*"

Rowan opened his unblinking eyes wide and stared at the cliff face not fifty feet ahead; it gleamed with spray from the falls that roared like a choir of lions, yet the disc hovered without so much as a wobble. "But I didn't..."

"*Never mind, you did great! I only helped a little at the end by stepping on the brakes, so to speak! Congratulations, you're an ace, a lionheart! See? I told you! Fun!*" She stood on the tips of her toes, and kissed the top of his head, right on the tattooed syx sigil now invisible under a thick mop of red mane. "*I'm so proud of you, Rowan!*"

His heart swelled at her touch. He wanted to cry – but maybe lionhearts should never show it. Yet clearly, achievement of the impossible had not swelled his breast, her touch had – he sat very still, eyes shut tight, his hands still immersed in the control desk, and breathed.

"*Let's fly across the farm fields now, Rowan,*" she shouted from behind him, her hands at rest on his shoulders. "*Let's take a tour of this land of wonders! You deserve a good look before our permit expires! We still have time to show you my special place!*"

"You mean your clan home?"

"*No, that's too far for a disc ride! We'd need portal tickets for that, but I'll explain what that is later at some point, unless your teacher does first! I want to show you my hidey-hole, where I go to think! It's my special place, a bit like the perch you watch the campus from! My retreat!*"

✦

"It's not exactly a hole, Samarit. It's a grove… so quiet. Only birds. And no bugs. What are these skinny trees across the lotus pond?"

"They aren't trees, they're giant grass stalks. Bamboo. I call it a hidey-hole, but that's only an expression, meaning no one ever comes here but me. It's a retreat. I found it by supplication."

"You mean you asked your sergeant? Or Madam Ellaern?"

"No, silly… I asked my inner being for it."

"Will you introduce me to her?"

Samarit puckered her lips into a rosebud as she often did, and peered at him before she answered. "You're looking at her right now."

"She's pretty."

"Thanks. I think you're pretty too. But don't get any ideas."

"Like what?"

"I don't think you got the chance to play in the orphanage, did you? You may have some catching up to do."

"I'm ready. Let's do it."

"Uh-huh. I think you're more playful than you know. When I'm with you I feel like I'm having fun even though you're a scaredy-cat."

"Am I? Should I be afraid of you?"

"You might find out if you try anything."

"For example?"

"Let's change the subject. When we're little, play comes naturally unless it's suppressed. It's so cruel, what happened to cubby Rowan. I wish… anyhow, Longbow children are taught to still their thoughts and withdraw attention from toys or whatever to touch their inner being, the spirit, the essence… the self." She stiffened a bit, and looked away.

Rowan had observed that Samarit straightened her back and shoulders whenever she felt unsure if he understood her. "Now that you mention it," he said, "at times I've seen my classmates sitting alone in the playground, usually under a tree. Their eyes are closed. Is that what they're doing? Touching themselves?"

"No, kitty baby." Samarit covered her nose and mouth with her palm, but her eyes twinkled at him.

He expected to hear her chuckle, something she usually did freely and often.

"I mean yes," she said, but did not even smile, "they're touching their inner self. Longbow kids call it the Friend. When you were a little cubby, the Heptas at the orphanage did the exact opposite. They could not have done any different, because they're even more enslaved as they get sucked into the system. They did their best, as they were taught, to prevent your natural self from being known. That's how the Reps operate. They're victims of the very same principle. With violence they make you focus on them and what they want. They break your will and embed self-hypnosis in innocent minds. They believe they can control everything absolutely if they just keep cranking up the fear. It's crazy, but it's their religion. It's what makes them happy."

"They didn't seem happy to me, Samarit. I didn't remember what that was either until you came."

They remained silent for a time, not really looking at each other, and remained seated in shafts of golden light filtered through green bamboo. A soft tone sounded from the disc that hovered beyond the bamboo birdsong lotus grove: time to return.

◆

The months went by and time stretched to more than a year. By now Rowan knew Samarit as the most wonderful being who ever lived. Yet she could be unpredictable, even difficult.

"You're weird," she said one day. "You know that, don't you?"

"Do you think so?"

"I know so." She lowered her gaze from his eyes to his torso, and asked, "Is that a fashion statement?"

"My new clothes?" He looked down at his outfit. "I like them. A lot. What about you?" He glanced at her skin-tight uniform, looked her in the eye and said, "Is *that* a fashion statement?"

"No, of course not." Her frown deepened. "I don't have a choice when I'm on duty. And I'm not going to change every time I take a break. But you obviously like it, the way you stare at me."

"I do, don't I? You're beautiful, and your uniform happens to suit you."

Silent for a long moment, she retained the frown. "Did Krumb pick that out for you? His taste is on the antiquated side."

"No. He's given up on me. I do what I like. Fashion can do what it likes too. My style is my own."

She relaxed and twinkled, much to Rowan's relief, although he took care not to show it. He felt he had just survived an ambush, like in the movies.

On another occasion, they had just been to a theatre and strolled near midnight past an alley. A woman cried out for help – a robbery of an ander woman by a large young man – she must have put up a fight, because the thief had her on the ground, and straddled her hips while he stuffed her small purse inside his shirt. Her little fists flailed in vain at his chest, but she tore at his clothes and ripped off buttons before he could grab her wrists. The purse fell out onto her concave belly. He shielded himself with a forearm, and snatched the purse from her grasp. He tried to stand up, and struck her face, hard. The woman cried out. The whites of the man's eyes showed. He reached into a pocket and pulled out a small object, which turned out to be a knife once he had pressed a button on it to release its shiny blade –

In an instant Rowan leapt a distance of twenty paces, bounced once for another ten and bowled the man over onto his back and pinned him to the pavement. In one motion he flipped him over and gripped both wrists behind his back in one hand. He got to his feet and lifted the man at the same time, and applied just enough pressure to let him know that his arms would break if he resisted. The knife fell to the ground and clattered.

Samarit arrived six seconds later. "What are you doing? I'm the soldier here, *not you!*" Her dark eyes shone.

"I can leap more quickly than you can run, Samarit. This creep is also twice your weight." He peered at her. "Should I have let you do it instead?"

She only glared at him.

Together they spent some time at the local police station to make a statement, where they had been praised and thanked profusely by both the officer in charge and the victim, and once again found themselves on their way down the street.

When they passed the alley again, Samarit stopped him, and said, "Rowan, I apologize. I'm sorry. You did the right thing." She took both his hands, and twinkled up at him in a way he had not seen before, shiny, but nice-shiny.

✦

The third instance, the most mysterious and difficult, had to be shelved for a long while. They had agreed to meet some distance from Jaspertown, the older part of the city where the university campus spread in the shadow of the White Tower, in between his rooms and her barracks. Their destination was a concert hall to hear a musical performance by a quartet of three young men and a young woman, who had risked the journey to Perkona Ola by travelling topside from a distant cavern nation east of Vugh Deep. They could have used portals, but the theme of freedom pervaded their innovative musical style. Intrigued, not only with their daring spirit but by their exceptional talent, he found Samarit's pre-performance critique even more interesting:

"Risking their necks topside," she said with her nose in the air, "is a gimmick to sell tickets."

"Spoken like a true security officer," he replied with a wink.

She did not respond, and only looked away without expression.

He waited in front of the hall until the beginning of the concert. Maybe an emergency had come up that called her to duty, so he went inside and enjoyed the show as well as possible with her seat empty beside him. He did not see her at the campus mezzanine as expected the next day, so left a message with her sergeant's office. The day after that Squire Krumb relayed her reply through Rowan's raven brooch. She could have done that herself.

"Samarit Longbow says to tell you, sir, that she had decided not to make a public appearance in support of illegal activities such as travelling topside without authorization."

"Why couldn't she tell me herself? *Before* I'd bought two front-row tickets."

"Unknown, sir," replied the squire.

"Apologies, Krumb, I'm just thinking out loud."

✦

A few days later, he asked her about what had happened. It did not occur to him to accuse of her of standing him up, fortunately.

"I didn't want to go," she said, deadpan.

"No worries." With great effort he took pains to appear completely neutral, and said, "Next time I'll go alone and save some money."

Her brows knit together. "Why do you encourage breaking the law? Don't you know how it makes me look?"

"You look lovely to me, as always. Even when you're in a bad mood."

"I'm *not* in a bad mood!" she insisted with a scowl. She stood up. Without saying goodbye, she went back to work early.

✦

More than once Rowan had been invited to move his curriculum forward to higher levels, at times to the envy of his classmates. Aided by regular sessions in a device similar to the "egg chair" to which he had been privileged for some unquestioned reason, he absorbed history, geography, politics, the basics of the sciences and the arts, as well as philosophy. In that subject he had grown especially fascinated by epistemology and metaphysics, and excelled. Physics made the workings of the silver discs and the infrastructure of the cavern systems no longer quite so mysterious.

The elderly meditation teacher, an ander contemplative, quickly got him up to speed with regard to what he might have learnt at a much younger age. Now he knew what Samarit had hinted at when they had visited her bamboo lotus grove. In fact he soon realized he had known it all along. The reptilians had methodically forced him to forget self-knowledge endowed to all by nature as a birthright. He chuckled when he understood he need do nothing to attain is-ness, or Being, the most obvious of facts.

✦

Nearly every day for two years he met Samarit at his own hidey-hole, the perch in the mezzanine above the campus square. This early morning she did not smile as usual, nor did she greet him, and only glanced at him from time to time.

"Rowan, let's take a ride," she muttered. "I want to show you something."

"In a disc? Can I drive?"

"No. But I'll explain on the way."

The meditation teacher had said he no longer needed to formally practise, but instead still himself whenever and wherever he desired, for pleasure or for concentration. A heavy feeling gripped his heart. The opportunity had come to test the ability.

The two friends descended to the ground floor, then out into the street. Traffic flowed as usual.

Samarit flagged a taxi. It weaved for half an hour between tall buildings unfamiliar to Rowan.

"So where are we going?" he asked. "I have all day."

"Yes, I know. To my tribal home. But first, I said I would explain what a portal is. Or did one of your teachers already do that?"

"Sort of. It was mentioned in my introductory physics class. The teacher said understanding it was impossible until later, and only for some of us, if we got past intermediate courses." Through the taxi's windows he gazed up at the modern architecture, quite unlike the old former borough of Jaspertown. "All I know is what everyone does. A portal is a doorway into distant places, even other planets some day, maybe other time periods. It could either be a natural formation or an artificial one. Or a combination. Sometimes it's only a window. But I have a hard time picturing it. I once saw the reconstruction of an ancient portal at the Hall of Memory on a field trip, but it's just a crumbling thing, just sort of an old stone gate. It doesn't function." He turned towards Samarit. "Are we going to look at a real one?"

"More than that. Remember I said we'd need portal tickets in order to visit my tribal home? We're off to the travel bureau in Eastport. Then we're going to Wishbone Warren for the day, back by tonight."

Eventually they debarked in a part of the city where buildings did not rise to such great heights, with wider streets too, and a major train station. Grounder traffic remained just as heavy. Rowan stopped to watch a sleek chain of carriages drawn by a bullet-shaped engine as it disappeared below street level.

"Rowan, we can look at stuff later. Right now we have to pick up the pace in order to time."

"I don't know what you mean," he said.

Samarit glared at him. "Come on, let's move. Here's the bureau."

They entered the station and moved through the crowd of travellers, no obstacle to his curiosity, however. "So, what is 'time'?" he asked. "I mean I know what *time* is... or maybe I don't, come to think of it, not since this past semester of physics... but what do *you* mean?"

"When you get to advanced physics, you'll learn that portals don't work like ordinary doors or windows. They aren't available to open or close at whim. It's not that they're locked sometimes, but sort of… the locks are natural functions of the matter structured by the flux of energy fields at portal points. But more than that, they're intimately 'timed' with the moon, the sun, the solar system planets, the galaxy we're embedded in, in fact the entire universe of galaxies and parallel universes to infinity, the entire cosmos. Otherwise they're unsafe. At my barracks there's a heuristic device that calculates a reduction of all that stuff that's reasonably close to the target site and gives me a readout. That's why I know the day, the hour, the minute, all the probabilities, within reason. Get it?" She straightened her posture as they waited in line for their tickets.

"It's like a vast clockwork? So we have to 'time' our trip? And what if 'reasonably close' is inside solid rock or underwater? Or outer space?"

She looked up at him. "By 'reasonably close' I mean within a millimetre, so relax. It's not as tricky as it might sound for people like us. I don't want to explain every last detail, but right now try to use your meditation skills to listen inside yourself. If there's any disturbance there, the vibes will interfere with our journey. I doubt very much that anything bizarre will happen, but you could get motion sickness. It might even kind of leak over into me because we're friends. Get it?"

"But if they're selling tickets here, don't they have everything under control? Isn't there some sort of high-tech scan to avoid problems?" He looked around at the children among the travellers. "Accidents?"

Samarit too watched the young and their parents. "Yes. The little ones are part of their family dynamics, their field of influence… information and energy. No one travels portals without special permission, meaning they're carefully scanned, examined each time before permitted tickets, even if they've qualified for passports. They must be psychologically sound, as well as physically healthy. It's believed that's why the Reps don't use them, because they can't. They're forced to take the long way everywhere. They must monitor portals in some way, so we have to be careful when going topside through one. But above all you have to have the right attitude. It's similar technology to what's used in hospitals. Attitude is half the battle, maybe more."

"But I don't have a passport," he pointed out.

"You'll be fine. I now have a special forces passport. Anyone I choose can travel under my protection. That's usually for diplomatic purposes or emergencies, like evacuation or suspect transfer, for instance, but today you're my guest."

"Thank you… but what if the criminal you've apprehended is putting out bad vibes? What then?"

"It's a risk I have to take. I'm trained to cope with it, but I'm not looking forward to the first time, that's for sure. Still, there's medication and other means of subduing a disturbed mind. People who aren't integrated on every level most often have trouble with their eyesight temporarily after a jump, even if they don't look directly at the portal exit, so that makes it somewhat easier. But if they're especially disturbed, they could be permanently blinded unless I knock them out."

"What should I do again?" The heaviness in his heart had not lessened. "To avoid travel sickness?" Samarit remained uncharacteristically serious. She must be the source of the feeling.

"Just look inside yourself. I know you share what I'm feeling right now. I feel what you feel too. I'm grateful for it, because it's a heavy burden and it's best to have someone to share it. It's the canid way. Once you find out why we're going home… I mean why I'm taking you to visit my warren… you might think it's a bit silly. But the truth should never be denied. It's fine to feel whatever we feel, even if it's crazy, as long as we know we're not the craziness. Or whatever feeling, even ecstasy. Get it?" She looked straight into Rowan's eyes. "You know you'll be fine with me, right?"

He nodded assent.

VIII
Clan Domain

Rowan took his place beside Samarit within a yellow circle on the matte black tread plate they had stepped onto when the uniformed attendant raised her hand in salute. Although not in uniform, Samarit must be known here. A flashing light and a soft tone, like the disc craft had emitted, indicated a change. The attendant instructed them to focus their attention on the thin circle of light suspended within a heavy brushed-metal frame half again his height and approximately square, studded with an inner frame of polished rivets. Without trying, Rowan felt he had synchronized his breathing with Samarit's. They stood very still before the waver of haze that surrounded the white glowing circle.

The attendant reeled off, as she must have done countless times, the correct steps. When the white circle had flashed three times, it would expand. Then they must step forward one at a time, Samarit first, and enter at the exact moment of countdown from ten to one, indicated by the tone also repeated at each count, as well as indicator lights. Once through to the other side – currently only a distorted version of the portal room's rear wall painted with diagonal wide yellow stripes on a black background to make the critical zone once initiated wavy and obvious – a different tone would repeat ten times and stop. They must not look behind them until at a distance specified by a cairn.

Rowan, tempted to ask the meaning of that word, thought better of it under the circumstances. Before them through the critical zone appeared a barren desert landscape, its flat far distance bordered by mesas of reddish rock under a pale blue sky, all reflected in a shimmery mirage.

✦

"Rowan, keep walking," ordered Samarit. "Don't look behind you."

"Yes, dear." *So hot and dry here.*

"I mean it. Do as you're told if you value your eyesight."

"The attendant never said anything about that."

"She can be excused for assuming you're a moron under my protection. It's my duty to explain it to you."

Rowan had not heard this especially tough tone in his companion's voice before. Until today emotions other than cheerful affection had been rare. So far he had at times been able to improve her mood fairly quickly by at a minimum not reacting like a child, if not a grown-up quite yet. He repeatedly examined how he might be at fault, but nothing he had done or said came to mind. He decided to only speak when spoken to, and to focus on their new environment.

◆

"Here's the cairn, so you can look behind us if you want," Samarit said. "But we must keep moving. If we spot a Rep drone, hide in the shadows immediately."

A stack of flat rocks, the cairn, stood beside them in an otherwise unremarkable arid flat area among large dusty boulders strewn about, which must have broken off and fallen to form a skirt of rubble beneath the vertical sandstone mesa behind their arrival position, a leafless landscape, only thorny skeletons of shrubs perished of thirst. Behind – no portal, only more boulders, the wide skirt of the mesa. Their footprints in the sand began about fifty feet behind the cairn.

Samarit's off-duty two-piece outfit conformed to her svelte form like a second skin in black leather that exposed her midriff, not unlike her on-duty uniform. She drew a small holster from her shoulder bag and attached it to her belt, withdrew a matte black metal pistol, and watched a series of tiny red lights on the short barrel as it powered up. "Come on," she said, "let's move." She remained a very much more serious version of herself. "My warren isn't far,

The badlands *of* Longbow Domain.

but it's a bit tricky to get there from here... there's a natural flux point for the portal. It used to be over there, about sixty feet away, but now it's here after all this debris fell off the mesa. It's in an exposed position, unfortunately. We could spend an extra hour climbing down that gully and back up the other side, a bit safer, but so far I've survived the shortcut."

After more than an hour's trek along a dusty trail, Rowan's throat grew parched.

Samarit remained cool and collected. "Look," she said quietly, and elbowed him. "See that cleft? We're going to skirt this canyon and enter it. But first, still your mind and listen. If you sense anything at all suspicious, let me know. Point or gesture, but don't say anything after this. Get it? Oh, and one more thing... let's agree on a vocal signal, the cry of an eagle. Listen." She projected her voice into the canyon such that Rowan could have sworn an eagle hunted high above. "Don't try it yourself, not yet. Practise when it's safe, maybe imitate an audio recording in your room when we're back in Perkona Ola. Get it?"

Rowan gazed into her dark eyes, much less soft with charm than usual, and nodded assent.

"Your size and red hair might attract unwanted attention. Nothing that's happened in the past makes me think that will happen today, but it has to be said. As a precaution. It's protocol." She grasped his forearm, and looked into his eyes to make certain he had heard. "Get it?"

⁜

"Sir Rowan Berry, welcome," said the old woman, a mature version of her grand-daughter in an indigo tunic over loose white cotton trousers tied beneath the knee, and shod with brown leather sandals. Her long braided silver hair hung well past the sides of her bosoms, between which hung a silver amulet with a crescent moon symbol. Chief Morningstar pressed her open palm to his heart. "A friend of Samarit's is a friend of the Longbows," she said, and smiled with her eyes in the same way his friend twinkled at him.

Rowan bowed his head in recognition of her status.

"Please, rest briefly," the chieftain said. "Refreshments are at hand. I still have a few things to attend to before the rite." She lowered her chin in a nod of departure, and retreated through a wooden door.

Samarit remained very quiet.

They sat together on a jute rug before a low round wooden table.

Rowan pondered what "rite" implied. Cooler air breezed across his skin.

Samarit poured a red liquid from a ceramic carafe beaded with moisture into slim conical hammered stainless steel flagons, and handed one to Rowan. She glanced at him, and said, "Sorry to not have explained what's going on. It's very difficult to speak right now. Thank you for your patience, and thank you for sharing this time with me."

He exhaled, and replied, "No worries," and waited for her to drink first, then tipped the flagon back and swallowed its cold effervescent fruity contents in one long draught. *Delicious.*

From inside the hidden village somewhere drifted the slow pulse of a drum.

Samarit's eyes had closed; she remained seated with legs crossed.

Rowan studied his friend. She had warned him that all this may seem silly. Her grandmother's gravitas contradicted that. He knew that Samarit had lost her parents at an early age, like his murdered by reptilians. Her late mother had also been an orphan. Samarit's maternal grandmother Morningstar and grandfather Rider had raised her until her rite of passage into maidenhood, several years before she had become "legal." Grandfather Rider had also died in battle, along with her paternal uncles Dio and Urhülinen, the latter an adopted ander from a region called Finnmark in the far north.

Samarit rose from her seat on the rug, and left the room, to change she said. When she returned, solemnity remained, now dressed in a calf-length white linen dress with a woven beaded sash, and over it a russet short suede vest lined with white fleece. Blue reptilian feathers, not the long ones, hung from its edges at the front. Suede ankle boots matched her vest. She had braided her dark hair from her hairline and wound into a coil at the back of her head, and exposed her pointed ears Rowan found so beautiful, tufts on full display.

At last Morningstar opened the door. Attired in similar fashion to her granddaughter, she gestured that they should follow to a larger room, a cave really, only slightly altered by excavation. The three strode past the hushed crowd of Longbows to the middle, to a rectangular stack of firewood. Higher up, warriors lined a ledge, all armed with bows and quivers, and other traditional weapons no longer in use except for ceremonies: elegant antler-hafted knives and swords, sickle chains and star-shaped steel throwing discs of various styles, their similar clothing also of skins and woven fabrics. Morningstar bowed her head. A small bell pealed. Samarit turned away, and hung her head as well.

Morningstar spoke: "It is the canid way to mourn our grief to the wind and the fire. Let us remember our lost ones gone ahead, but after today do not stand at the grave and weep. We do not die, we do not sleep. Do not stand at the grave and cry. We are not there, we do not die." Beside the stack of firewood a small torch aflame waited in a long metal funnel. Morningstar lit the kindling; some of the company quietly shed tears, despite the chieftain's advice. All joined hands and hung their heads. The wood burnt well; only faint pale smoke wafted through an opening in the ceiling.

Their emotions, expressed or not, resonated strongly within Rowan's breast. His own buried sorrow joined with theirs. Tears of solidarity poured down over his upper lip and dripped into the tuft on his chin. Thankful the fringe of hair that hung over his forehead hid his eyes, he soon understood the benefit, a purgation, grateful to not be all alone in it, not this time. However, the stack of kindling flamed, as soon did the logs beneath the wrapped bundle – had a young child died? Samarit had never mentioned any such person close to her, only her beloved grandmother, little of her grandfather and uncles, and even less of her late parents.

Over the next hour he contemplated the hot flames in silence, and his felid hearing ability eavesdropped on the quiet conversations within range. No one spoke to him. He listened closely for the name of the deceased. A few times the name Mog repeated, apparently a wonderful person, kind and wise. The rite ended with a chant in the Longbow native language. Samarit had told Rowan that in recent centuries it had been largely replaced by Common Tongue as the clan adapted, assimilated by the League of Domains. Many old names had been translated, but she took pride in her retained given name, which meant "watchkeeper" as in guardian, one who takes care of others in many ways, from motherhood to medicine and territorial security to warfare.

Chief Morningstar provided all a delicious traditional meal of stone-baked cornbread, savoury drupe loaf, pickled cactus, fresh greens with purple berries, and fermented mare's milk sweetened with peach nectar or honey.

Samarit, now back in her two-piece outfit, but with her hair still plaited and coiled, stood long with Morningstar in tight embrace.

Rowan choked up, turned away, and took care to swallow his tears.

Morningstar embraced him as well, and touched his heart with her palm in farewell, turned, and retreated to her chambers.

Still inside the cleft, Samarit drew her pistol. The strip of red indicators streamed as before, and stopped. The travellers moved into the lengthened shadows of the canyon. Soon they headed in the direction from which they had come, in silence as before. Samarit did not seem so tough now, but to Rowan more like one of the little girls who had been his early classmates, when they grew sad after they had lost a toy or found a dead bird. He wanted to take her into his arms. But they had to cautiously keep on the move until they saw the cairn.

61

✦

"Rowan, I want you to close your eyes on my command. Normally, portals are much like the one we entered at the travel bureau, at least the artificial ones, but this one's been here since forever, created by Mother Nature. So it's a bit on the wild side once activated. There are dangers. I know how to triangulate its exact location with this scanning device. Watch where I'm pointing it. See?"

"That's amazing… I can sort of see… what must be Eastport Station…"

"But you don't know that I've now been nanoid-augmented during my train-ing. I volunteered as a test subject. It's safe and effective, nothing to worry about. It's becoming more common among soldiers, particularly special forces. You may know it means tiny machines, called nanoids, nanites, or nanobots, have been injected into my bloodstream. My eyesight is protected, and made equal to yours in that I can see in the dark too. Not only that, but I'm able to leap as well as you now, maybe higher because I'm only less than half your weight. I bet my reflexes are as quick as yours, and I'm quite a bit stronger than before. The biggest difference between you and me, other than gender and colour, is that I'm a smaller target and need far less armour in battle than you would… perish the thought… but you never know…" She paused, blinked, and looked away. "I'm talking too much," she said, stowed the scanner in her bag, reached up with both hands, released her hair from its coil and combed it with her fingers. Afterwards it looked not much more untamed than usual. "I've activated the half-key. Put your hand in mine. I'll lead the way. You're safe with me. Close your eyes. Now."

Rowan stopped when Samarit squeezed his hand. He waited, happy to feel her slim fingers entwined in his. The rustle and babble of people in the portal station grew louder.

"Open your eyes, Rowan. We're back."

✦

He continued his studies, now with a major crossroads in sight. Rowan loved to learn about the world, a path he might continue if he wished. On the other hand, he might choose a career and play a part in it. One benefit: the past diminished in importance to vanishingly small. He felt like a new person, ready to create a new life. He had been so busy that the goal of going home, wherever that was, whatever it meant, retreated to the background. But since the return from Samarit's own tribal home, he had not seen her again for an entire week. He sighed heavily often, daydreamed about Wishbone Warren and the desert landscape, and found himself binging on chocolate. His training in meditation provided the tools to deal with it, but it proved a constant uphill slog. Books and solo trips to the Hall of Memory did nothing as distractions.

His classmates were all young anders, far younger in years and younger in psychological development, within a few years of Samarit's age, but still quite childish. The boys avoided him, possibly intimidated by his stature. At times he caught them spying on him, oblivious that his keen ears picked up their mockery. The girls at times flirted, but obviously only meant to enlist him as an orbiter, a boy who might boost their self-esteem if they made him think he had a chance with them as an actual boyfriend, their aim to make the most of their charms to snare as many boys as possible to see and be seen with as status symbols. Hence Rowan lacked companionship. It did not occur to him to seek adult company or perhaps find other felids to befriend. He assumed they were too busy to spend time socializing, absorbed in their activities and goals. Small talk seemed, well, small. Felids by nature tended to be independent, and besides, as a cub he had been strongly conditioned to isolation, one of the methods the Reps cultivated to discourage revolt. His most recent psychological evaluation showed that he needed to develop social skills. By its standards, his childhood had left him handicapped.

◆

He first felt her warm slim hands over his eyes, and her chin on his crown.

"Guess who."

"I give up. Is it Krumb? Please bring me a cup of tea. I'm parched."

She pulled his ears. "Get your own tea, kitty baby. I ain't your squire, just your friend." She spun around and sat on his lap and clasped her hands around his neck. "What are you doing? Watching the hive as usual?"

"Hive? It's more like an ant hill. Or better yet, a community of termite mounds, complete with castes."

"Oh? You must be well along in zoology." She leaned back to look up into his eyes. She grinned, and pulled the tuft on his chin. "And of what caste am I?"

"The friendly warrior caste…" He placed his hands on her hips, which made her stand up. But he said, "We haven't seen each other for a while. How have you been?"

"It's been difficult. I've needed time to lick my wounds." She turned her back to him to look out over the square. "I don't expect you to understand. It's the canid way." The evening darkened, and the square's lighting activated.

"We're not so different," he said. "Are you all right?"

"I'm getting used to it… maybe I'm growing up. I can't believe how long it takes. Compared to Grandmother Morningstar, I'm a big baby."

He closed his eyes for a moment, and listened to her spirit.

Eventually she turned towards him, half sat on the mezzanine railing and braced her hands on it. She peered at him intently in silence for a moment. "Remember… remember I told you it might seem silly?"

"The rite was anything but silly. It touched me deeply."

"But you don't know who it was for, right? You couldn't, because we wouldn't speak his name, neither me nor Gran."

"Samarit, who's Mog?"

"So someone did speak. He's gone, so it's not considered proper. We have to try to let him go. Names have power…" She turned away again, placed her hands on the rail, and bowed her head.

Rowan waited, and listened.

"You've got to understand something, Rowan. The Longbows are no different to other people. They only have slightly different values, and of course their unique history. They value each other as they value themselves, no difference. At least that's the ideal. Gran says that maybe one day they'll do the same for everyone. She often gets the argument that canids are considered second-class citizens, only good for guard dogs, what people call us sometimes. But she doesn't budge from her interpretation. I'm still working on it myself. But you know, really the clan bond is rooted in the environment. That means nothing there belongs to anyone, it belongs to the land, in our case the desert. The Wishbone Longbows belong to the desert, not the desert to us. Even the vipers and cobras, spiders and scorpions are our kin. Even the mesas have souls we used to commune with. Things changed long ago, but the connections remain in the background. Your teachers would call it animism… and Mog… well, Mog was my soulmate." Her voice had grown very quiet. "He came to me when I was little, a gift from my parents just before they were killed."

Rowan nodded acknowledgement. "Animism… I've come across the word somewhere before. I thought a soulmate was someone you're meant to marry."

"They may be." Samarit turned around, raised her dark lashes, and peered at him, and added, "But soulmate has a broader definition in our clan. You could say our tribe is a soulmate, a big one. Or all the Longbows are soulmates." She stood straighter and stiffened. "Get it?"

"Sort of." He recalled the small pyre. "Was Mog a sibling?"

"Yes." She paused, and murmured, "Mog was a kitten when I was a toddler myself. A little tiny baby desert wildcat, so unbelievably sweet. His mother had abandoned him… or had died. We bonded immediately." She quickly slipped back into Rowan's lap, clasped her arms around his neck and searched his face. "Do you see why I said you would think it was silly?"

"No." Rowan placed his hands lightly around her waist. "Should I?"

"People here often do." She peered into his left eye, alternated to his right one and back again. "They think pets are just dumb animals, a bit more intelligent than houseplants. They have no idea what intelligence is. If the ignorant think of animals that way, the animals act that way. Or seem to, as far as they can tell, if only because they don't speak in the same way we do. But Mog and I were as good as telepathic. I was as much Mog's pet as he was mine. We looked after each other. He taught me that and more, almost as much as Gran did." Her dark eyes teared up, and she melted her whole body against him. She pressed her face to his chest, and sobbed until the skin under his tunic grew wet.

He waited, and listened. "I think I understand," he said, and caressed the back of her head. "I've never been telepathic with animals, but I've tried to see through their eyes in imagination, to see the world from their point of view. What you say reminds me I have the impression that anders at times think of me as beneath them, like the Heptas did. Sometimes I hear whispers of 'alley cat' behind my back, even 'pussy.' Never to my face. I ignore it, because it's ridiculous. Look at Madam Ellaern, a genius. All the felids I know of, though fewer in number, are accomplished people."

Samarit remained nestled against him, very still, and murmured, "It's called xenophobia, fear of the stranger. Racism. Envy by another name, in my opinion. I get it sometimes too, even from my friends. The boys… not that I have any friends now, because I'm a law enforcement officer… it's sort of like dentists, especially before the new anaesthetics. And because my skin is only a little browner than some of theirs. And I come from a different culture… or at least it was quite different in the past. I overhear boys call me 'brown sugar,' 'dark meat' and 'doggy style'… even 'bitch' and for no reason at all. I often think the one favour the Reps have done us is to be our common enemy, otherwise we'd be at each other's throats."

"Do you? Why are we like that?"

"We've been genetically modified of course, long, long ago… designed to be divided against each other. War is the organizing principle in all societies. It's crazy, but that's what special forces are taught, as well as how to cope with it. I hope you'll learn that yourself in future studies, before you graduate… what will you do then?" She lifted herself, and brushed her long dark lashes with the edges of her palms. "Oh…" She touched his vest. "I've made you all wet."

"It's nothing. What you're talking about, I've studied it a little, what are called the Primordial Architects. Who do you think they were?"

Samarit stood up, and smoothed her skin-tight black bodysuit, although impossible to wrinkle. "I don't know for sure, but suffice it to say for now there was a race of higher-dimensional beings who used Eorthe as an experimental biology lab zillions of years ago. Forget the Reps' lies. They did *not* make us." Moment by moment, Samarit morphed into the familiar version of herself. "They themselves are products of some perverted experiment gone wrong. But that's only a footnote. Anyhow, those otherworldly beings thought of us like some of us do lab rats. Who knows to what purpose, but they left a big mess."

"This is supremely interesting." Rowan watched her lean on the railing. "Tell me more of how you see it. So they landed here? In discs or something like that? After travelling light years from some other star system?"

"Can we get some tea? Or where's Krumb? Get him to bring it," she said. "Blue tea, please."

"The lady has spoken," he replied, and pressed the brooch beside the wet spot. The raven symbol flashed a backlit glow of cyan in response.

Samarit sniffled, and reached into the top of a boot for a handkerchief. "For some reason I don't mind you saying that." She peered at him, the same way she did usually, but now it lingered even as she blew her nose like a little trumpet.

"I hope you don't do that when you're on sentinel duty," he said. "You may not notice the laser beam that targets your forehead."

The squire spoke through the brooch: "Yes, sir. How may I serve you?"

"Blue tea for two, please. We're at the mezzanine." A light tone like a bell chimed, receipt of the order. "Coming right up," Rowan said. "Now, what about those ethereal beings from another dimension?"

Samarit sat down beside him, and they both looked out across the campus square below. She lifted his arm over her shoulders, and snuggled against him. "Well," she said, "it seems incredibly nasty, but maybe we just don't understand why yet. Anyhow, that's right, they did not land here in discs or any kind of spacecraft. Nobody knows how they got around."

"Go on, I'm fascinated…"

Squire Krumb arrived with a cardboard tray in hand, with two paper cups inserted. A stylized symbol of a mermaid with her tail entwined around a sailor she submerged beneath the waves decorated each, the sigil of the shop that brewed the tea. Whether the mermaid had amorous intentions: a mystery.

"Wow, that was fast. Thank you, Krumb," said Rowan. "That will be all." When the squire had gone, he continued, "The campus tea shop must still be open. You know, I've never got used to having a servant. I almost never ask him for anything anymore. Madam Ellaern won't let me give him back. She won't say why… maybe he needs the work. But please, Sam, continue."

Samarit twisted her body to gaze up into his eyes. "You never called me that before, kitty baby." She puckered her pink lips into a rosebud shape and twisted her mouth to one side as she often did – and twinkled her eyes at him.

He said, "You've given me all manner of nicknames, from fox face to cubby to kitty whatever. Can't I give you a diminutive?"

"Hmm," she hummed through her smile, "so I'm being diminished now, am I? Just because you're a big superior cat-person? I'll have you know I'm your equal or better." Samarit squinted at him now, her dark eyes alight with a twinkle of mischief. "You'd better watch out."

"Are you going to finish the story of the invading extraterrestrials or are you stalling for some reason?"

"No," she replied. "I'm just dragging it out as long as possible in case you have more important things to attend to."

"You're always immediately next to number one on my list of priorities."

"What could be more important than *me*?" She punched his shoulder.

"*Ow!* Brushing my teeth. In primary school we were taught that it was the most important thing. In fact we should brush after every meal."

"Oh, that's all right then." She chuckled, and relaxed against him once more. "But to continue the tale," she went on, "I believe the ETs in this case were not physical beings as we think of them. In fact they weren't even from off-world. But they weren't from Eorthe either."

"I see. You know that doesn't make a lot of sense to us morons, don't you? How can this be? Were they from nowhere special or what?"

She groaned, leaned over, and set her cup on a side table. "Apologies for calling you a moron that time, kitty baby. I didn't mean it. I guess I was just upset, but you know it's not your fault, right?" She curled back into his side again, and hugged him. "Forgive me?"

"Of course. Right after I brush my teeth tonight. I promise. Or at the latest tomorrow night. Now, please, carry on. I'm dying to know what our mutual history is, going way back to our ancient ancestors, whoever they were."

"You're right, we do have a common ancestor, a hominid. I don't know that they're technically extraterrestrials… we call them the Primordial Architects for lack of a better term… they used that primitive bipedal knuckle-dragger as a foundation, then mixed and matched bits and pieces of other ETs with local raw materials, like wolves and lizards, crocodiles, birds, elk and deer, even dinosaurs, until they came up with all the various races of hybrids, some extinct now. At the same time they got the idea to try the technique on other species, such as your fuzzy-wuzzy feline ancestors. Mine were canine. Of course we're ninety-nine per cent hominid, therefore don't look it at all, just like felids, apart from the lovely patterns in their faces sometimes, like yours, and body hair, some of them… maybe like you…? Anyhow, it may explain why canids used to worship the moon. Howl-fests are still among some tribes' rituals as a way of letting off steam, although we got our ears from some other planet, Vulcan… I showed you, remember?" She lifted herself to twist her upper body and pull her dark hair back with both hands to display a perfect pair of pointed ears, tufts still unshaven. "I think it was just for show, because they're so distinctive, though some people's teeth are set on edge by the sight of them for some reason. That's why I cover them up when I'm not at Wishbone Warren, and of course it's illegal to bare your tufts if you're a canid, especially if you're a girl. Without any scientific evidence, they say it incites licentiousness, as if a bit of fuzz would cause orgies in the streets and the security of the realm would be at risk. Ridiculous."

"Absolutely. That's absurd. I think your tufts are really pretty."

"You do? Anyhow, old prejudices die hard, even though everyone knows it's stupid. But anyhow, the Primordial Architects even tried genetic blending on insects and plants. It must have been a jolly time for them on Playpen Eorthe."

"Nice… bugs and flowers with pointy tufted ears." Enchantment inflamed his heart. "I always wondered why my toothy smile is just like yours except for the long sharp sabre fangs, perfect for penetrating primate skulls. *Grr…*" He placed his palms gently over her ears while she still had her hands full of her hair pulled back, and pretended to bite her forehead – but kissed it instead.

Samarit grew completely still. She did not move away. She only looked at him with great solemnity. "I love you, kitty baby. It's wrong, but I do."

"I've always loved you, Sam." Rowan gazed into her dark eyes. "Even when I thought you were a boy."

Samarit's eyes opened wider.

"Wait…"

She giggled, dropped her hands, and tickled his ribs. "Oh? I didn't know you were that kind of kitty… so disappointing!" But she sighed, hugged herself, and leaned over to look at the toes of her boots. "But it *is* wrong. Oh, I don't know how to say it…" She slid away, and jumped to stand up, and lifted her palms to cover her eyes. "For a special forces officer it's a disgrace to be such a cry baby."

"No, it's good to grieve as long as you need to."

Samarit sniffled, and reached for her handkerchief. "No… Mog is fine." She blew her little trumpet, and continued, "I see him in dreams. He's forgiven me for going away to school. All is well with Moggie. It's me…" She hugged herself again, and gazed steadily at Rowan through welled tears. "You know we can't be together, right?"

Rowan's brows knit nearly into one. He forced himself to breathe. "But we are together, aren't we?" he asked. "We've been together for a long time, only it's grown bigger than we are. In fact it was always bigger than us. We only just figured that out. Aren't we soulmates? Like all the Longbows? Does it matter that I'm a bit different? Just a bit fuzzier and all that?"

"Kitty baby, I may have to reinstate your moronhood. We may be soulmates. Yes… we *are* soulmates. But… oh, I can't say it… but I have to." She straightened her back and squared her shoulders. "I'm promised. I'm promised to a prince, from the Touchstone tribe. It's our way. Our clan must stay pure and strong to be of service…" She reached to touch his shoulder, but withdrew. "Oh, I don't mean… I mean you're strong, beautiful and pure…" She turned away quickly, and gripped the railing. "Not long after Mog came into my life, my parents and his parents made a deal. Not a business deal exactly, but sort of because a dowry was discussed, and after much examination of bloodlines, histories, the constellations, as well as discussions with the chieftains and who knows what else, a ceremony tied our futures to one another when we were little. I don't remember any of that. Gran tried to talk about the future once, but I didn't let her tell me his name. I still don't know it. She didn't force the issue, because her hands are legally tied and she's an optimist. In other words, it's my fate. Maybe I don't want to know because names have power. If I know, I won't be able to prevent imagining a variety of outcomes, none of which I'm ready for. I don't know which particular prince is the one." Samarit wrung her hands; tension constricted her voice: "But I can guess… I will know it for sure one day, when we meet at last a second time…" She burst into tears in earnest now, and blubbed, *"On our wedding day…"*

Rowan watched Samarit's slender silhouette run along the mezzanine floor, down the staircase and across the square to disappear into the night. And he raised his hand to his breast and rubbed the damp spot.

IX

At Baile Ghrommet

Rowan's studies suffered. His teachers, who usually praised his diligence, silent in that regard now, more often criticized. The idea of a career or further higher education had lost its appeal. An entire month, five days, four hours and twenty-seven minutes had gone by since he had last seen Samarit. He got into the habit of skipping classes to walk the streets. Sleep had become erratic; additional long night walks often supplied the only remedy. When the dome overhead mimicked dawn, at times he fell asleep for a few fitful hours after he at last stumbled into his room. More often he lay in bed and stared at the ceiling until dark. The prefecture of Perkona Ola and the old borough of Jaspertown fell far behind when at other times he flagged a taxi, not caring where it took him, just as long as it kept moving. Many hours passed in this manner daily. Views from train windows drifted like the movies in the theatres and the displays at the Hall of Memories, now as devoid of interest as everything else.

He debarked to stretch his legs one night, very far from the city, drawn by what looked like the remnants of a derelict company town, called Baile Ghrommet according to a sign fallen to the ground, the discarded seed shell of one of the modern metropolises of Vugh Deep long since sprouted and transplanted to a more hospitable location. Until now he had never heard of it.

Baile Ghrommet, *an early prefecture of* Vugh Deep.

70

The lighting of the main dome did not penetrate the shadows of dripping stalactites and drizzled stalagmites at the perimeter, many of which had broken. The mineral formations cast long criss-crossed umbras from the few street lamps still alight, a sign the town may even be inhabited. Everything here had been blackened by soot, which had mineralized on exposed surfaces. The many steaming pools necessitated meandering trails that no longer corresponded to the old cracked roads. Puddles glowed an eerie toxic green, polluted by mining or primitive nuclear technologies of the past. But in the distance the echo of an occasional metallic screech, a truncated clang or a dull clunk signified this early settlement still had a purpose. A tired old factory whistle somewhere honked a breathy nasal squawk and reverberated. At times a long jet of steam hissed from a fissure or a rusty pipe or a clogged vent.

Weak with the sudden onset of fatigue, Rowan crouched to gaze into one of the wretched pools pungent with filth.

"Hello, love." The husky rasp of an overripe female voice drifted into his ears from somewhere behind him. "Looking for a friend?"

"No," he muttered, "I don't have any friends… if that's what you mean." He did not bother to look at the woman, and remained crouched, and stared into the glimmer of light emitted by the strange murk.

The woman circled the pool to stand beside him. "Oh? Well, you know, that's why I asked. I could be your friend… for a while."

He looked up at her – a felid, an old one, even elderly – or maybe aged by her diseased environment, but it suited his mood. He watched her face, hooked on the spooky neon-green lighting from the pool below, how it made a bizarre mask of her features. Her frizzy pale mane glowed bluish in the flicker of the street lamp that buzzed above. "I'm thirsty," he said, dimly aware he thirsted for more than water.

"Sure you are."

The thought arose that she might be on her way to a costume party dressed as an eccentric geriatric.

"Let's go to my place," she said. "I have mother's milk."

"I don't like booze much," he explained – alcohol only made him feel worse.

"Well then, I've got something else that may interest you, and it's a lot better than these nasty bitters you were just thinking of drowning in."

He raised himself to a round-shouldered slouch.

"Let's go, kitty cat." She put her hand in the crook of his arm, and led him from the crossroads up a slick track to a street-level flat adjacent a charred section, part of a much larger building, its windows now broken and dark, some

71

still boarded up. It took her some time to unlock all the various contraptions that kept its secrets intact. Inside, a more comfortable scene embraced the senses. The ceiling and walls had been covered with patterned floral fabrics, old sheets, some of them moth-eaten silk. Warm and humid, tidier than the cold littered street, it smelled better too, of incense and cheap perfume, and only a hint of blended mould and mildew. A lamp with a sheer red scarf over the shade cast a toasty glow that softened the old woman's wrinkles somewhat.

"Sit," she said, and pointed to the narrow bed. Concave, its springs creaked in response to his weight.

"You're quite the chatterbox, aren't you?" With a sly grin she reached for a slender unlabelled bottle. "Try not to bend my ear so hard." The cork popped. "This'll cure your blues. It's the Lord of Darkness hisself. That's why it's blue, but long on black of night, like this here old town. It's always night here… fight dark with dark, they say." She filled a small metal cup halfway with the blue demon, and handed it to him. "Bottoms up, pretty boy," she said, but did not partake, and instead chose another potion from an array of bottles – a ruby-red something in a chipped crystal flute.

"I had no idea the Dark Lord was blue," Rowan admitted. He expected blue fire as he poured the midnight-coloured limpid liquid down his throat in one gulp, just as in his travels he had seen barflies do. Instead it tasted earthy, but his innards warmed soon enough. He even felt better – a little. "How about another?"

"Oh?" The old woman glanced at him. "Here you go then, soldier."

Soldier – he must stop to think. But it meant nothing – and he downed the second shot. "This is great stuff… what is it?"

"I told you, it's the Lord of Darkness. You'd better pump the brakes now if you're smart." She glanced at him out of the corner of her eye. "We can do something else if you want."

Time drifted – backwards, and he alerted to it by a change in the timbre of her voice, less frayed at the edges. Fascinated by the strange effect, he peered at her more closely, and asked, "Like what?" He had forgotten his first impression completely, and noted that she looked good, a very good-looking female felid. He particularly admired the random array of beautiful spotted markings on her shapely thighs, now that her clothing lay in a disorderly pile at her feet. She embodied the radiant picture of youth, smooth and firm. He gazed long at the flattened mound of her soft belly – she smelled wonderful even from across the room. "Madam," he asked, "where are you from? I didn't know there were felids out here… or even that there *was* an out here out here."

"I'm from hell." With sinuous grace, she stepped closer. "I'm *joking*. Get it? The Lord of Darkness? Hell?" She shoved him to make him lie back on the bed, and climbed on top, clasped her hands to his, pushed them to the bedspread and lowered her full firm breasts towards his face. "Come on, handsome," she murmured – and her hot mouth sought his neck – "Let's have some fun…"

Shocked by the swift turn of events, he saw her words drift through his mind like smoke, legible if he concentrated – *Soldier kitty, get it?* – so mysterious, magical, of potent high strangeness. He asked, "What's your name?"

The girl's undulant embrace came to an abrupt halt.

"Names have power," he pointed out. "What's yours?"

She whipped her hands out from behind his mane and sat up, bare thighs astride his waist, in fact bare from head to toe – apart from the scowl she wore like a shield. "You're a freak, right?" Her voice had morphed from smooth to rough, as when the pavement ends and the gravel begins. "I thought you were just some heartbroken rich college boy, in love with some spoilt girl who's dumped him for someone with more class. Do you want kinky? Let me know right now so you don't waste my time. It will cost you. My potion ain't cheap. Neither am I." She clenched her hands into fists, and set them on her curvy hips. "So, partner in crime, what's it to be?"

"I like you," he said – and looked her over. "You're pretty. I just want to know your name, so we can be proper friends. Names have power, you know." His laughter sounded hollow in his ears. "Get it?" He sighed, and his heart grew heavy.

The woman leapt backwards like an acrobat. She barely jiggled. Before the bed she stood with the knuckles of her fists still on her smooth, perfectly rounded hips. "You're pretty too," she said. "You're also a weirdo. Get out. *Now.*"

An inner voice asked: *What did I do now?* He rested on his elbows, and watched her hypnotic spotted backside, the lovely round fleshy mounds. They quickly hid behind a silky belted garment decorated with abstract floral designs, so beautiful. He wanted to eat those artistic flowers. "I guess I am pretty," he admitted. Tears of glass formed and tinkled off his whiskers onto the bed, where they dissolved into nostalgic little wet spots. He stood up, and tried to make his way to the faraway old door – its woodgrain waved in wild worriment – he might *never* reach it. The immense effort exhausted all reserves, every breath like a cast iron anchor for a three-masted barque, despite his never having even glimpsed the sea. His shoulders sagged under the weight.

"*Wait!*" she commanded – or pleaded? – and took a step towards him.

He turned and looked at her pretty young face, and down at her slim outstretched palm. His mood brightened, he took her small hand in his own and shook it in greeting. "Pleased to meet you. My name is…"

The girl yanked her hand back clenched, and stamped her feet.

For some reason he grinned, but –

"You moron," she snarled. "*Get out!* But first the money."

Moron – that meant a great deal, everything in fact – but what? He scratched his head, and asked, "What *is* money?" He really wanted to know. He even thought he had the answer, but it slipped his grasp into the outer darkness, into the deep shadows between the broken dripping mineral formations.

Apparently the fumble enraged the poor girl – her stiffened shaking arms even made her robe fall open to reveal her beautiful, beautiful, incredibly stunning goddess form again – "*Freak!* Get out, get out, *get out!* Forget it, just get your hairy backside down the road or I'll… *I'll brain you!*" She drew her fantastic flowered robe tight to her bosom. It swallowed the two round breasts that glowed with a life of their own. They had not been consulted and strained in protest against the fabric in a desperate bid for freedom. She stepped back, but never took her sparkly dark-rimmed golden eyes off him. With the rosy lamp behind, her bright mane flamed like pink fire. One hand reached to and fro for something out of sight behind her scrumptious bottom as she retreated, her luscious red mouth pouted like an angel's kiss, so lovely – her ruby lips glistened in any mood, like a close-up in a larger-than-life advertisement he had once seen in a shop window somewhere –

No one had ever called his backside hairy – but then only Squire Krumb had ever had the opportunity, that time he'd given him groom. Maybe she felt frightened rather than angry. *But why?* He liked her – very much – *a lot.* He might still make her happy, so he said, "You know, you look a bit like Sam's teacher. Your eyes I mean. Pretty!…"

She found what she had been reaching for and threw it – a heavy thing that crashed behind him.

His quick reflexes served him well, but sorrow arose for the wall, now flawed by a deep dent in its astonishing array of faded but still gorgeous patterned flowers. Yet perhaps the flaw added something too – he cocked his head to one side to contemplate it, as if in an art gallery.

◆

The echo of her slammed door jarred his eardrums. Bolts slid and locks clacked –

so familiar. Her window grew dark. Were those two bright points her hypnotic golden eyes? A change of heart? Maybe not. *Well,* he thought, *I will miss her. So pretty. Oh, I didn't get her name… money… but she could have had all the money… just because. It's only paper. So impatient too. But, come to think of it, not really so friendly either. Maybe it's for the best…*

Slouched in the dark damp road, he noted his excellent vision had grown extraordinarily enhanced in other ways: patterns of fractals waved in a translucent paisley layer – no, the patterns had actually *embedded* in surfaces, inlaid like animated marquetry. And they in no way disguised anything. They only gave life to forms normally dormant. Many of the pictures in the gallery wing of the Hall of Memory looked alive, but here three dimensions had become sentient, aware of his attention. All looked more than alive and rippled in glee that someone had noticed – such a waste that he might be the only one of generations of passers-by who truly appreciated the neglected surroundings.

"Pay no mind, lad," said a gravelly grizzled growl. "She gets that way at times, spooked. There's no point trying to figure it out. Still, the old girl has a heart o' gold, that's a fact… if you can figure out how to see it that way."

Rowan's ears peaked and swivelled. Was the growl his own? No – it had drifted from some distance away, but sounded like it came from inside his head. His eyes followed his ears.

At the corner under a dim street lamp slumped a silhouette, another felid, possibly.

Rowan lumbered in the direction of the growl for a better view –

A worn old face – its baggy eyes half closed, a vague smile played across the thin lips beneath yellow-white whiskers that drooped over a mostly toothless mouth. The elderly felid raised his lids, and glanced up towards Rowan, and added, "I should know."

Ah, epistemology. "Yes, one should know," agreed Rowan, "but how?" Soon lost in philosophical contemplation, specifically how to justify belief as opposed to opinion, he loomed over the old man.

The gravelly growl rumbled into a moan that trailed off into a hoarse cough. "You know, she's been at it one hell of a long time," the old geezer went on, "two hundred and seventy-five years… thereabouts." The bleary old eyes rolled to his left and upwards as he apparently reconsidered. "Maybe it's more like three hundred. Anyhow, this town were something afore this. So were she. Aye, but she still is in my tally. Too bad we had no cubs… they'd have looked after us now."

"Do you mean to say you *know* that beautiful young lady?" Something struck Rowan as not quite right with the words that tumbled out of his mouth like stones that, if polished, might have been quite nice.

The man guffawed, but coughed and hacked. "Pardon me, young sir... I ain't had a chuckle in cave salamander's years. Aye, more than knowed the girl, did I, and a beauty she were. In fact she be the wifey, if you ain't figured that out yet, back when I be the constable of this once fair town, decked out in me shiny copper buttons and pointy helmet and all... quite a feat for a non-canid back in them wild old days." He coughed again, and spat. "I weren't so bad meself." And the slump resumed.

Perhaps the industrial ambience deserved the credit, however in decline, but great cogs of discovery creaked and geared into unoiled motion beneath the deck plates of Rowan's mind. "Interesting," he managed to say.

The man rallied somewhat, and continued: "I watch over her still, you know. I'm her watchdog." He chuckled. "Maybe watch*cat*. Only I've lost me bite." He lifted his white-tufted chin, and grimaced.

Rowan peered with care, and confirmed the truth: only a few long chipped and stained teeth remained.

"No chain can hold me. Only *she* won't let me go. It's a lucky thing I can take care of meself, always have done." He lifted his reddened watery eyes in the direction of the girl's dark flat. The old orbs rolled back to look at Rowan, and cleared as they penetrated reality – "I see she fed you the blue juice," he pronounced like a clairvoyant. "Your pupils be huge and round. She should know better. It only works the way she wants on anderkind. Us felids only go mad, though we see what once was just as well. Muffy just don't get that, the old bat... I mean old *cat*. Old anyhow... if you get me drift. She just won't let it go... of her youth, that is. Ah well, I reckon I fathom that. Poor old girl."

The old man jerked, as if something crawled up his backside. "I told her, I says, '*Go find yourself another chump to take your bruising*'... ah, but them bad words can't let me go neither... I'd take 'em back from the Devil's ear in less than a nanosecond... she wants looking after, does the old misery." The old fellow sighed deeply, and his thinly maned head slumped into his slumped body, which proceeded to broadcast loud snores.

A great vision unfolded in Rowan's inner view. Biology classes had only erected the easel and set a blank canvas on it. He stooped for a closer look at the man. Yes, the constable might be a fallen angel, but had not abandoned his post. Love had conquered all for the loyal defender, and neither would the Lord of Darkness win the battle Rowan fought. The blessed old woman spoke rightly about that: fight dark with dark, she had said. Muffy took her rightful place as the corresponding element in this vision of the marriage of two halves to form a perfect symmetry greater than the sum of its parts. Man and wife's disguise as the decayed remains of a long-gone day could not hide their timeless beauty, rather the beauty that makes beauty beautiful. He had seen it in her perfect undraped form, and now in a different guise in her faithful guardian. Grateful for this insight, Rowan's heart swelled. He crouched, and pressed his palm to the old man's own sleeping heart in imitation of Grandmother Morningstar, and silently blessed him.

X
The Volunteer

ROWAN HAD BEEN thrilled by the intricate fractal patterns lit from within, as well as others that waved, spiralled and curled in and out of everything as he made his way back to the city in a taxi. They eventually faded as he drew near, in part because the dome's morning light overpowered them, in part because the opening of perception the blue elixir permitted closed like an inner aperture as its influence waned. But not before he had noticed unusually bright gemlike objects that hovered in the sky at the perimeter. An uncanny sense that they had him under observation gripped his mind. Sentient beings in the form of minerals were not inconceivable in this utterly wondrous underland revealed during the rapturous night, now slowly adrift behind and away in the taxi's wake. The otherworldly apparitions did not wave in shimmers like the patterns, nor did they change position. Only their shapes morphed from diamond-like transparency to globular translucence. At times they pulsed and grew more opaque. They might be visible to other eyes – Samarit came to mind, not that she ever drifted far from his thoughts. Augmented by nanoids, she might be on duty right now with her eyes on them too. The strange objects linked the two of them. The ache in his heart flared and invaded his soul, and he closed his eyes.

◆

An insistent knock at his door startled him into the twilight zone between dream and awake. Groggy, he rubbed his eyes. The brass chronometer on the mantelpiece told of the approach of noon. Whoever politely asked for entry loudly demanded it now. As he crawled out of bed, his head promised to split under a driving wedge of pain. Dehydrated, he reeled, and opened the door. "Sam..."

"Rowan Berry, this is not a social call. I'm ordered to accompany you to our appointment with the minister. You're late." Her new uniform, form-fitted and black, included a short jacket with red piping, silver buttons and red epaulettes that emphasized her shoulders – hard, cool and professional – a triangular silver badge pinned each corner of its stand collar. The black turban of a specialist armed forces officer contained her formerly untamed hair. It even covered the tops of her ears – and the tufts had been shaved per regulations.

His heart soared at the sight of her, but his head made him nearly faint. He grasped the door frame for support, and mumbled, "I am?... I'll be ready in a tick." He only managed to peer at her out of one half-open eye. "Please, Sam, come in… it's been a very long time since we've seen each other."

"I'm Major Longbow now. And I prefer to wait out here in the hallway."

◆

On their way through the familiar campus square to Chancellor Ellaern's office, an unfamiliar wall of icy silence divided them. Samarit's use of the word "minister" suggested to Rowan that the meeting had something to do with the government, of which Madam Ellaern ranked minister of the Crown, as well as chancellor of Vugh Deep University. They negotiated the crowd that traversed the square below the mezzanine. Rowan noted that she did not look up at it as he did. But then this soldier did not look at him either, only straight ahead.

◆

Directed to sit before Madam Ellaern's desk, as soon as Rowan sat down, his yawn died, aborted by the stern look in the chancellor's intense golden eyes. The tireless headache throbbed his entire skull as if to crack a breach the perished yawn may have opened.

"Rowan Berry, you are late," she pointed out, a statement of the obvious. "But we are not here to discuss your deplorable ongoing lapses in attendance nor your plummeting grade point average, however close to graduation you may have been."

Knight Commander Diss *of* Vugh Deep.

If only he might be allowed to close his eyes and go back to sleep –

"Knight Commander Diss of the armed forces base will be here any minute. I had intended to brief you, but your tardiness prevents that. He has something important to discuss with you both. Please remain seated." Minister Ellaern's golden eyes acquired an intensity of focus Rowan had witnessed before – in fact he did not notice she had exited by a rear door of her office until he realized he had stared at her empty chair for some minutes at least.

What seemed long ages of strained silence later, her secretary held open the main door for the commander, who penetrated the room rather than entered it.

Samarit stood at attention and saluted.

The knight commander, in a barely modulated lion's roar, shouted: *"At ease, major! Be seated!"* Diss stood tall, a felid with broad shoulders made even wider by silver pauldrons with four gold stars embossed in each. Several badges of high rank adorned his dark blue uniform jacket, with a column of rounded silver buttons from the stand collar beneath his brindled chin tuft down to a wide brown leather belt with a long curved sheath attached, out of which protruded a knife handle of reindeer antler. His large face with its hooded dark eyes and crooked whiskers bore scars as testament to a long career forged in combat. Only a lion in the wild might have been more intimidating. That comparison underestimated the man who stood like a tower above Samarit and Rowan, because his every word came wrapped in a deep growl:

"I am informed, Berry, that you were late and that it is I who now must waste my valuable time just to brief you. To begin, your rescue, Berry, by your friend Major Longbow some years ago was one of her early assignments in the Surface world. You never questioned the welfare the nation has provided you afterwards, Berry. Perhaps it was because you were conditioned when even more immature to concede to authority." His voice grew more quiet as he leaned closer, but remained intense: "But," he snarled, "by *now* you surely should have overcome it!"

Rowan did not know what to say. *Major?* Until today he had assumed Samarit remained a security guard and sentinel, only recently qualified for special forces. At least the commander had called her his friend.

The lion-man sat down in Madam Ellaern's chair and folded his big arms, and restored his words to full volume: *"Vugh Deep has paid for your education, your room and board, as well as any other expenses, such as regular medical and psychological examinations."* He unfolded his arms, clasped his big hands together on the desktop, and leaned forward, and spoke more quietly: "By the way, Berry, you have also missed your appointment with the psychology department clinic." And back at full volume: *"Each of the above had been appended to a special act of parliament, in case that is news to you, thanks to the nomination, testimony and the unstinting support of our esteemed minister of education, chancellor of this university and one of our very finest citizens. Apparently she saw something in you worthy of investment. We shall see, however! You owe this great lady a very large debt of gratitude."*

Rowan replied, "But I am grateful…"

"The elderly woman by the name of Muffy, no surname like a celebrity, if you can imagine, of the condemned town of Baile Ghrommet scheduled for demolition, as well as her husband, an unemployed ex-police officer and unpaid bouncer, have been taken into custody on charges of operating a bawdy house and trafficking in Schedule

One narcotics. The pathetic old tart names you as a client. Despite that most recent failure of judgement, however, pending a negative test for venereal infection, we now wish to extend our tremendous generosity even further to present an opportunity to repay it. What's more, you may evade jail time for patronage, you naughty boy."

After a stunned moment, and a quick glance at Samarit's rigid face, Rowan realized the commander must expect a reply. "But I didn't pay… uh, thank you for all that you… I mean the… the kingdom has done for me." To compensate for the stutter, he explained: "I've been unwell lately, although I understand that's no excuse. If I can redeem myself somehow, I am happy to do so." His face grew hot. "And yes, it's unforgivable why until now I have not questioned my good fortune…"

"I am told you did try to return your squire, but failed to ask why you deserved one in the first place! You must have discovered early on that only knights of the realm are granted such assistants. Correct, Berry?!"

Rowan rallied. "Pardon me, Commander Diss, I mean no disrespect… but an explanation would have been welcome when I offered to release Squire Krumb from duty. Or even when I first arrived here. I didn't feel I had the right to insist on it. I was just… but that's no excuse… ignorance…"

"You are correct, Berry, there is absolutely no excuse! Perhaps the government is too solicitous to orphan abductees like you. But you should have asked! You may be contrite now, but your education has suffered a great setback. That will have to be remedied later. If possible! There is a much more immediate issue." The commander stood up, leaned forward, clasped his hands behind his back, and murmured: "Do I have your complete attention, Berry?"

"By all means, yes, I'm all ears… I mean, so to speak." Sweat formed on Rowan's brow, and he wanted to cough, but swallowed instead.

"Good! Now… as you see, Major Longbow has been officially requisitioned to attend this meeting. I have been well-informed in minute detail as to the nature of your relationship, which, I have to say, is really none of my business except that it may greatly affect the outcome of the mission. You have been informed of her social status in her homeland. Correct?"

"Yes, sir." Rowan looked away to the wall. "I understand that Major Longbow has been promised to another of her clan." He glanced at Samarit, who stared straight ahead as if still at attention, her seated posture exceedingly straight and her shoulders apparently permanently squared. "She will be married to him." He looked at Diss, and blurted out, "And not to me… ever." It had to be spoken aloud, although his throat choked tight. Worse, Samarit's shock at his admission surged and sizzled, resonant in his own nervous system like electricity.

81

Commander Diss continued: "*Good! Mixed-race offspring though not strictly illegal is frowned upon by everyone. You might in addition consider the difference in life expectancies between canids and felids. The major is relatively of the same maturity as you are now, of course not in solar years. Persons of her race can live a long time by their standards and achieve the same degree of ripeness and consequent wisdom, if all goes well. A life expectancy of a century for a canid is equivalent to one of four centuries for felids as you know.*"

"Oh, yes… of course, I hadn't really thought it over carefully, I admit. It's true that I would just be getting started when the major is far older than her grandmother…" Rowan's palm wanted to rub the back of his neck, but did not. He just wanted the commander to get to the point – whatever that was.

"*We are slow learners, Berry, but we go deep! There is nothing superficial about a felid! That is why so many of us who are free are leaders and teachers or high achievers in many fields. Our hopes for you were high, I repeat* WERE! *In your case, however, you have experience with special technology. I speak of what is colloquially called the 'egg chair,' which has facilitated your development arrested when your parents were murdered.*" The commander stalked Rowan like a hunter certain of the kill: "*We shall take advantage of your experience for a special mission, partly because of your background as an insider growing up under the Rep's thumb.*"

Rowan's head nodded agreement, and blinked as his eyes glazed over.

"*Berry, you shall be tested to train as Major Longbow's bodyguard!*"

In an instant Rowan's attention focused.

"*Your close relationship with her has the potential to maximize mission success, but not without absolute acknowledgement of her commitment to her tribe, her clan, the kingdom and the League of Domains. And not without strict training, for which your personality assessment on file shows potential aptitude.*" The commander's eyes hardened with an intense focus he had witnessed before – somewhere –

Rowan stared into those eyes, but found his voice: "Me? A bodyguard?" He tore his gaze away, and glanced at Samarit: her tough attitude – shaky now – she trembled, but did not show it. He squirmed in his chair, and tried to sit more upright, but blurted out, "I… of course, I will be happy to do whatever is necessary. Above all I want Sam… Major Longbow, I mean, to succeed."

"*Are you absolutely certain, Berry? You are under no obligation! It is my duty to inform you of your rights, although you may have your own lawyer present if and when we continue to set the wheels in motion. Until now you have been granted, unofficially, the status of knighthood, yet you will not be an official member of the armed forces, only a civilian consultant, and eligible for legal citizenship if the mission succeeds, but your training will be to the highest military standards and above top* secret. *You may be killed in the performance of your duties, Berry! So may Major Longbow. This is not a game! From this moment you are to remain silent regarding anything that has been or will be said here today, regardless of what happens next. You still can refuse. It is your right. No one will judge you.*"

Again Rowan's head nodded assent of its own volition.

"*As I have said, the kingdom has invested heavily in you because of your assessed potential and, moreover, thanks to Minister Ellaern's generous support. You can continue here as a civilian and contribute to the life of the land in whatever manner is your inclination and aptitude. We need strong and wise felids, who can sustain responsibility even in the face of the unacknowledged racism that prevails here, yes, even in the land of freedom. But, I am forced to insist, there may be no land of freedom unless you succeed! This mission is of the utmost importance. It would be a good time to grow up a bit faster than you may prefer. In fact the egg chair will force you to whether you want to or not!*"

Rowan the hapless hare, helpless in the claws of Diss the relentless lion –

The commander leaned closer, and spoke much more softly: "It will be painful, Berry… that is, if you accept."

Despite the murderous headache, for the first time Rowan knew he would die for Samarit. His weighty thoughts came to rest on the indelible memory of the night before, of the grizzled old constable and his headstrong and wayward Muffy now behind bars because of a young man's childish self-pity.

"I accept," he said. "What's the next step?"

＋

"*Slime dogs!*" the canid sergeant barked. "*That means you too, Berry! Get your hairy pussy ass through that wire now!*" The drill sergeant referred to razor wire strewn across the obstacle course. "*Are you a man or a midge!*"

Rowan's body ached all over. Even his whiskers ached, right to their very droopy tips. The strong young felid strained under physical training on the military field all day long, often wakened in the middle of the night to repeat the day's exercises. Fortunately, the bespoke edition of the egg chair that Commander Diss had specified took him away from all that, a blessed relief he looked forward to for half an hour each day. The modified chair became a haven of solitude and peace. Yet its programming insisted a little too insistently on making of him a super soldier, more and more a monotonous impersonal version of the barking sergeant.

But after he had been driven in an unmarked grounder to a clinic off-base, where injections introduced nanoids to his body over a week's time, success looked more plausible. At first it made him very ill, which invoked speculation whether Samarit's occasional moodiness had been provoked by her own augmentation. But his illness proved brief. After the third treatment, he felt much better prepared to face his mission into the unknown, whatever that might be. He only knew he would see Samarit again one day; that he would be her bodyguard; that she understood the mission in detail; that he would be informed of such on a need-to-know basis; that she would be his superior officer; that they would travel incognito as a two-person team after a certain strategic position had been reached. Until then Squire Krumb would accompany them.

On a rare break, one of the more hard-boiled assistant graduates told him he knew Krumb: "Your squire is famous, Sir Rowan. He'd disposed of a baker's dozen Reps unaided before retirement from the infantry, not all in one go of course, but on several raids and skirmishes topside. Even his medals have medals. And he's such a gent, that's what gets me, but a real man's man. Old enough to be my dad, he is, but he could trounce any of us here and take the trophy. And he's so damn smart. He wins smart contests, he does."

This came as news to Rowan, but it made it all the more perplexing why he had been bestowed the privileges of a knight, without merit and without ceremony. Isolated due to the top-secret nature of the work, he kicked himself for not asking Madam Ellaern when he had the chance: Had she not said she long looked forward to meeting him? He believed she had spoken of not just any generic orphan, but him specifically – or had he misunderstood? Had he inherited some entitlement? No – knighthoods had to be earned – not inherited. The deeply rooted belief in the sinful nature of curiosity obviously remained a handicap. He had, however, little energy to spare for speculation or thought about anything other than to pass the final examination.

Early on, Krumb had taken him to a prestigious bootmaker, which put an end to going barefoot for the first time in his life. Fashion dictated elegant footwear in the city, but now he needed something more robust, enhanced by nanoids as well. Vugh Deep Armed Forces issued specialists custom-made five-toed boots of the highest quality, adjusted as often as necessary by laser analysis until broken in to perfection, as well as checked and maintained on a weekly basis by a cobbler, and the podiatrist if need be. At times he imagined he rode on them an inch off the ground without slippage, especially when he ran long distances. In addition, nanoid-aided swim mode at the press of a button decreased relative density and deployed webs between the toes.

Visual acuity had been upgraded by nanoid therapy to blue-fungus standard, minus the patterns, fractal or otherwise. Rowan now reacted before external stimuli demanded a response, thanks to meditation training early on. He had deflected a live bullet, powerful enough to nearly penetrate his breastplate as he twisted his body at just the right angle to hit a bullseye. His teammates had cheered loudly at this.

But the sergeant yelled: *"Keep your pretty gobs shut, slime dogs! In combat at sea, in the air, in deep space or on any battlefield, when and if you survive elite training to actually perform like real men instead of little girly-babies – unless it is to acknowledge orders!"*

The soldiers had shouted in unison: *"Aye, sir, aye!"*

Rowan tried to think of the female recruits as real men – but failed.

Disc pilot training at first came slightly easier for him than some of the others, thanks to Samarit's generous sense of humour that day she had surrendered control of her craft to his reluctant paws, hands rather. In any case, disc technology had become so refined that the major skill in operating one turned out to be faith. The suspension of belief in its impossibility permitted experience to give rise to confidence. The disc then became the pilot's second skin, and how to travel obvious and easy. The next challenge: overconfidence, especially during the second phase of training. After an intense series of virtual exercises, the sergeant and his unit of recruits transported by military portal to a large uninhabited region of the Uaimh System carefully cloaked to avoid unwanted attention. Training began with holographic enemy craft in staged battles based on military history. Gradually random factors from inferences made from recent intelligence data were introduced to increase the challenge. As Rowan had already guessed, technical briefings confirmed the only partially mechanical nature of the disc he piloted. Its mostly biological framework of mycelial-metallic composite based on back-engineered extraterrestrial craft crashed in the ancient past had been theorized as potentially sentient. In actual battlefield situations, a module the size of a deck of playing cards inserted into the control array tuned it to the pilot's personality profile for a true symbiosis even better than the synergy with nanoid boots. With this initial experience behind him now, Rowan understood a little more deeply what the bright strange objects in the sky might be, living beings aware of his presence. Perhaps it had not been just his elixired imagination.

◆

The remote-viewing training officer asked, "Can you taste anything, sir?" The young ander woman studied her equipment in the darkened room to assess his subconscious responses.

Rowan sat in an egg chair similar to the ones familiar to him. He wore an eyeshade with convex protrusions so that his eyes opened at will without discomfort, and imagined that to her he must look like a bug-eyed insect. "Negative," he answered. "Major Longbow isn't in the mess with the others. She's in her quarters, sitting still with her eyes closed."

"That's interesting, sir. This could be important. What do you feel?"

"Anxiety," he replied, "a tightness in my throat, and especially in my chest. Soldier, is the major aware of this? I feel like a voyeur."

"The major may very well be, sir. We will have to assess her response later. In any case, she has signed off on whatever is necessary to the objective… so don't resist. Good, sir, very good. Now, ground yourself per the technique I demonstrated earlier. If it doesn't work, we can try something else." The trainer leaned towards her workstation, and carefully examined the readings that moved horizontally on its holographic monitors.

Despite the blindfold, he visualized the young officer so intensely he may as well not have been blindfolded at all. But he focused on his feelings. "Aye," he said, "I'm beginning to feel more relaxed. It's warm and humid now. I hadn't noticed that before. I'm breathing more deeply. What I feel within her has nothing to do with me personally."

"Excellent, sir. With respect, theory says it has everything to do with you, especially in a case like this. You have an empathic bond with Major Longbow, a very strong one. I've personally never seen anything like it, so I'm privileged to participate. This is what we like to see in an elite bodyguard, though it has its dangers as you've been briefed, unless training like the series you're undergoing here at the lab is successful. Would you like to continue? We can take a break if it's difficult or exhausting."

"I'm fine, thank you. In fact I feel highly energized." His limbs and especially his spine tingled.

"Excellent, sir. Do you see anything now? If so, please describe it in as much detail as possible. Take your time. I won't interrupt if you're silent. Signal in some way when you want to stop." She never looked at him, only at the monitors.

Although his eyes had been closed beneath the convex eyeshade, he opened them now. An unusually large Rep stood in plain sight, and breathed in long, slow draughts. Its gaze searched. Yet it seemed unaware of him, only suspicious. "I see a big Rep. It's looking down at me… no, not me exactly."

"Excellent, sir! This is good. Is it looking at Major Longbow? Or something else?" The trainer shifted her weight.

"It's scanning the environment without moving its eyes. I believe it may be using some technology, some hidden security device… or nanoids? I see no other Reps. I feel their presence in the near distance, however. There is no sound, only its breathing."

"Very good, sir. We don't want to hear any alarms going off, that's for sure! But how do you feel?" she asked. "What are your physical sensations?"

He noted the trainer breathed more quickly. Her uniform where it touched her skin – as if he were not her, but inside her unaware of him. "I feel more calm," he answered. "My mental state is steady, determined to summon will-power, to use however little means I have at my disposal to cloak my emotions." He paused. "Negative, I understand now that's impossible. Instead I must… not control them exactly, because they must be totally absent. Only then will I remain undetected."

"That is absolutely excellent, sir. But may I suggest that emotions cannot be eliminated. They can only be harmonized and sublimated. This will not diminish their power, as they are necessary for action. Does that makes sense?"

"Soldier, what do you mean by 'sublimated'?"

"Sir Rowan, as a technical term, it means to pay total attention to whatever presents itself to perception, with no evaluation in terms of whether whatever object you are aware of physical or mental is to your personal advantage or disadvantage. If you know it completely, the correct action will take care of itself, provided you are responsive, with no hesitation. This is not impulsion; it's more like the whole field of energy-in-motion, powered by the information matrix, wills, so to speak, whatever action will reduce entropy in the system. That's the theory, sir."

"Thank you," said Rowan. "I think I understand, if you mean the universe rewards intentions of peace and order."

"I'm not sure… that may not be a bad way of putting it, sir. I will ask my superior. My opinion at the moment, for what it's worth, is that the universe, if it can even be anthropomorphized, is unbiased. It improvises rather than follows a score note by note… I guess we would have to agree on some precise definitions in order to discuss it, but that's above my current certification, so… well, I'm not qualified. Anyhow, I can say you and Major Longbow are an ideal team, 'synergetic' is the technical term. Whatever your objectives in the field, the probabilities of success are optimal, according to my estimate." She stood up, palms on her desk, and studied the displays, first the right one, then the left.

Rowan's attention had deepened considerably as he listened, acutely aware of the trainer's actions, again as if he were inside her body. Her mouth pursed. Her tongue stroked her inner lips as she inhaled and exhaled in rhythm. A lock of hair at the nape of her neck softly slid an inch to the left. She shifted her weight, and the little toe of her right foot pinched. *She should report that to the cobbler.* Inertia decreased in parts of her anatomy as she moved, supported by her skeleton. Some muscles tensed, others relaxed, while fleshier parts swayed more freely, bounced subtly, and came to rest. Rowan confirmed her youth and health, but her body mass index could be improved. The flexible fabric of her uniform lightly brushed skin surfaces as it expanded and contracted, yet it chafed a little where it furrowed. She may be slightly allergic – a vague itch in one armpit – but she ignored much of this feedback. For the most part, like a musical performance, each element responded to the others in exquisite harmony. Together they synchronized as a whole, as in a dance, not unlike his male form.

In addition, until recently he had been surprised to find that he had only been dimly aware of the sensation of his own physical body, even while exercising intensely, for example, in negotiation of obstacle courses or climbing rock faces without ropes. The body's image in his mind had grown more whole and integrated, thus responsive. *But I must focus on Sam.*

"Aye," he agreed, "Major Longbow's skills, I appreciate them better now. No wonder she's a star." And something else, something he would not have guessed of such a charming spirit as Samarit: killer instinct. He felt no need to say so, as Major Longbow, a professional soldier, had been born to a tradition of warrior culture. But he understood why she had been chosen for a special mission. He must be one of the qualifying factors as well. *We're a team, synergetic, like the trainer said.*

The young officer turned to look towards the egg chair where he sat nested blindfolded and hidden from view. "Sir Rowan, this is a great advantage. Thank you." Her attention returned to the monitors. "One last question. What else do you sense, smell, feel, hear or see?"

"My thoughts… I mean *her* thoughts… are less scattered. Breathing has slowed. She's tired. She's hungry, but missed breakfast in an experiment with something called… intermittent fasting, I think, and must not indulge in carbohydrates after the evening meal. I feel…" Rowan gasped and held his breath as Samarit looked up and gazed into his inner eye.

The officer waited for a long moment. "Aye, sir, what do you feel?"

"It's nothing," he said, and exhaled. "Are we done for today?"

XI

Strange Skies

THE DAY FINALLY came. Rowan had been summoned to the commander's office to receive his orders. He had waited for this day for months, now well prepared and unfazed by excitement. Afterwards he would see Samarit at last, and together they would go to meet their destiny. He would defend her to the death and ensure her survival to return a hero and a bride – just not his. What would become of him he dared not think of. He had only ever wanted to go home, a childish dream, a costly fantasy, so he refused to think about it at all. A man's duty comes first, how he feels about it comes last, if at all.

✦

"*Berry!*" she hissed. "This is no lark in the park!"

He knew that look, like she might stamp her feet at any moment, her arms stiff and straight at her sides, her fists clenched – signs that he should watch his step. At once he deferred: "Aye, major." A mental review of the previous hour before the twilight of dawn failed to discover where he had gone wrong –

"Our lives depend on it. You *know* that."

"Aye, sir," he replied, and glanced at Krumb.

The squire looked away without expression, resumed his work and packed up the last of their camp: rations, gear and weapons.

Plain clothing disguised their mission: belted woollen tunics, thick fleece vests and loose canvas trousers, somewhat threadbare and worn in Samarit's and Krumb's case, tucked into boots of brown or black leather tall enough to thwart snake bites.

When the squire had finished, he threw a brown hooded cape around his shoulders. Of oilskin, it remained crinkled and stiff due to the cold.

Their beast of burden, a sturdy black horse, had been bred from ancestors rescued in centuries past from stranded alien visitors. With no means of escape, the humanoid extraterrestrials had grown enamoured of low technology to make a virtue of their plight, ultimately to their demise despite their exceptional skills at breeding animals. The official narrative stated a deadly toxin had wiped out their colony before they gave up on the vision of their illness healed by faith, but too late to benefit from outside medical aid. Not as high-strung as its more handsome equine cousins, this breed of packhorse was valued for steady nerves under duress. It too had been enhanced with nanoids to make it even stronger and for stamina at high elevations. A similar breed remained in common use among the few hardy souls who refused to live underground, the defiant, perhaps claustrophobic nomads who scratched a living on the Surface. They usually journeyed alone, more rarely in a pair. However, a felid slave tracker travelling with a canid and an ander with criminal records, and with a bounty on each of their heads, who allegedly prospected for gems and precious metals illegally, would not be unheard of in this volcanic and granitic wilderness rich in minerals.

"Just because we're still far from our objective doesn't mean we're safe," Samarit pointed out. "We were never safe really, even back in Perkona Ola." Her dark eyes softened a little. "We must be strong to be of service," she murmured.

And pure, added Rowan in silence. As always when he thought of the Longbow clan betrothal law, his heart grew heavy as stone. As his training had taught, he rallied and replaced the thought that had provoked the weight. "I have checked the perimeter, sir. We are all clear to proceed. Squire Krumb has extinguished the firestone to specification." He referred to the cylindrical rock the squire had rolled into place and ignited with a plasma gun to a controlled glow for their camp the previous nightfall. The black desert mountains they traversed remained bare of snow at this late summer season, but cold, especially at night, despite nanoid enhancements that compensated for temperature extremes. "The firestone's signature has been restored to natural," he added. "All weapons have been checked, recalibrated if necessary and on standby to fire. The packhorse has been fed and watered. Is there anything else, sir?"

"What about the beds?" The major referred to the shallow flat beds of gravel they had laid out and ignited with a wide weak beam of plasma fire to make the frozen ground radiate heat through the cold night.

"Any remaining energy has been retracted and the gravel scattered, sir. Krumb has carefully filled in and concealed the depressions he dug."

"*Squire* Krumb, Berry. Show some respect to a veteran. If there's nothing else to report, let's move out. No more talking unless I say so." Samarit straightened her posture. She checked her pistol. Its row of indicators on the barrel showed full charge. She quickly holstered the weapon, wrapped a heavy silk scarf around her abundant hair, and threw on her stiff oilskin cape.

Silence had been ordered, so Rowan replaced his potentially whiny inner voice with a review of the briefings back at the base. The canid staff sergeant had pointed to charts on the wall, and explained:

✦

90

"Reptilians value canids for their vibrations, especially if they can be tortured as a group, a psychic delicacy exploited by a crude telepathy that has the effect of a stimulating inebriant much more refined than the arrowthorn that makes them aggressive beyond the point of exhaustion, as its toxicity is rather high and easily exceeded. In addition, they employ an undisclosed method of storage of the harvested high-quality psi energy, at least temporarily, by that I mean mechanical, in addition to their occult rituals.

"Anders the Reps exploit for their technical abilities in the manufacturing plants, of which the Mudredd Vale region has several important ones, across this entire zone…" The sergeant's pointer had sought out large cloaked facilities as rendered by a staff technical illustrator, not aerial photographs, but artist's conceptions: "Here, here and here. Anders are extremely valuable as slaves when educated in mining technologies and materials handling, as well as digital and mechanical engineering. Training them without providing the opportunity to discover knowledge that could incite them to revolt is an investment of years of careful conditioning and systematic education.

"Felids certified as totally domesticated are dispatched as bounty hunters to retrieve, preferably alive, slaves of any species clever enough to escape the factory prisons, farms and other facilities. Bounty is in the form of increased freedom of movement, although tracked by the Eye in the Sky. Permission of a small quota of slaves to run away is intentional. If possible, escapees are rehabilitated after recapture, as any who demonstrate greater intelligence than the herd average are even more valuable as problem-solvers and technicians, especially in the research and development labs, often as subjects of experiments themselves."

♦

The travellers marched in silence. Their custom footwear disguised as ordinary boots muffled their footfalls. Rowan recalled their final mission briefing and the shock at learning of the enemy's depravity. The sergeant on that occasion stated:

♦

"We do not refer to Reps as persons ever, though technically they are. Never doubt they're the worst of the worst, demons from hell. There is such a place, and it's called Mudredd Vale. It is where you are going. I have detailed how they love to torture canids and why, to wit the young and therefore innocent of the slaves are prized as most potent, and they're given high priority as raw material. The Reps have devised occult and other techniques of cultivation and harvest that raise select vibrations… fear is what we call it… generated by canid and ander nervous systems to a pitch they value as exquisite and essential to optimal health. When distilled, the end product extends their natural lifespans, possibly the basis of their touted immortality. We believe there could be many applications to technology that can run on this type of pure energy superior to what they currently employ. Or at least supplemented by it. Felids' lifespans are long, as are the decades of investment to break their will and train them once physically mature, so Reps unless angry only reluctantly waste their time torturing free felid cubs, let alone the stubborn adults, as they do not frighten so easily. Or, I should say, so exquisitely. It's also said they taste unpleasant."

✦

Rowan remembered the sergeant's eyes on him, likely in order to gauge his reaction to this information. Apparently he had passed the test, but afterwards realized he had been just slow to react. In fact he had been and remained truly appalled, even though he had known of it since Samarit mentioned it when he had first met her. The sergeant had added:

✦

"All the same, felids have important roles in labour management. They are highly valued, only not as a food source if there are options. So, warriors, that's it for today, apart from an update. As you may know, Kirzaka has begun construction of a very large base on the moon. We do not yet understand the technology involved, but the Reps collect the psi energy they extract from terror and are able to store it, as I have pointed out, although we do not yet know how it's even possible. All we know so far is that the moon is said to be ideal as a storage battery, as well as the best environment in which to refine it as potent fuel for hypothetical FTL starship bio-drives… perhaps psi-drives is more accurate."

✦

Here and now the three travellers marched. The sergeant's mention of Kirzaka and the moon in the same breath evoked a suppressed memory of blood on the floor of the orphanage shrine room of Rowan's childhood. He shook his head to dispel the image of Fuzzy's execution. At the time, Syx had been conditioned to replace the memory with the Rule: bigger is better. The dogma insisted that at the top of reptilian hierarchy dwelt Maçina the Artificer, Creator of the Sacred Sun, from which their superior race had been born, the same sun they said illumined planet Eorthe during the day, rarely glimpsed by the orphans, and never with impunity. Next in line loomed Kirzaka the Deathless, Talon of Maçina, the father figure and guide of the reptilian races, the manifestation of the Creator on the material plane. His will equalled the Creator's will. The only painting Syx had ever seen before he arrived at Perkona Ola had hung above the orphanage altar, and showed the Talon victorious as he vanquished his bloodied foes, whose heads, arms and legs flew off into the sky. He towered above his reptilian horde at twice the others' size, with a long tail, unlike their stubby vestigial ones, and absolutely massive razor-toothed jaws in his gigantic head. His forelimbs, proportionally thinner than theirs, in comparison to his huge claw-footed legs, looked tiny, yet must be bigger than a giant's. Instead of the little orange eyes, his gleamed brilliant yellow. Lunah, the reptilians claimed, had been built as an artificial satellite of Eorthe to serve as his fortress. In each of the other worlds in the heavens, they taught, Kirzaka incarnated as a separate entity who managed the lesser species his genius had created by modification.

The teaching stated that on Eorthe these creations had been designed to remain undeveloped, puny and weak compared to the reptilians, the felids no less than the other inferiors. The creatures that walked on two legs capable of speech had all been based on an indigenous species, now extinct, tamed after Kirzaka put the moon into place, and landed on Eorthe in his magical flying chariot. He had mixed that primitive creature with other Eorthely and off-world species for various purposes, ultimately all for the benefit of *Reptilia sapiens*, the only one of his works whose superior ancestor had been sun-born, a being of light who had suffused an ancient form of velociraptor with beauty, intelligence, vigour and strength. The mere thought of his unimaginable power had been enough to provoke sufficient fear to keep order, supplemented by the unpredictable threat of inspection by Lord Boss and the Heptas' corrective measures of cane and whip. Rowan sighed and shook his head, and marvelled at how far he had come – all thanks to Samarit Longbow, cadet, now officer-class.

The road ahead for the squad of three in disguise as hunter and captives proved long, dusty and, very fortunately, frigid. Less cold-blooded than reptiles, due to hominid heritage, the reptilians nevertheless avoided cold weather whenever possible, even with nanoid enhancement and heated but more weighty armour. The three League soldiers looked out over an endless range of hills that rolled towards the indistinct horizon. Above, the dome of the sky shone clear, but only blue at its crown, a very dark blue at this elevation. Its lower portion faded to a greyish dusty haze, a blend of the various blacks, browns, reds and yellows of strata of rock that comprised the deforested foothills spiked with stumps as if broken off rather than sawn or axed. Behind the trio towered snow peaks, far beneath which and long leagues to the rear, like a cluster of crystals in an immense geode, hid Perkona Ola in the heart of Vugh Deep. Ahead and below now lay Mudredd Vale, said to look like an active volcanic zone.

They spoke only when necessary, which allowed freedom to think. Among Rowan's thoughts gratitude arose for not being forced to cross the only pass between the Uaimh System and the foothills on the other side of the Kéo range, some of the tallest mountains on the planet, especially at this season when glacial ice hundreds of feet thick grew slick with slush from monsoon rains. The foundation of this range comprised types of stone so dense no known tunnels bore through beneath it. Fortunately, one of the natural portals had stayed stable enough to allow the team a shortcut. Unfortunately, they witnessed it distort and collapse behind them not long after their exit. Rowan remembered the suppressed panic when they had inadvisedly looked back in dismay, even though they had expected the portal to be fickle. Again he recalled the sergeant's lecture as he had pointed to a regional map:

◆

"Major Longbow, as we know, on this side of the Kéo any tunnels or caverns will be patrolled by the more snakelike reptilians, colloquially known as Snake People, bred much smaller, thus untroubled by passages too confined for their larger humanoid cousins. Nevertheless, full-grown they can swallow a large adult ander whole. As we know, the *Reptilia* class they consider sacred, yet they have made experimental exceptions, specifically on the crocodile family in hot wet climates, as well as the occasional tortoise for their shells as shields, but elsewhere it is the Snake People. They're extremely dangerous experts, but only intelligent enough to execute their specific duties effectively with neither complaint nor question.

"Major, any other means of travel for you, cloaked or not, is too risky. There will be no roads until close approach to the highly secured Mudredd valley, where the Reps' factory prisons spew tall plumes of toxic soot like artificial volcanoes. You will be able to see them from a great distance.

"Air travel is out too because, even when cloaked to maximum, League discs are still detectable by advanced scanning devices the Reps have deployed from space for the magnetic field more near the Surface. They can count the hairs on the head of a parachutist in a tornado, and at their leisure, from far off. These scanners only work, however, to within approximately twenty feet of the Surface on the western approach to Mudredd because of the pink granite's natural radioactivity due to an unusually high uranium content in that area. They must know this and try to compensate for it somehow. Although you and your team will carry a portable cloaking device that generates a sphere of frequency invisibility around your group, aircraft and satellites too might spy it if they happen to analyze anomalous data, a risk you must take.

"Your death squad's destination, for you, Major Longbow, and for you, Sir Rowan Berry, in that distant vale is a facility within the central factory prison complex, a mill where rare metals are smelted and advanced alloys created. Nearby is the infamous biogenetics laboratory, where experimentation on a range of hybrid mammalian species is ongoing, which, if time permits, you will investigate. Intelligence has revealed a meeting between an underling, the chief executive officer of that mill, and the lizard king himself, Kirzaka. This rare type of event by itself indicates something of supreme importance to League interests and security, and an opportunity to assassinate our enemy, a choice opportunity to behead the dragon, thus killing its body, the Rep civilization, because of the large mammalian slave population, which you, major, and your bodyguard will infiltrate. This may be the League's first and last attempt to penetrate an otherwise impregnable fortress, the Rep world, before Kirzaka returns to the moon and beyond our reach at present.

"Major Longbow, as we know, reptilian government is totalitarian, the chain of command from the top down. Chaos will reign until internal strife forces a new dictator to arise, for the wounded dragon to grow a new head, as it were, should it not self-destruct. This will give the League time to enact our plan to further weaken and eventually annihilate every last Rep in existence. The League aims its needle of doom at the dragon's head with one canid, Major Samarit Longbow, and one felid, Sir Rowan Berry, with the invaluable support of ander Squire Änur Krumb, as its deadly sting." The sergeant had ended with a salute. "Warriors, the League thanks you in advance. Good hunting, sir!"

◆

Rowan understood well this tremendous responsibility tested Samarit to her limit. For that reason the courage he had discovered within must not waver. His energies must be paced and not flag. She must be able to trust him absolutely to trust herself to accomplish the unlikely if not the impossible. If she criticized and demanded and tested his mettle, he must not take it personally. His devotion to her must be unconditional, no place given to sentiment. He had been advised by Knight Commander Diss to grow up faster than he might like. Growing pains pervaded the daily background of experience now.

He reminded himself repeatedly of the inherited skills of her clan distilled to perfection in her being: Samarit Longbow, a nearly flawless specimen of her race, essential to future generations through the pure-blooded children she would birth, hence promised to the best-bred noble of her clan. Rectitude demanded that Rowan let her go. He must. He must. He *must*.

✦

At their next camp, Major Longbow broke her silence. "You should know, men, that I've decided you may benefit from the above-top-secret intelligence I was privy to just before we left the base." But she said no more.

Rowan, lost in admiration, nevertheless averted his eyes. He did not want to look into her soul and expose her vulnerability that resonated in his own being. A warrior leader must present as fearless, even if shaking in her five-toed boots. "Permission to speak, major," he said.

She did not look at him either. "Denied," she replied. Her posture even grew more rigid, her shoulders more squared.

A rock-solid tension gripped his belly, his own resistance too, not hers alone. A wiser part of his being respected her privacy; they both knew he could force his way into her mind. *My designation is intuitive empath,* he thought, *but that's like a receiver. I wonder if I can send information too.* He glanced at Krumb on the far side of the firestone, who watched Samarit. *Thank you in advance, Krumb, for saying something helpful now.* The tension relaxed a little.

The squire asked, in the very same words Rowan had used, but in a more deferential manner: "Permission to speak, major."

Samarit glanced at Krumb, and replied: "Granted."

"If I may make an assumption, I suggest that I not await your return to the rendezvous. Instead, permit me to accompany you all the way to the objective in Mudredd Vale. I am experienced with Reps as you know."

"Thank you, squire, I will consider it." Samarit stretched her arms behind her back. "Now... let me try to explain..." She extended her palms towards the firestone and leaned forwards, eyes focused on something in inner vision. "As we know," she continued, "the portal closed behind us. Whether it will be open again when we need it is unknown until we're within scanning range. By then it may be too late, if we're pursued, which we are wise to expect, assuming our mission is successful. We must take advantage of the ensuing chaos down there. But once we escape back up this trail, we can't wait at the portal site for rescue." She sighed. "Obviously." Her gaze turned to the southern distance, away from the firestone, this night a spherical boulder.

"As we also know," she added, "far to the south the Khémians' pyramid construction has begun, the biggest they've ever rebuilt. Living beings fear time, but they say time itself will fear their upgrade. It will last forever. Khémia has long been shielded on all sides, above and below as well, by telluric technology. From that Vugh Deep has benefitted too, except that we went underground. Black Land remains on the Reps' list of targets to assimilate, not that the evil monsters are interested in natural forces or their pyramidal power generators. This isn't news to anybody either, as the Reps of course tolerate no independent states. It's just that Black Land seems to be low on their agenda."

Why is she banging on about Khémia?

"So," she continued, "Khémia has sent an infantry unit our way. They could help us. But now a new factor's been thrown into the mix… this is my personal observation, gentlemen."

Krumb and Rowan leaned towards her.

She at last glanced at Rowan. "There's a stranger in our midst now, men, strange to Khémia, the League and strange to the reptilian empire, possibly strange even to the gods of all tribes, clans and nations."

He knew in instant of what she spoke. His sighting of the eerie objects in the sky at the fringes of Vugh Deep on the way back from Baile Ghrommet had been confirmed, not that he doubted it really. It just made him perversely happy that Samarit knew of them too.

She continued: "What's more, the stranger may be related to the legend of the Khémians' ancient ancestors, the survivors who took refuge in Black Land, their North Afaran delta kingdom, as well as in other parts of the globe, after the Great Mireflood millennia ago, the Antediluvians of course. The progenitors of even they have returned, the ones who made us all. That's my speculation."

Rowan wondered if Samarit circled these details or sketched a picture in an attempt to get her mind around the implication.

But she closed her eyes and withdrew into herself again.

He waited patiently – but not for long – and followed her inwards to look for an opportunity to support, whether she asked for it or not. His empathic skills lacked steadiness; he must step carefully inwardly as well as outwardly. Her anxiety mounted, so he applied the grounding technique. Psychic quills

97

covered her inner being, electrically charged; she did not want him to come any closer. *How am I to protect her when she's so distant? Anything could happen.* Then he understood. She felt as unhappy about their friendship's end as he did – for her a big unwelcome distraction.

"*Berry! Pay attention!*" Major Longbow whispered harshly: "*I keep telling you, our lives depend on it!*"

He looked up – her dark eyes glared at him like fire marbles. *Now what have I done? Or not done?*

"Permission to speak, major," asked Squire Krumb.

"Granted."

"We are as prepared as can be for the mission. All has gone to plan so far." He stood up, squared his shoulders, and added, "Please, if it's permitted, tell us how we can be of service." At attention, hood tossed back, long dark beard like a flag in the chill breeze, he looked straight ahead, one hand at the ready in front of his cape thrust behind him, the other on the curved dagger in his belt, knees slightly bent and feet planted solid, and said, "Sir, we stand ready to defend you and the League." The orange glow from the firestone illumined his face from beneath and cast deep shadows in his stern mask.

"At ease, squire, and thank you. All right then, I'll tell you." She got up, and walked a few paces to stand behind Krumb, now positioned between her and Rowan compelled to stand as well. She circled the two men as she spoke. They remained motionless. The packhorse also pointed its ears in her direction. Even the stars in the midnight sky above stopped their twinkling, hushed in order to eavesdrop. She spoke clearly, but quietly: "Squire Krumb, of the three of us you may know the history of Khémia and their ancestors in better detail than I do because you've had contact, so please feel free to interrupt and correct me if I get it wrong. I'm going to start at the top, for my own sake if nothing else. I need to review, the more the better."

Rowan sensed that something else lurked beneath the very charged bundle of thoughts and feelings caught up in the twisted tornado of her mind –

"Now," she said, "what we know, from the archaeological remains and from inferences made from myths and legends, is that the ancestors of the Khémians, the Antediluvians, were much more advanced technologically than any civilization on the planet today. The Reps argue otherwise, but they're victims of Kirzaka's dogma. However, nature had no mercy when its forces swallowed the Antediluvian island homeland in a single day and night. The seagoing survivors on its west coast rode the tsunami, where they flourished in a sparsely inhabited new world. The ones on the east coast did the same, and found safe harbour past the gates of the Inland Sea well known to them from their earlier colonization expeditions. Some went north, but fewer survived those journeys due to the intense storms that formed from the disruption of the atmosphere. Colonies to the south in the Afaran interior welcomed the stragglers, although in time we know what we now call Antarktikos gradually froze solid as the poles shifted. It's possible there are still remnants of that worldwide civilization there, under the deep glaciers where geothermal energy may make life possible, like it did for us when the Reps drove us underground. We just don't know."

Come on, Sam, what's this about?

"It was a huge disaster, but something grew out of the scattered debris, the great civilization of Khémia for one thing. We've adapted what we can interpret of their knowledge to whatever works for us, for instance the power of the giant crystals in Vugh Deep and similar great caverns around the world."

We know all this already…

She stopped to stand behind Rowan. "Am I boring you? This is primary school stuff, but like I said, I need to lay out everything in my thoughts for review. If we were in a library in the Hall of Memory, I'd drag out atlases and history books, and spread them on a table."

"No, major," Squire Krumb replied, "it's fascinating, but if I may interrupt, not to correct, but to anticipate. Is it confirmed that the ancestors of the ancestors, so to speak, have returned? And *who* are they exactly?" The squire maintained his pose, hand on dagger.

"Good. I was getting to that. I hate to bang on like a schoolteacher about stuff everybody knows already. Now, where was I? Oh yes. The world as we know it has grown out of seeds scattered from a mighty tree shattered by lightning." A little smile enlivened her soft pink lips. "You didn't know I was poet, did you? Neither did I."

She stood behind him out of sight, but to Rowan her faint smile resonated in his heart like a ray of sunshine that pierced a darkly clouded winter sky. Tempted to relax his stance, he did not, however.

"Anyway," she continued, "I believe the ancestors of the Antediluvians are here, everyone's ancestors, they whom we've called the Primordial Architects, the original… whatever… scientists, geneticists, farmers, breeders, meddlers, demigods, demons… it's hard to know what they are. But we may find out soon, assuming we live through the next week. I don't personally know any more than that, though I have seen evidence at the edges of the perimeters of the skies of Vugh Deep when on sentry duty before my promotion. Civilians have reported nothing yet, nor have they been officially informed via the media."

Rowan's heart leapt. He wanted to shout that he had seen them too! But he remained silent and still, all ears and no mouth.

"As I mentioned, I've been briefed," she said, "that the Khémians insist on sending a unit of warriors through the vast honeycomb of tunnels under the sea, then its northern mountain range, under the forests and north through the substrata of the continent to some location in the vicinity of Mudredd Vale, our destination. But I do know it's a hell of a long way, so it would be great if functioning portals will speed them up. Otherwise they just may as well stay home and put their feet up while they still can. On the other hand, I for one had not expected any assistance, so am prepared to wing it after job one is completed."

Sam! Get to the point!

"In conclusion, men, this mission only makes sense if the League is totally desperate. Maybe no one in the leadership discusses it with the likes of you and me because it's too grim to admit. Military history shows assassination of a major world leader never makes sense, because total chaos will ensue. The outcome is absolutely unpredictable, except inasmuch that it will not be what either side wants." Her voice grew more quiet. "Therefore we must prepare to mercy-kill each other if necessary, gentlemen… I just don't know how else to put it…"

Shock imposed silence for several minutes.

At last Squire Krumb spoke: "Major, you are in charge. I for one will follow orders to the letter. It is quite understandable that euthanasia be preferable to torture, as I know the enemy well. I have never heard of this as official procedure. Therefore I suggest that we decide now that if necessary I be the executioner of you both, then end my own life." He glanced from Samarit to Rowan and back to Samarit. "My kin are few and without exception staunch League patriots."

Rowan's power of speech failed when Samarit looked to him.

"Agreed…" she muttered, and looked away. "But let's be optimistic. I've never met a Khémian. But you have, squire. I read it in your record."

Krumb clasped his hands behind his back. "Aye, major, once, near the border of Vugh Deep and Greater Uaimh System, Sector 17. One of my first assignments in search-and-rescue as a young man was to escort him to safety, as he'd wandered off the path into a wilderness of uncharted chasms in search of petroglyphs, with only an antique piezoelectric torch, a few biscuits and a flask of some sort of… sacrament, I think he said."

"Who are you talking about, squire?" she asked.

"Apologies, sir, he was an elderly scholar called Amenken, an alchemist on a long underground journey around the world, a tough old geezer who knew how to get past the Snake People. But he was most personable, and gave me a favourable impression of Khémians. He'd vast learning acquired over a very long life, and told me many things, including little-known details of the legend of the Antediluvians. It was a long way back up to the main track.

"Oh, and he mentioned whom we call the Primordial Architects, but said it was believed they at times took physical form. He called it 'dissociation.' He said in that state they also once employed crystals as energy sources, only they came to know a great deal more about the higher-dimensional physics involved. I remember having the impression that perhaps they'd discovered something that took them away from their experiments here. Possibly they'd lost interest in planet Eorthe because something more interesting turned up." He moved his hands from behind his back, one hand on the dagger again. "That's just my personal speculation, major. No one knows for certain, in my opinion."

Rowan remained stood at ease before the firestone, but gazed at Samarit behind him with his inner eye as he had been taught. *This is more displacement activity. What else is she holding back?*

She said nothing. She did not move.

"Permission to speak, major," asked Rowan.

She remained silent.

"Sir, I believe we need to hear the rest."

She did not respond.

Rowan turned about to face her. "With respect, Sam! What else is there? We need to know everything if we're going to risk our necks. Please tell us!"

Her dark eyes glared. "What did you say?" Her dark brows lowered.

Rowan crossed his arms, but then slipped his thumbs into the top of his belt, and spread his feet apart a little. He spoke quietly but firmly: "I say you're hiding something. Tell us."

Her fair face hardened. "I will tolerate no insubordination, even from you," she hissed. "*You swore an oath!*" Her fists clenched at her sides, she stiffened her body, leaned towards him, and glowered.

Rowan remained firm and impassive.

Her eyes moistened, and the frown deepened. She looked away. Her body slumped in increments. In time, she spoke: "My people… the Longbows… incommunicado. No one can reach them."

"But, major," asked the squire, "are you saying encryption has failed? That would be a first in centuries. Have they been compromised, sir?"

"I… I don't know how to answer that… I haven't a clue. Silence, nothing, no distress signals, zero. No regular surveillance reports for days. I don't know…"

Her shoulders sagged; she sank to a boulder, elbows on her knees, palms on her forehead.

The pressure in Rowan's head eased a little, and his attention went to her long fingers that poked through the dark hair hung over her eyes. "Sam, are you all right?"

"I *told* you…" she muttered, but did not move, only sighed. "Oh, Rowan, are they all dead? No wonder they sent me instead of a senior Longbow." Tears spotted the dust at her feet.

Rowan dropped on one knee, and placed his hands on her shoulders. "We don't know that, sir."

She trembled beneath his touch.

"All we know is that communication has been interrupted, nothing more. There's no cause to jump to conclusions."

The trembling lessened. She clasped her hands to the backs of his. Her fair countenance tilted up towards him.

As a senior Syx, he had witnessed many sad young cub faces dulled by despair as they grew older. But he saw her canid dismay at separation from the pack. Alpha female she may be, but no lone wolf.

She remained silent.

Krumb stood at attention, hand on dagger. Meanwhile the cold wind tugged at his dark beard.

The stars above resumed their cold twinkling.

The ground-zero approach *to* Mudredd Vale.

102

XII
Viper Pit

THE TERRAIN REMAINED barren, but temperatures increased with decreased elevation, a most welcome difference. It also increased the likelihood of crossing swords with enemy rangers. Volcanic rock mounted in evidence, including deep drifts of grey-white ash and cinders in the hollows. The assassins drew ever more near the great valley of Mudredd and the target mill.

"Squire Krumb," ordered Major Longbow, "set up and calibrate the long-range scanner. If you spot any interference patterns, stop immediately."

"Of course, sir. Will do." From among the saddle bags the squire withdrew the long heavy leather instrument case, carried it into the shadow of an ash dune, unfolded it with care and followed orders.

Samarit looked up at Rowan, her face a study in indifference.

But he noted the light of a smile in her eyes, her unique twinkle. It confirmed that, in her mind, he had joined her clan, his foregone conclusion long ago. Yet she must master the roller coaster of emotions if she were to remain undetected. Reptilians thrived on the negativity they provoked, they fed on it, they could smell it from a distance. Fear equalled danger, sadness no less, but the warmth of happiness, no matter how fleet a flicker –

"Thank you, Rowan," she said, "for your support."

He took her hand, but released it when Krumb powered down the scanner.

They watched him quickly fold it and slide it into its case.

"Major," the squire said, "we're on track and remain unplanned visitors, as well as uninvited."

"Excellent, Squire Krumb. Soon we'll be unwelcome ones too."

◆

Despite gas masks, the temptation to cough persisted. The wind whipped dust from tailings high into the sky in dense clouds that diffused as debris and hung in the air and sagged in tall pillars like the legs of a giant made of reeking dust, and spilled over the travellers in pale sulphurous fits and starts. Cloaking set to maximum increased danger of detection due to range shrinkage. Covered in fine yellow powder, forced to walk close together, they took care not to suffer their toes trod upon by the packhorse, who luckily did not seem to mind the stink.

His mask may have been more effective. Or else equine nanoid augmentation deserved the credit.

A few hours later, masks now stowed, the assassins drew near a crest, approached with slow caution, and peered over the rim.

Far below, a wide windy scalloped yellow desert streaked with char stretched into the distance, still not a tree or even a bush in sight. In the middle ground, many cylindrical exhaust towers billowed clouds of deadly toxic fumes, now fortunately diverted from the crest by winds from the south that corroded the vale. Waves of dusty sand blasted the complex, which often hid portions of the grim factory prisons, even the facility in closest proximity: the biogenetics laboratory. In addition, the vale hosted a launch site for space satellites and spacecraft to the moon, as well as an airport. Why technology factories had been set up in such a difficult environment puzzled Rowan. The positive air pressure inside the buildings and vehicles must be extreme to keep out dust. Unwanted humidity would be low, but perhaps the cool-blooded reptilians collected the daylight heat and stored it in some way for night-time distribution.

Krumb said, "We're a bit ahead of schedule, major," while he checked his chronometer, "by about twenty-three hours."

"Are you absolutely certain, squire?" Samarit continued to peer through field glasses at what looked to Rowan like a swarm of airborne "pteros" (pterosaur-shaped Rep fighter aircraft) near the airport.

Krumb replied, "Atomic clocks come with a lifetime guarantee, sir… if it's wrong."

Samarit turned towards him, placed her glove on his arm, lowered her brows at him and shook her head.

A white smile shone through his big dark dusty beard.

She continued: "Unless anyone has any objections, orders are to sneak a look at what goes on in the lab if we have time. We have time, says our squire. And we certainly won't on the way back out of this viper pit. Our rears will be in enemy sights from all directions in spite of the chaos that's ahead." She gazed out across the wide valley. "If we're lucky."

The sunset that strove to penetrate the smoky haze cast Samarit's fine profile in a paradoxically soft rosy glow. Rowan's heart leapt. A compulsion to writhe in agony threatened to swamp his mind – but he tore his gaze away to focus on the scene below.

She said, "Krumb, either you stay here and guard our steed or, if you agree, follow us down, after you program his bots to guide him back to the portal. It's his best chance."

"No one can stop me from coming along for the ride, sir. I can hide the gear, the long-range scanner and the cloaking device, but we need all the weapons and ammunition we can carry, what will fit under capes." The squire grinned as if he anticipated a holiday, not a confrontation with the possibility of a grisly death.

"Very well, squire. Take care of that now." She turned to her bodyguard. "Sir Rowan… are you ready?"

"Aye, Major Longbow, as ready as I'll ever be if you are. Down into the pit of vipers we go then." A smile played under his whiskers, whose tips curled as they never had.

"Very good, Berry." Samarit snickered, and her dark eyes twinkled freely. "Very, very good." She held his gaze until Krumb reported that the horse had headed back up the trail.

·

The wind had dropped. "I can't see much," whispered Samarit. "Can you?" The night had fallen double dark under the filthy blanket of smog – even nanoid-enhanced vision had dimmed. The heavy air hung slack, as still as if entombed.

Rowan replied, "I can see well enough… in greyscale."

"That's a relief. We're not here to play hide-and-seek. Where's the window?"

"Above my head. If I stand, I may be able to see something." He shifted his weight, and stood up.

Samarit tugged on Krumb's sleeve, and whispered in his ear: "Aren't you glad you came? Can you see in this murk?"

"No, major. I'm blind as a cave salamander as we say where I come from. But I'm cheered to have made it this far. I could even whistle a jolly tune."

"Please don't." She looked up, and asked, "What do you see, Rowan?"

He had tried to rub at least some caked dust off the glass of a tiny window beside a small pipe that extended a foot from the wall, presumably a means to visually verify its throughput from the inside. "I can just make out rows of trans-lucent vats. Inside are blobs of darkish stuff slowly circulating…" He ducked his head. After a few minutes, he looked again – the door opposite the window closed behind a technician in orange coveralls, an ander. "I don't know what I'm looking at. Let's try to find a better view." He took two steps, halted, and looked back. "No, stop. Why not wait here? I'll scout up ahead a little first. If I'm not back in three hours, call it a night and go home."

"Ha ha," whispered Samarit. "Proceed."

The other two soon disappeared from view as Rowan inched his way for an hour or more, until he approached a vertical rectangular depression in the wall. It turned out to be a door, one with a window in it, tall and wide. Dead weeds had collected at the door sill, but that meant nothing in a place so windy during the day. It might open at any time. He stood on his toes to look over the window sill at eye level. Through the dusty abraded glass criss-crossed with embedded wires, he peered into a garage for vans, flatbeds, dump trucks, bulldozers, graders and other road-building equipment parked in rows. The genetics laboratory must be in the section more near his starting point.

Rowan decided to retreat, but a powerful lamp switched on where several Reps stood in a circle under its conical spotlight, which cast their bare bodies in dark shadows and brilliant highlights that reflected in their iridescent scales. Many anders stood in the darkened background, all in orange coveralls and rapt attention, spectators of a game the huge reptilians played as they tossed a bundle like a large beanbag back and forth. That went on for some time, until one of them fumbled a catch, tried in vain to correct, but dropped the bundle on the concrete floor. Its wrapping came undone. It did not bounce, only rolled once and stopped. The other Reps threw their massive blunt heads back, opened their salivating maws and roared.

Rowan could not hear anything coming from that garage, only a drum beat – correction, his own heartbeat, he soon realized.

One of them, not the one who had fluffed his turn, got down on all fours and grabbed the bundle in its jaws. It stood up with a jerk that tossed the thing to a point twice its own height. The bundle spun towards the lamp in the high ceiling and came undone completely at the crest of the trajectory.

Rowan made out arms and legs – an ander infant.

The Rep let it splat on the concrete. The other one, not the loser, took a turn.

Rowan looked away, nauseated and dizzy. *But,* he reminded himself, *each moment since we left is my chance to do my duty and recover self-respect, to complete the mission and, above all, to protect Sam.* Therefore he must crawl back to her and Krumb immediately – but he stopped – duty demanded that he take one last look, even if it meant watching a baby being ripped to shreds. But that's not what happened.

The child served as a tool to provoke the ander onlookers, who stood and quivered or fell to their knees, and in one case, flat on her back, likely the mother. No one dared help the poor woman. Rowan absorbed their terror into his own being as if he were too near a raging bonfire, a radiation of pain and anguish that passed clear through the wall.

The Reps obviously revelled in it: their small orange eyes dilated to black. They danced around the inside of the circle, faced their victims, roared and rushed at the crowd.

Rowan looked no more.

·

Samarit and Krumb sat silent. Rowan's glimpse into the Rep world had been very difficult to report, apparently equally difficult to hear.

"Our duty re this building is done for now," said Major Longbow at last. "If we can rest, let's rest. I'll take first watch. Krumb, you take last watch so Sir Rowan can lead us while it's still night. To review, we know Reps don't see well in the dark, unless equipped with night-vision gear. Or if they're nanoid-enhanced, which may be too costly or too risky a procedure to waste on the menials here, like those… baby-killers. But they do sense shapes in low light. What's more, they can mentally construct and project what those shapes mean in some detail, thanks to their incredible heat sensitivity. It makes it easier to fool them, but not without special gear that's not all that portable. We can crank down our nanoids somewhat to compensate, according to our squire, with some experimental dope he brought along, but it may chill our bones, so chattering teeth could be a dead giveaway… pardon my poor choice of adjective. Fortunately, it's bound to be hotter than hell once the sun comes up."

"Aye, major," said Krumb. "Just one thing… I suggest a weapons check, as it's a dustbin we're sunk in."

·

The uppermost of the sky in which the stars refused to shine transitioned from inky black to several shades darker than the hue of deoxygenated blood. Rowan deemed it soon time to move out. The vale's flat plain offered no natural cover, only outbuildings with no fences. Above, a hard holographic dome disguised and protected the vale, not exactly a sealed environment and quite draughty during the day, frayed at the rim where it touched the rugged edges of the mountains. The flaw had allowed the assassins to penetrate it without trigger of an alarm. Most likely an aperture opened as necessary for launches. Ptero fighters patrolled the perimeter of the wide valley, no doubt with heat-seeking weaponry. Well-armed rangers surely must be on patrol and stationed in the hills as observers, despite typical reptilian overconfidence. And the biogenetics lab may have engineered creatures of the desert to serve as sirens, booby traps or mines when stepped on by the unwary. The squad had better try to stick to footpaths and roads, the more shadowed the better.

Rowan had declined the thermostatic drug. Beneath his cape Samarit nestled in slumber, and even snored a little. The squire lay still as well, possibly asleep. Dawn would not come for another hour.

✦

Krumb very carefully pulled his face mask up over his bushy black eyebrows caked with dust, and spat quietly. Orthomolecular supplements balanced a supersoldier's deficiencies. On the battlefield, however, they carried synthetics for a quicker onset, so he swallowed another little yellow pill to lower his body temperature.

Samarit did the same. "Krumb," she whispered, "this thermostatic nostrum is the absolute worst. Maybe it's not so bad if you wake up in a five-star lodge afterwards. At least this dust is sort of soft."

"Sympathies, major, as it deserves its minus-ten stars, but it seems a better alternative to being sniffed out."

"And right you are, squire. How are you, Sir Rowan? At least you feel toasty." She yawned – and stifled a sneeze.

"With respect, sir, it's you who feel toasty," whispered Rowan, "especially on one side." He flipped back his stiff oilskin cape to allow her to stand, thus created a reason to smother another sneeze.

They stretched their limbs. The men turned their backs while Samarit watered the dust, and they watered the building's wall, however at risk of detection by the sensitive reptilian snout. In a few minutes, they slipped across a patch of shadowed ground to a stone shed nearby; inside whined a bearing that needed oil or replacement. In time they had crossed a quarter-mile of the stronghold complex. The strange organic-looking burnt-ochre stone buildings, admirable for their aerodynamic curvilinear and scalloped shapes made by wind and sand, showed bright irregular windows here and there, especially on the lowest floors.

Rowan noted vague movement within. But all outdoors remained silent and still – until the sky brightened subtly: its dull cobalt assumed a more optimistic hue, and rapidly lightened; a thin breeze arose – followed quickly by clouds of red dust, then a buffeting sandblast, with little dust devils that stabbed at the ground as the sun's red shafts penetrated the desert gloom. Along the deep

108

shadows of the structures the assassins crossed, the wind whistled in baleful hollow tones, as if it moaned a long drawn-out warning.

"Krumb, orientation. Are we still on track?" Major Longbow peered through her dusty face mask. "Let's get this over with."

"Aye, major, look here." The squire held forth a small hand-held display in dark mode. "The blue dot… our course is less than a mile straight ahead, then at this slight angle. We're blessed with the mounds of slag and junked equipment strewn along the path to hide us too. The red dot is of course the target."

"Timing is everything. Again, are we on track?"

Krumb checked his chronometer, and replied, "Aye, our timing is good. Not too soon, nor too late… so long as the Reps haven't changed their plans. That's unlikely, as they're a bit rigid about that sort of thing. Inflexible, you might say. They're naturally impulsive, so the law forces them to think twice about every decision or pay the price if they blunder. The powers that be get the bad vibes they generate during penance as a bonus. I imagine it must be the vibrational equivalent of junk food. Where I come from we say they're too serious, and graceless on the dance floor to boot."

She wiped her mask lenses with gloved fingers. "Let's hope the highest-ranking reptilian on the planet is a typical specimen then. A meeting of this rarity must take complex logistics. It's very important for some unholy reason. May the angel of inflexibility be with us. Right. No talking from here on in. Get it?"

Another noise trumped the wind: the smokestacks' blowers winding up. Little clouds of black from their flared tops drifted into the sky, now as dark blue as a bruise, each time with a compressed chuff that battered the assassins' eardrums and body cavities.

Samarit raised her arm prior to the command to move out, but first she turned to Rowan and twinkled a message with her eyes: *I'm so glad we got to sleep together again."*

XIII

Lost

KRUMB SAVED HIM –

But one of Kirzaka's bodyguards in one bite decapitated the squire – the monster's little orange eyes dilated to black – the thing hopped and salivated and sprayed mucus, a sign of reptoid glee – so Rowan had heard.

As if to destroy all doubt of that, the Talon of Maçina, twice the killer's size, looked on and spewed mucus from his little round nostrils in tenfold measure. His jagged fangs remained clenched in a grimace, but his thoughts penetrated Rowan's mind: "*You freakish miscreants are puny and stupid, hardly worth my time to torture in small quantities.*" His tiny yellow eyes drilled into Rowan's mind from

Kirzaka *the* Deathless,
Talon *of* Maçina.

high above. "*Yet the female's criminal carrion,*" he added, "*may be of some small use when ripened.*" The Talon's maw opened wide, a guttural grunt scraped, grated and stretched out far too long before he sprayed mucus of pleasure again.

Rowan collapsed onto his knees, and writhed as the boundaries of his mind frayed under telepathic attack –

"*You, felid, stink,*" jeered the Deathless. "*Your place is the dunghill, but for some small pleasure we can extract from your still-breathing corpse. I anticipate with a thrill the conflagration of terror I shall bestow on your doomed world through you.*"

Rowan lifted his face to the monster who towered over him, and peered directly into the widely separated tiny yellow eyes.

"*Arrogance! It is suicide to look upon the Talon of Maçina! I grant you divine dispensation. Why? You shall return with a message. You shall crawl on your pathetic soft underbelly to your felid master, the ignorant follower of darkness. Tell her this: the meagre tribute is rejected, worthless. It was too little too late. Yet it is a delight to anticipate the vibrations that will ripple through your domains. Now go.*" Kirzaka abruptly spun about to leave, but the whip of his metal-spiked tail ripped off one of his bodyguard's upper limbs. Dark blood spread a stain where the creature's weapon clattered to the floor. The many orange eyes dilated to black in unison, but the reptilians followed their king as he went on his way. Krumb's murderer, the last in line, stopped to choke – and slowly disgorged a matted dark hairball.

+

Nothing had changed but everything: the stillness of the dim Mudredd night, the dunes of dust punctuated by the odd dead weed – wretched, hollow, quiet. And Rowan now alone, exhausted, sick and blind, no longer the self he once thought he knew. A final torture: the Reps had extracted the nanoids that had bestowed enhanced vision, strength and stamina, that which allowed him to do his duty without sufficient rest since long before the would-be assassins' sturdy packhorse retreated to the portal. The wounds from their rough clawed grip stung with the salt they had sprinkled on him. Lashed in place, he had squirmed in agony, and choked and vomited. They told him they looked forward to the light entertainment as they watched his progress to see if it were even possible without his fancy boots (shoeing the feet, pathetic, they said, for the feeble, the weak). Besides, the handicap would make it more interesting. Wagers would be made. They had remarked on his wounds, how they festered so nicely because they had licked the foul-tasting lesions to infect them with bacteria-ridden saliva.

But the blood of his comrades, especially the female, would serve to cleanse the palate. They wished him recovery nevertheless so the hideous scars might bear witness as tokens of their bad intentions.

True to their word, he had been left alone beside the pools of black blood to find his own way out, then from beneath to the dome's frayed edge where the failed assassins had first stepped onto the desert plain. From there he looked up to the crest – and passed out cold as awareness drained away.

✦

Rowan peered down from the crest, and measured his progress. It had taken an entire day to crawl this high. Now the sun plummeted behind the peaks in the west. One thought and one electrified thought only tortured his rankled nerves: *Sam*. He could not – would not – believe she was gone. This thought held power, nowhere near nanoid augmentation's equal, but enough to keep him going. He *must* find her – his clenched teeth ached in his aching head. Again and again he recalled the vision of her lovely profile in the setting sun's rosy glow – she had looked out over their objective in this very spot likely only twenty-eight hours earlier. His heart ached to breaking point. Another hour darkened, and he wrenched himself away in grim resolve, and stumbled up the rocky trail, crucified by his own roiled mind –

And noble Krumb, how he had underestimated him at first! The loyal squire had saved his life, but for what? An agony of guilt, and the bearer of bad tidings to his "felid master" – that could only mean one person. It made sense that Kirzaka cast her as ignorant, a "follower of darkness." Rowan knew little of her religion, only that it looked forward to an age of enlightenment, whatever that meant – but it implied current and ongoing endarkenment. He knew little of reptilian religion either, although he grew up with it, if not in it, only that it took licence to dominate so-called lesser forms. Nonsense. Science had revealed undeniable evidence that *Reptilia sapiens* had been the outcome of just one experiment among many. And what did the ogre mean by the rejection of the "tribute"? Rowan himself? Or all three assassins? But how were they a payment – he a civilian, an unimportant one at that, just a foul-tasting felid – *but Sam* – she had standing among her people, a top-tier warrior, potentially a world leader – Krumb too may have been on some reptilian most-wanted list, the bounty now paid.

✦

Delirious and raving after a couple of days of endless rumination, sick, wounded and famished, he fell to his knees. Something primal within defeated him utterly, took control and released a roar appropriate to a depraved beast, while his spirit stood to one side and observed uninvolved. Shock in echoes resounded on the cliffs and assaulted his sensitive ears. Gravel rolled down a creode in the flank of the mountain – *something, someone out there* – he crouched behind a boulder. The air smelled of fresh blood. Silence – but there on the frozen gravel – a small mountain goat, its throat slashed, its white breast stained brilliant red, its slotted pupils blind. He fell on it and sated the belly that chewed on itself until then, his mind thoughtless and uncircumspect. Again the loud roar as strength returned. Only much later as he peeled congealed blood from his face did he wonder at it, disgusted. What crazed frothing beast lurked within? Had the Reps watched from the shadows and heard him, and decided to lend a claw despite their cruel mockery? Perhaps they enjoyed the white-hot raging fire of animal craving. No matter. He stumbled on, albeit in agony –

✦

The skeleton – undoubtedly that of a horse. Its bare white bones lay scattered, some missing, no doubt dragged to some den. Sorrow for the poor beast welled and flooded Rowan's eyes. He fell to the ground and let grief give way. Fortunately the death squad had taken care not to name the animal. A long interval of silent exhaustion later, another thought came: *I must be near the portal at last.* He stood up on sore feet, and surveyed the surroundings. Yes, the topography remained burnt into memory – not far off they had watched the shimmery portal crackle, distort and vanish behind them. *This is it.* But so what? He had no scanner. He had nothing but the thin, ill-fitting orange coveralls of an impersonated slave, and cold cracked feet unshod of their symbiotic nanoid boots. Worse, he slumped under the weight of unforgiveness and the endless question: *Sam… where are you?* To die here beneath the snow peaks – just deserts. No one would know, except the Reps somewhere to confirm who among them had won their bet. No doubt they watched from the Eye in the Sky high above –

✦

"Sir Rowan Berry, I do presume," said the voice – of a man.

Rowan peered in the direction from which the words had drifted –

113

Captain Masudah of Zau, Khémia.

"Forgive the, how you say... encroachment, the startling." The voice, strongly accented, identified itself: "I am Captain Masudah of Zau, in Khémia. That place you as well call the Black Land, I believe."

Rowan did not trust his own eyes. The rough ground where he huddled and shivered remained hard and cold, powdered in a light skiff of snow during the night. The sharp peaks under a leaden sky looked down just as frozen and indifferent as before. His feet still ached cold to the bloody bone, near to useless with blisters.

The man tilted towards him, smiled and extended an ungloved hand. About ten feet behind stood others, like the men in uniforms Rowan had seen before listed in his bodyguard training manual: longish off-white winter overcoats with brass buttons, belted at the waist with wide brown leather, from which hung various holsters and sheaths. Jackets and trousers: twill and tan, tucked into tall brown boots – red piping down the outer seams. Some wore close-fitting knit caps with a tassel on the crown – others off-white pillbox hats with a sigil, a small red circular field with a triangle in gold – and star-pentagonal gold on the leader's collar. All appeared to have visited the barber this very day – and spent the rest at the beach in deep tan-enhancement drill. The speaker, Masudah, wore a black moustache, wings on the upstroke like a bird in flight, turned up at the tips, beneath a long straight nose and above a square jaw. He peered at Rowan through very warm brown eyes that saw more than just a barefoot loser lost in the wilderness. A distinct possibility: these fresh-faced men must be a troop of greeters at heaven's door – no, wait, not here where the poor packhorse's skeleton lay scattered like a shipwreck on some Anggh-forsaken frozen rocky coast –

"Sir Rowan, if you may forgive my saying so, we come to save you from a pointless fate. Please, let me shake your hand and introduce my men." The hale and hearty Masudah gestured behind him, and offered his ungloved palm.

Rowan allowed the man to pull him up. Stood up now, but less straight and steady than ever, he looked down from a height a half-foot greater to meet the man's eyes.

"No... yes... I'm Rowan Berry." His voice had gravel in it that no cough would loosen. "But the title is..." he rasped, "unnecessary."

114

"Ah, but allow me to employ it in your honour, Sir Rowan. It is our way. In our land there are also what one may call knights, and we are they. We know of you from before we left Khémia. Such a long way… it is to our great sorrow we had not arrived some days more soon, but we suffered an unexpected delay, attack by our common enemy the Apep, those devils you call *Reptilia sapiens*, the Snake People kind." The man's pleasant face grew solemn, and he bowed his head. "Apologies."

Rowan said nothing, too slow of wit to assess these soldiers' true intent, but watched the man straighten, and shook his hand.

"Sir Rowan, we must attend to your feet, as they are unfit for travel. And we wish to offer, how you say… grub, hot, as soon as possible. Please, come away from these sad bones. We make camp beyond. When we have rest, the journey moves on. It is to your land we go."

◆

Rowan and Masudah had seated themselves before a small firestone of their own and out of earshot of the other men.

"You're most generous, Captain Masudah, thank you." Rowan's irritated gravelly vocal fry had cleared to less-frayed. "You found me at my wit's end… but I now feel up to hearing your plans, especially as they seem to concern me. I'm a bit lost in every way at the moment. Things have not been going well for us… it seems a fool's errand now… all was lost…"

"You are most welcome, Sir Rowan. As you know, no doubt, as a League ally Khémia's duty is not only to protect its borders but the entire world from our common enemy. For long we have been able to prevent their trespass without too much trouble, even ignore them. Our methods from times of old still work well, of which the Apep remain uninterested… they have larger fish to cook, so they do not trouble to understand how we do it. But us small fish, how you say… they have us for breakfast one day, if we do not supplement with material science."

Rowan glanced up, and murmured, "Our technology is in a way similar to that of the reptilians… we see nature as a kind of machine. I'm not a scientist, but to me it means if we understand its mechanisms, we can take advantage of it. Khémia is reputed to be a mystic land. Do you mean to say your science is different?"

"Very different, Sir Rowan. I as well am not a material scientist, thus will not try to compare in detail. You see, I am a priest as well as a soldier. My duty as warrior includes defence of our science. We may as well call it that, as it has

115

something in common with your idea of it, that is, experimentation. To us the Source is primary. All else is secondary. We believe the universe is one. The material machine you speak of is non-separate. Objects, the machine, are at one level of order, but secondary. There is a primary level. I do not say 'high.' No, not above it. But, how you say… inclusive. The whole includes its parts. My duty as priest is to actualize identity, the whole. For that the parts, the secondary level of order, must respect the primary, the whole, and above all cosmic law. If I succeed, it is like a stone thrown in a pond… it spreads like that, to all. And if the people come to me curious, I teach… Sir Rowan, is this clear or is it mud?"

"Clear, Masudah. But I have to be careful not to mix up what I think you're saying with religious ideas. I was raised an orphan, under the thumb of the Apep as you call them. So that's what religion means to me, a way to control."

"Understood, Sir Rowan. For us religion is not like that, yet a convenience, how you say… institution, a form that allows one like myself the freedom to experiment. Like a scientist. Faith pending results! We need not speak of this further if you wish. But it is good to get to know one another, not so? We are comrades in this battle between good and evil after all, my friend, if one may put it thus."

"Yes… Masudah, if I may presume on that, what do you know of a woman called Chancellor Madam Ellaern, Vugh Deep's minister of education? Was she somehow connected with our mission?"

The Khémian tilted closer. He raised a forefinger to his lips, and stood up to check on his men engaged in quiet conversation around their firestones. Hands clasped behind his back, he bent towards his listener. "I believe you can be trusted. But you must not speak of this again. You see, I have no proof, only a priest's, how you say… intuition. Through your embassy in our capital the minister in fact informed us of your mission. She was always much interested in Khémia and its ways. I know her since many years, yet this is most suspicious, as she must have a private means of communication, perhaps a hold on a high bureaucrat in some way. For long now there is no official safe channel between our respective domains. She asked my superior that it be I, Masudah, who must stop you from going down into that demon hole, that lizard pit Mudredd. We did not come to help you kill the king of the Apep."

Rowan's curiosity sparked to life. He stared at Masudah. "You didn't? And, if I may, what's your opinion? Off the record."

"Of the minister? As I say, I have no evidence." He sat down with both elbows on his knees, bent close and murmured: "I suspect she may be under the claw of the Apep, in fact the mighty Talon himself."

Rowan grasped at the idea to keep afloat. Did Diss abort the mission? Why not send his own troops to retrieve the death squad? But Kirzaka had called Ellaern his "felid master, the follower of darkness" – she had enlisted the Khémians –

Masudah watched him, pressed his hand briefly on Rowan's shoulder, and said, "Now you must rest, sleep well over firestone gravel under wool in a tent. Tomorrow we open the gate." The evening ended with a simple ritual led by the warrior-priest, to focus their collective will, he explained, to sleep in peace and strengthen their shield.

✦

In the twilight before dawn, the company packed up their camp. By brilliant early morning sunshine, they marched the short distance to the skeleton, including Rowan on bandaged feet and supported by a walking stick. Some of the soldiers collected the remaining bones and buried them in a grave lined with stone. On top they placed a flat oblong rock engraved with a hieroglyph, the sigil of blessing and good fortune in the afterlife for a hero fallen in battle. And they sealed the grave. To all appearances neither man nor beast had ever set foot on that ground.

After a few words in Khémian from Masudah spoken over the burial, the warriors lined up to form a chevron, its tip directed at the location of the portal where Rowan remembered it having vanished: jumbled boulders beneath a cliff, above which jagged white peaks loomed. Masudah asked that Rowan clear his mind as well as possible, and that he stand directly behind his own position at the tip of the chevron.

Rowan imagined the men as the arrowhead, and the warrior-priest, along with himself and several others, as the shaft. Whether the metaphor had any bearing on the reconstitution and activation of the portal he did not know, but it made him feel that he contributed something. However, without the aid of nanoids, he wobbled. Even a hand-held scanner's relatively quick effect compared to the Blacklanders' natural methods would have been welcome.

At presumably some unseen signal from Masudah, the entire contingent got on their knees, faced the still invisible gate and bowed. Other than the thin keening of the wind, silence reigned, unlike the crackle when scanners activated nature's portals, but the same wavy circular pattern, like a stone thrown into a clear pool, distorted the rocky background in a pattern of rings. In a loud voice Masudah ordered his men in the Khémian tongue. The company of soldiers passed through the portal.

XIV

Inkling

COMMANDER DISS STOOD at his metal desk, palms down on its surface, and glared at Rowan seated across from him. "*You look like warmed-up Rep shit, Berry! Worse, your report leaves a great deal in doubt! I refer to the fate of Major Longbow!*" His loud voice grew more insistent and louder, if that were even possible: "*You graphically describe Squire Krumb having been decapitated by one of the Rep bodyguards after he deflected a blow that would have killed you! Of course he did his duty like the decorated military man and hero he was! You, however, wasted precious seconds by preventing the major from striking her target! Why? She was your superior officer! What was your intention?*" He leaned forward further, but lowered his tone to a murmur: "*To sabotage the mission?*"

Rowan glanced up, all the way up into the commander's stony gaze, and replied, "Negative, sir. I believed that she would not only miss the target, but stood in the line of fire. Therefore I felt it necessary to save her life if possible... I... I was her bodyguard."

"*So you say!*" yelled the commander. He backed off, sat down and glared at the report lying on his desk. "*Were you not trained to follow orders?! She was in command! If her life was in danger, that is simply the nature of a soldier's existence! Often short! It was your duty as bodyguard to defend her! Acknowledged! But it was her job to execute the order to assassinate the Rep leader! Your actions aborted the mission!*" More quietly, he hissed: "*And it failed the major.*"

Rowan stared at the helpless guilty hands in his lap – *his* hands.

The commander continued, louder: "*I repeat, there is significant doubt as to what happened next! What did you observe of Major Longbow after witnessing the squire terminated?! You say you were sprawled on the floor some eight feet from your position at her side, after you pushed her, and after the squire saved your life!*" He slammed his fist on the desktop. "*Well?!*"

"Everything happened very quickly, sir." Rowan stared, eyes wide. "After Krumb, Squire Krumb, knocked me over... Sam... Major Longbow... was no longer in my line of sight. The Rep bodyguard made sure I looked directly at it before it bit... before it decapitated the squire. Then it... it laughed."

"*Reptilians do not laugh!*" shouted the commander. "*That is anatomically impossible!*" He leaned towards Rowan, and said more softly, "Please speak more concisely," but maintained the relentless glare.

"I mean, sir, that's the impression I… received. My unofficial designation is intuitive empath, as you know, sir, despite my official capacity as a civilian consultant and bodyguard. Because it's a secret program, it takes years of training to achieve unacknowledged first-class certification, yet my natural abilities seem to be evolving on their own. Either that or the reptilians' empathic powers are greater than assessed. In my mind I perceived the Rep guard mocking me. It spewed mucus. In our terms, that translates as laughter."

The real Diss.

"*Of course Reps are empaths, that's why they torture their victims, to somehow harvest the energies generated by fear to power their damn resonance generators when they put their ugly heads together in their infernal black magic rituals! All right, so the Rep mocked you, according to your definition! I hope your warm fuzzy felid feelings weren't hurt, but that's no excuse for ignoring your duty!*" He slammed the report to the desk. "*What of Major Longbow? What happened to her?!*"

"Commander, I don't know!" Rowan's wide-open stare grew wider. "I saw nothing. I don't know what happened to the major. I recall looking into Kirzaka's eyes in defiance. The next thing I knew he had me by the balls… I mean as if a… a tractor beam had hold of my attention. At that point I was aware of nothing but the presence of a power greater than my own will… his… as if… as if nothing existed but him. Him and what he wanted… of me."

The commander relaxed somewhat. "You say Kirzaka gave you a message to forward, therefore spared your life. The message is, and I quote: '*Blah, blah, blah… the meagre tribute is rejected, worthless. It was too little too late. It is a delight to anticipate the vibrations that will ripple through your domains.*' You were to deliver this message to a female, '*blah, blah, blah… your felid master, the ignorant follower of darkness.*' *Who is this person?!*"

Rowan glanced at Diss. "I can't be sure, commander. Kirzaka could have projected an image into my mind, I'm sure of it. He forces us to speculate. Felids such as yourself throughout Vugh Deep are very often leaders of one kind or another, including teachers, the ones referred to as masters, unlike the others. I've had many such masters over the years of my education…"

"*And?! What else DON'T you know, Berry?!*" Diss shouted. "*Speculate then! Please, answer my questions without wasting more time! Who is this 'master'?! We need to know!*" He leaned back, clasped his hands behind his head and growled low: "Until you can confirm a name, you will be detained here at the base under strict supervision."

"Confirm, sir? Do you have a suspect?"

119

"*I ask the damn questions here!*" Diss slammed the desk with his fist. "*We know your profile inside and out, Berry! We know the names of all your contacts since you arrived in Perkona Ola, including your teachers! We want you to name a name! If you do not cough it up like Krumb's hairball, you will be subject to interrogation by the same technology we use on spies! Have no doubt the truth will be wrung out of you, Berry, but you'll wish you never drew breath in this world if you resist! Who is the 'master' you are to deliver the message to?! Dammit, who is she?!*"

"I failed Major Longbow… and the mission… but, commander, I have nothing to hide. I accuse no one, but if you insist, my best guess is that it's Chancellor Ellaern. She's known to follow a religious faith, though I'm not sure which one exactly. The Reps see ways of understanding the universe other than their own as darkness, so they would call her ignorant. While she wasn't involved directly in my curriculum as far as I know, I had several meetings with her. She may have taken special interest in me from the beginning. As you may know, she was one of Major Longbow's teachers in the early years, before she'd been promoted to chancellor and then elected to her current ministry. She retained an interest in the major's military career. In addition, one of the major's first solo training exercises as a cadet prior to military college was to rescue an orphan felid. Major Longbow said the minister especially recommended my orphanage to the major's sergeant at the time. What's more, she specified that I be that orphan to rescue, I'm sure of it, based on something Sam mentioned about green eyes. I mean Major Longbow, sir. The minister said she'd known of me for most of my life… I think. More than that I don't know."

"*You 'think'?! But we know all this already! You were one of many unfortunates, felids and others who were and are bereaved and abducted from their homes by the Reps! You have said nothing of the fact that Captain Masudah of Zau, the Khémian, brought you back from that hell-hole Mudredd Vale, or at least the nearest quirky portal! He told us what brought him here! What do you say?! Look at it from our point of view! You may have been specially conditioned by the reptilians to breach our security, an ostensibly innocent victim but programmed to sabotage us like a time bomb!*" The commander sustained his unblinking power pose, but murmured, "To be fair, Berry, you of course may not even be aware of it."

Rowan straightened his posture and protested, quietly at first but with increasing volume and intensity: "With respect, sir… then why was I trusted to train as Major Longbow's bodyguard? Why was I given an unmerited title and assigned a squire in the first place? While it's true that I failed to question it at the time, I believe due to my earlier conditioning that authority never be doubted, and the impact of my unbelievable good fortune as if it were a wonderful dream

I feared to wake from, it's *not* something I asked for. In fact my record shows that I tried to release the squire! An assistant was quite unnecessary after the first few months! And *why* were we, inexperienced for the most part, sent on such a hopeless mission? *Why was Sam promoted? She hadn't even graduated yet! She was only a…*"

"*Enough, Berry!*" The commander stuck his arms straight out palms up, ran his fingers through the sides of his brindled greying mane, stood up and stepped to the office window. Beyond and below, troops marched in formation, and military grounders rolled along in the broad light of the cavern's illumined dome. All this he observed intently, hands clasped behind his back. "These are good questions," he said at subdued volume. "They all have answers. For now, you will be confined to base. At all times you will be accompanied by two armed guards. You are to repeat our conversation to no one. Understood?"

"Yes, sir. May I ask a question?"

"Just don't expect an answer. What is it?"

"With respect, sir, I remind you that you said that if I hazarded a guess as to whom Kirzaka referred, you would let me return to Perkona Ola…"

"*I did not say you could return to Perkona Ola!*" The commander turned away from the window to glare at Rowan. "*I only said, Berry, that if you refused to confirm a name you would be detained here at the base and subjected to interrogation until you caved or wish you'd never been born! You have acceded to my demand and proffered a name! Thank you! But for security reasons you will remain here until we investigate further! Return to your quarters! Now!*"

◆

"Masudah, how's your visit going?" The two sat among many others in the mess at their meals in noisy conversation, apart from the two armed guards who remained within close range at all times.

"I am happy to see you are well, Sir Rowan. But I am sad also, as we are soon to leave, but it has been most interesting. Our hope of sharing our alternative technologies was politely heard, but it seems there is too much, how you say… at variance. It may not be compatible without a shift in, how you say…"

"A paradigm shift?"

"Ah, yes, paradigm. Perhaps rightly it has been criticized as too slow to be effective under pressure, despite our long-standing freedom from the Apep. It may be that if they truly desired it, Khémia would soon be theirs also. It is very sad if so, and our long tradition, so beautiful in many ways, would be lost. It may be your ways will be victorious, but who knows? Yet the defence minister promises to take our offer to parliament at least. That is something."

"Do you remember our conversation on the other side of the portal?" asked Rowan. "I mean the gate."

Masudah casually looked around the large and busy room, then briefly crossed his lips with a forefinger when the guards' eyes followed a shapely young female soldier as she headed for the exit, as did several whistling and shouting men around them. She turned and blew her admirers a kiss, after which the men made enough noise for the Khémian captain to whisper: "We have learnt much, but time will tell." He shook his head, which meant "say no more."

Rowan nodded assent. "And due to my unfortunate lack of presence of mind when confronted by the powers that be, I forgot to ask about the Longbow clan when I had the chance. They were said to have been cut off from Perkona Ola, but I'm not allowed to speak to most people, especially canids."

"Yes." Masudah peered at Rowan for a moment, and stood up. "As a priest, I am against hiding truth. But as a warrior, it is my duty to honour our allies. Yet I believe you will discover all in due course." He placed his left hand on Rowan's right shoulder, and with the other hand shook his hand in farewell, and smiled with his entire being. "You must, my friend. You must!"

◆

Released now, Rowan rode in an unmarked grounder en route to Perkona Ola. The commander had said Kirzaka's message must be delivered to Madam Ellaern verbatim, but an appointment must not be made first. He must show up at her office unannounced, and say that what he had to discuss must be for her ears only. He need not explain why. He must recount the events of the failed assassination attempt just as he had officially reported them to the military. No one else must be present. No report need be made of this meeting afterwards, as it would be transmitted and recorded via the raven brooch he always wore, now modified by a military technician for the purpose. He examined it closely, and pondered the inscription that encircled the stylized raven, *Fjkwi' mar ljljl*, which he had once researched. Translated from the language native to the late extraterrestrials who had bred the ancestors of the death squad's packhorse, it meant: "Down, but not out."

Surely Ellaern must be implicated in the failed mission, but how? And why? Worse, how had he been duped into taking on such a foolish task? Well, maybe that was clear enough: *a fool for love is a fool like no other*.

✦

The minister listened with great attention, dignity unruffled. She appeared to think carefully before she spoke in the pronounced Lyran accent that made her sound so intelligent, sophisticated and gracious: "I am very sorry things turned out the way they did, Rowan. Squire Krumb was well-known as a valiant warrior. Samarit Longbow was my very best student in the early years, a truly gifted child." Ellaern looked down with a wistful smile at her clasped hands rested on her office desk. "And so beautiful, the cream of her race. She had been destined to be her tribe's chieftain, a princess, then a Longbow clan high chieftain one day, perhaps their queen, although these days it is only a ceremonial title… better to be mayor of Perkona Ola, possibly a prefect… or even the first canid prime minister of Vugh Deep come to that. Many doors would have opened to her."

"We don't *know* that she's gone," said Rowan, his whole body tense. "I didn't see what happened to her, as I said. I believe she's still alive." He forcefully stopped his mind from imagining under what conditions, however. He clenched his jaws and ground his teeth to compensate.

"Yes, we must hope." Ellaern looked at Rowan with a little smile. "As well as remember." She stood up, stepped around to the front of the desk, and looked down upon him. "May I tell you again how this news sorrows me, Rowan, but you must know that a warrior accepts the risk of death at any time. Her identity as a canid was bigger than the merely individual. She would have only been happy in service of the greater whole, just as her pre-therianthropic ancestors did as pack animals. As an alpha female she was destined for ever greater leadership upon victory at each test…"

"You keep using past tense." Rowan scowled, and griped in wounded tones: "*Why* were we sent on such a futile, hopeless, stupid mission? *Why* wasn't someone more experienced or more dispensable… *why*?"

"Why? Why, to strike a fatal blow at our enemy! There was no way we could have made such a major coup in a show of force. We have not the strength. It would have been the end of our world." Her tone firmed as her gaze hardened. "And I should probably not tell you this, but it may be the end of our world in any case. Yes, we are very vulnerable since Kirzaka's technology has made major advances in recent months. This I know, although you will not hear of it in the media, not yet. Kirzaka is overconfident now. We had to try. We had to try something so audacious it would be more easily overlooked, a deadly mosquito to bite the dragon…"

"And I can tell *you*, minister, having been there, having looked into Kirza-ka's beady yellow eyes, it was impossible. They *knew* we were coming, *before we even left!*" Rowan stood up and glared at the minister, fists clenched. "How do *you* know so much about a top-secret mission? Did *you* knowingly send us to our deaths?"

"That is preposterous. Why would I do that? And how?!" Ellaern backed away to retreat behind her desk. "I valued Samarit!" Tears welled in her dark-rimmed golden eyes, yet she tensed her lower jaw, and focused until only her golden eyes remained. Her voice soothed, balmy as a summer breeze: "Look into my eyes, Rowan. Relax completely. You are very relaxed. You forget your false accusation just now. You forget it. It was Diss. Madam Ellaern only did her duty, like any patriot."

Rowan fell back into his chair, and slumped.

Ellaern tried to speak, but crossed her arms instead. A moment passed, and she said, "You should remember whom you are talking to. Until now I have been your benefactor." She sat down and riffled through papers on her desk. "Now, if you will excuse me, I have much to do. I am going abroad. Thank you for the message, although I do not know what it has to do with me." She leaned forward, glared at Rowan's brooch and raised her voice: "You can tell *that* to Knight Commander Diss!"

＊

Once again Rowan without mercy beat himself for failure to ask how Ellaern, as he believed she had once implied, had known of him for most of his life. It must be a clue. *Why am I such a foolish, dense, stupid, slow-witted, idiotic moron? I'm just a half-witted, brainless twit, thick as a brick...* but the incompatibility of "half-witted" with "brainless" – *Which is it, half or none?* – no answer, yet the brief interruption of his scathing self-scorn enabled the resolve to seek professional help to penetrate the remaining dark cloud of self-hypnotic Rep programming still in operation and delete it or upgrade it, and fast. He simply must learn that an authority figure need not be a switch that kills circumspection, curiosity and proper investigation. Free of that, he intended to qualify for the highest degree in the martial art he had already trained in, to test whether his mind had been freed and to increase fitness. Internal chaos decreased, as this resolution alone gave strength to the will, by fair means or foul, to rescue Samarit, thus the hope of repaying his debt and doing his duty – come what may.

XV

Revelation

"M<small>Y VIEW IS</small> that sentient beings have something truly fundamental in common," the doctor said, "beyond genetics, beyond species, beyond the body and mind altogether. When this essential factor is allowed free expression, unhindered by a cloudy mind and a troubled heart, the light of truth does the work, eliminates dysfunction by replacement with natural order, reconnecting body, mind and spirit. The religions of the land also profess to literally 'relink' per the definition, to effect reunion, but a model of the psyche such as the one I employ allows freedom to experiment, even when the prognosis is poor. Thus I never give up until the patient has given birth to an improved version of themselves, assuming the old one has failed in ways large and small, usually repeatedly."

Doctor Sola looked like what some racists, specifically the ander sect called the Sannir, were pleased to call a "true man," in their opinion superior to both *Canis sapiens* and *Felis sapiens*. Hence also known as the True Men, a term that supposedly included women, they claimed to represent a large fraction of the population of Vugh Deep, the fair-complexioned *Ander sapiens*, secondarily those of other hues of skin and conformation of ears. The therapist's impressive shock of blonde hair and penetrating blue gaze behind tortoiseshell eyeglasses gave him an air of intellectual authority, which unavoidably alarmed Rowan at first. Authority figures triggered submission, thus loss of mental acuity, the very flaw he sought help to overcome.

But when researching whom to consult, Rowan discovered that Sola did not subscribe to the Sannir ideology that claimed the races of Eorthe should be classified in a hierarchy, not even based on cranial capacity. To his credit he was renowned for his effective methods as a transpersonal psychologist, a practitioner of a discipline that did not believe identity began and ended with its most obvious presentation, the body-mind. Most other sub-fields of psychology agreed that unconscious factors informed the personality, but Sola had acquired a reputation as something of a mystic, a mark against him for some, but he believed identity extended far beyond the individual into the archetypal, a selling point due to Rowan's training in martial arts founded on practical principles discovered long years before the current age of reductionistic materialism, or what one of his tenured university professors had called "nothingbutism."

The doctor continued: "Thus I am very interested in your experience with the blue fungus you mention in the exploration form. It's quite familiar to me.

Of course smugglers trade in exotic substances for which there is no end of demand. Why? Because the psyche has an inbuilt drive towards wholeness, and most of us feel that we are missing something, thus we seek that something and often come to grief. Chemically bypassing the brain's filters is one method of temporary disabling this belief, but also of glimpsing its workings, not that most users and abusers are interested in that. They only want relief, even if their pain is merely in the form of boredom. But do you know blue fungus spore casings are stronger than steel? They can survive space travel. Perhaps they're ancient intergalactic adventurers drifting on ionic winds in search of new worlds to share in telepathically and to seed. This fungal species has little in common genetically with native varieties on Eorthe. Our pre-industrial ancestors even claimed to have symbiotic relationships with this extraterrestrial race…"

"*Doctor…*" With great effort, Rowan interrupted: "Doctor, that's very interesting, I do apologize, but I very much want to disable the hypnotic commands I was forced to make my own. As I've already said, whenever I'm in the presence of an authority, my attention narrows to a cramp. I automatically assume every word such an authority speaks is unquestionable truth. In fact, if you'll pardon me, I'm experiencing it right now when I listen to you speak! It may very well be the truth… I'm not contesting that… it's just that I can't help but put the representative of that authority on such a pedestal that I neglect opportunities to think for myself. I don't believe it's fear, only stupefaction. I make myself vulnerable to manipulation as well. I want to disable the programming or else convert it to a better one. Can you help me?"

"Unforgivable!" The doctor threw up his hands. "I've been talking too much. My role is to listen. It's only because I'm so intrigued. You see, I don't often get patients like you. Indeed, Sir Rowan, I can help. In fact this is why I mention the blue fungus. Since you already have some experience with such materials, I propose we try something that will, as mentioned, bypass the inhibiting hypnotic command so we can examine it, something of much more benefit than the so-called egg chair the establishment here prefers. In my opinion, these chair technologies are easily manipulated to limit what one can learn, so I do not recommend them for our purpose. My method allows for total freedom of the unconscious mind to reveal the truth, really a question of trust in it. This by itself may disable undesirable hypnotic commands, saving much time."

Rowan shifted his weight, uneasy in his chair. "But my experience with the blue fungus showed me a distorted view. It made an old woman, who had lived a long hard life, look young, fit and hot… as in attractive. If my particular felid chemistry had allowed it, I would have been totally seduced."

"Ah, this is the interesting bit," said the doctor. "Was your vision distorted or was it clarified, even deepened? What if there is a deeper beauty beneath all appearances deemed good or bad by our likes and dislikes? We are all hypnotized to some degree since birth, some say before that, born into a field of information and energy that makes constant suggestions as to what is valuable and what is not. It punishes us for not conforming, rewards us if we do. I say 'suggestions' and not 'commands,' as in short order self-interest makes us internalize all that, similar to how the reptilians forced upon you self-hypnosis, thus it is we who become our own worst enemy. Perhaps what you saw by intuition in that old woman was innate, that very beauty shining through your disabled filters, a great but fleeting gift she was born to literally embody in youth, but clung to as her only virtue, sadly. She didn't learn from its loss to grow into psychological maturity. And yet, your unfiltered perceptual apparatus revealed the beauty as tangible and true, at least while you empathically shared her world."

Rowan pondered. "Do you mean to say the elixir somehow stripped off the blinders to, in some chemical way, see back in time? That's bizarre. Even if it doesn't, it implies that what I'm seeing right now isn't the whole picture."

"Is that not precisely why you have come to me? One could argue that all and any experience is chemically modulated, as if our nervous system is a biological multimedia receiver. The elixir allowed the frequency, the channel, to change briefly. All we must do is understand it as well as possible and learn to live at peace with ambiguity and not knowing everything, in other words, the mystery that is the twilight zone of our life in this world. One of its greatest mysteries is how it is possible to pretend it is banal and not a mystery of astounding and unfathomable proportions. But let us not get ahead of ourselves. We must take a small step, then another, and so on. And do not discount that you were rewarded an unexpected insight when you met her husband the constable," said Doctor Sola. "Shall we begin?"

◆

Sola's assistant, a friendly young lady called Marika, led Rowan to a windowless room at the back of the clinic, carved out of the solid granite of the cavern wall. She assisted as he entered a large tank that contained a heavy saline solution at body temperature, where he floated weightless in complete darkness. The anechoic chamber dampened all sound but his heartbeat and the whisper of circulating blood. Time trod water. Even gravity lost its usual effect. He could not tell the difference between horizontal or vertical. His head had been positioned in the middle of an array of purple crystals in a regular pattern fixed to the interior of a stainless steel cowling, much like a geode sliced in half, but without contact of the cranium, supported by a small antigravity pad. He had been told the experimental technology replaced the former drug therapy, as it could be controlled more precisely by the therapist, but only if necessary in case of an emergency, such as terrifying hallucinations. Yet even these, if they emerged, should be explored as symbols if possible.

"Go towards the pain, should it appear," the doctor had advised. "Running from it makes it more intense and entrenched. Simply remember you are more dangerous than danger. All this is within you, within the scope of awareness, however convincing it may seem as external, either as a blessing or a threat. When the lid has been removed, so to speak, we will then release and examine destructive repressed elements so as to convert them for constructive purposes." Rowan had been forewarned too that he would encounter more recent memories before moving on to deeper strata.

A lucid nightmare immediately came to the fore: Kirzaka's staring little yellow eyes and the bloody dismemberment of the squire. The hideous strength of it nearly made him call for help, but Rowan processed it quickly in order to dive deeper. He waited, and floated, for a lengthy period interspersed with minor suppressed memories come to life of racist slurs directed at him behind his back. At last: a dim orphanage interior, the stable in fact – nothing unusual about it, however, only the familiar humdrum sights and sounds of childhood, not even the bullying of the Heptas or their torturous skin-grafting rituals, let alone heads on the hook and blood on the altar, even Fuzzy's. But then –

The honeyed light that pervaded the fields and wooded hills under the warmest and bluest of skies – love itself – *Berry!* – Mama, Papa – he searched full-circle, but only their little hut appeared, nestled as if in a cot of shrubbery. Behind him, the long grass rustled, so gentle – not a breath of wind, so he turned to look. A lithesome young felid girl approached, not a woman quite yet, not like Mama, but obviously blossoming. Her long mane, alight with gold, glowed with the luminescence Berry bathed in. Her limpid eyes, also golden, the lashes long and black – exquisite. Her name –

✦

"*Let me out, let me out!*" yelled Rowan, and banged his fist on the inside of the tank enclosure. "*Let me OUT!*"

"Relax, Sir Rowan, you are perfectly safe," assured the doctor through the intercom. "Try to face down your fears. They cannot harm you here."

"You don't understand. I'm *not* afraid, I need to get out now. *Please!*"

Marika opened the door.

Rowan burst out of the tank like a felid cannonball.

The doctor applied the utmost persuasion to get him to at a minimum shower off the salt before rushing out into the world again. The man shook his head in dismay at the passions of youth. "Please, Sir Rowan! Take the opportunity while the experience is still fresh to examine what has presented itself. It is no accident and needs to be assimilated properly to be of any benefit. Worse, the lid is now off. There is unstable psychological danger!"

"Thanks, Doc, but that's not my problem at the moment. I may be back to do exactly that. But right now I just don't have the time." Rowan hurried towards the exit, but glanced back and explained: "*It's an emergency!*"

✦

At one of the libraries in the Hall of Memory, salt-encrusted and damp, Rowan dived into a book titled *Cult of the Dawn Cat: Mission from Lyra*, about New Dawn, the religion to which Ellaern subscribed, or so he had heard. At the time her religious views had been of little interest, but now they may provide a clue. Or at least her whereabouts – abroad, she said – he searched for any lead. He chose a selection of political histories that might make it possible to chart her route, if one there were, from the hinterland of Berry topside to the subterranean world of Vugh Deep and Perkona Ola. How had she risen to such a position of power? What did that have to do with him? With Samarit? The general information on the subject of League religions had only explained that New Dawn fell under the category of sects that believed the Primordial Architects would return one day. Academics, such as philosophers of science, assumed these beings, in their opinion mythical of course, existed as elements of an origin story for immature minds or the uneducated, mere projections of superior, all-knowing, internalized parental figures as an extraterrestrial or extradimensional race, even specific figures among them, but hardly to be taken seriously by any educated adult. *Nothingbutism.*

In the case of New Dawn, these forebears, insectoids allegedly, came from the distant Fédora Galaxy, which resembled a hat with a curled brim. Science had shown that *some* intelligence had taken the hominid that had reached the peak of development permitted by its natural environment and combined it with other species' genes very cleverly, which had resulted in monsters at times, but culminated in the various iterations of *sapiens*. Some evidence remained in dispute as to whether the tinkerers had introduced even their own bequeathal into the mix before they had mysteriously vanished millions of years ago. Evidently New Dawn devotees identified the insectoid pioneers as their creators, an unlikelihood, but claimed logic and reason were secondary to intuition, i.e. theirs.

Moving on to the classifications of known extraterrestrial races, he found interesting references to intelligent insectoids visited by a voyeuristic cloaked research spacecraft in the remote past, somewhat near the Fédora, said to be incapable of high technology, but had instead cultivated a complex cosmology and a physics incomprehensible to contemporary science, which dismissed the ramblings of an obviously ignorant and perhaps insane species lost in cerebral delusions, who lived without any artificial devices, even for communication, let alone space travel – few details, except one of interest. Rowan sat up straighter to read of the obsession with physics believed to be planet-wide and debated thoroughly until the people reached a consensus, who only then undertook further research using their unascertained means. Obviously, they had no issue with communication. Nor did their social structures and economies suffer as one might expect of the demented. The theory suggested their environment had become toxic, that the insectoids had not yet had time to adapt, hence had gone mad. *Speculative nothingbutism.* Rowan sighed.

Spurred on nevertheless, he moved on to Ellaern's history, according to the official annals first. Perhaps someone had written a biography. Maybe even an autobiography – but he suspected public figures often invented themselves. She had come from another star system, the Lyra constellation, according to one encyclopedia – the youngest daughter of a noble house, and her mother had come from Eorthe. She had trained as an educator – and sent to Eorthe and the Lyran embassy to study local languages, as well as diplomacy – Lyran interests included any planet that hosted feline species, as they believed they had in the very distant past seeded them with their own kind.

Rowan noted that her birth date as listed reasonably corresponded with the likely age of the felid girl in his vision in the doctor's tank, and roughly agreed with what she had told him. The portrait of her in the encyclopedia quite reminded him of the girl in the meadow, especially the eyes. Ellaern did speak with a Lyran accent, but that may be fake. She looked like a felid, not a feline. Her nose was not triangular, for one thing, and she had no leopard or cheetah spots, only a few little ones near her hairline at the temples, like large freckles – a Lyran-feline-Eorthe-felid hybrid?

So far all the information had disappointed. Either he guessed wrong or the official documentation lied. Intuition provided the only evidence that she had known him in his earliest years, because she had been there in Berry, perhaps grew up with him. Maybe she had been a childminder during the late stages of the reptilians' reconfiguration of the Surface world, when his parents among a few other felids still retained some independence. *Why oh why didn't I think to ask her when I had the chance?* Rowan smacked his head, hard. Maybe she would have lied about it anyhow. He had not trusted her from the beginning. Maybe he had just hallucinated the scene of her in the bright fields of Berry, thanks to Sola's strange contraption. But it had been so vivid, easily as vivid as his experience right now in the library confused –

He looked for and found a directory of New Dawn meeting places, temples and shrines. He closed his eyes and planted the tip of his forefinger on a page – his first stop. He must find Ellaern. This time she would not get away until he had the truth, assuming she had not already vanished.

◆

In vain he had visited nine of Perkona Ola's New Dawn temples, but then came to New Dawn Fane Clach Beò. Proportioned well, it accorded with the classic sacred geometry he had studied in art history classes, and was situated in a treed neighbourhood of residences and parks just off a main thoroughfare. Built of dressed red granite in the architectural style of the early past century, when simplified classical forms were popular – without windows, its only signage a circle of gold plate above the portico, just like all the other temples. He had copied the sigil into his notebook, along with a word to be translated later: *càradh*. The circle enclosed a symbol shaped like a pennant, a vertical stroke with a triangle at half-mast that extended from its middle to the right.

He leapt the three steps to the heavy wooden double doors elaborately carved with incomprehensible spidery marks that may have been pictographs, but looked like pith fleck, worm tracks – maybe like a stereogram; the longer he gazed, the more likely a clue might appear in the image that would emerge. After some minutes, he decided perhaps it was just pith fleck after all. He did not know whether to knock or not. So far he had been in too much of a hurry to learn more than what the brief synopsis had told him of New Dawn beliefs – no handles, nor a button or pull for a bell – but the doors opened silently on their own. No one anywhere – but then from the foyer the inner sanctum remained a mystery. The doors closed behind him with a quiet thump. An aromatic fragrance of incense like sandalwood pervaded the space. He listened with great care, his ears swivelled, and he proceeded.

He took the three steps to the next level, and the lighting switched on. Softly lit in the same manner as the cavern's ceiling, the fane's dome displayed the night sky spangled with brilliant constellations as seen from the Surface world. He recognized the Fédora Galaxy at the very top of the cupola, here made a fixed pole the other constellations orbited in slow motion. A kind of compass rose had been inlaid in the stone floor directly below – and in the middle of that the same sigil seen in gold leaf above the portico, this time inlaid in honey-coloured stone.

He passed between two highly polished cylindrical marble pillars that extended to a rectilinear limestone lintel just before the circular inner temple. The place dreamed – still and silent, not like Doctor Sola's anechoic chamber, but with presence as if the air itself vibrated at such a rate it activated the solar plexus. He examined other details: unlike the other temples, no altar here, no other images, only four identical inner entrances. Pleased to remember to retain his wits should they be challenged by an official, he looked for some point of reference so that escape through the front door might be easier – however, nothing unique suggested itself for that among the four entryways.

From deep inside the building – the faint click of a latch and its echo. Soon through the entrance opposite appeared a being – tall, of indeterminate age, in a long robe of velvet black embroidered with golden stars linked by thin lines – surely the Fédora if laid out flat. A cowl covered its head. Its face showed the beautiful dark patterns of a leopard. Its eyes – the most pale green, rimmed in black, emanated intense concentration – something more than predatory attention made Rowan wary, as it resembled a big wildcat native to Eorthe's wildernesses. It pulled the cowl back – its fur, very short and, apart from the black spots, the common straw-blonde of many felids – only it evenly and densely covered its whole head – no bare skin and no mane. Long thin white whiskers shot from the sides of its muzzle, and short white tufts sprouted from its ears – its nose, dark and triangular, much like a cat's, unlike any felid's. It opened its mouth to speak – sharp cuspids, including four long sharp fangs between its thin black lips. Altogether striking. "Welcome," the leopard-man said, his voice a rumbling growl. "How may I help you?" His speech – elegantly accented, like Ellaern's.

In the hope that fortune favours the fearless, Rowan replied, "I seek knowledge. I'm a pilgrim at the moment. Perhaps one day I'll find the true path." He imagined that the priest, or whoever he was, could roar him out of the place with that deep voice.

But the leopard-man looked Rowan over with care before he responded. "Ask, felid brother, and you shall receive."

"My name is Rowan Berry..."

The being raised his paw. "Àrd-Sagartus am I," he said, and pressed the paw to his chest, "high priest of this fane. Please, follow." In the twinkling of one of the stars that lit the temple dome, the priest vanished into the shadows out of which he had emerged.

◆

Behind closed doors of bronze, in a walnut-panelled chamber, also softly lit by a hidden source, Àrd-Sagartus sat on his cushioned divan like a sphinx rested on its side. A long spotted tail snaked out from beneath his robe. With a nod of his leopard head, he gestured that Rowan should take an armchair.

The high priest closed his eyes; a more feminine voice, like his own but an octave higher, through his fanged mouth said: "Well, well... you've found me."

Chills flashed through Rowan's body from his crown through his soles.

The female voice continued: "It's time. This is the truth... try to understand. Our parents were so... they would *not* listen... I had no choice... but step by step I'm making my way to freedom. The Talon tried to cheat me. Again and again he demands tribute to bind me to him. I have cheated *him*. My spy is in his house, one of his own. He believes me to be his slave, little brother. No longer."

Àrd-Sagartus' eyes opened wide and stared into nothing. He opened his mouth again, but failed to speak. His tongue lolled. He shook his head, bent down and scratched with fury at his ears. He leapt to the floor. On all fours, he arched his back, and his voice exploded in a blood-red jungle roar that must have been heard blocks away.

Rowan's mane stood on end. He sat paralyzed. A high-pitched shrill ringing pierced his ears. Only his mind remained in motion, and reeled. *So this is it!* His voice no longer his own, he struggled to speak: "What are you saying? You're my... sister? That you... you murdered your own parents?"

Àrd-Sagartus leapt off all fours and up on two legs towards Rowan – but only to grasp him by the shoulders. His pale green eyes trembled – *"She is a demon! But she cannot control us both. Help me!"* He fled the chamber down a long hallway. At its apparent end, he put his paw into a depression in the wall, which slowly withdrew into the ceiling. By the time it reached halfway, the priest passed beneath. In what seemed a silken bedchamber, they confronted a smaller female leopard-being pressed against the wall, likewise in a black spangled robe.

"*Stop!*" she shrieked. "*I am in command!*" Her form wavered, and at intervals broke into geometrical patterns of lower resolution. Her voice distorted and crackled. She turned to look over her shoulder, and said: "*They're coming…*" After a short burst of static, she vanished.

"She has *not* gone!" The priest growled. "Unless…"

◆

Rowan eventually found the priest, who stood in the middle of the circular inner sanctum beneath the starry temple dome, leopard feet on the New Dawn sigil inlaid in the floor. Forelimbs spreadeagle and his eyes closed, he faced the slow revolution of the constellation in the ceiling, opened his leopard eyes wide and roared – this time the building really did shake.

"*They are here!*" their voices shouted from a single throat, the priest's and the leopard-woman's blended.

The two poles connected the floor with the ceiling and vice versa – brilliance burst from the representation of the Fédora Galaxy at the apex. The star system rotated like a wheel – its separate points of light formed contiguous circles that streaked around the upper pole – while the other depicted constellations in the night sky remained relatively motionless by contrast – and the inlaid stone symbol, the lower pole, spun synchronized, lit from within, blazed up the high priest's robe from below and shone white rays out of its embroidered stars –

XVI
The Invitation

À*rd-Sagartus in the* inner sanctum had been absorbed out of sight by the intensity of the glow projected from the cupola, which grew incandescent and shortened Rowan's shadow as it approached. Blinded, he turned away, and beheld, in the spotlight it cast, a giant insectoid, like nothing he had ever seen, even in a mad surrealist's dreamscape, as much as one of the bugs called praying mantis he had watched on that last rare occasion he had been allowed outdoors as an orphan cub. Indoor insects had been familiar enough back then: flies, moths, ants, termites, silverfish, weevils, cockroaches, spiders, bedbugs, fleas and lice. Some of the cubs had tried to keep them as pets, much to their cost when caught out. But this monster was no one's pet at easily nine feet tall, on its hind legs. Its forelegs had folded into its thorax, and its pincers opened and closed, behaviour inappropriate to the situation, like hand-wringing, displacement activity when resolution of options in conflict fail – confusion, in other words. Its body brown, but so dark as to be nearly black, glistened with oil or buffed wax. Trapped between it and its brilliant craft, if craft it were, Rowan's backlit silhouette reflected wherever a highlight glanced off the being's form.

The two largest of its five black eyes bulged huge, almond-shaped and wrap-around. Out of the depths of those dark optics sentience peered, and examined him in detail like an organic scanner. The air acquired an acidic odour. Clicks emitted from its insectoid face – at times in a pattern – then it spoke, in falsetto with a metallic inflection, as if filtered through a grater: "*Fascinating.*" The giant mantis tilted forward, possibly to inspect its object of interest more closely –

Rowan backed away with great care to keep the two biggest eyes in view.

"*Much like to the hominid aboriginal of old, but with pelt more fine, stature greater, but less perhaps robust is it. Wonder we do if survive it can encounter an aurochs with, a test of fortitude, skill, stamina, strength. Perhaps a boar, wild… or a saurian, a raptor. Alert is it, but fears not. Suppression? Will? Daring of the fool? Attributes of Panthera leo has it, think we possible.*" It stretched forth one of its upper limbs, and opened a pincer –

"*Back off!*" Rowan roared. "*Who are you?! What do you want?!*" He tried to peer into the huge black eyes, but only his reflection doubled peered back. A growl gathered force deep in his diaphragm.

The mantid's reach came to a dead stop, and it withdrew the pincer to its mandible. "*Small cuspids such, like much to all therianthropes similar. Interesting.*

135

Intelligent it somewhat is, mental potential capacious… experiment make we must." It bent even closer, which made Rowan's defiant reflections in its eyes enlarge. *"Defender, the male is. Female hostile is, impulsive, aggressive, psyche isolated, unindividuated, lonely ideation dominant, unbalanced, impaired reproductive organ, fear suppressed, inhibited, regretful, compensatory. So see we shall if mate they do."* The mantid vanished as if by the wave of an invisible magic wand.

And a shaft of white glitter flashed forth, gripped Rowan and drew him up into the sphere of light.

◆

Samarit in her skin-tight black uniform, and her beautiful grin – and the twinkle, the incredible twinkle – he the dreamer, she the dream? The vision disintegrated into jagged horizontal lines, like a translucent overlay behind which stood – that felid woman, the minister of education, her hands balled into fists – and undignified for a public servant: ruffled mane, designer business attire tattered and torn to shreds, glasses missing. She hissed and spat like a wild thing, and glared at him like a cornered wolverine.

Rowan, torn between hate and he knew not what, struggled to speak a whole sentence, but managed to croak: *"You… Why* did you send us into the jaws of certain death, to Mudredd?"

Ellearn jammed her fists into the curves of her waist, and stiffened as if to reinforce her glare, but blinked.

Rowan growled a warning: "You're not going anywhere until you answer."

She sighed, rubbed the back of her neck, and dropped her chin. "I was the dumbest smart girl ever," she muttered. "That girl was a sociopath. She wanted what she wanted when she wanted it." Madam Ellaern's Lyran accent had vanished. She crossed her arms, raised her chin and continued at normal volume: "I disown that bitch. Me, I just wanted to survive. I needed information, for an escape plan that did not involve attracting the attention of the authorities, so I found a way to get around late at night. Sleep was impossible anyhow, because the axe could fall any minute. See, I'd already found out about our mama and papa not so secretly going around stirring up revolution. Sedition. We were slated for the chopping block. Even a stupid little bud of a girl like me could see that. I tried to tell them about what had already happened to me, but it was embarrassing as hell. Not one word dared pass my rosebud lips, because my inner good girl I'd damaged refused to admit it to herself in the first place. That their sweet baby firstborn had turned out to be an ordinary underage slut would have been bad enough. I looked into their nice faces and knew they would not believe me. Or if they did, it would break their hearts. So they just patted me on my tongue-tied head because they only had time for their bloody stupid resistance to the tracker colonies that sprang up after the Reps made all the species of their class the untouchable law, destroyed our cosy way of life and replaced it with slavery in the local mines they tore out of the pristine hills that surrounded us. That was the end of the beautiful hamlet of Berry, for generations a happy place for naiveté to live and awareness of evil to die. I had no choice but to hang out with the young reptoids, for one thing to show my friends how cool I was to confront the enemy. I thought of myself as a spy so I could form the big escape plan. And it smothered the fear a little, which I mistook for confidence. And the lizard boys weren't all bad, but mixed with a bad crowd. Perfect. I was in, ha bloody ha."

She had not answered his question, but with some anxiety he let her struggle to collect her thoughts and let her own conscience condemn her, if she had one, from the inside out.

"Look," she continued, "I'm not here to reminisce, never mind introspect. If you must know, I sent you to slay the dragon so I could get that maniac off my back for five minutes. Of course I knew it wouldn't get rid of him for good. It was just another deadline extension on a loan by way of a favour. Be grateful it's a good thing they don't much like the taste of us felids. They think we're too gamey." She glanced at him at last, but scowled.

Ellearn continued: "And your girlfriend has something, something she doesn't even know she has. But they know it. Kirzaka knows it for sure. Her unique vibrations are a delicacy. They can smell it. It's a drug, like fortified catnip is to a Lyran. It makes them crazy they want it so badly, without understanding what it is any more than she does. They feel they want to eat her brain, see, consume it to gain her power full-time." She glared afresh and scowled.

"Keep talking, madam."

"I'll make up own mind about that, little brother. But don't worry, Kirzaka the death-defying Talon won't give the brain-eaters the satisfaction. He has the discipline to hold her over their open gobs to tease their taste buds. Maybe he doesn't think her brain is even worth much, but his minions believe it. To them she's a thousand canids. Let them snap at each other for a spot at the head of the snack bar queue in the meantime. Divide and conquer is his management style. But there's one thing he does value in her. Virtue. That's what he wants, the joy of joys, the greatest of Rep pleasures, to co-opt and ruin a good thing. She's most likely in storage, marinating until she's ripe."

Rowan claimed his turn to glare. "Our parents were murdered. And to save your ass you sacrificed your innocent little brother. Did you ever stop to even imagine what that was like for me? Did you?"

Silence.

"*Answer me, dammit!*"

"I was a victim too."

Rowan's power of speech failed.

"Do you remember a raven?" she murmured. "When you were a young boy. In the tower window? That was me. I came to check on you."

He scowled at her.

"I came to check up on you, to see how you were doing. I was the raven. Your sweet little face looked right at me. Later I made sure they gave you free time outdoors. You were so pale. More than that was beyond my talent. But I hoped you might taste a little freedom and figure out how to escape somehow."

Rowan looked at her now too – and snarled. "Oh no," he said, "don't try to wriggle out of this. Whatever you were then, you still are. You sentenced the squire to death and delivered the best canid in the land to the enemy as a plaything and a snack. And for what? *To save your worthless…*"

"And yours!"

"How can say that with a straight face! I'd have been better off dead as a kid… and after Mudredd. I won't call you by your name, ex-minister. I don't remember what your real name is. I don't care. You're despicable, evil, a mercenary for a demon, orders of magnitude worse than an underage…"

Ellaern shrieked: "*Don't you DARE call me that! I'm the only one who can say that word and know what she's talking about!*" She wrung her hands. Her breast heaved. "They could have killed us too just as well as made us orphans. You have no idea what I had to do to…" Her words trailed off, and she actually blushed.

He nevertheless glowered, and muttered, "Lucky us."

She gritted her teeth. Defiance returned in force, and focused: "I was born without the religion gene, but New Dawn was a handy front, a good one in case I needed a hideout with the potential of an emergency exit. All it took was a bit of identity theft. Madam La-di-da never missed it. She gave up the ghost years ago on some out-of-the-way planet in the Lyra system. Her genetic data needed a little tweak, that's all, so I wouldn't have to go under the knife for a nose job in some illegal clinic. Full-time fangs might have been a bit tricky, but I figured out how to fake it when I really need to. It's amazing how people see only what they want to see. It was enough to get me access to the little portal in the high temple. I didn't figure out how to travel the stars through it, but I made contact with the Primordial Architects. Àrd-Sagartus made eyes at me non-stop in an exponential manner, but didn't have the balls to break the rules and experiment with it after hours. He's second-generation League-born, a high priest but a bit flaccid in the faith, you might say, so nor did he believe they'd be insectoids. But he's from the Lyra system. Lyrans are loud and can roar, but they're an airy-fairy lot when push comes to shove, the definition of pussycats. Not that I dislike pussycats, quite the contrary. Anyhow, I invited the mantids here. *Me.* Your big sister is more than meets the eye, that's for sure, though you have to admit what strikes the eyeballs is pretty sweet too."

"Sweet?! You're a *criminal narcissist, a psychopath! But you're no kin of mine!* So you learned how to shape-shift, to hypnotize your prey so they perceive what you want them to, whatever. You impersonated Commander Diss too, didn't you? You hypnotized key people at the base to get us through the portal. *For what?* And you convinced Sam that the Longbows were in danger, possibly wiped out."

"Got it one, little brother. You're not so dumb after all, are you? But then we *are* related. Not like those idiot military police buffoons. Do you know, they've been looking for me under every rock and in every crack and cranny for the past five days? It's a national security emergency and it's like they're blind." Her shoulders slumped, and she sighed, and added, "But I don't know why I did that to Samarit… I liked her. In fact I had the idea to throw the two of you together to see if there were sparks. She was such a lonely girl… fear that her clan had been wiped out would have encouraged it." But Ellaern stiffened and clenched her fists. "*You should thank me!*"

"*For what! You must have known she was already taken by that aristocrat!*"

"So I'm perverse, an opportunist. It made me feel good for a while. Maybe I thought it was a good idea to pump up her fear too so Kirzaka would be happy…" Ellaern scowled afresh. "Well… he's *never* happy." She looked away. Before he could respond, she glared with renewed fire and added: "Listen, if it weren't for me, the mantids wouldn't be here to clean up their mess. Have no doubt that Kirzaka now has the means to invade Vugh Deep and all the other caverns on Eorthe. This I know. And I let the mantids know what murderous freaks they created. I have ears and eyes in his house. I have proof. He and his slithery sawtoothed horde will dominate the world at last. Then they'll be happy to cleanse it of its inferiors to please their god Maçina. We don't have a chance. What's really funny is that the god of gods will delete the reptoids too. They're as biological as we are. That's the thing right there. It takes countless generations of breeding, the cooperation of Mother Nature over millennia and millions of years to upgrade. But biotechnology, now, that's more convenient, essentially immortal. Other than paranoia, the other thing the Reps have successfully sneaked into the entire system through double agents like me is nanotechnology. Nanoids are just the start. Even that will have to go eventually. Pure artifice, that's what Maçina is, a perfect self-aware principle, built right into the infrastructure of the universe from the start."

Rowan shook his head, and sighed. "You've lost your mind, Madam Ellaern."

"I guess I did at first, but you better believe I came to my senses."

"Which makes no sense…"

"It's not all bad news, little brother. The mantids can stop the madness. Only they can do it. With *my* help. My fellow academics call me a religious nut behind my back without me ever speaking a word about my assumed faith, so I don't expect any recognition for a service of such magnitude, let alone thanks, but who gives a damn. I'll be out of here. I'm off to Lyra where I can fit in. I'll have to put up with a lot of moronic religious missionary fervour with respect to feline dispersion across the galaxies, but I can work with that. The mantids will drop me off on the way back to the Fédora… or whatever region in hell they spawned from."

"You're incredible…" Rowan shook his head. "Didn't you, like me, get beamed into this soft-focus cocoon without your consent? You must have put up a fight by the looks of it. You know they're watching us, right? They probably think this is just a lively mating ritual. If we keep it up, expect the lights to dim, romantic music to play and pheromones to infuse the air."

"That's revolting…"

"So," he said, harsh as lye, "you *do* have a tiny speck of decency left, do you?"

Ellaern turned her back, and showed him her profile. "Blue," she said.

"What's blue? What do you mean?"

"It's my name. My real name is Blue."

◆

The giant mantid pressed the tip of one dark pincer to its dark mandible as it studied the hologram sliced into sections like the pages of a book it swiped with its other pincer. "*Cortisol, up. Adrenaline, up. Why present not oxytocin in nucleus accumbens is and paraventricular hypothalamic nucleus? Testosterone and estrogen,* low. *Mesolimbic dopamine pathway suppressed? Dopamine, up. Not good. Mate must they do. Allostatic load increased much. Analysis of deoxyribonucleic acid chains double helix do we must... siblings these be? What the...? Factor of risk... genetic defects. Social conditioning, intact. Disappointing... good, but not good."*

•

Rowan and Blue found themselves stood back to back in the dark. A prismatic diamond tetrahedron rotated high among the stars near the top of the cavern's dome in night mode. The object looked distinguishable from the crystalline stars only by its slightly larger dimensions. And he knew it watched the two of them.

Blue, a faint figure under the dim starlight, apparently did not. "Thank the gods we're out of that claustrophobic love nest," she said, "or I'd have puked and risked your good opinion of me... but how the *hell* am I supposed to get them to take me away now? The one thing I bought into at New Dawn was the doctrine of reparation and rescue. It's an utter load of utter crap."

Again a precise beam of light widened into a feathered circle of luminescence on the ground. Within its sparkling motes appeared a most beautiful felid. For the first thirty seconds unclothed, her stripes like a tiger's stood out on her head, except her face, but on her shoulders and upper chest, between her breasts, on her upper forelimbs and thighs, likely her upper back and hindquarters as well. Fine downy fur faintly covered the rest. White whiskers sprouted from her face like optical fibre, and a short white tuft appeared on her chin, but vanished when a purple silky gown wrapped her hourglass figure tight to the skin. A magnificent mane of platinum-tipped silver adorned her head at the same instant. She gazed at them each in turn like a tolerant mother bemused by her naughty children, a soft smile in her large black-rimmed sapphire eyes, which transitioned to emerald, and her lashes curled. She spoke in kind resonant tones of maternal love: "Better? Not to worry, little ones. No harm shall befall you."

The sparkly spotlight widened to include all three of them. She took one elegant step forward, and fixed her gaze on Blue. "Thank you for the invitation." She tilted her glowing head a little and roved her gaze from Blue's tousled head to her scuffed toes and back, as if in appraisal of a work of art. "An invitation is necessary to potential intervention. Law decrees that we must not interfere once certain parameters have been fixed, unless there is a misevolutionary emergence that threatens to cross boundaries of adjacent regions of the cosmos."

"You're... welcome," murmured Blue. "What are you... a projection, a hologram? Because giant mantids are too intimidating?"

141

The tigress-felid pressed the tip of a finger to the softly full sensuous lips that gave her face such a blossom-like beauty, along with her other perfect increasingly flowery features lit from within. She smiled in her indulgent maternal way, and replied, "We have no particular form, but are fond of kittens and flowers, thus we project a tangible body for your interactive pleasure. We, as you, are projections within a master hologram called the cosmos."

Mouth agape, Blue croaked: "Did you create us?"

"We did not." She observed Blue with care. "Perhaps I shall tell a story. Long long ago in a place not far away, in our infancy we were given a toy planet, a learning laboratory, but great fun. Then the Primordial Mother, one might say, called us inwards to rest. Too much fun is not good for growing ones. They must learn to let go so that fun can return renewed."

She turned her attention to Rowan. "Noble one, fearless you are. We admire and take pride in this. Fear creates fallacy. Like bamboo in the forest where the tiger hunts, it is strong, but it is hollow. It is *false evidence appearing real*. Your green eyes, lovely are they, and see clearly." The lady's own emerald orbs glowed from within. "And will do ever more so as you grow."

Blue snapped out of her revery. *"Hey! Look at me! Take me with you! Now! I want to go to Lyra!..."*

The tigress being's flowery benign smile vanished. "This demand will not be met. Little one, you have lined your den with thorns. You know what is meant. You cannot run from yourself."

"Dammit," cried Blue, "I don't want to run from *myself*! I want to run from this crazy planet... *take me with you!*" Tears poured over the dark rims of her golden eyes. "They tried to kill me from the beginning. I've got this far, *take me now!*" She fell to her knees, and wept into her palms, awash in melodrama.

The lady floated towards Blue, crouched, and stroked her tawny mane. "This one is damaged." She looked up at Rowan. "Try not to despise her, only her wicked ways." She turned back to Blue, and stroked her tawny tousled mane. "She is strong, but she is hollow."

⋆

Rowan stood alone with the tigress-flower lady, and looked down through a facet of her craft, the floor of the prism of diamond, the stellated polyhedron he had seen earlier high above in the clear night sky. The urban sprawl of Perkona Ola looked like it splashed the cavern floor with phosphorescence from this dark height. *That's odd, no vertigo.* Neither had he curiosity, only absorption.

142

"We hear you, noble one. It is satisfaction, yes? The field of force we ride within makes it so. It is a living entity, you see, complete order in form, symbiotic with us. You share in it by virtue of my presence. Wonderful, is it not?"

Rowan had to agree, that is, when he figured out how to stop purring so an answer might form. "Yes, it's... there are no words." He purred again, inhaled deeply, stroked his chin tuft, and in a moment added, "I never want to leave... but I don't belong here."

The lady morphed into a living gem, a shining flowery jewel, and gazed up at him. "Your destiny in time is elsewhere," she said, "but no less perfectly satisfactory if you choose wisely. I share with you what I have gleaned from my own explorations and suffering. It is this: what you seek is not of this world, nor another. It is within your own heart here and now, mirrored by this geometry. By that I mean your essence, that without which you would not be you. It is never not here, your true home, where you have always longed to be. It is independent of any outer circumstance in space-time, liked or disliked. It is freedom itself.

"The disliked, your enemies, are manifestations of ignorance, as are all entities, only more so, more purely benighted, one might say, an oxymoron. This is their role. They worship a god, a coherent projection of an intelligent but inverted abstraction, a mental image to which they unknowingly assign power. This power allows them to penetrate beyond this world, yet blind. Not knowing they are blind, they see in the mirror of a higher dimension, a twin universe one might say, what they are, and believe it is the ultimate truth. It is only their interpretation, nothing more. If they understood the infinity of the mirror in which this mere speck of their true potential reflects, they would be humbled and ask for wisdom so as to grow into it with integrity. But arrogance allows ignorance to slumber undisturbed, even while they sleepwalk naive.

"You too were naive. You saw what you wanted to see in the mirror, but you were misled by the misled. The blind led the blind into the pit. Now they have taken your mate. This is their nature, but not yours, as you are humble, thus can grow."

"She's a canid," Rowan replied, "I'm a felid. Her years are short, mine are long. She's promised, she belongs to her clan, not to me. I belong to no one."

"You are of her soul family. Love is your bond."

That pang again. Rowan's eyelids drooped and threatened to close in sleep. His skin itched due to the salt from Sola's tank, an irritant he had successfully ignored until this moment. It had been a long search, with no end in sight. The perpetrator had been found, but that was all. What good had it done? Justice eluded him.

"Your kin would have us cancel your challenges," the lady said, her tigress aspect in decline, and illumined from within, the floral aspect in ascent. Still patient as a doting mother, she explained: "This we must not do. Yes, we had a hand in creating them. Ever so long ago that it is near to immeasurable, the forces were set in motion. But we avoid regret as toxic. We played our game for countless aeons, many more than this world has existed. We played our part. Now you must play yours. Take heart that it is a drama, a very serious one, like any great work of art, yet it is play at the same time, a paradox you must resolve. You must learn to perform well, like the noble artist you are."

He shook his head. "I'm only a runaway from an orphanage, as naive as you said. She rescued me and gave me everything… but I failed her."

The flower-lady pivoted to stand before him. Her eyes glowed crystal-green and penetrated his mind, with Samarit's face as a mask, with alabaster skin, a crown of petals made of ruby, leaf-shaped pointed Vulcan ears and perfect rose-quartz lips like budding segments of a corolla about to unfurl, so alive.

His breath stopped.

She took his fingers in her translucent radiant hands. "Your kin sent your mate to elevate you from a low place, from the Surface world to the underworld we see beneath our feet. An irony, yes? You must acknowledge this. It is because it is an image within you, a potential to unfold, called 'entelechy,' like the dream of the mature oak within the acorn, which must be buried in deep darkness in order to flourish. Or, to say it another way, you are now the lowly crawling immature form, but the wingèd imago is your natural destiny.

"Your kin believes she is evil, corrupt, so she acts consistently with her belief. To cope, she projects the pain of that onto the world, a tragic delusion that hopes to escape the truth. Guilt, this is the legacy of her captors. They tortured her, forged their purpose in her, but could not break her spirit. She is indomitable, like you, but her only inner support in her search for freedom from shame is arrogance and pride, and lonely desire for revenge. Yet she through deceit and, yes, honest labour, had you made a noble, had given you a title, had given you a servant, had given you wealth greatly in excess of that of the state, had given you learning. She is strong but she is hollow. Yet something long hidden knows that you, if sufficient wisdom is gained, may overcome her enemy, and she will be redeemed."

XVII
Commando

BEFORE HE ENTERED, Rowan stopped to examine the sigil above the temple portico, the vertical stroke with its triangle, the pennant. This time he knew its meaning: "gateway," and below it the word *càradh*: "reparation." As before, the pith-flecked doors swung open unaided. He passed between the marble pillars, stood and peered at the currently inactive columnar portal zone in the rotunda, the inner sanctum, and shouted: "*Àrd-Sagartus!*" and it echoed in the hollow –

"She is hidden." The high priest's throaty growl came from behind. "They will never find her."

Rowan turned about, and said, "But *I've* found her. Please, I need to see her. Vugh Deep needs her. The world needs her. Please, it's urgent."

Àrd-Sagartus' face remained stony. He crossed his heavy spotted forelimbs.

"Reparation," Rowan continued. "If that's what you want, what New Dawn wants, there's only one way. And she's the key."

"*Càradh*," Àrd-Sagartus scoffed. "We once believed. No longer." The pale green eyes in the leopard face betrayed nothing. "The way is closed." Only his monotone let slip despair.

"I understand," said Rowan. "You feel cheated, deceived. But it's only a setback, not the end." He took a step closer and urged, "We can make it happen…"

The priest dropped his forelimbs to his side. His gaze released and focused beyond, at something behind Rowan –

"What do *you* want?" the leopard woman asked.

Rowan turned about.

She too scoffed: "Can't you see it's a bad time for a social call? We're busy commiserating. Self-pity is all that's left."

"I'm here to enlist your assistance," Rowan said. "According to you, only the Primordial Architects can save us, with your help. They can't or won't do that. Only *we* can, with *your* help."

She sniggered. "Little brother, your imagination is racing away with you on a bullet train. Have you already forgotten what the woman said, if she even is a woman? Get lost, basically. We're done for. I have the proof."

"Exactly," Rowan replied. "The proof is what we need to convince the League to mount a pre-emptive strike. You said yourself the Reps don't understand the situation they're in. They've sold themselves out. They're doomed, not that they'll buy that idea until they're forced to. It's actually in their interest to cooperate with us…"

"Little brother!" She scoffed anew and shook her head. "Are those flowers I see stuck in your ears? Listen to your elder: we're goners… *dead meat*… soon to be brains on carbon-fibre platters, at least the tastier among us. More likely our felid skulls will be made into fancy blood-wine cups. I've seen that kind of tableware first-hand. They're building a scanner that can penetrate *four hundred miles* into the ground and trigger quakes. Talk about shock and awe… at the same time it can disable our shields. The prototype will be online any day now. In fact any minute you could find yourself sprawled on the floor looking up at a smirking Rep standing where you are right now. The only upside is that at last they need me no longer. *I'm free…* ha bloody ha."

Rowan sighed. "You're right. They're too stupid to cooperate. But you're wrong too. I want you to teach me how to shape-shift."

"What?" She mocked bafflement with a palm pressed to the side of her face, and her black-lipped fanged leopard mouth agape and pale green eyes wide. "You want to impersonate an officer to get your crazy idea off the ground? Naughty boy… you do know that's highly illegal, don't you? On second thought, maybe I should do it. I'm on the most-wanted list anyhow. What can they do? Execute me for the same crime twice?" She glared intently at Rowan and sneered: "*It would give me something to do other than bite my nails waiting for my head to get chewed off.*"

"Nice try, Blue. While you're teaching me how to shape-shift, I want you to contact the Khémian embassy. If that's impossible now that you're a fugitive, I know you can find another way to ask Captain Masudah of Zau to come here as soon as possible to teach me the secret of invisibility."

"You said *what?*" She peered from beneath raised lids and leaned away.

"I said you're in a position to turn this bad situation around. We don't have to stretch our necks out on the chopping block and wait for the axe to fall. We can be proactive, just as you've been your whole life. You called yourself an opportunist. I hate to admit it, but it's your gift. Don't waste it now. You can still come out on top."

"Hey, you called me Blue…" She paced back and forth, stopped and ran her fingers across the sides of her smooth leopard head as if she still had a felid mane. At last she looked at him and added, "…the most evil bitch in the whole world. But the cat, *ha bloody ha*, is out of the bag. Everyone will know. My neck will be in a noose… or my head stuck on a sharp pole in the dirt for the masses to spit at…" She grimaced, winced and looked away. "But… speaking of which… I've got dirt on everybody that matters. Maybe you're right, I can twist that to

146

my advantage. I might maybe, just maybe save my pretty ass. Come with me, little brother."

◆

"Your concentration is very good," Blue said. "Now for the next step, very important if you want to fake a heavyweight convincingly…"

"No, wait. I'm not going to impersonate anyone, but I am going to project an image into any mind or group mind. It will ignore me as one of them. Or at least think I'm a rock or a piece of furniture. And I want the ability to take the driver's seat, so to speak, in the mind of one if need be."

"I see." Blue's brows raised. "Well, that's even easier, although less stable than shape-shifting per se. Reps are good at hypnosis, as you know, but they're also easily hypnotized if you know how to do it. And I know how. I've studied Kirzaka, and he's a master magician, the blackest. In fact I used it often to defend my dwindling virtue… anyhow, I was never caught at it. But let's focus on the task at hand." She hesitated for a moment. "You know, you're a brave one, little brother, if I can guess at what you've got up your sleeve." She smiled at him for the first time since he had known her only as Chancellor Madam Ellaern, minister. "But then we *are* related." She even winked.

Her friendly vibration resonated within Rowan's breast. This had never happened before. A great pretender she may have been in her role as mover and shaker in the government of Vugh Deep, yet he never had thought of her as a warm individual. This time he relaxed and grinned back in response.

"Put this on." She handed him her pendant; engraved in its black obsidian: a raven in flight. "Even the most brain-ridden scientists think it has too weak a field or is only a placebo at best, but they don't know everything. You don't seem to have a problem with pessimism, except maybe a little about your big sister, but it will help to deflect negative energy directed at you from the filthy bastards as well. I believe it saved my pretty *glutei maximi* at least once or twice. You need all the help you can get where you're going."

"Thanks, Blue…" Rowan looked up from the gift. "I may not get another chance to say this, and I must be direct. You're right. I am still a little wary of you, if only because you were forced to fake your way through life since you were very young, not something you're likely to grow out of now. To be honest, more than a little wary. But I've been thinking. The mantid-tigress-flower-architect-whatever made a big impression on me, more than I understood at the time. Faking it is just fine by me. Selfishness is totally okay. Possibly you think I judge you harshly, which I admit I did. It was obvious. And you deserved it. But those are footprints in a bygone winter's snow. The past can't be changed as far as I know. Maybe the flower lady would disagree with that too."

Blue's brow wrinkled. "What do you mean faking it is good, selfishness is good, little brother? That doesn't fit with any code of ethics I know of. And before you make some smart-ass comeback, I do know the code, if only the better to violate it. I'm the minister of…"

"Ex-minister. Past tense. But I didn't say it was good, only fine with me. And you can call me Rowan, not 'little brother.' It's my name. We're all grown up now. We're equals. You'll never be minister of anything again, so I call you by the name our parents did. It's just a label. Status is bogus anyhow. We're all just here, in the now, whatever our so-called rank. The only question to ask ever is, so what? What does it mean? Kill or be killed? I don't think so."

Blue peered at him as if he really did have flowers growing out of his ears. "You're a better person than me, little… Rowan. Thank you for your generosity. Really. I respect that. But I know better than anyone I'm a self-absorbed cunt. Of that there is no doubt, nor does anyone doubt it once they get to know me. Kill or be killed is my motto. The only reason I'm helping you is to save my pretty ass."

"That's perfectly fine, Blue. Think about it. Just expand that incredible selfishness to include me, Àrd-Sagartus cat-napping on his divan in another chamber and the passers-by in the street. I doubt any mice hang around in a place like this for long, but by default include the dust mites chewing on the dander on his bed, include any other creature overlooked, the tardigrades swimming in the boiling water below us and their next of kin riding on the Rep space station high above the stratosphere. And fake it till the mountains wear down and the real sun shines through cracks in the dome. It's only what everyone does day in and day out anyhow. I heard it from your own lips early on when I audited a lecture you as chancellor gave a graduating class. And you were right. That's the secret. You have the power and you know it better than anyone. Your focus has been too narrow, that's all. Until now, that is."

"Interesting. So… I can remain a cunt?"

"Once you understand that you're bigger than any nasty label you're hiding behind, that sort of negativity will drop away naturally. What you really want more than anything… more than just to save your pretty backside… is to live large, to be somebody, a real person. Admit it."

"*Ha bloody ha! Listen to you, loser…*" Again, she stopped, stared and sighed. "Well… I guess for the moment I'm a flop. I'll think about it… this is a new idea to me."

"Try it is all I ask. Try faking an honourable version of yourself. Or at least an upgraded one. You're a great actor. Just rewrite the script to include more and more of life itself into your sense of identity. And you're on your way as we speak, starting with helping me. I'm not saying the past won't creep up to bite you on your fabulous fundament, but you can jam a stick between its teeth. I'm not the only one who'll be grateful."

She gave him a quick glance, and said, "You should be in sales, not saving the world. Right then, let's get on with it. Reptilian Hypnosis 101." A wry smile formed on her lips. "But do I really have to include Àrd-Sagartus? For a pussycat he's a bit arrogant and demanding."

✦

Rowan grinned and asked, "How did you get here so fast, Masudah? I take it you didn't meet any Snake People en route this time."

"We did not." The warrior-priest of Zau bowed with a flourish and smiled broadly, which made his trim moustache a blackbird in flight that contrasted with his very white teeth. "I am told by one who must remain unnamed that I am required once more. As well, it is a mission with two, how you say... two prongs perhaps, as I am sent again on a diplomatic mission, our case to update. My visit to your fair city before was most enlightening, Sir Rowan. We had thought to bless our ancient wisdom on the materialistic society, yet in fact by the time we returned to Khémia we had understood that time is of essence, even though it is only, how we say..."

"A construct?"

"Just so, my friend. What I try to say," Masudah continued, "is that before it is too late we too must adapt to conditions as they be, not as tradition dictates. Thus we have borrowed a page from your book, so to say. An expedience, a shortcut, is necessary for the time being. We have used a scanner for the first time to open the gates. This is more quick. But, and it is most fascinating, by applying our so-called magical techniques we have increased its, how you say... efficacy, as it makes the gate more stable. This can be of benefit to you as well, you shall see, yet we are concerned that it violates the cosmic law, ultimately, as it uses force. But no choice there may be."

"However you did it," said Rowan, "I'm very glad to see you. You're right, we have little so-called time, so I'll get right to it if you don't mind. I need you to teach me the secret of invisibility."

"I see… *not*." Masudah winked. "How you say… a jest, not so?" He scratched his head. "I must practise this skill, I think. Ah well, it is said the danger it is grave and howls at our door. The proof has been secretly passed on to the government. I agree, victory must be seized without delay. For this they prepare."

"Yes," added Rowan, "I was the one who anonymously delivered the proof. They must not yet know anything of the one who must remain unnamed, nor of the original source of the documentation. All will be clear later, assuming our success. But I'm serious. Really. If you consent to teach me the secret first, I'll return to the armed forces base to apply for elite training as a commando. That's all anyone need know for now."

"Sir Rowan, my presence here is neutral. I am a diplomat of Khémia under direction of the ambassador. Consider well. You should not be telling me these things. I may be a spy, you do not know. Yet I see your soul is open, in danger of misstep, so if this teaching will help you, I will help you. But… and this is the famous 'big but'… to achieve such mastery over one's own mind, not to say the minds of others, takes even a gifted one months, often years. It is tradition that it is greatly aided by a ring or a helmet of special metals… ah, a *talisman*. I could have brought one! But perhaps there are such things here as well. Even then a talented candidate must be qualified. He or she must be dispassionate, alert, forgiving, forbearing, tolerant, wise and unafraid. This is not for a young person, only one who has absorbed life's lessons and is free to concentrate for a length of time to not only create the effect, but to sustain it under difficult conditions. Other than that, one need not be an intellectual giant, only pure of heart."

"I understand, Masudah, that's a tall order, but completely reasonable. I have no idea whether I can qualify, but I must try. I'll search for a ring as well or have one made. At times like this I wish my squire were still with us to do that discreetly. Krumb was good at that sort of thing."

"We shall begin as soon as you wish, Sir Rowan. The loss of your servant must be difficult, but please, my adjutant will be happy to search for a ring. Furthermore, she knows what to look for, not something one can find in the shop of an ordinary smith! But be forewarned… I say again, unless one is pure of heart, this power may result in permanent invisibility. You may live a long life in this world, but no one will see you. They may feel your touch, see objects move as if on their own, when it is you who moves them. Your voice they may hear… at times… or perhaps never. It depends on their sensitivity and the conditions, such as the weather, fields of electromagnetics and so on. This is bad enough, but you may gradually lose your, how you say… vitality. You could feel as if a living corpse, without soul. And you may go mad in addition to that dire fate."

"Is that all? If I must pay the price, Masudah, so be it. I've tested my hypnotic commands on a few unwitting subjects here. At the insistence of my teacher who must remain unnamed, I stole a large amount of cash from a bank, not that I need the money, nor does she. Of course I replaced it a few days later. No one noticed in the meantime, but then they weren't the Apep. I'd feel better if I had a backup technique. Maybe they could be combined as you've done with the scanner."

"It is true, Sir Rowan. This can be done, by an adept."

"One more request, if I may. It's said that Khémian magic includes the oracle. I understand that to mean a gifted adept may not only divine hidden current conditions, but he or she can read alternative histories and probable futures. I intend to conform to whichever future is most beneficial to the common good as it unfolds, if you understand me. I am really most interested in the related ability to see remote locations in real time, which I've had some basic training in, with minor success."

Masudah nodded recognition. "'Star-travel' is the translation from Khémian. Remote-viewing is, how you say… an element, a facet. Now, that is rather more easily achieved. If we had much time, I would teach you accuracy. You may already have naturally had some experience, perhaps in dreams?"

"Yes, dreams do come… but only rarely with great clarity. I don't know if they can be trusted. They may be mere wishes or meaningless illusions. Or they may be just mental vomit, release of hidden anxiety, all the bad stuff."

"Ah yes, dreamwork is a long study, and requires a subtle intellect. In that case I suggest that I, Masudah, accomplish the task. I shall prepare. If you give me a target, I shall then transfer to paper what the inner eye does reveal."

◆

Commander Diss expressed his usual intense and dubious self, more so now because of preparation to mobilize the armed forces. His habit of shouting even in casual conversation at close range persisted, not that this meeting could be considered at all casual: *So you want to train as an elite commando now, do you? This is the REAL me talking this time, not some hallucination! I commend your bravery, Berry, but in my opinion, another misadventure is more than likely. The best commando in the League is no match for a Rep, let alone the lizard king. I am only signing off on it because…"* As before, his volume dropped considerably when he concluded a statement, nearly to a growling murmur: "Because I must. But bring her back. *If* you can."

⁙

Rowan passed inspection for an unusually expedited course of commando training. Nanoid replacement, however difficult, had been a great aid – and he hoped without penalty – as the urgency of the situation demanded physical fitness. Fortunately, his earlier training gave him a leg-up. Cross-country runs and wrestling the strongest of the other trainees, along with boxing matches, increased it. Exercises conducted with live ammunition and explosives made training as realistic as possible. Speed and endurance marches conducted up and down the nearby mountain ranges of the Surface world over assault courses included a zip-line over a three-mile-long lake at the bottom of a deep basin. All the while he carried arms and full gear. Training continued by day and by night, with river crossings, mountain climbing, weapons training, unarmed combat, map-reading and small boat operations on the syllabus. Living conditions were primitive in the camp topside. Housed under a light narrow tent so small he felt like a Khémian mummy, he also assumed responsibility for cooking his own meals. The Surface world remained a dangerous environment at the best of times, but exploding devices and plasma weapon fire proved the most difficult to cloak due to their extremely rapid onset, an energetic signature somewhat like the technical term "attack" is to an audio tone, more easily detected by the reptilians' Eye in the Sky. Even firestones provoked constant worry, but not an option, as the season had grown cold.

A special forces consultant native to the mountains of the East had been brought in to teach volunteers an unofficial alternative: mind control to thermostatically adjust body temperature. To test this ability, Rowan dived into a hole chopped in the ice of a high-elevation lake at night, swam one hundred yards beneath, and emerged from a second hole in the frozen surface. After that he had been wrapped in a wet blanket and timed as to how fast the rapidly freezing wrapping thawed and dried by his body heat, ready to be stowed again. After some debate about whether necessary, given that his provisional goal was penetration of the same desert stronghold as before, Mudredd Vale, it was decided that Rowan be quickly transported along an underground river to the northern coast to train to swim frigid heavy seas. Samarit might be transferred anywhere in the Rep world at any time, so any environment must be expected, even outer space, thus zero-gravity combat skills were added to the list.

He returned to Perkona Ola, and exhaled in relief upon hearing Masudah's remote-viewing sessions report. Samarit remained alive and still incarcerated at Mudredd Vale. He relied on Masudah to update him twice daily as to her likely location. He had to be prepared to adjust his target in a heartbeat and to monitor the conditions of portals. To that end Masudah also taught him what the warrior-priest had discovered regarding the combination of his traditional magical methods with high technology to open them, not only more quickly, but to sustain their stability afterwards.

"The secret, Sir Rowan, as always, is in the integration of spirit, soul, mind and body. Now that the body-mind-sense complex is balanced and tuned as well as it can be at this time, you must completely surrender to the spirit. You cannot control it, as it transcends time and space, but you can earn its grace by consecration of every thought, word and deed. If you clear your mind and purify your heart, the odds of reaching your goal are good… provided success is in the best interests of the Totality. Our little desires must be in harmony with the will, so to speak, of the Whole, not the other way around. This is the ancient teaching, but timeless, and is as true today as ever."

Rowan nodded consent. "I can now better appreciate what's made your civilization great, Masudah. From the beginning its order has been based on the big picture. I hope to visit your land one day to learn more."

"Indeed, we have seen how it is from the start, long ages ago. And even today constant vigilance is necessary so that the knowledge does not corrupt. I have become more or less a policeman in this regard. Or perhaps a temple guard dog. One day, I fear, Khémia will descend into an era of magical thinking, having lost its true sacred vision. But it is not easy to follow the spirit. Not only is there no followed and follower to follow it… that is, the two are not easily discerned as one and the same, a paradox… but personal nature is fickle. Why? The way of nature is fickle, if we take the personal viewpoint, as it is ever in, how you say… flux. One can never set foot in the same river twice, to quote a great sage. If we adopt the Totality's viewpoint, all is in perfect order, not a subatomic particle out of place. How could it not be thus? This is solid ground. Nevertheless, in the experiential order all is ever in transition. It must be so. If not, an event could stretch on and on like a note of music that lasts too long, and ruin the melody. Illusion. Delusion. Entropy. Chaos. The great god Apep! All is in motion, thus the great skill of an adept is transaction based on virtue based on natural law. But yes, we must make plans for your visit to Khémia, not so? Did not a great sage say to plant a tree on the last day of the world?"

XVIII
Stasis

Rowan stood at the exact spot on the crest that Samarit, Squire Krumb and he had last looked out from over the dusty desert plain, the viper pit as they had called it – his heart swelled at recall of her beautiful profile lit by the desert sunset – the memory had tortured, but now it inspired with equal fervour. Yet the image of Kirzaka's massive smug grimace as it towered over his head still held terror undiminished. However, he had prepared for the worst as well as possible, and renewed faith in the best.

Storm clouds dark on the horizon diffused, then smothered in deep gloom the last of the sun's red-orange fire.

He only wished he'd had time to learn the art of remote-viewing better so he could track Samarit's movements, as well as gather other intelligence without delay. Masudah's guidance would have been welcome in this shadowy place, but his current role as diplomat prohibited greater involvement.

Two commandos experienced with reptilians, Tòrr and Ballista, brothers, accompanied him, but only one would have been sanctioned by the Sannir. Tòrr Hornblower, the elder, heavy-browed, stocky and dark, not a man one should make an enemy of, may have inherited *neanderthalensis* ancestry. Younger brother Ballista Hornblower stood taller, a handsome, fair-haired mesomorph, always cheerful and consistently professional.

At the last minute Commander Diss had decided that Rowan should not attempt the mission alone, although he could not help but remind him, at full volume, that it was against his better judgement to risk valuable assets on a doomed expedition. The thought of a soft spot beneath Diss's hard exterior evoked a smile. It soon faded as Rowan reminded himself that reptilians were all hard spots, from stiff feathered comb to razor-clawed toe.

Intelligence now several days old confirmed Kirzaka's presence, this time to inspect the communications and reconnaissance manufacturing plant. No doubt the expected deep-mantle scanner remained at the top of his agenda. He would want to celebrate its deployment first-hand. Updated intelligence on this could be gathered from afar, just not communicated with impunity to the commando squad.

While Rowan had benefitted from Blue's hypnosis training and Masudah's knowledge of Khémian invisibility magic, his comrades the Hornblowers had not, nor had they specialized in remote-viewing, an unacknowledged program regarded as somewhat suspect by most military personnel, if they had even heard of it. Ballista would wait in this high place, the crest, their best option for observation of the enemy. Tòrr would follow Rowan as far as he deemed secure and of use, on standby to assist. After that Rowan would be on his own. Both would be needed to assist escape to the portal, as Masudah had assessed that Samarit would not be fit for travel unaided.

A couple of wild cards: Masudah had ordered, he did not say how, a squad of his own men to be deployed from Khémia through the same underground passages and portals they had used before, but as expected, blocks had since been put in place after they had disposed of the Snake People. Detours would have to be made now. They would get as close as possible, as well as monitor the situation with their magical methods, remote-viewing among them. They could not communicate with Rowan until further notice, but they could watch his progress from afar. Since no safe channel existed between the two domains, he guessed that Masudah must have got Blue to relay a message to Vugh Deep's embassy in Khémia via her secret method.

The other factor: Blue's, or rather Madam Ellaern's, inside contact, the "ears and eyes in Kirzaka's house." She had not been able to confirm whether this person would be of assistance or betrayal.

One advantage, if there could be said to be one: the particular facility where Samarit was believed to be held stood in the desert dust relatively near their current position, only three miles from the edge of the plain.

◆

The stench remained as pungent, the dust as deep and the smokestacks billowed smog unabated. Of a sudden the sharp chuffs stopped, and the plumes sagged and rained to the ground as scattered grains of coarse sand and pea gravel. Night fell. The air cooled rapidly. No alarms triggered, but whether the commandos had been detected remained unknown. Surely perimeter security monitors had been upgraded since their first raid, but then reptilian confidence must be at an all-time high now that they teetered on the verge of a major step towards achievement of their goal of world domination. Perhaps the intruders were expected – as before – Rowan did not know. He stopped to direct a prayer of supplication to the Totality that his mission harmonize with it, and another prayer of intercession on behalf of Samarit. It could not hurt. More than that was up to what he could contribute personally.

155

The thought of seeing her again made his heart sing. But a fighter aircraft, a ptero directly overhead, nearly silent, silenced it fast. Updated intel reported that the reptilians had, via the black arts of their genetic technology, incorporated the flight capability of a super pterosaur until now thought to be extinct, and merged it with the new model's fundamentally fungal-metal alloy framework. League ordnance experts tended to regard this advanced reptilian technology with indifference as mimicry of their symbiotic methods. Their assumption may be wrong, perhaps arrogance. A reptilian pilot remained a necessity, as the highly instinctive craft only lacked an intellect, which made it a much more formidable foe than their drones when fitted with plasma weaponry. Air moved over its perfectly sculpted aerodynamics, which pushed the thick airborne dust back. Only that made it visible to the three commandos.

Perhaps they had evaded it, as they had for some minutes before already stood dead still in the shadows to assess the field of operations. Personal cloaking should have been sufficient to make thermal signatures transparent, yet the chance remained that emotional vibrations Reps relished so would trigger some device. The commandos relied on strict mental control, standard procedure in the battlefield, to minimize that risk.

Rowan brushed the dust from his face mask, and checked his hand-held map device, touched two fingers to one goggle lens and signalled Tòrr to move out. About a hundred yards from the target, he halted and signalled to stand by. He skirted the junked machine parts and equipment in the shadows of the strange wind-sculpted building. A glow of alternating red and blue filtered through its ground floor windows and brightened the drab clouds of dust outdoors with shafts of dim luminescence. The raiders had been covered in the fine powder, but that could only help.

Handholds and footholds proved not difficult to find. Soon he had ascended in silence like a spider to a point where he could see within. He carefully wiped enough grime from a pane to spy an army of ander slaves in orange coveralls, many with their heads covered completely, as they looked out through narrow darkened horizontal visors. The less covered might be old or weak, expendable, punishable or slated for entertainment. Several roving Rep overseers towered above their slaves, who laboured at tasks on long production lines in motion on conveyor belts, and assembled components into larger ones.

Rowan climbed higher and found ladders and catwalks, and the lee side of the curvilinear roof, very steep to allow some of the caked dust to slide off. He hoped to find Samarit there, or rather beneath it, once he located the correct dormer window, all currently dark. He brushed dust away with care, peered within and spied a metal cylinder horizontally mounted on supports, about eight feet in length and with rounded end caps. The capsule's bottom would be at eye level if he were inside, but of a height perfect for a Rep to peer into the top without the need to bend over too much – portholes at one end, the top and sides, hoses and cables attached – a row of indicator lamps in an inset panel – one flashed blue intermittently. Masudah had said she lay inside deeply asleep, possibly in a coma. Or most likely in stasis. He must release her from this coffin. Masudah had suggested possible entry points. Rowan tried them all. Finally, one yielded. He opened a hatch with care; hinges squeaked drily as years of dust slid off in layers and released a puffy cloud. Silent and still, he listened. Within he focused, to expand attention, to widen its scope. Breath at near standstill, and no one else evident yet – *except Sam!* When ready, he extroverted attention to the objective. He passed through the hatch. He had entered the building.

•

Samarit, no longer a firmly muscled female canid at less than half his weight, likely a third less than that now, had been strapped to Rowan's back. He barely noticed the burden. His equipment included a search-and-rescue framework with straps designed for the purpose. He easily scaled down with her to the ground, but traverse of the shadows required care, as everywhere lay much junked equipment, apparently abandoned to the elements, scattered around the building's ground level.

In time he encountered Tòrr and transferred his precious cargo. He checked the perimeter with care, and could not believe his luck. This time he offered a prayer of thanks. But they were not safe and sound yet. More long shadows must be crossed before the steep climb to the crest. Even then it would be days of marching uphill to reach the portal, at constant risk of discovery by rangers, as well as aircraft and satellites. But this time he knew how to open it quickly and safely. How it could be soon enough, he dared not question.

He repeatedly checked her condition. Breathing – erratic. Heart rate – slow and weak. Body temperature – normal. He checked her eyes. The pupils remained extremely dilated – but still no glazing or excessive tearing up. Before enclosure in the cylinder immersed in some sort of greenish-grey gel, she had been stripped naked, so he had been able to confirm that the skin of her hands, knees and feet appeared basically normal, apart from minor wounds, but emaciated, and her natural pigmentation had been bleached to uneven pallid and mottled chalky tones. No bones had been broken. One of her upper front teeth – missing. Her skin had wrinkled – flesh once full and firm had shrivelled. If he had not known otherwise, he would have assumed her to be a half-starved woman on the verge of old age. Dark bruises and large but uninfected scrapes disfigured one haunch. Cuts on her palms and forearms had nearly healed, but abrasions on her elbows and knees remained chafed – and a raw burn mark on her left shoulder – branded, with the Eye of Kirzaka – her eyebrows and lashes had vanished – her thick dark hair had lost its curl and much of it came out if he combed it with his fingers. The sight of it in his hand clenched his teeth, but his eyes teared up anyhow. He suppressed a deep growl with force, his body heated and his vision blurred.

A deep breath followed. He cleared the gel from her unseeing eyes, with care removed the plugs and hoses from her mouth, nostrils, ears and other orifices, and thoroughly wiped down her entire thin body with a towel. After application of antiseptic ointment and bandages from his first-aid kit, he calmed his mind to dress her as quickly as possible, no small feat in itself. Among his equipment had been one of her customary skin-tight black uniforms, but a thermal version, and a knit ski mask to cover her entire head. He wrung out and bundled the remainder of her wet dark hair into a thin topknot. After he had slipped her feet into woollen socks, he wrapped her in a cloak before he strapped her to his back. He had brought hiking boots, but left her unshod for now.

◆

The waxing crescent moon at last rose above the dark clouds on the horizon just as Rowan and Tòrr reached the crest.

"Welcome back, Sir Rowan," Ballista whispered. "Congratulations. Let me take the major now." The corporal unstrapped Samarit, and with great care laid her down on her back on a flat place he had cleared on a shelf of stone.

Rowan peeled back her cape, rolled the mask up to inspect her eyes, and confirmed that her condition remained stable.

Tòrr said, in a low voice, "Sir, we've had extraordinary good fortune so far. It's uncanny. Something must be wrong, I'm sure of it. How were we able to so easily withdraw from the field without detection? Aye, we were careful, but

158

I've never seen the like of it, especially at an enemy installation and the lengthy course we had to negotiate. Is it a trap, sir?"

"I've been wondering the same thing, corporal, when I've a fraction of a second to spare. They just don't care, if you want my opinion, if they even know we're here. They've got other things on their plates. It's possible Major Longbow would have died of neglect in that chamber within a few weeks and rotted for months. Few would have given a damn, except for the poor bastard eventually ordered to clean it out."

Ballista reported: "Sir, you should know that I dispatched a ranger two hours ago. I buried the body under that dune." He pointed to a large pile of slightly disturbed sandy ash, one hundred feet off the trail. "It was easily done. As soon as I spotted it, I set bait to lure it towards the dune so I could dispose of the evidence after eliminating the threat. The constant wind up here is already filling any marks or tracks. I think it was old, possibly just retired, maybe a rogue unwilling to quit. It reacted more slowly than is my experience of Reps, but still a very dangerous geezer. In any case, I don't think it reported before it attacked. I found no communication device in its possession. I believe we should move on as planned without delay regardless, sir."

Rowan smirked. The Heptas had taught that reptilians were immortal – but they were not. "I agree, corporal. Good work. But we can't presume anything. Let's move out, men. We'll take turns carrying the major and won't stop, except for brief rests to check on her, until we reach the portal. Maintain your boots at maximum output. We recharge at base."

◆

As the elevation increased, the temperature plummeted. Moonlight brightened the path, but exposed their presence. Rowan checked Samarit every mile or so now, wherever enough shelter appeared. Although her skin draped her frame in wrinkled and saggy near-leather, she did not appear dehydrated, possibly a residual effect of the gel. She must not get too cold, covered only with each of their capes in turn while in transport, in addition to her own. He found the small cave noted on his first expedition to this part of the world, and ordered Ballista to ignite a firestone. Tòrr dozed. Ballista took first watch.

Rowan held Samarit close to keep her temperature stable. The partially frozen gel still in her hair stank of something indescribably rancid, and possibly diffused for many yards and drifted with the wind. The towel soaked with gel had been left inside the capsule, which he had taken care to seal again, so he did his best to comb it with his fingers, but more hair came out with that method. With one hand, he dug a small hole in the ground at his side and buried it. Task completed, with his back against the uneven concave wall, he realized he had slept only when he heard scuffles outside and the sharp crack of breaking bone. He strapped on the rig with Samarit in it, under his cape, his weapon charged and aimed at the mouth of the cave –

Tòrr stood at the ready, just ahead inside the entrance, pressed against the wall, plasma pistol in hand. His silhouette in an instant absorbed into a more massive one as a large shadow darkened the entrance. Blackness – the familiar sniffing – the creature withdrew and revealed the moonlit mountain trail once again, and Tòrr's silhouette intact. They waited –

His attention withdrawn into the silence, Rowan expanded it to include Tòrr, the cave and the immediate surroundings.

The Rep loomed outside, only ten paces from the mouth of the cave and to the left – and there lay Ballista – his head, arms and legs twisted into an impossible mess.

Rowan could almost breathe with the giant humanoid lizard lungs. He definitely sensed the creature's thoughts, just as he had Kirzaka's:

"Slave spawn. One felid, a second ander. And one canid. The one! Merit or kill and consume? Difficult. Talon may punish… if… What is that?"

Rowan had by now unstrapped the rig, exited the cave, invisible to the Rep or to anyone, and silently positioned himself further down the trail, intent on drawing attention away from the cave where Tòrr guarded Samarit.

"Nothing. It is nothing. So cold up here. But it is… what?" The huge reptilian sniffed, again and again. *"Rocks? Nothing. But the cave… the mammal sleeps there."* The beast sniffed and snuffled. *"It smells so good…"* The lone ranger swivelled its beady orange-eyed stare at the cave mouth again –

Rowan jumped straight up, swung his pistol's plasma beam in slice mode and decapitated the enemy. The vile stench of burnt flesh and a puff of smoke from singed nape feathers followed. A thud and a cloud of moonlit dust confirmed the kill. Across the gravel a black stain crawled and spread.

No others appeared – yet. Apparently they monitored their territories solo and dispersed widely. Perhaps this giant had been the buried one's replacement. If so, a fatal contest between elder and youth may have ensued had they met this night. Rowan dropped from the ledge and checked the dead Rep for a communication device – it wore a badge – maybe that was it. Of stainless steel, it too had been embossed with the Eye of Kirzaka, a sight that made a growl form in Rowan's throat. He took the comm badge in case the Eye in the Sky tracked it. That may buy some time and disguise the fact that the beast had stalled too long on its rounds for whatever reason. More near the portal later, he would throw it into a fissure, a deep one.

But Ballista must be looked after. Rowan dashed back to the cave, where he found Tòrr looking upwards in his general direction. "Sir, I know you're there. I can see the Rep badge, as it's not absorbed by your field yet. Permission to find Ballista, sir."

Rowan, intent on visibility again, found it difficult. It took longer than expected; his body intermittently faded in and faded out. He clasped the obsidian pendant in firm grip, and calmed his mind to concentrate to the exclusion of all else, and repeatedly whispered the spell of crystallization into the ring of gold on his finger. Finally, Tòrr made eye contact, and Rowan propped Samarit up and took his place. Tòrr went in search of his brother.

◆

Burial of the remains of the massive ranger proved hard work. A large grave dug out of the hard mountain would take too long, so they decided to drag the stiffening bled-out corpse and severed head into the cave and block the entrance, with Samarit all the while strapped to Rowan's back to keep her warm and in case they needed to run for it. Fortunately, they carried climbing rope and pulleys, which helped. With no pickaxe, only a small collapsible spade, they dug up and buried its bloodstain, which had soaked deep into the stony pathway.

And they buried Ballista. Stood at attention afterwards, Tòrr conducted the last rite. He stammered recital of victories and a prayer for his brother the fallen warrior, for his long journey to the Otherworld – wherever – Rowan did not profess to know. Like Blue, he felt he had not been born with the religion gene. Of the two burials, Ballista's had been much more difficult.

◆

Back on the path now, they ascended the long steep flank to the portal area. They encountered frost, then snow, hence their tracks grew plainly visible, but with no sign of another tracker, not yet. For the past hour under an overcast sky near midday Rowan carried Samarit. They had planned to stop at a level enough place if they could find one to use fresh snow to clean her hair at least a little better, then dry it quickly with a small firestone in the wind somehow, as long as it would not give her a chill, nor scatter lost hair far and wide. But

161

the load on his back moved. A soft moan emerged. Before he could properly halt to check on her, hard little fists pummelled his ears, sharp elbows jabbed his neck and knees tried to crush his ribs, while her feet and ankles kicked his backside. Unconcerned for himself, as strapped in Samarit could not strike with much force, he worked her struggling form loose, but forgot to suppress his joy, which may have been a beacon to any ranger nearby. Too late to prevent it, she slipped his grasp and vanished among the boulders.

Only a few bootless footprints in the snow remained.

He quickly followed, as did Tòrr, who had been slightly behind them.

But she had disappeared, nor were there tracks. The rocky ground here had been swept clean by the wind.

They stopped to survey the talus of tumbled scree beneath the cliffs. Many possibilities presented themselves. How far could she get in only stockinged feet? She must be hiding nearby. The nanoids would have been extracted from her system months ago as well. They must find her quickly. A minute lost could mean her life lost. But even now, thin and weak, Samarit had no equal. They searched for a good half-hour but found nothing, although her stinking hair, if nothing else, should betray her even when frozen. Meanwhile, snowflakes increased and the wind picked up. Noon grew nearly dark as midnight.

"*Sam!*" shouted Rowan, at risk of being heard by the enemy. "Sam, it's me, Rowan! Where are you? *Sam!*"

Only the north wind answered in whispers and whistles that it could not care less if she froze to death.

Once more he withdrew inwards to widen the scope of attention to include the entire field. Within he scanned for any sign of pain not his own, any emotion. Nothing. He did note that Tòrr hurried to inspect every crack and crevice.

The cry of an eagle echoed between the cliffs.

Rowan opened his eyes wide.

Tòrr rushed to his side. "Sir, there's no open water nearby for feed. It's too late in the year for an eagle at this elevation anyhow. What do you make of it?"

Rowan, tempted to grin, answered: "It's good news, corporal. We've found the major. Did you get a fix on the source?"

"Negative, sir. But I believe it's this way… aye, there's a whiff of something rotten." He scrambled down a slope of scree and disappeared into a hollow. "*Sir! She's here, the major's here, sir!*"

Rowan followed.

Wedged between two large splintered rocks, barely visible – eyes as wild and mean as a badger in a steel-jaw leg-hold trap – Samarit crouched and shivered.

162

"Sam! You're safe. It's me, Rowan!" He moved closer, only to be pelted with stones. "This is a friend, Tòrr, a League commando. *You're safe!*" A rock hit him between the eyes and made him reel. He touched his forehead. A smear of blood dripped off his fingers. He threw back his head and let forth a reasonable impression of an eagle's cry, which reverberated in the ravine where they clung perilously near a crevasse at the edge of a glacier.

The whites of her eyes showed through the openings in her mask. The dark red-rimmed irises stopped their rapid sweeping motion and made contact, and welled with tears. She had seen him as himself. But the emotion she displayed was not relief. In fact she screamed – only once, but loud – and the echo repeated.

Instinct made both Rowan and Tòrr survey the environment, weapons drawn, aimed in arcs that followed their lines of sight. Nothing suspicious seen, Rowan signalled Tòrr to stand watch – and inched towards Samarit. At risk of another injury, he raised his forearm to protect his eyes, and quietly said, "Sam, you know it's me. *Please*, you need to get warm. Please let me near. I won't hurt you, Sam."

Her mouth opened and closed, shrunken lips cracked and dry. Her breath fogged in little puffy clouds. Frost rimmed the mask's mouth. Her dark wet lashes froze together as her eyes closed. Her head dropped, she huddled into a ball and rolled to her side against one of the big splintered rocks.

Rowan carefully reached in, fished her out, bundled her into his forearms, and furled his cape, his midsection pressed to a woman-shaped icicle. "*Corporal! Firestone! Now!*"

XIX
Plaints Observed

FOR AN ENTIRE day, even after recovery enough to try to walk on her own a little despite the series of large scrapes on her backside, Samarit remained silent. She did not allow Rowan to apply ointment to it nor to her other wounds as he had before she regained consciousness, not even to the suppurated brand on her shoulder. At times extremely enervated, her bruised face a pale mask of fortitude, at other times she seethed.

Rowan's heart burned with it like a heavy hot stone had lodged within. He only once suggested that radiating such a powerful emotion might attract unwanted attention. She gave him a black look then that made him tremble. He tried in vain to hide his disquiet. Commando or not, he had been cowed speechless. They made little progress, slowed greatly by deepening snow – and Samarit's wrath.

They rested now in a sheltered lookout, where she broke the silence. She ignored Tòrr, her voice forced to rasp, its familiar timbre inflected with a lisp by the missing tooth, and said: "*Why*, Rowan? *Why?* I had a clear shot. You ruined it… and Squire Krumb was killed. *For what!*"

The weighty smouldering stone within grew incandescent. "Sam, I only did what I thought was right… I saw danger, I tried to protect you…"

"You only ruined my *life!* You're the worst thing that ever happened to me. It's all gone now. Nothing will ever fix this." She moved as far away from him as possible beneath the overhang, just where a small cornice drooped below its jagged icy edge like a fang. "I can't trust you."

Tòrr looked to Rowan, saluted and said, "Sir, permission to answer a call of nature, sir."

Samarit turned in an instant, winced when her clothes brushed her festering wounds, cheeks flushed, and said, "*I'm the senior officer here, corporal!*"

Tòrr glanced at her. "Aye, Major Longbow, sir!" He stood at attention. "Beg your pardon, sir!"

"Granted then," she muttered. "Vigilance, corporal, vigilance."

"Aye aye, sir!" And Tòrr disappeared.

Samarit looked out from beneath her cowl into the far distance.

Rowan examined the gravel dusted with snow between his feet, forearms rested on his knees, and leaned back against the rock wall. "I'm sorry, Major

Longbow. I can never apologize enough, and I know it can never… Squire Krumb was the best… I witnessed his murder. They knew we were coming…"

Samarit did not look at him. She crossed and uncrossed her arms. She fidgeted with her collar and grimaced, leaned back against the hard cold rock, and at last sighed, and trembled. She looked at the ground in silence for a long moment, but murmured: "Thank you for saving my life. It was very brave."

Rowan looked up, but only to glance at her. She had faced away. Her body language did not encourage a response.

She added: "We were stupid to follow orders that make no sense. I don't want to discuss what happened. Not yet. Maybe never." She stamped the snow off her boots. "I stink like shit. *Where in bloody hell is Hornblower?!*"

✦

The north wind picked up speed and howled. They passed the grave of the pack-horse the Khémian soldiers had buried. Rowan said nothing of it to Samarit. In any case, the unmarked last resting place had long since been hidden under a drift. He silently bade the nameless steed godspeed nevertheless.

In twenty minutes they reached the portal. Rowan stood at the left, Tòrr took the vanguard. Samarit rested her meagre weight on one leg on the other side, supported by a stick. They formed as close to an arrowhead formation as the squad could make, only the tip of the head, but sharp enough, they hoped. Rowan powered up the hand-held scanner and passed it to Tòrr, who attached it to a small tripod, and stood behind it. When its indicators stopped their chorus-line dance, the three warriors got on their knees in the snow, bowed and faced the still invisible portal.

Rowan reminded his comrades to clear their minds, and stilled the surface of his own to a clear mirror as Masudah had taught him. The gale roared louder as the temperature plummeted, the scanner crackled in the dry cold, and a wavy circular pattern, like a stone thrown into a clear pool, distorted the rocky background. Rowan directed in a loud voice: "*Sir, major, sir! Corporal! On your feet. The portal is stable. Corporal, pick up the scanner; when I command march, take the lead. At the ready. On my signal… now! Forward march!*"

✦

Commander Diss, obviously vexed, displeased, more than irritated, shouted as if to the deaf as usual: "*You lost one of my best commandos, Berry! What is it with you? Can you not manage to avoid casualties? I told you it was… Well, I suppose it wasn't a total waste of time! You did manage to rescue Major Longbow!"* He stood up and stepped to the window, placed his palms on the frame, but dropped his arms and clasped his hands behind his back. *"For that I thank you. The League thanks you. Her tribe thanks you, no doubt. Whether they forgive you is not bloody likely. Yet she will be rehabilitated in time, according to the medics."* More quietly he added: *"But I wouldn't want to marry that girl, not if I valued my peace of mind. The fiancé, that Longbow prince, will one day have his hands full."*

"Sir, you're most welcome. I only did what was right, my duty. And in my power. I'm glad to hear of Major Longbow's prognosis, sir. Corporal Hornblower was a good man. Tòrr's brother Ballista died valiantly doing his duty. I'm very sorry for his loss and for yours, sir."

"Listen, Berry, you failed in your duty on the first mission to that hell-hole! But I'm forced to cut you some slack. You were duped. We all were. Amazing. When we find that woman, that snake in the grass, her head will roll snake eyes, I guarantee it!"

The volume of his last statement had resumed its test of loudness tolerance, but Rowan remained undisturbed. His heart dwelt elsewhere. Only his ears listened politely.

"One thing you must explain, Berry. Why did the Reps let you get away with it? They let you go the first time, now a second. Your report states your opinion as expressed to Corporal Hornblower. Do you still maintain it? Or have you further ruminations you would like to share?"

"No, commander. I have not revised my opinion. And it's only a hunch. I believe the enemy suffers from hubris, sir, excessive pride and overconfidence, if they even cared we were there, just like the first time they permitted ingress unconcerned. We were no threat, in their view, no more than three little black crows that had landed on their rooftop. I don't mean every Rep, sir. Maybe most individuals are iterations of a type, a programmed unit. Only their supreme leader is independent enough to make decisions, but even he's subject to a repressive ideology of his own invention."

Commander Diss turned around, stepped back to stand behind his desk, leaned over it and spread his hands over its surface. He glared at Rowan and roared: *"My, but you do use a lot of big pricey words, Berry! Are you saying the thieves allowed you to steal back their loot? The major was a prize! That suggests a lack of discipline, let alone pride, not the opposite!"*

"Commander, I simply mean they have more important things on their minds. Or at least on Kirzaka's mind. I believe he'd basically forgotten the major. She would eventually have died in that tank. She was only briefly important to him as a temptation to withhold from his underlings. What he really wants is what she represents, what he can exploit for sorcery. For that the entire Longbow clan and other canids around the world, as well as the anders, are on his agenda. We felids are less valuable. He's the only one of them barely patient enough to wait until terror is maximized, and only then will he harvest what he wants. Without that, the Rep forces alone are insufficient. His followers only want to satisfy their appetites by adherence to a prescribed way of life. Dogma and hypnosis are part of their culture. They do what they're told and don't question it. Their entire civilization rolls in a well-worn rut, and they want to drag the whole world down into it with them, once they've stolen what they want."

"*Interesting, Berry! Tell us more of what we already know! What is it that they want for us? No, don't tell me, I will state the official position! They have depth scanners now that will break down our doors so they can murder us in our beds, according to the evidence YOU passed on to the minister of defence! It took a while for him to cough up his source, but we have our ways, including that fancy brooch you always wear!*" Diss sat down in his desk chair, and muttered, "Unfortunately, it shorted out somewhere along the way."

With relief Rowan remembered having splashed brine on his raven brooch when he dressed in a great hurry after release from Doctor Sola's tank. Incredibly, he had forgotten about it activated as a wire. "Sir, that seems a reasonable inference. In fact it's incontrovertible." Rowan looked up at Diss. "Sorry, sir, I mean it's undeniable, based on the evidence. It's only a matter of time."

"*I do know what 'incontrovertible' means, Berry!*" He straightened and crossed his big forearms. "What I do NOT know is what you're hiding."

"Hiding, sir? I don't know what you mean."

Diss truly shouted in earnest now: "*You know very well what I mean, Berry! WHERE IS SHE? Where is your dear elder sister? The dishonourable minister of education! Now, that's incontrovertible! Did you think your records do not include genetic information? Think before you speak!*"

"I don't know where the minister is, sir. I believe Madam Ellaern hoped to be evacuated to the Lyra system by the Primordial Architects. It's part of the New Dawn belief system. She's a follower… maybe she was successful."

The commander stood once more. "*Berry, I do know all about the Primordial Architects, thank you very much!*" He bit his lower lip. "*We have even spotted their strange craft. I do not know how they got in here, and they're turning out to be very difficult to shoot down, but we'll disable them in time. Of course we searched all the temples of that sect, the whatever… New Dawn! We nearly tore down the musty old headquarters where that feline cleric presided. In lieu of deportation, for now he*" *will be detained for sheltering a fugitive, have no doubt about that! After a trial, a fair one of course. Then back to that lackadaisical star system goes he, if and when the Lyran embassy transports him back there, expurgated!"* He leaned forward and spoke more softly: "Is that the right word, Berry?"

"I don't know, sir."

"Perhaps you prefer another one, bigger! Super polysyllabic! See? I can talk like a brainiac too! Now… there is something about that place that defies logic. Our forensic investigators suspect she was there for some time." He banged his fist on his desk, which made all the objects on it jump like acrobats in a circus. *"What do you know about that, Berry?! WHAT!"*

✦

Diss confined Rowan to the base, this time locked in the pound. To be released, all he had to do was denounce Blue, but he really had no idea where she had disappeared to. If not Clach Béo temple, then where? Even Àrd-Sagartus had no idea, probably. She could be anywhere – or anyone – anywhere except on a Primordial Architect outbound craft, certainly not in the Lyra system – yet.

Rowan found himself caught on the sharp horns of a dilemma: either condemn her as a traitor to be hanged or even beheaded – or say nothing and condemn her to possible permanent invisibility and madness. The first option would save him from a prison sentence for complicity. But the second gave her a slim chance of survival intact, and hope of a cure. Obviously she was extremely clever. Nothing would surprise him less than that she would find a way.

✦

His five-toed boots had been confiscated. For a week he paced the concrete floor of his cage until his soles blistered. But a visitor had been permitted –

"Ah, Sir Rowan, it has come to this. One wishes to help, but you must not succumb to despair." The warrior-priest and Khémian diplomat winked. "I come to offer unasked-for advice, to wit all is not as it appears, as I have said to you before, a timeless truth even if I had not. It is, as are all things temporal, how you say… transient. But there go I again, this is a topic for another time." He chuckled, which made the wings of his moustache take flight. "Forgive the jest… comedic skill, it is yet small."

Rowan gripped the iron bars between them and asked: "Have you seen or talked to Sam… to Major Longbow?"

168

"No, I have not. But rumour is that the major, a false title, by the way, bestowed by the ex-minister posed as a commander, is soon to be released from military hospital. It is said a full recovery is expected, although it will take some work… some difficulty with the nanobots. To that end, she will return to Longbow clan tribal territory, Wishbone Warren, where her grandmother Morningstar is chieftain. I believe, when she is well, a wedding will take place, at another warren. The time is as yet unannounced. As you know, she is betrothed to the youngest of the House of Touchstone princes, Pineshadow by name, if memory serves."

Rowan failed to heed Masudah's advice – despair crushed his soul – the groom's name, like a snowflake that triggers an avalanche, flattened any remnants of resilience. He dropped onto the cot and sat with his face buried in his hands.

"Apologies… I sorrow to bring this news, my friend, if it be the cause of such pain…" Masudah waited for a response, but none came. "Let me tell a fable, if I may." He pulled a chair closer and sat beyond the iron bars. "It is a timeless tale of love, called *Licking Honey Off a Blade*. What I am about to tell takes place in Iawi, the Antediluvian home world, the Olden, long ages before it was lost in the Great Mireflood. Of this land great debates rage among the archaeologists, who very often are, how you say… reductionists, simplistic, dismissive. None are mystics. They should be well advised to learn how the mind projects its beliefs. Then they may decide which of the histories to prefer, yet none is truth. But I, how you say… digress.

"The events of the tale occur before the Olden came to pass, in the Time Before Time. The scene is the gravesite of a great god worshipped by the Antediluvians' warlike ancestors. Here lay Sojhalin, killed in a duel with his brother Oçh. Their fight was over Tanuta, daughter of the Eye of Duw, divine mother of all that was, that is or ever shall be. Tanuta's father is Duw the Immeasurable, god of infinity. Tanuta and Sojhalin had been born on the same day. On that day it had been decreed throughout the cosmos that Tanuta's title would one day be Queen of Heaven, and that Sojhalin, destined to be the best of the gods of war, would be king. But Tanuta did not love Sojhalin. She loved his younger brother Oçh, god of music, poetry, truth and light. From the first moment of meeting, their hearts had merged into one without their consent.

"Ah, there is no song that can tell of Tanuta's otherworldly beauty, and none that can tell of the great soul of Oçh. But, to be fair, none could do justice to Sojhalin's courageous heart. Yet he could not forgive Oçh. He felt it not only his birthright to wed fair Tanuta, but that heaven and earth would fall into the claws of Apep, god of chaos. Thus we call the reptilia *apep,* demon.

"In the anguish of passion, Oçh felt it impossible to surrender Tanuta to such a fate, to Sojhalin. Their hearts, heart rather, would break. They would die of it, thus the cosmos would die along with them, heaven and hell both. The only solution, he believed, was to kill his own brother, come condemnation, cataclysm or catastrophe.

"The Eye of Duw witnessed noble Sojhalin's dead body in a pool of blood on the stones of Eorthe. She knew the other gods would demand that she restore his life and punish Oçh by making him Apep's slave. This she would not do, for she could not break her own laws. Why? Because she *is* the law. All must be exactly as it is. It can be no other, not once it has gone to all the trouble of the long journey from the limitless to the becoming to the existence. Oçh would meet his fate on the road he took to avoid it, to paraphrase a great sage. She knew the consequence of his violation of her law would unfold exactly as it must, that he and Tanuta would live in guilt, thus the whole cosmos would share in misery at her coronation, but without a king."

Rowan had sat with his head in his hands, as still as a statue. "That's the saddest story I've ever heard," he muttered, and followed with a sigh.

Masudah continued, "There is more to it, my friend. It concerns forgiveness, of self, then other. In the end it concerns renunciation…"

"So I'm supposed to give her up…" Rowan sighed ever more deeply.

"More than that, my friend, much more. You must give up *yourself*, not your actual self, but your false identity. This is renunciation, surrender to *what is*, not what one *wants* to be what is. Tanuta and Oçh had to not only desire, but to discover true love within, to forgive themselves, then each the other. At last they had to renounce their passion for expanding into limitlessness in each other's arms, the endless forbidden craving, and along with it the guilt. They were now free to love in truth, but free of binding attachment. The cosmos was most grateful. The honey, it is not love. And the blade, it drips with more than blood when the tongue slips."

Rowan remained embedded in sorrow like a bee in amber.

"When first we met, Sir Rowan, I explained that, when in Khémia, I am a priest. In times of conflict, I am a warrior. My duty is to maintain and defend our ancient tradition. I conduct rites and ceremonies. I tell stories like the one I just told to you. I also said that if I am a proper priest and a proper warrior, that is, simply do my duty as well as I am able, that should anyone on that basis become curious, well, then I teach. The teachings are not mine, as they are truly of the Time Before Time. By this I mean they are of an unbroken lineage ancient even in Iawi, the Olden, destroyed, our myths say, by Apep. These teachings belong to no one, not even Iawi, never mind Khémia. You once told me that as a boy you were taught to believe curiosity is a sin. This is one of Apep's so-called truths he does his utmost to force down their throats to choke his victims into compliance. He wants them dull, ignorant, afraid, how you say… divided, complacent, quiescent, lazy of mind, heavy of heart and weak of will. I speak, how you say… figuratively, but I say now, *resist Apep! Stand up and fight, O mighty warrior!*"

Rowan remained unmoved. "If there's something you can teach me, Masudah, now is the time. Curiosity is beyond my ability, however, no offence. You taught me the secret of invisibility and how to better open a portal. These skills were practical and life-saving. But my heart is crushed, like Oçh's. I won't kill the Touchstone prince, obviously. What *can* I do?"

"At last, your question permits me to teach, Sir Rowan. This is curiosity precisely. Now, this is what you must do… love Samarit Longbow."

Rowan's hands dropped onto his knees. He peered through the black bars at the diplomat, and said, "*That's* the teaching? With respect, Captain Masudah of Zau, that's precisely the problem… what on Eorthe do you mean?"

"You must love your way through this, how you say… impasse. Remember how I told of craving the honey of limitlessness. Strange to say, our nature is honey already, but to crave is precisely limitation. To want what is not. At best it is a tongue licking at the wind. Samarit appears the living honey in the world outside, not so? She is so different to you, so opposite. She is girl, you are boy. She is canid, you are felid. Her years are short, yours are long. She is promised, you are not. You feel you are missing what she alone is. All these mean the honey is an object of temptation, irresistible, just beyond reach, about to be stolen once more, not by that monster Kirzaka, but by the force of Longbow law, that is, if you listen to your mind. I say listen to your heart."

"But it's broken…" Rowan failed to restrain a moan, and his voice broke. "How can I… listen to it without wanting to die?"

"Ah, but here, Sir Rowan, is the secret… the feelings that torture are *not* the heart. They are the reflection of mind in the body. Mind desires to act, it whips the body. But it cannot act, causing a, how you say… jam of logs. As is said, irresistible force meets immovable object. Thus the pain, the cramp, it is deep. But here is the teaching much *more* deep. The mind's thoughts, most perhaps, we are unaware of. Some were formed before we knew words, when we were babes. Some were of great beauty. But some were of fright or of disgust, of shame and suchlike… and longing for mother-honey seemingly denied, through no fault of her own, but by our ignorant little mind if she were slow to rescue us from our lack of peace! So they are hidden in a dark place, out of sight, out of mind… so it seems. But they do not go away! They are like the pigskin sewn into a ball the poorest peasants of my homeland float on to cross the canals in defiance of the jaws of the crocodile. The ball, it will not stay under. It floats like a raft. Try to push it down, up does it rise. Just so, the forgotten thoughts *cannot* hide.

"Now, permit me to change the picture, how you say… the figure of speech, the simile. The thoughts, like the director prompts the actor from the shadows off-stage. The actor thinks he must act so as to be judged worthy or appear a fool. He must follow a plan, a script. So far so good, but if he simply repeats what he is told, he is a machine, not an artist. You see? But a machine has no skill, no imagination, it but repeats what it is told. A real actor must know the tale, he must understand its world, know his lines and make them his own, suspend his idea of himself as if he is indeed the character he portrays as he shares in the playwright's imagination, yet each moment he knows he is free of its pain. And yes, its joy. But he does not need his role's joy, he has his own. Some say he is a mere child to pretend, to spin a falsehood. So what? Critics are consumers, not creators. His accusers have lost their innocence, their imagination. They have no authority in this matter. Let them seek to recover it in vain through their worldly pursuits of wealth and power. The actor's art, his great art, the art of living, is a model to the audience, who see themselves reflected in him. But only if he knows who he is. He hears the director, yes, but interprets the direction in the light of self-knowledge. It is knowledge of the truth of his freedom that sets him free to perform well. And to demonstrate *how* and *how not* to live well."

Rowan lifted his head, nodded acknowledgement a little and said, "I've heard talk of art, play and freedom before, Masudah. I'll try to… 'how you say'… make it my own. But you said the feelings are not the heart. It sure *feels* like it though, right here in the middle of my aching chest. Its claws are ripping my insides to shreds, only a sorry hollow left… so what is the heart you want me to follow?"

"The claws will retract, the wound will heal." Masudah's eyes twinkled. "The heart is that without which you would not be you, your, how you say… essence, that which is real, which does not change. The essence of honey is sweetness. Its heart is sweet. The essence of self is love, more pure than the purest honey, revealed reflected by the loved one as if in a mirror. The essence is the heart, the innermost, beyond which there is no whicher. It knows not the future, nor the past. It knows the eternal now alone. It is complete. To young people, love is outside… 'in' the other… first mother, father, family, pets, friends, then mate, perhaps children. But the ancient teaching is that love is nowhere but 'in' you, *as* you. Sir Rowan, this is the Divine, no difference. You cannot force a razor blade between you and the Divine. You are one, like actor and role, like fire and heat, like honey and sweet."

XX
Underworld Onslaught

OVER THE SEVERAL days that followed Masudah's visit, Rowan sat on his cot with his arms wrapped around his knees pressed against his chest; or he paced the floor and stared unfocused at nothing in particular. At times he lay on his back with his hands behind his head, eyes open, unglazed by insomnia – open, but vision looked within. Rowan Berry, only one of the characters in his life story – the script reinforced in memory each day and recycled each night in dreams. His backstory, one element, defined the limitations of form and flaws of character. The big-picture narrative, the background scenery and props: cosmology, geography, species, race, history, society, status, language, philosophy, religion and science; social constructs and contracts. The script – a work in progress, with arcs of personal growth, arcs of other developments, plot, tension and so on. The theme – somewhat vague until the last act, perhaps. But he thought it possible to make suggestions to the playwright and the director, even going so far as to clarify, to improve the arcs, not to revise the ending to a happy one necessarily, but to be honest, true to life as it expresses itself in every possibility in the spectrum of experience, the bitter and the sweet, and to bless and honour the sacred beauty that makes beauty beautiful beyond both.

His story's cast of characters – indeed remarkable and interesting, including his own persona, the actor's mask. He saw that at this moment his character on the stage had snagged on an unhappy point on the through line, if getting what the character wanted meant what it appeared to mean – a big conflict. Suspense. He may as well be Oçh as Rowan. He could only have compassion for both – his mind came to a stop – he sat straight upright, eyes wide. *That's it, the secret. The actor is more than just the inert mask, the man is more than just the inert actor… he's the sentience; more than that, he's awareness of the sentience.* A brilliant light blazed in his mind. *That's it. Masudah's right.*

✦

"I'm very sorry to see you in here, Rowan. It's not right. I'll do everything in my power to help. Only… only I don't know what that is yet…"

He glanced through the iron bars at his visitor. "Thanks, Sam. You look well. A lot better than the last time I saw you." And he looked away again, but watched her in peripheral vision. He still loved to watch her.

The corners of her mouth turned up a little. "I'm still a wraith," she replied, "but I feel better. They say the nanoids that were extracted… well, I need complete rest. I'm going home, to Gran, to my tribe… she'll look after me." She did not look at him directly either.

He glanced at her – but stared at his hands clenched to the bars.

Strained silence fogged the space between them.

"Rowan, thank you for what you did. You risked your life for me. I don't know how to repay you… if I can."

Their eyes met.

"No need. How could I not? Listen, Sam… I want you to be happy, to live. Go home. Be happy. Be strong… be free."

Samarit's dark eyes welled and spilled over. She stepped forward and reached through the iron barrier; slender arms encircled Rowan's waist as well they could. She pressed the side of her face against the black metal, eyes closed.

Her silk scarf loosened and fell back to reveal that her head had been shaved, but even without hair – familiar, sweet, fragrant. He released his grip on the bars, and stroked the back of her head as well as possible, his forearms too thick to reach very far. *Razor blade or not*, he thought, *it cuts like one*.

They stayed locked in limited embrace until the guard entered, a canid by the look of the curved tips of his ears that protruded through his mop of shaggy dark hair. The time had come to part.

◆

Three days later, the same guard closed the door behind him and returned to his post. A familiar visitor had returned –

"Masudah!" Rowan leapt up and grasped the iron bars with both hands. "I'm very glad to see you so soon! I have something to tell you. You were right…"

Masudah darted his gaze about the room, and said, "Hey, brother."

Rowan squinted. The warrior-priest-diplomat did not sound quite right. And his accent –

Masudah glanced at the outer door, and did again several times in quick succession.

Rowan, brows lowered, gripped the bars, and said: "*What* is going on here?…"

"*Quiet, you idiot!*" The wings of the dark moustache froze on the downstroke. Pseudo-Khémian accent now vanished, he whispered: "Listen… we're going to blow this brig, like they say in the movies. Just keep your furry face shut and follow me like a duckling and I'm your mother. I'm not completely certain how long I can make this last. Talking burns up a lot of energy." He fumbled with a clinking ring of keys, and tried each one in the lock. "And the guard… he's one of those rare ones impervious to my power of persuasion."

Rowan whispered: "Is that *you*? This is incredible!"

The winged moustache contracted. "Shut the fuck up… *right*?"

The lock clicked. The gate creaked loud enough to wake the long-dead. They both froze, eyes on the outer door. The guard would investigate, once he came to and found his keys were missing. The pseudo-Khémian pulled a pistol, a small phaser smuggled in, aimed at the door, and gestured to Rowan to step quietly.

Instead, he sat down on his cot, looked at his would-be jailbreaker and crossed his arms. "No, Blue. This is madness."

"What the…? Come *on*. What's *wrong* with you?"

Rowan shook his head in defiance and stared. So clever she was, but clearly only a caricature of Masudah now that he peered at her with more care –

But the room spun – until it went dark.

·

He stood, apparently. Something heavy in his hands. Environment – very dark. The air reeked of acrid smoke. Something had been vaporized. And mixed in: the stench of burnt flesh and death. But he made out dim shapes: mangled grounders, buildings in ruin – a war zone. The nanoids – still in effect, and enhanced his already excellent night vision, which revealed nothing but a black night as black as black can be – although – everything looked very flattened – poor depth of field. The heavy object in his hands – an assault rifle, charged and ready, its row of indicators unlit; only the green one glowed dimly grey in this light – or lack of it. Quick flashes like sheet lightning, echoes of thunder – percussive buffeting, rumbling in the distance. He looked down – five-toed boots on his feet. "What is this?" he mumbled.

"*Shush!* Do you want to get us killed?"

Commando training kicked in. He crouched to make himself a smaller target. Rowan peered in the direction of Blue's voice. He whispered back: "What happened? Where are we?"

"You're such a bonehead. I had to hypnotize you too of all things. I do my best to spring my little brother from the slammer, and what does he do? Sits down on his bum and refuses to budge! Don't thank me, I'm just the last of your kin. That reminds me… here, take these."

Afloat towards him on its own drifted the faint impression of the obsidian pendant she had given him. His gold ring followed.

"You're welcome," she said. "You didn't know I'm a safe-cracker too, did you?"

"No…" He stared in her direction. "So you abducted me. I shouldn't be surprised at anything you do, Blue. You're a black witch."

"No. *Stop* that. *Don't call me that*, not when you've seen what it truly is up close. I'm your only ally in this crazy world remember."

"It certainly looks crazy at the moment. Crazed, cracked and shattered. What the hell happened? You could use some tactical training. Please brief your ally on the conditions on the field of battle before argument."

"*You* started it by calling me names. Well… never mind. Anyhow, as soon as I got wind of what was coming, I made a beeline for where I knew my little brother must be. That meant leaving my hideout, but it was now or never. All hell was about to break loose. It was easy to infiltrate the base, easier than before. I won't bore you with the details."

"Please, Blue, *where* are we? Still at the base? Somewhere outside it?"

"Right. We're at the perimeter, the eastern boundary of what's left of the base. It's not ideal, but nothing is… I mean nowhere is… I'm really tired. My grammar is deteriorating."

"I will excuse your poor grammar just this once," he said. "Now please, what the hell happened? It's obvious the Reps have penetrated the dome, and sooner rather than later. But is the enemy within range? If so, what's their position?"

"What do you mean by 'just this once'? Fine. The enemy has flattened the base, thanks to that turncoat Diss. Funny, right? He alerted the media to what was coming, then mobilized the military into perfect position to get clobbered. Ironic, to say the least. It makes one wonder what they could have bribed him with. Maybe they had him by the gonads. I thought I did… for a while."

"Blue! The enemy? Their position? I need to know. *Now!*"

"Right. Most of the troops are dead or deployed elsewhere. Where exactly, I have no clue. And I don't know why the whole system isn't totally cooked. I guess they want to loot its industrial-strength crystals. We're lucky if so. There may be, probably are, wounded soldiers here and there. Most of the Reps who survived have moved on to the city. You can smell the ones that didn't, and mighty malodorous they are too. Some are still hanging around to steal whatever they can… heavy weapons, munitions, stuff like that. They probably don't want to destroy Perkona Ola completely… my guess… as other resources may be valuable, especially all the corpses scared to death and ripening as we speak. They're likely planning a vibe party to end all parties. I would."

The gloom could not hide Rowan's scowl.

"Hey, don't look in my general direction like that! I just mean if I were them I'd party my pretty ass off too."

"Speaking of which," he pointed out, "it's invisible, in case you didn't know. How long have you been like that?"

"Do you know, I can't remember? I've had too much on my mind since I decided to risk the trip to save my baby brother's bacon. *Right?* I wouldn't be surprised if that wasn't yesterday. Or… the day before."

"All right, Blue, thank you. Really, I mean it. I'm grateful. Otherwise I might still be in that cage waiting for my last-ever visitor, the Grim Reaper. But that's far too long to remain invisible. You didn't tell me you could do that too. You know the danger, don't you? You could have a hard time getting back to normal."

"I gave up 'normal' when I was a sweet young thing… well, young anyhow. But yes, I know all about it. It's just that I can't seem to find the off switch or… or maybe it's the on switch."

"We have to fix that. One more thing… my chronometer says it's late evening, but I don't see the artificial stars. It's neither night nor day, because the dome is defunct. But I can see somewhat. Can you?"

"*Duh*, of course it's defunct. I can't see as well as you, because I'm a nanoid-free model, but I can make out the odd large obstacle… if I squint."

"Good. I think we should look for a hand-held scanner, find a portal and head for the Surface, the only one I know of that might take us to a place I've been before. Eastport Station is to the east of our position, not that far once we skirt the downtown area. If the Reps haven't flattened it yet, we have a chance."

"Sounds like a plan. Only… I'm awfully tired… maybe… a nap first…"

Rowan's ears sensed a soft thump. A vague puff of dust rose from the ground. *So there she is.* He carefully felt for the transparent weight of her body and carried her to a patch of relatively untouched lawn between two wrecked grounders. He stretched her out, and the blades of grass beneath flattened to a silhouette. She flickered in and out of sight. He checked his chronometer: 21:10:03. He withdrew attention inwards and surveyed their surroundings. No signs of the enemy – free to focus. On what exactly, he had no idea. He surrendered to the inner world, and all reference points on which hung the description of the outer one fell away, including his own body. Attention deepened inwards, and an alternative imaginal body formed, a sphere of light, which gradually became just as tangible – light everywhere now. He trusted that the physical body would still be waiting for him in space-time, but a great temptation arose: to never go back. *Hyperspace is so free…* but he did not forget his intention to find Blue and bring her back, and fast.

The all-pervasive light slowly lost its even tone – spots of brighter hue here and there. He examined them more closely, and recognized what, or who, he sought. His attention embraced a glow that pulsed like a heartbeat, and sensed the profundity of her state, on the verge of the sleep of – "death." He struggled to understand the concept. It meant little here. A spontaneous vibration emitted from the exact centre of his spherical form, and encompassed Blue – the duckling now, enclosed in a shell of light. Safe.

Aeons passed. Every thousand years or so, he stirred from meditation to check on her. The hollow had grown brighter each time, and warmed the unhatched within. He remained as patient as a midwife.

◆

He checked his chronometer: 21:10:33. Exactly thirty seconds had passed. Little had changed, only Blue's slight translucency. A search-and-rescue rig like the one he had used to carry Samarit out of Mudredd Vale would have been handy. He must remain patient. When she awoke, he would search for supplies.

Twenty minutes later she cast a shadow in the gloom, soon stirred, rolled over and yawned. Her eyes opened wide. She sat up and stretched her arms. "Wow, I feel great…" She looked around – and her gaze landed on Rowan. "What did you do to me? I had the weirdest dream."

"Nothing much. If you're fine to wait here, I'll find food and water. And a scanner. Then we should move out."

"No way. I'll be a sitting duck. You're my decoy. Anyway, I feel like dancing, definitely not eating. Am I dead?"

"If this is the afterlife, maybe we deserve it. Let's head out. We can find what we need on the way. Follow me."

Only a hundred paces beyond the two crushed grounders, snuffles, grunts and sniffing alerted felid hearing. A flash of an explosion like sheet lightning lit the horizon and backlit the silhouette of a big Rep fifty feet distant with its snout dug into in a mound of dead troopers, the corpses which it sliced open with its fangs. It had not yet seen the felids yet, but certainly would if it glanced their way.

Rowan put his hand on Blue's shoulder and gently pushed her to a prone position. He crouched and raised his assault rifle – and waited for the right moment to strike the Rep between the eyes – difficult – gore and intestines disguised its entire skull and made it hard to guess the position of its sutures, as well as the beady orange orbs. He must find a chink in its body armour – or better, strike its brain through its palate when it opened its mouth.

Meanwhile it gnawed noisily on a dead soldier's leg.

The viewfinder's crosshairs moved into position –

At the sound of a sharp whistle, the monster's head turned, its mouth wide open and dripping with ander and canid blood –

A thin pulse of plasma sizzled in its direction.

It fell to its knees, then flat on its lower jaw with a solid thud in a cloud of dust, and bit off its own tongue.

Rowan's mind boggled. He had not pulled the trigger yet, so looked behind.

Blue remained frozen with a little phaser in both hands, eyes still sighting along the barrel at the target.

"*Blue!*" Rowan whispered hoarsely. "*Are you insane?*"

She pretended to blow smoke from the barrel. "You were dragging your bum, little brother, taking far too long. I'm not ready to give up the ghost just yet, thank you very much. I may not deserve it, but I plan on a long life, even for a felid." She twirled her weapon into its holster.

"You're incredible," said Rowan, and shook his head. "Just incredible."

"I know. Well, I'm peckish now!"

◆

The explosions and flashes of light far to their left receded into the distance on their way to Eastport, the same portal station Samarit and Rowan had taken to visit Wishbone Warren. He hoped it remained intact, only abandoned ahead of incursion. The city core offered the greatest resistance as well as the greatest plunder, hence the station surely ranked lower on the reptilian agenda. The Reps would have their claws full for the time being. On the other hand, perhaps the portal had been sabotaged by the League on the off chance the invaders had figured out how to use them. Whoever may be in hiding in the gloom, if anyone, did not betray their presence. Neither did the two felids, a pair of silent shadows blended into the deep dark of an unlit underworld.

"This is it," said Rowan. "I remember." The portal mechanism to his nanoid-enhanced eyesight resembled only a vague blocked-out sketch of itself. Under lighting it might prove undamaged, only missing the throng of travellers. "We're unbelievably lucky to find a scanner earlier. Now we'll charge it."

Together they watched the row of tiny indicators pulse, which blinked in succession and blinked off. The last one stayed on and turned greenish-grey.

"Blue, get down on your knees and bow. Clear your mind as well as you can. Then face the portal and open your heart. I mean your essence, but your body will express an openness in the chest area as it relaxes. It's only pent-up energy releasing; it feels good, but don't get too attached. Just keep going deeper. I'll do the rest. While you're doing that, I'll set up the scanner. You'll hear my voice when it's ready. Understood?"

She peered at him, and said: "Listen, little brother, I've been through portals before. I used to be somebody. I got around. So tell me why I have to get down on my knees. That's stupid. What the hell does that have to do with anything?"

Rowan sighed.

Arms crossed, she stood stiff-necked and glared.

Blue, he thought, *we don't have time for this nonsense. What is it with you? Invisibility sickness still? Pride in hitting the bullseye? Do I want to stick a razor blade between us right now? Don't tempt me.* But aloud he spoke in reassuring tones: "Of course you were important. You're still a somebody. You're famously infamous and most wanted, not least by the police, the armed forces special investigators, the intelligence agency and Kirzaka. And okay, by me. When the media found out, well, there was no limit to what people everywhere wanted to know about you. If you like, look at it this way: you're bowing to yourself. You're getting down on your knees and kissing your own bottom. You're asking the mirror of your mind who's the fairest in the land. It will shout back it's been you all along, 'appearances to the contrary notwithstanding.' All it means is that you admit you've got a lot more going for you than is generally perceived, by others and by you. Say, 'Yes, I accept that I am complete, a partless whole. I'm free of all limitation. Love is my nature. It's all me, and I love myself because there is no one and nothing else.'"

Blue uncrossed her arms. "Well, I'm not sure what you just said. It sounds like solipsism, but whatever. You've got another sale. Let's not waste any more time. Really… I'll do whatever it takes."

With more light, the yellow circle on the matte black platform she had afterwards stumbled onto would have been more obvious. The flashes of light and the soft tone signalled power filtered down from hyperspace initiated by the hand-held scanner and the mystic technique Masudah had taught Rowan. He reminded Blue to focus attention on the narrow band of light suspended within the square heavy metal frame with its inner border of polished rivets. He spontaneously synchronized his breathing with Blue's as they stood very still before the shimmery rainbow haze that surrounded the white glow of the circle that reflected in bright glints off every smooth surface in the room. When the white circle had flashed three times, it expanded.

They stepped forward, Blue first, at the exact moment of countdown from ten to one, indicated by the tone that also repeated at each count, as well as indicator lights. Once through to the other side – at first only a distorted version of the portal room's rear wall painted with diagonal alternating wide black and yellow stripes – the tone repeated ten times and stopped. Rowan had also reminded Blue, very politely, that she must not look behind her until they had reached a distance specified by a cairn. Otherwise, she could be blinded temporarily or even permanently. The landscape gradually come into view and wavered in the distance – a mountainous desert scene at dawn.

At *the* edge *of* boundary country, *the* badlands *of* Longbow Domain.

XXI
Boundary Country

"MY EYES HURT," she said, touched one hand to the cairn briefly, and pressed the heels of her palms to her eyes.

"You're fine. I watched. You didn't look."

"Of course I didn't. I've been through portals before, you know, even that one at Eastport many times. I mean the sun is blinding. And it's so hot."

"Of course it's hot. It's a desert. And it's only dawn, so just wait."

"Deserts can be cold as well, you know. I'm the minister… never mind. It's topside, obviously, but where the hell are we?"

"I've been here before. What matters is that for the moment we're safe, touch wood." He tapped his forehead with his knuckles. "It's Longbow clan country, specifically Sam's tribe's territory that surrounds Wishbone Warren."

"It is? Not good. Can you see? Doesn't the sun hurt your eyes too?" Blue squinted and scrunched up her face. "I can't see a damn thing."

"We can rest while your eyes adjust. They've been forced to contend with total darkness for an extended period. I'm fine. Nanoids, remember? They take care of a lot of stuff, touch wood." Once more he tapped his knuckles on his skull.

Blue, fugitive *from* justice.

"I could dimly make that out, blockhead," she said, and tried to squint in his direction. "The clunk of wood is a dead giveaway. So you expect the Wishbone Longbows are friendly? I imagine there's a warrant out for your arrest in their neck of the wasteland, not to mention my reputation having preceded me." She groped for the cairn, and dropped to a resting squat.

The pink sunrise revealed her tawny mane as dusty, wild and tangled. Until now Rowan had seen her dressed only in designer business attire. The elegant and dignified Madam Ellaern persona now of no use, he wondered if she had grown more honest and authentic. Her white satin camisole, still fairly clean, but the short red leather jacket and black cashmere leggings, smudged with dirt and ripped where she must have sat on something abrasive, spoke of forfeited dignity, never mind elegance. She had complained earlier that somewhere along the way she had lost the matching mini skirt to a tangle of metal. In its place, the remnants of a torn yellow silk scarf had been tied around her waist.

Before he could respond to her question, a slight movement appeared in peripheral vision twenty yards distant: a Longbow ranger, who had drawn her phaser and aimed at his head. Another silently appeared behind him, then two more off in the plain; one carried a rocket launcher while the other scanned the cloudless morning sky, all in desert camo gear. The first ranger touched her comm badge and spoke inaudibly.

◆

The sun grew even stronger among the huge boulders. Perhaps they acted like capacitors and retained the legacy of yesterday's heat as well. Chief Morningstar Longbow appeared cool and collected, however. "You may stay, Sir Rowan," she said. "We will not cast you to the reptoids, nor to your superiors." Her silver twisted plaits framed her wise old sun-browned face, and she added, "If they survived. This time we really are incommunicado." As before, the amulet with the crescent moon sigil hung from the silver chain around her neck, the sign of her status, this time over leather armour. She had not pressed her palm to his heart in greeting, however.

Rowan bowed. "Gratitude, Chief Morningstar. May I present my sister, Madam Ellaern of Vugh Deep?" And he turned towards Blue.

Morningstar did not look at her, but at him, and replied: "Your kin may stay. She is well-known to us. And we have met in years past." The chief did not speak the ex-minister's name.

Blue did not bow, but nodded politely enough, although she had not attracted even the chieftain's glance. "Gratitude, Chief Morningstar," she said. "I remember well, grandparent of Samarit Longbow. When last we met, at the annual state-of-the-kingdom symposium two years ago, we spoke of the Longbow children and their curriculum." She parted her lips to say more, but wisely did not, nor did she betray the slightest embarrassment at her dishevelled and unwashed appearance – nor the resumption of her best Lyran accent.

With no response, Morningstar turned to others who waited to speak to her.

Two men in skin-tight League uniforms under leather armour, phasers holstered in their belts, led the two felids to their individual quarters in another part of the hidden village, where also sheltered the few dozen others who had fled through the portal before the power failed.

•

Rowan fretted. Would he ever see Samarit? He had believed she rested in the care of her grandmother, and lived at home again. But Samarit had not so far made an appearance. Since no one mentioned anything of her rescue, although he had not expected it, he did not feel justified to ask about her welfare either.

Socially isolated from the Longbows, as well as the other outsiders who shunned them as the traitors the media had denounced before the invasion, they endured one distraught and bitter ander, who had taken it upon himself to act as spokesman, and accused them in a harsh and repetitive public taunt: "*Go back, Rep-lovers! Killers! You're only fit for the vibe circus! Murderers!*"

Officially neither ally nor foe, Rowan thought perhaps he had regained some credit, a little. With any luck he and Blue may be classified as refugees, the last to have escaped through the portal into clan territory. Time would determine their standing with the Longbows. However, privy to declassified League intelligence via the rumour mill, via the guards, they learnt more of the local situation.

The Longbows' role in the kingdom did not generally include training in advanced physics, but they had tried to destroy the portal by any means. Portals, however, are not conventional objects. Rather they are hyperspatial geometric abstractions that manifest as folded vortices in relativistic space-time under certain conditions. The one in the desert had defied all attempts at destruction. The canid rangers had been forced to keep it under observation only, a very dangerous task, as the Reps surely mapped all portals from their Eye in the Sky, although they did not use them due to vibrational incompatibility.

The Longbows believed that over the past two days Perkona Ola had been for the most part demolished. Any survivors were kept herded in makeshift paddocks or served as bait for non-stop vibe circuses wherever they freed a space of rubble. Of course the dome had been disabled from topside by the depth scanner they called Skyfire, housed in an antigravity satellite in near-planet orbit. But a large searchlight fixed to the dome's apex now pooled a spotlight in the same square Rowan's rooms in the university campus had looked out upon. The shadows its cold bluish light cast had been described by one intrepid late observer as stark, livid and as sharp as shards of obsidian. The White Tower nearby loomed among the few structures that remained upright.

The Reps were reported to be surprisingly unorganized, and leaders few. The beasts sported and wallowed in uninhibited lust for blood and vibrational titillation, leapt and danced in their ungainly way, intoxicated with arrowthorn, deadly to all but them, graceless and naked in iridescent scales, having discarded their customary metal armour, confident of total victory. Fights were common among them, sometimes to the death – an orgy of chaos. Kirzaka the Deathless, Talon of Maçina, had not made an appearance yet, and likely would not. Apparently he had more important affairs to attend to, perhaps on Lunah.

The Uaimh System and others had been conquered in similar fashion. League caverns worldwide under threat raced to finish devising the technology, if they had the means, to reinforce their cloaking grids to defend themselves from the scanner in orbit, of which there was still but one. Many caverns were said to be still intact, although most locations were by now exposed, and destruction an inevitability forecast for all soon.

The belief spread that the reptilians had succumbed to their infamous impulsiveness incited by the power of their new technologies, but constrained by far fewer numbers than their census figures had touted. It would take time for them to conquer the world. Hope of their defeat had not died yet, however.

◆

"How do I look?" asked Blue. "I kind of like this tribal-peasant fashion… not sure about the hairstyle… it better suits pointy canid ears with cute fuzz poking out of them… I never did figure out why the law thought it obscene to expose it in public. It's not like ear fuzz is pubic hair… or I guess it is, since it doesn't sprout till puberty, but so does facial hair… anyhow, it's hotter than magma up here topside." She pranced back and forth on the jute rug like a model on a runway. "Casual and comfortable, but elegant… right?… hey, you, *come on*, say something! Nobody talks to me except that dickhead who yells at us in the street. He actually called me a slag this morning, the prick. And the guards, or whatever they are. I tried asking the older heavyset one, but now he won't talk to me at all… won't even look."

"Maybe," Rowan muttered, "he thought you were flirting."

"Me? Now, would I do something like that? Hey, you, *look* at me. Tell me… how do I look?"

Rowan glanced up from his book. "You know you look good in anything, Blue. It's the way you're made. You can't help it."

Blue stopped prancing. "Hey, thanks, little brother, that's the nicest thing you've ever said to me." She took the sides of her calf-length skirt in each of her hands and curtsied. "It beats the hell out of *'criminal narcissistic psychopath.'* Anyhow, it's a step in the right direction."

Without looking up again, Rowan replied, "You're never going to let that go, are you, Blue? Mythology states and theology confirms that the great god Maçina is a most attractive being and shines like his Sacred Sun. He's so beautiful he's never to be portrayed or the viewer will die even if the artist does not. But handsome is as handsome does. As far as you're concerned, I'm doing my best at unconditional positive regard. I've a long way to go, so please be patient. And stop calling me 'little brother.' I'm *Rowan.* It's my name."

"Will do, little brother. Tsk tsk, cross as two sticks. Do you need a nap? I can be grouchy too, so take your own advice and be patient with *me*… I mean, please?… What are you reading?"

"I'm not." He closed the book. "I'm trying to distract myself. It's not working. Meanwhile the lizard king is trying to destroy the world."

"Hey, it's only been a week, give him a break. It'll take a while." Blue pursed her lips and looked across at him.

He remained slumped in a bent-willow chair, silent and glum.

She watched him, and said, "Speaking of hairstyles, does your girlfriend braid hers now where it's permissible to show tufted ears? I thought you said she was here. Why hasn't she come to call?"

"Her tufts were shaved when she got promoted." Rowan's frown deepened. "If you're bored, poke at someone else, like that man who insulted you… but he's just in pain. Better to ask one of the Longbows to teach you basket-weaving… if they'll consent."

Blue stared at the rug. "Rowan, I didn't mean to touch a nerve. Did you break up? You never said."

"Blue… stop. You know she's betrothed."

She peered at him. "Listen, I'm doing my best to improve my manners. It ain't easy. I faked them for so long the real ones feel phoney too. I'm no good at compensating. Can't you see I'm trying to be genuine? I just don't know what that means. Maybe I'm just fishing for attention. I'm really the kingdom's biggest loser and terrified of the repercussions, so I say stupid things. I don't know how to ask for mercy. I don't believe I deserve it. I can't even say I'm sorry, but I am." She turned away to the window. "There… I guess I said it after all."

Rowan stared at the back of Blue's tawny head. The Longbow hairstyle exposed her neck, and a few strands remained unwrapped by the two twisted tawny plaits that hung down her front. The new linen outfit she had been given looked crisp and fresh outlined by the harsh desert sunlight that seeped in through the clefts in the grotto, softened by the translucent window covering. In fact she looked so slight and feminine that he wanted her to be harmless. *But how many times did she say "I" just now?*

"Sam is promised," he said. "Marriages here are arranged by the families concerned, in fact the whole tribe. Lengthy debates, consultations with astrologers, casting of the bones by wise persons and patient hearings of anyone who has something to contribute… it's like a court case. Longbow clan law is based on a traditional model that's served them well for centuries. It's said to work out most of the time. And her case is extra special, even for royalty. Her fiancé is some sort of prince. She's a catch too, so it's a done deal. End of story… Why am I telling you all this? You already know the protocol, ex-minister of education."

Blue spun around and lowered her brows. With her knuckles pressed to the sides of her new blouse to her trim waist, she set her sandalled feet apart and said: "Listen to me, Rowan. You can't let them take her. I know it's contrary to all common sense. We're under house arrest as the unwelcome guests of our only friends in the world… well, potentially our friends. I'm enough of a politician to understand that much. And I was never any good at the romance thing. I'm just too… oh, fine… selfish. Right?" She held one palm up and closed her eyes. "Please, no need to agree, I've secretly suspected it my whole life. It's more than obvious even to me now that you've given me permission to be more selfish than ever." She opened her eyes and dropped her hand. "As if I could hide it. Well, it's come round full circle to bite my pretty… never mind me. I talk about myself too much. As I said, win her back. Just do it."

Rowan stood up. He crossed his arms and uncrossed them, his turn now to pace the jute rug. He rambled, thinking out loud: "What you're suggesting is backstabbing. I respect the Longbows more than any other faction of the League I know of. But I hope to visit Khémia one day too. I want to know how they can remain topside freely… magic, the story of their past, first-hand. And other lands, the world, the solar system, galactic… whatever. They've forgotten more than we'll ever learn. Masudah's invited me. At least I hope he's still alive, somewhere. It's the one thing I've got to look forward to. It makes the future look less bleak. His advice was… what? Well, for one thing, Diss was right. When you and I are old, she'll be a centuries-old legend, long gone… yet to me like it was yesterday. There could never again be anyone like her… but, thanks to you,

I can't even *remember* what else Masudah said. What a flippin' crazy idea!" He walked out to stew in his own juices elsewhere.

⋅

On the evening of their eighth day in the village, they emerged from their hut to find the pathways busy with activity. Unlike previous evenings, when lighting of any kind was strictly forbidden, crystal torches blazed as Longbow warriors and others rushed to and fro. No one shouted. Only loud commands issued from leaders. The felids' guards had apparently abandoned their post, but the younger one who still spoke to Blue leapt out of the stream of passers-by and said: "Invasion! We are under attack. Follow me to the chief." He pointed to the front of the crowd and added: "This way. Hurry!"

Surrounded by Longbows, Morningstar's dignity as the great leader had been enhanced by armour and arms. She singled him out and said: "Sir Rowan, you are a League commando. This is an emergency. We need everyone who can help now. Never mind your history with us. I had not planned to speak of this so soon, but we know you regret your actions with respect to my granddaughter, although it remains undecided what would have been her fate had you not interfered with her command. But I believe you were misled into that no-win situation." This time she did glance at Blue.

To Rowan she said, "We acknowledge that you later did the right thing at great risk and loss to save her life. For that we thank you. We are a disciplined people, perhaps somewhat rigidly formal, so a clan law court would have made the truth plain one way or the other. But set that aside for now. It may be the end of Wishbone Warren, if not Longbow Domain, but not if we can help it. If we go down, we shall go down fighting. If you volunteer, your weapon will be restored to you, along with whatever other equipment we can spare."

"Of course, Chief Morningstar." Rowan bowed. "I'm at your service."

The chief faced Blue and stated: "Madam, pending the outcome of this battle a second court case will decide your fate. You shall stay here with most of the elderly, the ill, the mothers and our precious children, the young the reptilians value most. You will remain under guard. Passageways carved in times of old and deeper caves beneath these hills is where you will shelter. We have prepared for this day, so you will be held there until all is clear. Understood?"

Blue donned her most professional mask, although the Lyran accent had vanished. "Chief Morningstar, I admit I did wrong, and I deeply regret that your granddaughter was endangered by my actions. I deserve fair punishment. But don't waste a guard on me. I can help too. I'm as a good a shot as my brother. Ask him."

Rowan locked eyes with Blue, frowned and shook his head.

Morningstar stated: "The fact remains that you cannot be trusted. Even you must see that." She gestured to the guard to take Blue away.

✦

Ogna Longbow, the seasoned squadron leader, buxom for a canid, peered at the horizon through her dusty visor, and adjusted for long-range resolution. She dropped from the crest back into the trough of the dune, spindrift raining after, and pulled back the hood of her tight-fitting one-piece desert camo uniform, and spat. Sand had caught in the tuft of one pointed ear. She dealt with it, drew her hood up, and said: "Sighted, above that eroded mesa that looks a League government building in ruins. South by southeast, twenty miles distant, ten o'clock and hovering. This latest enemy foray is a futile attempt to lure us out to a more vulnerable position. The reptoids do seem to understand that our lands are part of us, that each grain of sand is family. They expect us to waste more ammunition and time on them, to wear us down. We are here to observe and report. Fire only when fired upon. Understood?"

"Aye, sir," replied Rowan, and brushed the dust from his own visor. "On the other hand, sir, if we can bring one down without damage, maybe we can commandeer the craft."

"Of course, Sir Rowan. That is why you are here with my squadron. You are a pilot. We can try, although it is difficult to avoid all damage. We have rocket launchers at the ready, fifty yards to the south, not that they are effective against their shields at less than close range." She quickly flipped up her lenses to peer at him more closely through clear brown eyes in her stern face. "No heroics. So far I have only managed to cut one a little before my soldiers chased it away. They have already killed and eaten raw three of us in other border skirmishes, good soldiers all. They prefer to ripen their kills by allowing the carcasses to rot for a time, so that repulsive act of crude barbarity was just to demoralize us, maybe revenge for the wound I gave. They are hard to distinguish as individuals, but one of them seemed to jeer at me, as it sprayed mucus... anyhow... I do not think the enemy is as strong as they try so hard to make everyone believe. Nonetheless, they are formidable. Even one survivor of a crashed dragon ship is literally a huge menace. As always, aim for the suture between the eyes where their skull is weakest. Or try for the eyes themselves, the rotating little orange eyes… but I waste words. This you must know already."

"Aye, sir, I know it well."

Longbow boundary country – even more arid than the portal site where at least there had been the odd dead thorn bush or sun-bleached skeleton evidenced that life might be possible in the desert, however remotely. Here stretched only wasteland as far as even an eagle eye could see, hundreds of square miles of broken wilderness with islands of ancient eroded bare rock. Baked by the relentless sun, its desert floor trowelled by the wind and sculpted into rippled patterns, from time out of mind it had been a natural barrier. But this meant nothing to invaders from the sky, except as an ideal killing field.

Sighted: dragon ship, Longbow Domain.

191

XXII
Woe Betide Us

"Lieutenant, how many?" asked Ogna.

The Longbow warrior reported: "Sir, only the one, stable in position. Other reports are unreliable. League Station Alpha should be in orbit at thirty degrees east of north and gaining on us, but communication is intermittent, sir. The station crew must have a better reading of all fronts. We do not know what's going on up there, but then it was still under construction, as well as recently attacked, so maybe something broke down. We'll continue to monitor, sir."

"This is difficult to explain. Why is that thing just hanging there?"

"Sir, unknown, sir."

"It was a rhetorical question, lieutenant… one with no answer."

"Sir, aye, sir."

"Has the scout returned, lieutenant?"

"Sir, the scout has not returned. There is no communication, sir."

"Inform Berry that I need to speak with him, lieutenant."

"Sir, aye, sir." The warrior saluted and slid down the dune, and raised as little dust as possible.

✦

Ogna flipped up her visor. "Sir Rowan, when training as a commando, were you given any instruction that involved remote-viewing? You may already know we call it 'far-sight.' But it is an art we lost long ago." The evening sky had grown quite dark at the zenith, with a few stars already in evidence. The squadron had walked and crawled ten miles closer to the arrowhead-shaped Rep craft that hovered above the sandstone pillars. "We have drawn a blank," she admitted.

Rowan had overheard her conversation with the lieutenant, but made no mention of it, and answered: "Yes, sir, introductory far-sight lessons only. Khémian diplomat Captain Masudah of Zau offered more, but there wasn't time. Instead he employed far-sight himself, remote-viewing, to locate Major Samarit Longbow at Mudredd Vale."

"Samarit Longbow is not to be referred to as an officer, Sir Rowan. That false promotion alone, in my view, is enough to warrant punishment of the ex-minister to the full extent of the law, regardless of her relation to you."

"Pardon, sir. Without remote-viewing, I would have searched thoroughly, but probably in vain. I did, however, learn something else of more immediate benefit at the time. It may be of value now, although I don't see how just yet, sir."

"Oh? And what was that?"

"Invisibility, sir."

Ogna's eyes opened wider, and she raised her dark eyebrows. "Do you mean the captain gave you a Khémian cloaking device? I did not know they even favoured such technology. Our own cloaks are no longer invulnerable to detection, you should know. In fact they have become beacons, so we do not use them at all now. They are worse than useless. We are totally exposed. Even camouflaged we are readily visible to satellite cameras, thermal and otherwise. They could be watching and listening to us right now. That is why it is so strange the enemy craft is just hanging in the sky in plain sight out there. I had hoped you might be able to spy on it from a distance in some way."

"Captain Masudah did not give me any hardware, sir. What he taught me was purely psychic, of the mind and its innate powers. I'm not a scientist, so I can't speculate how it works. I only know that I was able to become invisible to a reptilian ranger who had detected our cover. With that, I was able to sneak close enough to dispose of it. You can find the details in my record, sir."

Head turned to one side, she continued the cool inspection of his face. "Impossible." She rolled to look at him more closely. "Look, in case you have not noticed, there is a reptoid dragon ship not ten miles from our location. We are under threat, Berry. I should not have to remind you not to waste my time. Please remove your visor completely." She lifted her head, leaned on one elbow and peered at him. Expressionless, she searched his eyes.

"I am very serious, sir," said Rowan. "The diplomat, who is a soldier as well as a priest, taught me the basics of two secrets of his tradition. I employed the other one, in tandem with a hand-held scanner, to assist in opening the portal even after the power had failed at the departure point, Eastport Station in Perkona Ola, northeast of the armed forces base."

"Interesting." Her deadpan expression remained unchanged. "We knew power was down at the artificial portal. When I heard of it, I wondered how it was possible that two more refugees had emerged at Wishbone's end. We have not been briefed on this, Berry, so I can only assume the method you refer to is not approved by League armed forces authorities. You may know there are myths and legends among our people too of magical powers. But they are considered entertainment for the young nowadays, morality tales or fantasy literature at best. Education has improved over a couple of centuries now, though some anders still consider us peasants… or worse. Our old superstitions gave way to science. But remote-viewing is not officially sanctioned procedure by the League either. Off the record, I have heard from credible sources that it can be effective." She wriggled back up to the top of the dune and flipped down her visor.

"Sir," said Rowan, "let me try it then. Based on my experience with Khémian magic, there must be a connection between all powers of mind and spirit. I've experienced what may be the unifying principle. It can affect matter profoundly. Even material scientific theory teaches that at a fundamental level matter doesn't really exist except as mathematical descriptions of frequencies in potential states, the wave function believed to be collapsed into an apparent singular measurable state by observation."

Without looking at him, Ogna replied: "I do not understand what you just said and am not willing to go that far, Berry. I do not believe you understand it either. Matter is quite real to me. I have been wounded in battle. The matter of my body was profoundly affected by the matter propelled from the enemy's weapon. This morning I was happy to assimilate my breakfast, matter to replace matter. Whatever information you come up with may be a form of daydream and completely unreliable. We will find another way." She stared at the craft. "If only we had a disc of our own here. They are too few, three destroyed now, the other two engaged." Ogna sighed and flipped up her visor. "Remain at the ready in position, Berry. I must check on report updates of activity on fronts in other combat zones." Hesitant at first, she removed a sheath from her belt. "Here, you do not have a PUS. Take it. I can get another."

"A pus?… sir?"

"It stands for 'personal utility sword.' You may need it for close combat. I have not had time to clean the blood off the blade yet. Try not to touch it."

She slid down the dune and disappeared behind the next one over.

Rowan checked the blade, a little longer than his forearm and very sharp. He sheathed it and attached the scabbard to his belt, adjusted his visor, and for the hundredth time studied the arrowhead shape of the dragon ship – the hue of tarnished silver, it hovered above the sandstone pillars under the cloudless evening sky. The stars multiplied and traversed the heavens at their imperceptible pace, but the craft remained motionless by comparison. The squadron leader had not ordered him *not* to try, as he interpreted her statement, so he determined to keep his eyes on the ship while at the same time withdrew attention inwards, to see if it were even possible to divide attention that way. He imagined being inside it.

He knew military historians demonstrated that the Reps had pursued a more complicated developmental path for engineering their spacecraft and current range of aircraft based on them, with the assistance of enslaved ander engineers' and canid technicians' deft fingers instead of their own big clawed paws. It involved antigravity, but constrained to manipulation of unstable energies. Toxic radiation remained a big problem, as well as risk of unusually destructive explosions. Mechanical failures were common. More importantly, reptilian psychic abilities were believed to be too limited to accommodate the creativity ideal for symbiosis. They possessed limitless appetite, but limited imagination.

Rowan closed his eyes, awake in a dream – but – nothing there. In the out-of-body state he viewed the lacklustre silver arrowhead from all sides, even passed through it. Behind his visor his eyes opened wide. Beneath his hood his mane tried to stand on end. He roused, and slid down the dune to find Ogna.

✦

"Yes, yes, Berry." Ogna waved him away. "It is already confirmed that it is a hologram. Our territories are surrounded by them. Some even appear mobile, but they are decoys. The reptilians have projected the dragon ships from their station in space, simultaneously worldwide via new satellites, new to us, that is, but there are some real ones too, a clever tactic. We just do not know which is which right now. We are to retreat to our territorial bases as soon as possible. For you that means Wishbone Warren. Remain on high alert. Do not lose hope, but do not be its slave either. Good luck and safe journey."

✦

A long night across the desert into predawn now behind them, Rowan and those of Morningstar's warriors who had not remained behind as guards returned to Wishbone Warren. Even from a twilit distance the horizon had glowed in a false western sunrise. They had choked on the smoke, but pressed on, into the lingering radiation that had instantly baked the arid plain to the crests of the sandstone hills above the tunnels and caves of Wishbone, everywhere vitrified, semi-molten and brittle, dull red beneath the white ash and black cinders. The chief had remained with her people. The hot discharging rubble contradicted any hope of their survival. Their particular cave system had been neither deep nor extensive. For centuries the Longbows had preferred locations like this because of close proximity to topside, from where they could more easily monitor the Surface world.

The male officer in charge turned to the crowd and said, "We can only wait until it cools now. It could take months."

The entire group stood and gaped while the eastern sky grew minutely lighter behind them.

Another group appeared as vibrating dots in the distant shimmer of the mirage and emerged from the vanishing point on the hazy southern horizon. Among them: Samarit in the lead.

◆

With the others in a loose band behind her, she drew within ten feet, and spoke with a pronounced lisp as if she were alone: "They tell me I'm chief now, Rowan. It's not my time. It's far too soon."

He wanted to gaze at her to his heart's content, but only glanced –

She stepped to his side, and stared at the smoking ruin. Still thin and pallid, the premature crow's feet at the corners of her dark eyes appeared less deep, and more of her youthful self shone through than when he had last laid eyes on her. The scarf that protected her shaven head did not hide her lovely Vulcan ears he could look at forever if he let himself, tufts or not.

"Yes," he said, and looked away, "too much was thrust upon us too soon."

"I'm told Ellaern is with Grandmother Morningstar. She'll be under guard, confined as a criminal suspect."

Rowan did not know how to respond.

"I'm told she's your sister."

"It's true. She was."

"Gran is the last of my family. I will not give up on her."

Rowan hung his head, too tongue-tied to speak.

"Nor must you give up on yours, whatever she did."

"Her name was Blue. Our parents called her Blue. The Reps twisted and broke her. It's what they do. I can never go home now… they need to die."

"We mustn't give way to bitterness, Rowan. Revenge won't cure it. I know it sounds trite, but I know how you feel… I feel it too."

Rowan nodded acknowledgement – he breathed, and let her in a little, even though she must be in denial – or perhaps because of it. Blue had pointed out Samarit's essential loneliness, apparently a motivation for his sister's contra-dictory and inexplicable manipulations, absolutely narcissistic and irrational, but inflected with compassion for the little boy Syx, a little. And Masudah had pointed out that Samarit possessed something Rowan believed he lacked, which he identified now as her open heart, as well as the objectivity, inner strength and charisma of her grandmother. How was she a mirror? He did not know what she saw in him. But it raised his mind to her level, as it would others. She was right – revenge would make a monster of him too. So he let it burn like the molten scene before them, until the urge burnt out.

Samarit took his hand in hers, and they stood together and watched the glow amidst the smoke. "We have each other, Rowan. Always and forever."

Something like a dam collapsed inside. Hot tears streamed down the sides of his nose through his whiskers and soaked into his chin tuft, and found their way to end as brief wet spots in the hot dust and ash at his feet. Neither his expression nor his stance changed. He only drew a silent breath and held it, and blinked in an attempt to restore clear vision.

Samarit looked away, and said softly, "Before you arrived at Wishbone, I'd gone to Touchstone Warren. Gran thought it best. If anything happened to her and our tribe, I'd be protected by my future husband's family. They were royals, so their base was better defended, and I was still very unwell. It wasn't exactly correct protocol. Anyhow, you're right. Too much was thrust on us, too soon."

He listened to her as if he were only an ear and no more.

"I watched them die, Rowan. Whatever happened here happened there too. I can be stubborn as you know, so I wasn't sheltered underground at the time. Ready or not, my only thought was to be at the front, maybe not as a fighter, but just to know first-hand what was at stake. It's the way I am. I don't know now whether it was fortunate, not after all I've seen. My intended prince… his name was Pineshadow. He was a good man, I'm sure of it, not that I got to know him really, otherwise we would have violated clan law. He wasn't at the battle line, so he must have chosen to remain with his people.

"I grew exhausted out there on the front, watching the skies too long. There were several of those probably decoy craft flitting about. Something about it didn't seem right. They seemed like dangling baubles to tease a kitten… or taunt more like it. I didn't even feel too bad about returning to Touchstone to rest. But I was just in time and near enough to see the sky turn white… in the blink of an eye… a wide column of white fire shone down on Touchstone Hills, and instantly melted the surface and cremated to ash… everyone, all those people down there, children, animals, everything."

Rowan took both her hands in his own. They stood before the ruins of Wishbone Warren, and looked at each other.

XXIII
Sea *of* Stars

"I'll bet my badge of office you're happy to see me again." Morningstar had miraculously emerged from the smoking cleft unscathed, apparently, and talked like she had been away on holiday. Knuckles on her hips, a wide grin spread across her old face.

The Longbows as one body stared back.

But the apparition looked directly at Rowan.

"Blue," he muttered, "you're incredible."

"Thanks, little brother, you've blown my cover."

No one said anything, not even Samarit.

The apparition of Morningstar strutted back and forth against a backdrop of smoke, rills of lava, and ashes twisted into dust devils, set her knuckles on her hips as before, lifted her chin, apparently about to speak – but blinked once and froze, shattered into jagged lines, soon a low-resolution blur, translucent, like her voice – indistinct, muffled, brittle and cracked. And she vanished.

The crowd of Longbows, mouths agape, gasped in unison.

"*What insult is this?!*" shouted a warrior.

Samarit leap onto a boulder, arms akimbo, legs astride, and spoke: "*What we just witnessed is the evidence that our chief is with us in spirit!*"

In half a moment the tribe shouted back: "*Long live the Longbows!*"

She added: "Grandmother Morningstar would say we must release our grief to the wind and the fire, but to never give our power away. The Longbows live on. We shall fight again. Our enemy has tried to break our hearts and minds by murdering our most vulnerable and dear. But he will *not* destroy us!" She raised one clenched fist into the air. "The sun rises on a battle lost, *never the war!*" Samarit threw her head back and howled like an alpha she-wolf at the moon, and the sunrise cast her thin silhouette in backlit red-gold flame.

The Longbows howled back: "*Long live Chief Samarit! Long live the Longbow clan! Long live clan domain!*"

Rowan breathed in the solidarity, and nodded assent. *She was born for this. Masudah says the people are best ruled by the best. She's the best. We all can see it. Now we know somehow the suffering will end. Things will get better. All will be well in the end. It's just not the end. Not yet.*

◆

The survivors moved on. Wishbone Warren's ashes disappeared in their wake. In a few hours they camped in a canyon of ancient iron-stained hills treed with pinewoods, open to the sky. A few stragglers showed up from time to time. Above, the full moon coasted a sea of stars and flooded the desert with silver light.

Samarit and Rowan sat together at a short distance at their own fire. Under a copse of gnarled trees, their firestone shone up like an amber footlight.

He gazed into the midnight sky through black branches bristled with needles and cones, and placed an arm around Samarit's shoulders.

She leaned into his side. "I don't care," she said, "if the Eye in the Sky sees us."

"I wish I could say the same."

"I wasn't just cheerleading back at Wishbone, Rowan. I really do feel Gran near. Maybe I'm just in denial. But I don't think I'm losing my mind. Mog is here too… has Ellearn really disappeared?"

Rowan gazed at the firestone, and tried to understand the question.

"When I was a little girl, Gran told us kids fairy tales. In one story, a warlock called Hydan conjured a spirit and trapped it in a bottle. So the demon offered the power of shape-shifting with a magic talisman if he took the stopper out and let him go. Hydan thought this was the greatest stroke of luck ever, but while showing off, expanded to giant size and accidentally killed the king. At first he freaked, but because no one saw what happened, in a moment realized he could simply impersonate the king to cover his tracks, who would announce Hydan had gone on a mission of magical significance to the benefit of the land. To make the long story short, he grew bored with ruling the kingdom, but for a time delighted in playing pranks on his subjects. Of course the kingdom began to fall apart and everyone grew upset. Hydan lost his mind completely and vanished for good. The people down the years reported ghostly sightings… often they just heard his voice crying from a great distance."

Rowan nodded recognition. "Many a truth is hidden in fairy lore. Masudah warned that the wielder of powers must be pure of heart or there's big blow-back: madness, mayhem and misery. Blue's her own worst enemy… I'm going to say *was* her own worst enemy, but she's a survivor… Did you hear that? I said it again. Sam, I don't even know what 'appear' means, let alone 'disappear.' All I know is that Blue studied the Reps like a psychic naturalist. They didn't teach her. I think a power like that is not necessarily the reward of reptilian genius, just an accident of nature… anyhow, bitterness doesn't help, so for the sake of argument, if she still exists in some form, when and if they ever figure out that she knows something they could exploit, we're all in even bigger trouble." Rowan released Samarit, stood up, and took her hands, and pulled her up to stand too.

"Sam, look at me."

She peered into his eyes, and held her breath.

"Sam, whatever we have left of League technology is next to useless now. We have to find some other way to defeat the enemy. Khémia is the only part of the Surface of the planet we know of that's immune, or was."

She exhaled, placed her palms on his chest, and gazed into his eyes. "Yes…"

"What I want right now more than anything is to surrender to the beauty of the world because of you. It was there all along, but I never knew. Thank you."

"You're very welcome, kitty baby, but don't hold me responsible. Like you say, it was there all along. I think it's better to say we woke each other up to it."

He clasped her even closer, and heard his heart speak the words his mind would not: "You know I would die for you, Sam, but I must do better than that…"

He felt a tremor shiver up her spine. But he stood firm, and added, "You're a natural leader, like you were born to it… because you were… and you're well-trained as a warrior, better than me."

A quaver inflected her reply: "I know what you're going to say, kitty baby. If I'm not careful, I'll cry and spoil your flattering assessment of me."

"Don't cry, Sam. Where's your lionheart?"

"I guess canids can have lionhearts too." She brushed a tear from her cheek with her wrist.

"Sam, we can't keep running. There's nowhere to go. If you're still listening, despite everything, please know we *will* find a home, Sam, where we can be happy and free, somewhere in this big wide world. Kirzaka can only pollute the drop, not the ocean."

"Yes, Rowan."

He felt perhaps she took in not his words so much, but *how* he spoke, so took care to breathe, and ignore his fears, and focus with an open heart.

But Samarit did not appear to breathe at all; she watched him like a warrior on the brink of doom, resolved to endure a harsh fate with fire in her dark eyes – until they misted. She grew very quiet. With head bowed, she gazed into the firestone's warm glow.

The sailor moon cast its silver through the tracery of the pinewood canopy, and made a net of shadows on the ground.

She inhaled, sighed, and glassy-eyed, said, "Yes, you must scout ahead, go to Khémia, and search until you find a haven. You're our wayfinder, and our envoy. We'd only slow you down." Half her face in moonlight, the other half warm in the light of the firestone, she looked up and touched his face, and the unhealed

Samarit Longbow *and* Rowan Berry Longbow –
the adventure continues…

scar between his eyes. "I'm sorry I threw that rock at you. I was not myself that day. I promise, never again."

"Maybe I deserved it."

"You deserve the best. I love you. Our tribe loves you. You saved their chief. We must let you go so that you can return. You're a Longbow now." Her dark eyes searched his. "Your home is with us," she said, "always and forever."

Rowan gazed back into those clear depths – his breath stopped, but his heart beat on. He expelled a sigh, kissed her brow, and enfolded her in his arms. "Our exile has begun, Sam, but it will end. It's just not the end yet."

Please leave a review!

PLEASE CONSIDER LEAVING a review at Amazon.com or whichever site you purchased this book. Prospective buyers place more trust in the opinions of honest reviewers like you. George R.R. Martin, author of the epic fantasy series A Song of Ice and Fire, of which *A Game of Thrones* is book one, says that a range of reviews is helpful to the author, so I invite you to share your thoughts in a review after reading this book. Furthermore, I subscribe to reader-response theory, which recognizes the reader's role in creating the meaning and experience of a literary work. The theory argues that literature is a performance art such that each reader creates their unique text-related interpretation. That means you are a partner. Your opinion matters.

Thank you and keep in touch! You can do that on the contact page at my website. Also, consider signing up for my newsletter there to be informed when the next trilogy in the series will be published, along with excerpts and possibly illustrations from published and forthcoming books.

RupertSmithson.com

Book Two:

Bones *of* Silver, Bones *of* Iron

IF YOU ENJOYED *Lightning Seeds*, you will want to continue the adventure in The Stars Hereafter Chronicles with book two, *Bones of Silver, Bones of Iron*. Here is an excerpt from chapter 29, "Impression Ringrise":

◆

UNSEEN AND UNHEARD until then came the oncoming swarm. The things literally poured from the cliff caves in an unstoppable flow, a heaving Horn'd horde, swarthy, skittering – silent, at first. As they drew more near, a shrill, shrieking cacophony tore at his ears. He would have to swim for it. He extracted the portable scanner from his other gear, which would have to be abandoned, and strapped it firmly to his belt next to the plasma phaser holster. He pressed a couple of buttons in succession on his five-toed boots, swim-mode enabled, and dived into the surf. When he had swum far enough to look back, of course the filthy creatures were boarding their canoes in crews of twenty or so per vessel, and sported paddles aplenty now.

With no thought of capture to diminish concentration, under the waters of the Inland Sea he plunged, deep below the surface to make his way northwards. But was it north? The moon uncooperatively hid behind the clouds, but that may be a blessing in disguise. The current lower down flowed strong and steady. He hoped it favoured his intended direction, however murky in places. And unused to such exertion – he needed air. He poked his nose out of the water, which brought relief – and excited heightened shrieking – he had been spotted. *They must be able to see in the dark…* and with great acuity at this distance. He started to dive, but something caught his collar and pulled hard, and drew his head above water.

"*Quick! Get in! They come!*"

RupertSmithson.com

www.ingramcontent.com/pod-product-compliance
Lightning Source LLC
Chambersburg PA
CBHW070834120626
46556CB00002B/755